Sayonara

Sayonara

ELLIOT MARSHALL

CHAPMANS

Chapmans Publishers Ltd
141–143 Drury Lane
London WC2B 5TB

A CIP catalogue record for this book is
available from the British Library

ISBN 1–85592–018–2

First published by Chapmans 1992

Photoset in Linotron Trump Mediaeval by
Rowland Phototypesetting Ltd, Bury St Edmunds, Suffolk
Printed and bound in Great Britain by
Clays Ltd, St Ives plc

This book is dedicated to the memory of Gordon Instone. Wartime hero, father, friend. A man whose courage, tenacity and continual optimism in the face of adversity were a lifelong inspiration.

ACKNOWLEDGEMENTS

My sincere thanks to the many friends and colleagues whose expertise and constant support were invaluable in writing this book. In particular, members of the Far East Department and the Japan Research Council at London University's School of Oriental and African Studies. Also Keith Jackson, Beth Mason, Stewart Mitchell and John Turner.

My publisher, Marjory Chapman, and agent, Mark Lucas, believed in this project when it was 30 sheets of paper. This book would not have been possible without their creative input throughout its development.

PROLOGUE

Japan, 14 August 1945

The chauffeur leaned on the horn of the Hong Qui limousine, screaming abuse through the open window. Ahead, a group of farmers was struggling to free a hand-cart full of whining children from a deep shell-hole. He would have to wait.

An elderly couple sat huddled at the roadside, too exhausted to go on, too far from home to go back. The man eyed the limousine carefully through the legs of the refugees who continued to stream past. If he was going to die, better in his own town than here. And there were only five in that car, easily room for another.

With his last ounce of strength he staggered to his feet and flung himself through the crowd at the car door, twisting the handle and hammering on the window. Suddenly, the hand-cart came free. The car lurched forward, taking the old man with it, his knuckles turning white as it gathered speed. When the car hit the shell-hole his wrist snapped like dead wood and he pitched back into the crowd with a piercing scream. The faces of the car's four occupants registered nothing.

The Tokyo road seven miles further west had been so ravaged by Allied bombing that the chauffeur had to pull off to the right through a newly made cutting in the woods and ease the car over a rough track of low stumps and boulders.

As it wound its way down a steep escarpment to rejoin the stream of refugees, the four sombrely dressed passengers got their first glimpse of their destination. A mile and a half ahead in the failing light they could just make out a large, low complex of buildings surrounded by a high stone wall.

Towards the bay foreshore the road divided, leaving the refugees behind. Now the men in the limousine could see two ancient gabled roofs above the wall, their low, sweeping eaves reaching out against the darkening sky. Two heavy bronze doors swung open on the seaward side to allow them to enter. Inside, low buildings from many periods were arranged around an oval lake. A miniature garden with dwarf trees and delicately arched bridges was set out on an island at its centre.

The limousine moved up to join seven others parked in a courtyard at the western edge of the complex. The chauffeurs stood in a huddle, trying to catch the heat from a massive bonfire of papers and files being constantly fed by a chain of servants.

They all stood stiffly to attention as the four passengers emerged. A man in his mid-twenties hurried across the courtyard to greet them. He stopped a few yards off and bowed deeply. The four men of the Nashiba family bowed in return. The eldest stepped forward.

'Please accept my apologies for the lateness of our arrival.'

The young man bowed stiffly again. 'The road from Tokyo is a nightmare. My family is only relieved that you have arrived safely.'

The Nashibas followed their host's son wearily across the courtyard, up three cypress-wood steps, into the largest of the low buildings.

Minutes later they were ushered into a wide conference room. There were visible signs of relief amongst the eleven men seated around the large square table. The business of the evening could begin at last.

The importance of this gathering was lost on no one. For the first time since 1907, the four great dynastic families of Japan, the Tosas, Nashibas, Ishiharas and Kugas, had been called together to discuss their country's future. Every man in the room could trace his ancestry back through two thousand years of Japanese history. At the dawn of the nineteenth century, their forebears were feudal warlords. At its

10

close, they were the industrial giants behind the fastest growing economy in the world.

Though only the Ishiharas were known as politicians, no committee sat that the Four Families did not influence; the Kugas were the only avowed militarists, yet the Japanese war machine of the thirties could never have been conceived without the commitment of all. They lived reclusively, watching governments come and go, knowing that wherever the country's future might lie, they, the 'Four Great Pillars of Japan', would always finally hold sway.

Their host, Hiromi Tosa, a slightly built man in his mid-seventies, stood up to speak first.

'Tomorrow, at noon, the Japanese people will know what most of us here already know: the terms of surrender to the Allies have been agreed.' He paused in the almost palpable silence.

'At this moment, the Emperor is recording an address telling all Japan that the war is over; that we will not fight with bamboo spears to the last man, but will face up to our defeat and endure the unendurable.' Tosa put his palms against the edge of the black lacquer table, leaning into them to ease the dull ache in his arthritic knees. He studied his swollen fingers for a moment before continuing.

'Thirty-eight years ago, when our families last met, our fathers and grandfathers sowed the seeds of what was to be our "Great Endeavour". There are five of us here now who still remember that night. I think we should all be grateful that the others have been spared this terrible humiliation.'

He surveyed the expressions of the men in the room. Most simply stared ahead, their faces frozen. Only the youngest of the Kuga family allowed himself an intake of breath.

'We cannot know what form the Allied occupation will take,' Tosa went on. 'So it was imperative that we should all meet to discuss the future whilst we still have the opportunity.

'I know some of you must wonder at this moment if there is a future. But we Japanese are a resilient race. Our families

11

have been bound together since the beginning of recorded time. We have plotted and plundered, wedded and warred for centuries. But never have we lost control.

'We, above all, can view this tragedy in a larger context, as but another bend in the river of years. We, above all, can believe that in time the agony will pass.'

Itaro Ishihara, the second-oldest of his family, got stiffly to his feet. 'It's hard to talk of the future when some of us here may yet be hung as war criminals.'

On the opposite side of the table, General Kuga pulled at his collar, uncomfortable in civilian clothes. 'If we had stopped in Manchuria,' he started, 'no one in the West would have moved a muscle . . .'

'"We have awakened a sleeping giant",' Ishihara recited quietly. 'We are just beginning to pay the price . . .'

Takeo Nashiba, head of the banking family, spoke without rising. 'However many of us the Allies call to account for their actions, it will still fall to the Four Families to carry Japan into the next Era.'

'Yes, gentlemen. We cannot undo what has been done.' Hiromi Tosa broke in at last, his voice cracking with weariness. He sat slowly, some of the tension draining out of his face as he lifted his legs on to a footstool. 'Let us talk of the future. Let us talk of rebuilding Japan.'

He called for refreshments for his guests and turned to his nephew, a studious young man sitting at the far corner of the table. 'Isami, your father tells me you are a talented architect and engineer. I am certain you must have some thoughts on this.'

Flushed at being asked for his opinion in front of his elders, the young man soon gained confidence, pointing out that the Allied bombing had at least cleared the way for a new beginning – a unique opportunity to create engineering marvels that would not otherwise have been possible. A network of new roads, like the German Autobahns, a high-speed railway system, vast industrial complexes.

As small trays of green tea and rice crackers were served, the devastation of Hiroshima and Nagasaki by what the Emperor had called 'the Allies' cruel new bomb' and the shameful surrender that it had brought, were put aside for a brief hour and the mood lifted a little.

Senjuro Ishihara, a shrivelled, rodent-like man, kept his eyes on the tiny face of a geisha which was set in relief at the bottom of the delicate china cup in his hand. 'And where is the money going to come from for all this?' he asked. 'If we have to pay reparations, as the Germans did in 1918. Think of that! We will be lucky to be able to fill our bellies!'

General Kuga shifted his weight from one buttock to the other, to ease the knife-like stabs of his haemorrhoids. 'Ah, but great deprivation breeds great resolve. Within twenty years the Germans had built the largest modern army the West had ever seen. We could do the same — better! Isn't that correct?'

'*Chigau* — Incorrect!'

Every head in the room turned towards the uninvited speaker, a man of barely twenty-six, half-hidden in the shadows now creeping across the room. He was tall for a Japanese, with bright, intelligent eyes. Unlike the other young men present, whose hair was cropped to the crown in military style, his was worn full and combed back like a Westerner.

'Supremacy through military conquest is obsolete. It is counterproductive.'

The young man's father made a move to silence him. Their host held up his hand.

'No, let him speak. His is the generation that must carry Japan forward. You were educated in America, Tatsuya Nashiba. I am interested to hear what you have learnt.'

'Whatever the Americans take away from us, they cannot take away our energy, our ingenuity or our patience. It is true we must rebuild our country. But so must the Allies rebuild theirs. The difference is, as the victors, for every thousand houses they build, they must build a tank, for every hundred factories, a warship, for every ten cities, an atomic bomb.

'As the vanquished, gentlemen, that is not something that we will have to be concerned with. Fifty years from

13

now, the best of their technology and the greater part of their wealth will go into defence. Where might we be by then? The philosophy is a simple one: we have lost the war but we must win the peace.'

The faces of the older men began to soften. Nashiba knew he had his audience.

'Before 1941, nobody believed an operation like Pearl Harbor was possible. Since then technology has moved into a new era. Our aeronautics experts tell me that in ten years, an airliner will be able to make the Pacific crossing with only two fuelling stops. Within twenty years, perhaps only one. A Japanese businessman will be able to wake in Tokyo and sleep in New York in the same twenty-four hours. Within a generation, the rest of the world will have become so accessible that lands traditionally targeted by us for colonisation, solely because they are within military reach, will be irrelevant.

'Everything we value in our own culture now was taken from the cultures of others. We distilled the best of these cultures and turned them to our own use. This is a natural process for us. It is a process we can apply with even greater success to the American.

'In a few weeks' time, and far into the future, the American will be on our soil. We must use this time as an opportunity to study him.

'As in war, the first thing one must know is the enemy's greatest weakness. In the American, it is his insatiable avarice. We must learn what his needs and desires really are. We must learn to feed this greed. And if it takes years, even generations to get a grip on his appetite, so be it! What are a few decades to a nation that has survived for eight hundred generations?'

'Where is the honour in this? What glory can this bring Japan?' General Kuga's sudden interjection burned with indignation and loss of face. 'You can campaign for a lifetime, Nashiba, but I tell you, all battles, all wars, turn on the events of a single day!'

'But gentlemen,' Nashiba's reply was calm, 'there will be

14

a single day. We will need no armies, no atomic bombs. In that single day, we will take from the American all that he values most and leave him a wasteland that will not flourish again in a thousand years.'

Part 1

ONE

Detroit, 8 July 1995

Mack Lasky's head jerked back. His face contorted with pain.

'Okay, you made your point.' Mack felt his gut flatten out against his spine. Every nerve in his body said, *Reach out! Take control!*

'So?' Warren Steadman's small eyes twinkled with childish delight.

'I'm convinced.' Mack watched the co-pilot's control column, an inch from his fingers, move back as the six-seater turbo-prop pulled out of its steep dive and began to climb. The engine screamed as it completed the loop. 'It's a hell of a plane.'

'That's two thousand horsepower of pull you're feeling there.' Steadman eased the column forward and the plane levelled out. 'Fun toy, huh?'

'Sure.' Mack felt the pressure on his eardrums let up. *Might be, when you learn to handle the thing*, he thought.

'Still fly?'

Mack shook his head. 'Not much, I let it go. Like too many other things.'

He glanced at his friend. *For a guy who's having so much fun, you've aged, pal.*

Steadman checked his watch. 'Look, we got about an hour's more fuel, take her over whenever you want, okay?' Mack gave him the thumbs up. 'Okay, my place is coming up on your right now.'

Five hundred feet below, Mack could see Warren's new spread. It'd been too dark when he'd arrived the night before to take a real look around. Instead, they sat up talking long after Warren's wife had gone to bed; the Harvard years, old friends. Anything but the Chicago mess. Warren'd opened a bottle of ten-year-old bourbon and killed it almost single-handedly. Mack remembered smelling the last of it in Warren's coffee that morning as he was given the ten-cent tour.

Warren was justifiably proud of the rambling, ranch-style property that had been his home for almost two years, Mack thought. It had been designed with great taste and built carefully from seasoned materials to give it the warmth of age. Behind the house, there was a terraced area dominated by the Olympic-sized swimming pool. This was flanked by a guest-house, games room and changing rooms. Now, from the air, he got a complete view of the two acres of land-scaped garden; the tennis court and orchard to the west, the wide corral and stabling to the east.

'Some place you got there, Steadman,' he said. 'I'm impressed.'

'You could have had something like this years ago your-self. Never understood why you didn't.'

'Too busy.'

Yeah, Warren thought, *too busy playing 'Boardroom barracuda'. I saw that piece in the* Sun Times – *'Drum-mond's master strategist, Mack Lasky, holding the Bear at bay . . .'* He looked at Mack. 'I guess the recession had to be good for someone.'

Mack turned back to the window. He could see now that Warren's spread was part of a vast new development which stretched out beneath them in every direction.

'A thousand new homes – and that's just phase one,' Warren called. 'Not one of them on less than an acre and every one of them sold.'

'What's the catchment? I mean, I thought people were leaving this place by the truck-load.'

Warren shrugged. 'Well, if the Japs hadn't come to town in the seventies, I think we'd all be out of here by now. Okay, it ain't perfect but it's better than the way it was. At least what we're producing here is half American. Fifteen years ago, every other car on the road was Japanese. The old giants like DMC were being reamed. They knew the day of

20

the gas guzzler was gone, all right, but they had nothing to take its place.'

Mack listened to Warren jabbering away. Sounded like he was trying to convince himself more than anyone else.

'By the time I joined DMC the Japs could feel the pressure building up on them to cut back on exports. The rest you know. A strategic alliance with Mitsuda seemed the most natural thing in the world to me. They needed domestic plant and a work force and, God knows, we needed their designs and automated assembly plants. Some of the old guard thought lettin' them take a thirty-five per cent equity holding was too much. But they turned us around, Mack. In five years.' He laughed nervously. 'Christ, look at us, we got Japanese stereos, videos, cars, planes. Makes you wonder who won the war!'

For a while there was just the drone of the engines. Then Warren popped another white pill. It was the third Mack had seen him take that day.

'What you got there?'

'Aah, it was a heavy week – just helps me get that nice Saturday-morning feeling . . .'

Colombian coffee, Jack Daniels and Librium. Kind of short on roughage, but it was a diet. Mack's eyes wandered to the instrument panel, then to his friend. *Maybe four years on the board of DMC had been tougher than Warren'd made out.*

'Hey, look, Dad,' Tyler's voice piped up from behind as he pointed out an oddly shaped stretch of water to starboard. 'We're over Beaver Lake.'

'Yeah,' Warren lowered his voice, 'Saturday night after the bars close, that lake sees more beaver than you can shake a stick at!'

Tyler was craning his neck to get a better view of the windsurfers skimming over the lake's surface.

'Nah, they call it that 'cos of the way it's shaped. Never could see it myself.'

Warren pulled the plane up steeply through a cloud bank. The earth below fell away.

'I'm glad you came out, Mack. Really.'

21

'So am I.'

'You know, I used to think you didn't like me. When we roomed together at Harvard.'

'What are you talking about? You carried me all the way! I was on my knees after Princeton. Without you, I'd have flunked out the first year. You were the one person I could count on.'

'Look, I was the fat, squinty-eye little Yid, remember? No one would've come near me if you hadn't have written me in on stuff. You were the only one who ever gave a shit about me. You think I'm stupid? I knew. I used to see them screwing up their noses as I came by, like I smelt bad.'

For a moment, Mack wasn't sure he'd heard right. No one badmouthed Warren at Harvard, the guy was talking garbage. People liked him. He was funny, good to be with.

'What are you—'

'I used to look in my car mirror. You know that old Porsche I had . . . I could read their lips, Mack, see what they were saying about me . . . There he goes, the one Hitler missed. Oh, they'd smile when I looked straight at 'em, but I knew . . .'

Warren was going wacko. It was like he'd just jumped into a different personality. Mack turned to look at him. His face was crimson, his eyes were streaming tears.

'The only one who really liked me was Crystal Corrigan. She loved me. She used to come to my bedroom and fuck my brains out. You remember that, Mack?'

'Crystal Corrigan . . . ?' The plane started to pitch and roll like it was hitting turbulence. But Mack knew the only turbulence was inside Warren's head. *Crystal Corrigan. Hadn't she been in some TV series for a season or two? Warren always pointed her out. He'd known her in seventh grade, or something.*

Mack yelled over the roar of the engines. 'Where the hell are you, Warren? She wasn't at Harvard, for Chrissake.'

'Daaaad!' Tyler slid, half fell across the plane. 'I'm getting sick!'

Things started to fall apart badly. Warren shoved the control column forward, but too hard and too fast. The plane dropped out of the air like a stone. Their ears screamed with pain. Then he pulled up steep, in a high, stomach-wrenching turn. The engines started to shake violently like they were going to stall.

Somewhere inside Mack, a voice rationalised: *I'm travelling at 250 knots . . . 15,000 feet up . . . in a plastic tube flown by a paranoid schizophrenic.*

'Daaad, don't!' Tyler started to scream hysterically. Warren's eyes bulged as he fought for air.

He's having a cardiac! Mack's mind raced, *No, he's . . . he's too high! It's the altitude. It's all that shit in his blood. The pills and the booze. He's forgotten to pressurise the cabin. Every thousand feet we go up, the effect's doubling.* Years ago, when it'd happened to Mack, he'd only had a couple of Scotches. But he recognised the symptoms.

'Warren!' he shouted. 'Bring her down . . . down!'

They went into what felt like a vertical dive. Mack's limbs turned to lead. His eyes streamed and he could feel his sphincter muscle going. Tyler was rolling around the roof, in an apoplectic fit. By the time the nose of the plane started pulling upwards, you could damn near make out the faces of the windsurfers on the lake below. The over-boosted engines let out a long, tortured scream, then, inch by inch, the horizon reappeared diagonally in front of them. They were still moving at one hell of a speed, but at least they were now lower, straight and level.

'Slow down.' Mack tried to sound calm. He watched the needle of the airspeed indicator slowly unwind. A few miles ahead of them, slightly to the left, he could see the airfield they'd taken off from almost an hour earlier. He grasped the dual controls in front of him. 'Okay, Warren, let me land her.'

'It's all right . . . I'm all right.' Warren's grip was like iron. He looked terrible but the plane was flying normally.

A voice was calling urgently over the radio. Mack strained to hear it over Tyler's violent sobbing from behind.

'Warren, for Chrissake tell them you're coming in.'

It was too late. Warren, his eyes staring ahead, was going for a final approach, like it or not.

Mack started running instinctively through the landing procedure. Position: good. Speed: a little fast, but okay. His eyes scanned the instrument panel as he tried to remember what came next. He was vaguely aware of fire tenders pulling out beneath them.

They were twenty feet above the runway before he realised the three red lights right in front of him should have been green. He stared at them for a full second before he took in what that meant.

'Jesus Christ!' He felt for the lever he knew must be on the console to his left. As the ground rushed towards them, he slammed his hand against it. Immediately, the hydraulic pumps thrust the undercarriage downward. He gritted his teeth for the impact.

The plane hit the runway with a bone-jarring crunch the split second the wheels locked. It bounced twice, yawing violently, the starboard wingtip scraping along the concrete. Finally there was a comforting drag as the brakes bit and brought them to a halt.

Mack's head fell against his chest. 'You fucking stupid bastard,' he said. 'You nearly killed us all.'

Simmond's airfield was not a place to hang around any longer than necessary when you'd broken just about every flying regulation in the book. Warren was too shaken up to take in much of what the controller said but Mack reckoned he'd got off light with a report to the FAA. Taking Warren home in this state didn't seem like such a smart move either. Anyway, he needed a drink now.

A couple of miles from the airfield, there was a place called O'Connor's Steak House. Mack took the wheel of the red convertible while Warren sat hunched up in the passenger seat, lost in thought. He looked at his friend. His gut hung out over his pants, his shirt was stained. It seemed to sum up the way he felt about himself.

What had happened to make Warren this way? He'd

24

always been lumpish and poorly co-ordinated, but back at Harvard it seemed that what he'd lacked in physical agility he made up for in brainpower. He had that rare kind of intelligence that could cut through layers of irrelevant detail and go straight to the central issue of an argument. Then Warren'd been sharp, incisive. These days his mind seemed to be getting kind of flabby too.

Booze and tranqs: Mack had had his run in with them himself. When the good times came, he found himself living his life through a fog, his senses dulled, as though the world was still something to be kept at a distance. Facing the problem had been the key to solving it.

But Warren'd never had that kind of willpower. For someone so smart, he was surprisingly soft and gullible. It was what made him a sweet guy. But he'd gotten lazy, Mack thought. Had too much of an easy ride. Warren's family had had money, had backed him all the way through college. His had been a different story.

It had been a long hard climb from Kedzie Street, from the bleak alleys that ran up from Chicago's Arnold Canal. Making friends, real relationships; somehow that had got lost along the way. *Dead man's pass*, he thought, *Rafakowski, Gersh and me must've rolled a dozen guys there when we were kids.*

He'd been back a few times. Seen friends from those days; Rafakowski with his body repair and paint shop, Gersh, that dry-cleaning business a couple of blocks away. He couldn't really tell what they thought about him, just knew he had nothing to say to them any more. They were part of a world he was glad to have left behind.

Mack turned the wheel hard left and pulled up outside O'Connor's Steak House. They settled into a quiet part of the bar. Tyler, his face pale, his small frame shivering in his father's outsized golfing jacket, stared vacantly at his Coke.

Mack knew that Warren could feel the unspoken question: You got a beautiful wife, kids, the kind of home most folk only dream about. Everything. Why the hell are you so fucked up?

25

Warren's small red eyes swivelled away from his whisky and held Mack's for a moment. 'See pal, the thing is, I owe three million bucks.'

'How much?'

'Three mill. Nobody's fault but my own. I got crazy, got carried away.'

Mack took some loose change from his pocket and pressed it into Tyler's hand. 'Here,' he said, 'go see what you can win on that fruit machine.'

Warren didn't even seem to notice his son go. He was staring out of the window to where a young couple were lifting two small kids out of a hatchback. The man whisked the little girl up on to his shoulders and bounced her around like he was a rodeo pony. *That's what a guy looks like when he doesn't have his ass in a sling*, he thought, *when he doesn't spend every waking minute wondering where the hell he's gonna find the equivalent of eight years' salary.*

'I guess it started with the house,' he began, slowly. 'The Cedar View development was a Mitsuda project. The directors of DMC got a special deal, mortgages through the company at five per cent. Jackie and I went out and took a look. I tell you Mack, I never dreamed I'd live in a spread like that.

'It was a big squeeze for us at first. After we moved in, the place still looked empty. We got a lot of stuff through the Jap connection, I can't remember half of it now.' He leaned his head in the palm of one hand. 'That spring, I know we put in the hot tub and a games room for Tyler with all that electronic crap that kids love. We got it all way below trade.

'I should have waited a bit, but some of the directors were buying holiday homes in the Florida Keys through the company, and Jackie has family down there and, I dunno, I got sucked in. After that, I really started to lose touch with what I was spending. There were all the furnishings for that place too, and we needed cars to get around down there.' He tried to seal up the crack in his voice with a gulp of air.

26

'The biggest craziness was the plane. The plane! I've been trying to sell the goddamn thing for a year, and a lot of the other stuff too. Can you imagine what it costs to maintain all this? Most people just don't want the overhead.'

His shaking hands closed round his glass like it was warm. 'Anyway, I got so behind with repayments, after a while I had to take a slug of bourbon every morning before I even dared open the mail. That's when the real drinking began. My work started to suffer. I made a couple of screw-ups — one serious one, and things came to a head.' Mack watched him take a slug now for old times' sake.

'The Board was very understanding. We decided I should lighten my work-load for a while, step back a little till things straightened out. That's when the company doctor put me on the pills, to relieve some of the stress.'

There was silence while Warren fought to keep his tattered act together. When he started talking again, his voice was strangled. 'Days when I should've been really on the ball, I was a fucking vegetable. Like when the two Jap directors started pushing through a lot of changes. I should have been in there, Mack, fighting. But y'know, I'd open my mouth to speak my piece and I'd hear this voice inside me say, "Back off, Steadman. Don't push your luck."' Tears started to roll down the big, amiable face. 'Look at me! They got me every which way.'

Mack did look at him. The thought he'd had earlier in the day returned. This beaten down, overweight guy wasn't a day over thirty-three but if you'd just walked in and met him for the first time, you'd say he was pushing fifty.

Warren popped another pill. 'You know the only thing that makes it any better?' He looked back over his shoulder, as if he might be overheard. 'I'm not the only one around here in this kind of shit, not by a long shot.'

Mack looked into the flames of the fake log fire burning cheerfully in the corner and struggled for some straw of consolation that Warren could cling to. Finally, he managed, 'You're a survivor, Warren, I've known you a long time. Hell, you'll come through this – God knows I'll help you all I can. You'll make it, you'll see.'

But what he honestly thought was, *Buddy, you'll be lucky if you see the year out.*

TWO

Helmut Richter had known for months that today
would be one of the most difficult of his career. He
leaned against the temporary safety rail and looked down.
Sixty storeys beneath him, the doors of a grey limousine
swung open. He watched three men get out and walk hurriedly into the building.

The towering framework of steel, concrete and glass
where Richter stood rose out of what had been, five years
before, the mined no-man's-land dividing East Germany
from West. The foundations of buildings that would shape
the skyline of a reunited capital sprang up now from the
same bare earth that had once borne the Berlin Wall. A
forest of illuminated hoardings, each showing an artist's
impression of a completed project, ran the entire length of
this, the most valuable strip of undeveloped real estate in
Europe. 'The Nashiba Bank – Opening November 1995'
blazed the one below Richter now. The way things were
going, they could carve that date on his gravestone.

Richter looked across at the four other Germans who
stood in the centre of a concrete floor that was large enough
to take nine tennis courts. His site manager and his own
assistant were lifting a scale model of the Nashiba building
on to a trestle table. A few feet away, shivering in the cold
morning air, stood the two architects. Their names were
Franz and Beppo Schraffl, but to Richter and his team,
almost from the start, they'd been known as 'Dick und Döf'
– Fat and Stupid – the German for Laurel and Hardy.

Richter grimaced. It had to be admitted that 'Dick' had
done an adequate enough job on the main structure of the

building. There'd been no more than the usual number of setbacks expected on a project this size. But just what had inspired him to entrust the intricate upper section to that *arshloch* of a brother of his, only he and his God would ever know.

'Döf' would have made a fine job of the new public toilets on Friedrichstrasse, Richter thought, his eyes radiating scorn at the gangly Bavarian, might even have pulled off a new bus shelter on the Kurfürstendamm. But handing him something of this scale was like throwing a Rottweiler to a rabbit. Richter wasn't in a charitable mood. Hadn't been for a long time. He let out a sigh. Why this, of all projects?

When his engineering firm won the Nashiba tender against stiff competition, Richter had thrown a champagne party for his staff. Theirs was a young, energetic company and this was the most prestigious project they'd ever pitched for. It was the break they needed to lift them above the many to prosper with the few.

Until that summer he'd never really thought of there being an actual Mr Nashiba, any more than he'd thought about there being a Mr Boeing. It was now the summer of '95, the project had been on foot for two years, yet nowhere had he seen a press profile of the great man. *Mensch!* Richter thought. *I don't even know what he looks like.*

He wouldn't have to wait much longer to find out. The President of the most powerful bank in the world, the driving force behind the fastest-growing Japanese multinational conglomerate, was riding up in the rusty iron cage that served as a temporary elevator at that very moment, to chew his balls off.

The grille-work door slid back like a razor on glass. His guests had arrived. The tallest and youngest was Nashiba junior. Richter had met Akitō once before when the bank project was still on the drawing board. The Harvard law school education, the English accent picked up at Cambridge, the $3,000-worth of Roberto Lauria clothes, were all part of a Western skin he could shed at will. Underneath, he was Japanese to the marrow. Richter saw him and the third Japanese, now, only in peripheral vision. His eyes were locked on the old man at Akitō's side.

Tatsuya Nashiba walked towards the Germans. His dark eyes shifted slowly, betraying nothing; focusing on each face, assessing it and moving on. Finally the eyes settled on Richter, slicing into him. No chance act of nature produced this kind of charisma and none was going to snuff it out until it was damn well ready. Mr Nashiba existed all right.

My God, time has been good to you, old man, the engineer thought. There were no arteries hardening in that wiry frame. Seventy-five years had wrinkled the skin around the eyes a little, thinned the hair at the crown, but that was it. Richter inclined his head a little. He'd learnt enough about his Japanese customers to show the desired respect. Nashiba responded. Then, in a simple movement of his hand, the old man gestured that Akitō would be handling matters and broke away from the group to survey the view from what would soon be his European headquarters.

Richter looked around himself. This, the highest storey, was to be the building's showpiece, a cathedral-like atrium, a pyramid of alternating glass and copper panels mounted on a light alloy frame. The architects, in their tender, described it as 'a tree-filled hospitality suite, a conference area, an art gallery – a gemstone on the skyline of Berlin symbolising One Germany'. Right now, Richter thought as he took Akitō and the other Japanese over to the scale model, it symbolised one fuck of a big problem.

Akitō waved away coffee offered from a vacuum flask. 'No November opening, Herr Richter.'

'No November opening, Mr Nashiba. End of February at best. I'm afraid we've hit a design fault. This area, this . . .' He waved his arm around as if searching for the least offensive word. 'This *atrium*, is sound enough to withstand normal stresses, high winds, storms, that kind of thing. But unfortunately the framework won't take the weight of a power hoist.'

Akitō turned to Schraffl the younger. 'Power hoist?'

Richter was smiling tightly, now, right into the face of the man he'd come to loathe over the last eighteen months.

31

Okay, you dumb Bavarian cunt, he thought, *let's see you slide your way out of this one.*

'The copper and glass panels were heavier than we anticipated,' the architect started. 'We needed a power hoist to lift them from ground level. But the roof structure wouldn't take the weight.'

'Hmm.' Akitō put his thumbs together against his lower lip and looked almost sympathetic. 'So how has this much been achieved?'

The edge of Richter's mouth twitched. *Oh, this is good. This is really good. I've waited a long time for this. Let's tell the Japanese kid how we're spending Daddy's 250 million Deutschmarks.*

Schraffl reddened to medium rare. 'Well, we pulled sections up with ropes and a pulley.'

'Ropes and a pulley?' There was no contempt in Akitō's laughter, apparently just genuine amusement. He stepped back and looked around the half-completed atrium. 'Ropes and a pulley . . . to build a pyramid. How very appropriate.'

'If there'd been better communications,' Schraffl started, 'everything would have gone as planned . . .'

His brother beside him, who had been trying to look as if he didn't exist in any material form, shook his head once, quickly, indicating that this was not the best approach.

'. . . anyway, we will most certainly, definitely have everything completed by the end of February. Franz?'

Elder brother nervously checked his notes one more time. 'Correct.'

'Incorrect!' The change in dynamics in Akitō's voice made everyone flinch. The other side of the floor, it hit Tatsuya Nashiba, too. That same word had once stopped dead the most important meeting in Japan's recent history. He turned to look at the speaker now, seeing not his son, but himself almost fifty years before.

Ah yes, the room had rocked for him. He had presence, power and the inspiration of youth. The men whose attention he commanded then were powerful but old. Their era was over. His was at its genesis.

Akitō continued, but the old man was no longer listening to his voice.

'. . . This is Toshio Tada, Herr Richter, he designed our office in Paris. Please take your instructions from him from now on.'

Instead, he turned to look down on the massive earthworks below, the half-completed concrete foundations, the exposed steel reinforcements rusting in the light morning rain. To Tatsuya Nashiba, this spoke not of a reunited city but of a ruined one. Not of Berlin, but of Tokyo, as it had looked that night in August 1945.

The atmosphere in the limousine that had carried Tatsuya, his father, uncle and eldest cousin to the Tosa family compound had been funereal. It was not a human spirit they mourned, but a national one . . .

Akitō turned and walked towards his father, then, almost as an afterthought, turned back to the brothers Schraffl. 'Thank you for your work on this project, gentlemen. Please leave your security passes at the gate.'

In the time it took the young Japanese to take the dozen steps to his father's side, Richter observed a very satisfying transformation. The Schraffls hung on the air like Disneyworld automatons in a power outage. You could practically hear their brains shutting down cell by cell. Richter pursed his lips and quietly whistled the Cuckoo Song. Dick und Döf had just got their closing credits.

The Mitsuda limousine pulled through the Brandenburg Gate on its way to Tempelhof airport. Tatsuya Nashiba turned to look at the bare mound that had once housed Hitler's Chancellery.

'Lebensraum.' He turned the word over in his mind. 'Living Space.' That was the claim the Germans used to justify the war of '39, but what did they know about living space? The Japanese were a nation of 125 million people crammed into an area a fortieth the size of Texas. A two-bedroom high-rise apartment in Tokyo now cost the better part of a million dollars. Families had to spread the mortgage over three generations to pay off the debt.

Tatsuya had been a twelve-year-old schoolboy in Osaka when Japan invaded Manchuria in 1931. This foothold in the Chinese mainland had marked a new era of Japanese expansionism before. It was a propaganda exercise. A move calculated to excite nationalist fervour, to justify Japan's own need for living space.

And it disturbed the rest of the world not a jot. As the *Washington Post* remarked: 'Americans don't give a hoot in a rain barrel about Manchuria.'

But the mood changed with General Tojo's army's push into Shanghai. This, the commercial centre of the East, was home to thousands of expatriate Americans. Nashiba was beginning his second year of Economics at Yale when news came out of the mindless slaughter that followed.

At first he fended off the anti-Japanese jibes with a shrug. 'My family are in the mortgage and loan business! We're nothing to do with this.' In reality, he knew that the Nashiba family interests had extended far beyond banking a century before.

As the invasion force swept relentlessly south into Indo-China, and war between America and Japan drew closer, the jibes turned to physical violence. Tatsuya found himself counting off the days until his finals were completed and he could return to his homeland.

The same month the Japanese bombed Pearl Harbor he was given the job of co-ordinating the Nashibas' five electronics plants in Nagasaki. These factories had formerly produced consumer goods. Now, the same skills were turned to supplying the full range of electronic components necessary to keep the Japanese war machine on the move.

General Tojo's propaganda continued to feed the people a diet of matchless glory, but along the impenetrable lines of communication that connected the heads of the four great families, a starker truth emerged. Japanese, forced to colonise vast tracts of the new Empire, were sending back bitter tales.

The day Hitler was shown the wonders of a freshly conquered Paris, Tatsuya dined in Tokyo with his cousin.

Hiroki had been invalided out of Indo-China and sent home. He was twenty-three, but his hair was almost white. Pain shot across his face even at the sound of chopsticks on the thin china bowls in front of them.

'I tell you between ourselves, Tats, we are lords of thousands of square miles of jungles and swamps. At night we burnt the leeches off our feet with cigarettes . . .' He stirred the food aimlessly round his bowl. 'Half of my men have dysentery, malaria and typhoid fever.

'And Manchuria? That windswept wasteland, populated by savages, whose only contribution to mankind is endemic gonorrhoea? Living space? Tats, it's dying space.'

The Empire continued to grow and certainly there was gold to be panned with the grains of sand, but to Tatsuya, a man who'd seen more of the splendours and sophistication of the West by the late thirties than most Westerners had by the century's close, the pickings seemed slim.

The night after the destruction of the Japanese Navy at the battle of Midway he wrote in his diary: 'This was a campaign built on old ideas and limited technology. While we are still content to colonise only those territories that lie within the limit of military range, we must be content with an Empire that, at best, unites nations of primitives who will take generations to match the achievements of the West.'

Then in large characters: 'Militarism is not the sole answer. Perhaps it is no answer at all.'

It was this last thought which prompted Nashiba to speak that day in 1945. To dare question the authority of the descendants of those who had ruled Japan, unseen and unchallenged, since it was a nation of fishermen.

He had intended to speak, knew he must speak. He too was heir to a great dynasty. A dynasty whose fate, though inexorably linked with the other three, was in his hands. He had been taught that, through this war, these leaders, these old men, would secure the greatest honour in Japan's history. Now that honour was lost.

The old men knew that as well as Tatsuya did. They held their peace as he, the youngest of the Nashibas, shaped a vision of the future none of them could have conceived and none would live to see.

'... *As in war, the first thing one must know is the enemy's greatest weakness. In the American it is his insatiable avarice. All standards of success are set by his possessions: his luxuries, his ingenious toys.*

'*We must feed this avarice. We must feed him and feed him until he chokes! We must dazzle him with endless new technology, bring him everything he has ever hungered for, make it cheaper and more reliable than he could ever make it himself.*

'*We must throw our people into the factory and the marketplace with the same fervour that we threw them into the battlefield. We must wait and we must work together. And then, one day,* Kettei no hi, *the decisive day, we will strike our blow.*'

Nashiba settled back into the comfort of the kid leather seat and began to enjoy the shimmer of light through the frail leaves on the limes of Unter den Linden. That day would be soon now. Very soon.

THREE

Mack slammed his fist down on the desk top. 'Quit steaming your clams, will you, we always knew VideSet'd get ripped off sooner or later. It was just a matter of time. It was a cash cow, Bill, that's all it ever was. We were damn lucky to get the run out of it we did. It bought us eighteen vital months. Never forget that.'

He glanced down the passageway to where Warren sat in the den, slouched opposite the television holding a can of Labatt's beer in front of him like a phallus.

'Look, this is the first break I've had in a year,' Mack said. 'There's nothing we should do for ten days. Let's see what kind of impact this thing makes and take it from there. I'll be in New York from tomorrow. I'll touch base with you when I get in.'

He hung up and walked into the den. Warren plumped up his cushion and settled back into the old armchair. Mack remembered that chair. It was the last vestige of a simpler, more frugal lifestyle. It had been bought for the first apartment Warren took after leaving college. A succession of overweight sitters, small pets and boisterous children had taken its toll on the springs and upholstery and now, like its owner, it was worn and shapeless.

Mack went back over his notes on the week ahead. 'You knew Ellis Friedman at UCLA, didn't you?'

'Yeah. Cold sonofabitch.'

'Gutsy sonofabitch.' Mack ran his hand down his jaw, unaccustomed to the feeling of two days' growth of beard. 'You got to hand it to him, he's fought off the competition tooth and claw.'

'What's it to you?'

'He's had his head-hunter sniffing round me for a month.'

There was a long pause. 'You seeing him?'

'Tuesday.'

Warren made a hissing noise through his teeth. 'You and he'd tear each other's throats out inside six months.'

Mack watched Warren's attention drift back to the ball game. *Christ! He's changed,* he thought. *Time was when he generated all the positive energy I could take.*

Those last few weeks in Chicago, Mack had started taking stock of his life for the first time. Again and again, his mind had gone back to the Harvard days, when things had been simpler. Deep down, he knew he'd only come out to Detroit to top up on those times. Now, as he looked across the room at Warren, anaesthetised from a world of problems he could no longer face, it seemed that another touchstone was beginning to slip away. A sudden sense of isolation engulfed him.

In many ways, he'd always been remote, cut off. He'd made himself that way. The process had begun when he was eight, when his father was killed in 'Nam. His sister had been too young to understand what had happened, but to Mack it was as though his childhood ended that day. From then on, he knew he'd need to be a lot more than just another working-class kid with street smarts. By fourteen, he was operating a small mail-order business from his bedroom as well as editing a home-printed ad-sheet for second-hand cars.

All the time at college, Mack'd listened good and hard. When he walked out of Harvard at twenty-four with a masters in law and business studies, the scholarship boy stopped listening and started talking. By twenty-eight, he'd talked himself into the senior vice-presidency of Drummond Inc., a Chicago-based conglomerate with interests in consumer electronics and property development.

Driven; that's what Laurie'd called him. She hadn't been the first. The same frenetic energy that had powered him relentlessly through a dozen major projects, had worn out a lot of relationships along the way. Theirs was just one more casualty.

The snap of another can of beer being opened brought Mack's attention back to Warren's TV. The ball game was punctuated by a commercial break. Some actor, dressed as Davy Crockett and holding a camera, sang in a broad Tennessee accent: 'A vacation is for ever with Yamagata.' Mack shook his head. *The goddamn world's gone loopy*, he thought.

'I'm gonna call Morton in New York,' he said, suddenly. 'You wanna speak with him?'

Warren's voice answered from the far side of the planet Librium. 'Sure. Morton? . . . yeah.'

He escaped to Warren's study and dialled Morton's number in New York. The phone sounded like a cicada on heat.

'*Cirrr . . . Cirrr . . .*'

Suddenly Morton's voice was on the line. 'Yup?'

'Orson?'

'Who's this?'

'Eleanor Roosevelt.'

'Sorry, Eleanor, I was taking a dump. You in Chicago or New York?'

'I'll be in New York tomorrow, for a couple of days.'

'Laurie with you?'

Mack took a deep breath. 'We split, Morton, about six months ago.'

'You're kidding. You guys? How come you didn't tell me this before?'

'Oh, you know. Listen, I got a couple of offers I want to check out in New York, so I thought I'd give you a call.'

'When you going to be free?'

'Eight, eight-thirty.'

'Stop by. I want to hear what's been happening with you.'

'I'll bring the Hine.'

'VSOP.' The line went dead.

*

39

Mack lifted his case into the trunk of the waiting cab and turned, extending a hand to Warren. 'Don't forget, now, call me anytime if you need more help.'

'Thanks, Mack . . . for everything.' Warren flung an arm around his friend's shoulder.

' 'Bye!' Jackie and the kids were waving from the doorway. Mack waved back, then turned to Warren, gripping his hand firmly. 'You've got everything a man could want, Warren, for Chrissakes don't blow it.'

The American Airlines 9.15 flight out of Detroit lifted on to its flight path and turned south for Kennedy. Mack snapped open his briefcase and reached inside for the folded *Wall Street Journal*. He let his hand rest on it for a second, then leaned back in the seat, deep in thought. Calling Morton'd been like calling home.

It'd been at Harvard, in the spring of '85, when he'd first met Morton Totheroh. He remembered it plain as day. He'd been deep into a Federal Supplement, when Warren'd peered over the horn-rimmed glasses he wore in those days, and told him, 'I've put us down for the Morton Totheroh Lecture.' He'd looked blank and tried to place the name.

'Morton Totheroh for Chrissakes!' Warren said. 'He virtually pioneered cybernetics from the adding-machine to the twenty-megabyte personal computer. Well, him and a few others. If it wasn't for him we'd all still be counting on our fingers. I heard the guy talk at UCLA once. I tell you, he's like Thomas Edison and Victor Borge in one body.'

Mack tried to visualise the combination, failed completely and returned to The State of California versus Nathan Lubinski.

As it turned out, Morton Totheroh was entirely himself. Unlike most technocrats and academics who, for all their brilliance, couldn't have put over the Vehicle Code, Totheroh was a positively magnetic figure. He looked to be in his late forties but was probably half a decade older. His trim, stocky frame moved ceaselessly around a packed Sanders Theater, his fingers poking and stabbing at the air to reinforce each point. The wiry, salt-and-pepper hair had once shown some signs of grooming but, by the end of the evening, it seemed to owe its style mainly to the Busted Sofa School of Hairdressing. The intense blue eyes, with their permanent look of mild amusement, connected with every face in the audience at some point in the evening, giving the whole show – for that's what it was – a completely personal meaning.

Most affecting of all was his voice. It filled the room with a theatrical resonance, rising and falling with the bravura of a young Orson Welles. It was easy to see why graduates and undergraduates from all spheres flocked to his lectures. The man's grasp of his subject was not only total, his capacity to make it accessible and compelling was remarkable. His sweeping visions of the technology of the future, dire warnings of its misuse, his wit and enthusiasm swept all along with him.

'You know,' he said, to loud, disbelieving laughter, 'when radio first came in in the twenties, my great-aunt Florrie used to put a blanket over it at night, so the announcer wouldn't see her undressing. No, this is serious, and a lot of people feel the same way about the on-line computer now. They should. It poses a greater threat to personal privacy than anything yet devised by man. Once you're hooked up to that telephone line, any spy, fraudster, saboteur, or two-bit technopath between here and Taiwan can hack into it and be looking at the most intimate details of your life in seconds. While computer development moves forward it must also consolidate. Secure systems are the number-one priority now.'

'Can you build a hacker-proof computer?' Mack had asked, fascinated by the subject for the first time in his life.

'Not so long as you have human beings in the equation. Corporations like mine spend millions of dollars developing new security systems for our customers. And do you know the first thing that happens when it's installed? Nine times out of ten, their staff use their birth date or their wife's name as their personal entry code. Then they wonder why some dipshit who dropped out of school in ninth grade can hack into their new system before the ink on the cheque's dry. The guy I know who developed the encoder – that's a scrambling device that jumbles up data while it's being passed down the telephone line – he found out the other day that his own secretary had written her entry code to his system in lipstick on the side of her work terminal! That's like leaving the keys to your safe on the kitchen table.

'I don't know what lies ahead, but if the whole history of cybernetics, from beginning to end, was equated to one calendar year, my guess is that today we're somewhere around 12.10 a.m., January the first. I probably won't be there but some of you guys are gonna be responsible for 12.15. Don't screw up! Good luck, thank you and good night.'

Mack's thoughts were interrupted by the arrival of an air steward with breakfast and hot drinks. He put his briefcase on the empty seat next to him, folded down his table and set down the large black coffee.

He tore open the sugar packet and stirred some in. *That first night had been the start of so many things.*

'I don't know if you've eaten yet, Mr Totheroh,' Warren'd said, 'but there's this great little Italian place on Inman Square a few minutes from here. We'd really appreciate it if you could join us for dinner.'

'I'd have liked that.' Morton wiped chalk dust off his trousers. 'But I'm afraid I've already made plans. Unless . . .' He called over to a tall, slim Japanese sitting alone near the door. Mack had seen him before around the campus. He was a freshman law student. 'Akitō, do you have any objections if we make it a foursome?'

The smooth, chiselled face broke into a broad smile. 'I'd enjoy it.'

For a second there, Mack's street antenna had detected a sense of relief from their burly dinner guest. It would be nearly ten years before he'd find out why.

Late into the evening, the party sat talking in a corner of the otherwise empty Italian restaurant. The food was good and Morton was feeling relaxed. 'This soldier,' he declared

42

over the fourth bottle of Frascati, 'having given valiantly of his best, will be buried with full military honours.' He laid it gently to rest in the middle of the table and piled paper napkins on top.

Mack made a cardboard tube out of what had been the menu and blew the Last Post through it. As Morton continued, reciting the eulogy in suspect Italian, Warren completed a cross out of breadsticks and stuck it upright in the butter. This was duly placed in position as a headstone.

A bemused Italian waiter, anxious to lock up for the night, tried once more to clear the table. Akitō Nashiba held up a hand. Exhumation of the deceased, he explained in his immaculate English, would cause needless grief to the relatives. If the waiter could bring the check, they'd be happy to pay a little extra so that the departed could remain interred at least until the following morning.

Finally, the party retired to Akitō's small rented house in Avon Hill. Like Warren, he received a generous monthly allowance from his parents, but he chose to live alone, off campus, with his books and records. As he started to have a good time, the natural shyness, so often mistaken for coldness, slipped away. The warmth of the evening, the high spirits and the low comedy, brought something that he hadn't felt in his adult life before – a true sense of camaraderie.

Akitō poured out cognac brought from the restaurant while Morton settled himself into a large Chippendale chair, loosened his tie and asked if anyone minded if he smoked. Without waiting for a reply, he produced a large, fat joint, lit it with a silver lighter and drew on it deeply.

Mack raised an eyebrow. Ecstasy, crack, LSD tabs and raw heroin had been commonplace on Chicago's mean streets, but marijuana was something of a novelty to him. He took the joint from Morton's fingers like it was an artefact from a lost civilisation.

Warren usually tripped out reading the speeches of Clarence Darrow. Akitō, whose older male relatives often took opium, preferred to lose himself in classical Japanese poetry and Sibelius. But even for them, taking a couple of hits on

43

a joint was something different. Hell, it counted as inter-active social history!

As the smoke of the joint hit the back of Mack's throat, he calculated that if Morton was now in his early fifties, he must've been about their age when the Flower Power thing broke. He tried to picture Morton in a beaded headband and kaftan. Somehow, it didn't fit.

Soon, the quality of the conversation reached a new low – Mack's and Warren's favourite at the end of any drunken evening: bad horror movies.

'Not the Spielberg things with all those expensive special effects,' he explained to Morton. 'The real turkeys, the black-and-white jobs made on a budget of about eight dollars.'

So, with great solemnity, the friends weighed *Plan Nine From Outer Space* and its reputation among film buffs as the nadir of American film-making, against the glori-ous inadequacies of *Jesse James Meets Frankenstein's Daughter*.

Akitō soon joined in the argument. He'd been sent to boarding school in America at the age of twelve. There'd been enough lonely weekends watching the *Late Late Show* for him to be familiar with the genre. But, despite his heated protests that the Japanese classic, *Godzilla Versus The Smog Monster*, should be considered as a Golden Turkey, Mack insisted that the quarter-scale miniature cities, built to make Godzilla look colossal, were much too well executed to be considered. Privately, he'd always felt sorry for the craftsmen who must have spent months making those cities only to have some fuckwit in a rubber dragon suit stomp them all to bits.

'QED,' he said. 'Disqualified on the grounds of some redeeming quality.'

'Okay, fantasy buffs, what's this?' Morton drew on the last of the joint as he leaned forward, the voice that was so nearly that of Orson Welles becoming exactly his.

'The projectile has buried itself in a large hole about twenty yards from where I'm standing. There's a sound! Like a hatch being unscrewed ... I can see now, a small

circular section of the projectile is lifting up ... Something's coming out of it ... I can see a tentacle, a black tentacle ... now another, and ... Holy Jesus, it's got a body the size of a bear, glistening like wet leather ...'

Morton's voice boomed through Akitō's little living-room. *'... Its eyes are black, like a snake's eyes. The mouth is V-shaped, rimless ... The whole thing's pulsating ... Whatever this is, it is not of this planet, it has evolved in a different time, in a different place in the galaxy.'* Morton sat back and sipped his cognac through the applause that followed, a huge grin of satisfaction on his face.

'H. G. Wells, *War of the Worlds*,' Akitō said immediately.

'Originally,' Morton's eyes twinkled.

Mack turned to Akitō. 'It's the radio version, broadcast in the thirties. Haven't you heard of it?' Akitō shook his head.

'Caused a sensation at the time. Folks who switched on in the middle of it thought it was for real, thousands of them packed up and fled to the hills.'

Akitō stared at him incredulously. 'They really thought they were being invaded by Martians? Come on!'

'No, Mack's right.' Morton got up suddenly and started to look for his car keys. 'My Uncle Jack and half the Milwaukee Gun Club went up to the woods and waited for the damn things to land. It was a long night, I can tell you.'

Akitō shook his head. 'Only in America.'

There would be many similar nights over the next two years, often in different restaurants on Morton's home ground in New York. By popular request, *War of the Worlds* became the evening's traditional finale. Akitō's fascination with it never diminished.

Often the wisecracking would give way to more serious discussion, usually with Morton taking up his own position against the other three. He'd start an argument calculated to inflame his young companions, then pursue it with a doggedness that left them exhausted.

A typical line of his would go: '... Thirty years from now, lawyers'll be able to programme the details of a case into a computer and, in minutes, get out all the relevant law plus a full legal opinion, more carefully researched and objectively reasoned than any human could ever do it.'

Warren would stick his thumbs deep into the pockets of the vest he took to wearing in his later years at Harvard and take the floor. 'You'll never replace the human element. Nothing can rival the technique of a trial attorney in cross-examination or the persuasiveness of his closing address.'

'If the judge just bought the same software he'd know pretty much what both sides were going to say before they even opened their mouths.' Akitō's voice would come in a whisper. Always did when he was irritated. 'Up to a point he does now. That's how you get to be judge.'

'All right, take the State of Chicago versus Loeb and Leopold, Nineteen Twenty-four,' Warren would go on. 'Clarence Darrow's closing address to the jury was one of the finest pieces of oratory in the history of American jurisprudence. Those guys would've fried without him. You can't tell me some software package can replace that!'

By this stage, Morton would be enjoying himself. 'Never,' he'd say. 'Never will. Those kinds of cases are the stuff of history, in a class of their own. I'm talking your everyday story of homicidal folk, here. Ninety-nine cases out of a hundred conform to one of half a dozen scenarios: kid holds up a gas station and panics; guy finds his old lady in the sack with the neighbour; jerk blows his old man away because they wanna watch different TV channels. Same stuff, over and over again. Technology can and will help with those.'

'Nothing can allow for the effect on a jury of a defendant suddenly breaking down on the stand . . .' Mack would try. And so the argument would roll on, until either the booze or the stamina ran out. Sometimes they'd come to a point, and only Mack knew how to judge it just right, when he could say, 'You don't believe a damn word you're saying, do you, Morton?'

Then Morton's booming laugh would fill the room. 'Nah! Just like to give you trained monkeys a run for your money, make you look behind the issues, not just take everything you're handed as holy writ.'

Over time, the group became a kind of private club with

reciprocal benefits for all. The guys gave Morton back a sense, not just of youth, but of family. Whether he consciously acknowledged it or not, Mack and Warren were the sons he'd never had the chance to have.

What Morton gave them all was a heightened sense of the value of analysis. One time, he said, 'Once you can take something apart – even *Plan Nine From Outer Space* – right down to its smallest component, understand how it works, individually, in combinations and in combinations of breakdowns of like things, you can start to figure out what makes that something great, unique . . . or a failure. From then on you can utilise different combinations to create something unique of your own.

'You can apply it to anything. An electrical circuit, a mechanical rig, a painting, a pop song, a meal even. Take it apart with your eye, your ear, your hand or your taste buds until the process becomes second nature.'

It was this jewel of his wisdom, above all, that would be his greatest gift to the three; destined to be absorbed and grafted on to their personalities.

The air steward returned to clear away Mack's coffee cup and untouched breakfast tray. Mack refolded the table and took up his briefcase again. Inside, under the newspaper, was a sheet off a legal pad he'd used for telephone notes at Warren's place. He re-read it, then turned it over. On the reverse was a jumble of figures, pencilled frantically at all angles – Warren's tally of what he owed, totalled again and again in the vain hope that, somehow, next time, it'd come up different.

Mack stared at the paper. In a way, he thought, Warren hadn't changed at all. One time, he'd booked dinner for The Club at a new and highly recommended French restaurant in New York when Nouvelle Cuisine was at the height of its popularity. He remembered how Warren'd stared down at the portion of food in front of him in deep shock; one tiny noisette of lamb lay in an artistic pool of delicate pastel sauce. Three snow peas were arranged lovingly around a radish rose.

'This,' he'd said, 'I don't believe. This is an insult to the notion of nourishment. This is *downright un-American.*' A few heads turned in Warren's direction. 'It's food, Jim, but not as we know it.'

'What's the problem?' Akitō, so familiar with the minimalism of *sushi*, was puzzled.

'It's not the American way. America is about more, plenty. The whole idea is to have too much. Listen, you're talking about a nation of displaced peasants here. In the countries our grandparents came from, a man's success was measured by how much food he could put on his family's plates. He couldn't hold his head up in town unless his wife had a double chin.'

'You develop that argument logically, you have why we're a nation of consumer junkies,' Morton commented, pushing his noisette around an acre of empty plate. 'It's like that gag – hot-shot executive takes delivery of his first Porsche 911 Turbo; that night, he hits a curve too fast and spins down a ravine. When he comes to he's lying smashed up on the rocks, surrounded by paramedics. He looks over to this heap of tangled metal and moans, "My Porsche, my Porsche . . ." Then one of the paramedics says to him, "I have some bad news for you, sir. On the way down, your right arm was torn off." There's a pause, then the guy sits bolt upright and cries, "My Rolex, my Rolex!"'

They all laughed as Morton stabbed the noisette, the radish and snow peas with his fork and swallowed the lot, in one.

'I can relate to that,' Warren said, with mock gravity. He lifted his wine glass. 'Gentlemen, I give you "Plenty".'

Mack stabbed the legal pad with a sharp pencil. So much for plenty.

Morton Totheroh lived in the slightly faded splendour of a nineteenth-century apartment block on New York's Upper West Side. He peered round the door as though he expected to be sold some new brand of Christianity. Mack pulled the dusty bottle of cognac from its paper wrapping with a flourish and put the label an inch from Morton's nose. Totheroh squinted at it.

'Seventeen years old! You were still playing with your dick when they bottled this. C'mon in, there's Chinese food in the oven.'

Mack followed him into the kitchen. 'You cooked?'

'They cooked – I sent out. It's been in there a while. Couldn't remember what time you said you were coming.'

They extracted half a dozen steaming foil containers from the oven. The crispy duck was a charred carcass. Morton sniffed at it. 'Jesus, we're gonna need the dental records on this one. Get the glasses, kid.'

Mack crossed to the spacious living-room Morton never seemed to use. Nothing much had changed in that apartment since Betty died. Except for the study. This was now a state-of-the-art workshop, identical to the one that Morton occupied during the day across town at the company he had founded thirty years before. He joked that even the coffee cups were the same.

The living-room with its elaborate drapes, delicate oil paintings and Dutch marquetry furniture was kept clean and polished but somehow the welcome had gone out of the place. This had been Morton's and Betty's room, they'd spent their evenings together here. The evenings had been too few.

Mack set the brandy snifters down amongst the debris on Morton's workbench. His old mentor was hunched over his notes, already chewing on dried-out noodles.

'So how's Warren? DMC still coming out every morning to jump-start his liver?'

'He's in one hell of a mess, Morton.'

'That bad, huh?'

'How long have you got . . .' Mack picked aimlessly at the aluminium food container in front of him. 'Jeez, you don't get many prawns with your monosodium glutamate these days.'

Morton studied the implacable face for a moment. 'An' how's things with you?'

'Looking good. If either of the guys I'm meeting this

week makes me a serious offer . . . who knows?'

'Not before time, either. You've been with Drummond way too long.'

'Tell me! I need something new, Morton, something I can get my mind around. Get my juices flowing again.'

'You'll find it. Talking of juices flowing, what sort of action you been getting lately?'

'I get lucky now and again.' Mack's eyes showed the hint of a smile. 'Had a couple of hot nights with a little PR girl in Cincinnati a week or so back.'

'They have orgasms in Cincinnati?'

'She seemed to enjoy herself.'

'How could you tell? What'd she do, turn her spot-welder down to low burn?'

Mack shrugged. 'Didn't check. She's history, anyway.'

'Ever the romantic, Lasky.'

Mack picked up his coffee mug and walked through to the kitchen for a refill. On the wall above the coffee-maker was a cork noticeboard covered in domestic correspondence: scribbled notes and invitations, many for functions long past. Mack had seen it a dozen times before. The faded photographs pinned into the corner hadn't been changed in years. He took a closer look. There, among them, half covered by a postcard, was one of The Club. Warren, slimmer, with a full head of hair, stood squinting into the sunlight, his arm firmly around Jackie's waist. Akitō was half turned away as though in conversation with the short, dark-haired girl at his side. Morton stood centre frame, grinning in the forced way people do when they've run back from a camera set for a time exposure. And then there was Mack, his wine glass held aloft, oblivious to all around him, Laurie's face pressed tight up against his, her bright eyes creased into a smile.

Morton came up behind, watching him from the doorway. 'Wanna talk about it?'

'No.' Mack lifted the steaming coffee jug off the hot plate, poured himself some and stirred it, slowly. All the while, Morton's eyes were boring a hole in the back of his skull, willing him to open up. 'Look, she shacked up with my best

50

buddy and business partner, that's all there is to it.'

'Is it?'

'Sure . . . sure it is, what do you want, chapter and verse?'

'And where were you while this was happening?'

'Taking care of business.'

'So well that you weren't taking care of her, right?'

'Give me a break, will ya?' Mack banged down his mug, sending coffee over the breakfast counter. 'Look, Morton, I gave it my best shot, I was out there busting a gut, staying ahead of the curve, an' while I'm doing all that, while *I'm keeping the whole shooting match together*, she's in *my* bedroom fucking *my* partner. That's *not what I call a deal!*'

'So did you fight?'

'Fight? No, the hell we did. Wouldn't give her the satisfaction. Why should I be the one to bleed? She made her choice, what's it to me?'

'What is it to you, Mack? Seems to me you had something good going there.'

'Well that's what I thought . . .' Mack reached for the kitchen towel and sponged up the mess.

'And what do you think now?'

'That maybe I didn't listen enough.' He paused. 'You know, thinking about it, I guess she did try to say . . . explain how it was for her, but I didn't really take it seriously.'

'Times like when you were shaving in the morning or getting ready for bed? Kind of unimportant times?'

Mack turned. 'Yeah . . . yeah!'

'They always pick those times, figure you won't get so mad.' Morton's eyes held the sadness of unshared memories. He turned away.

The two stood in silence. Then Morton put an arm round Mack's shoulder.

'You know why I love you? Know why?' Mack shook his head. ''Cos you're dumb and you're human, that's why. You just got to remember that sometimes, you know? Remember you're human too. Quit giving yourself the macho crap, it's okay for a guy to give in once in a while.'

Mack shrugged and moved off for the study. Morton followed. He picked up his chopsticks. 'This stuff should be good for wallpaper paste by now,' he said, taking another taste of the carry-out and shoving it in Mack's direction.

'Who gives...' Mack slumped down in the chair as Morton turned back to the computer screen. 'The latest creation?'

'Yep, this is my baby. I gave birth to it. Eleven years' work went into getting it to where it is. You're looking at the world's first two-and-a-half-gigabyte computer.' Morton stretched himself and poured them both a brandy. 'Course, I'm a lot less involved with this side of things than I used to be. You can't be everywhere, not these days. It's all too specialised. Kids up in the office, younger than you, came up with half the stuff in this thing. I kept out of their way, concentrated on writing programs and software packages.' He warmed the glass over his cigarette, turning it carefully in his hands. 'I still feel it's mine nevertheless. I mean, who ever understands their children when they're all growed up?'

'When does it hit the streets?'

'The spring.' Morton sat at the computer and started to put it through its paces.

'What are you calling it?'

'It's two-and-a-half gigabytes, so it's the G250. Catchy, ain't it? I've learnt to stay out of the marketing side too.' His fingers ran deftly over the keys. 'It's all changed, Mack. I was my own boss for twenty years. Now...? I tell you, the last few years've been hell on a handcart.'

'Oh?'

'Yeah.' Morton prodded one chopstick at the keyboard. Data on the computer screen flickered and changed. 'You know what the Japanese are like when they dig their heels in.'

'What are you talking about?'

'Nashiba have been major shareholders in AmTronics for nearly ten years.'

'Akitō's old man? I never knew that.'

'Didn't seem important. You know what they say: if you

52

can't beat the bastards, join them.' Morton hovered over the keyboard for a second. Every time he got into his real feelings about the Japs his blood pressure went through the roof. He didn't often admit his depth of loathing for the Japanese, even to himself. It was a loathing that had haunted him his whole life. His father, a commodities dealer in the South Pacific, had been taken prisoner in 1940 at the fall of Shanghai. He'd died of starvation in Changi jail. By the time Morton got his last letter, he'd been dead for a year.

Carving out a relationship with the Nashibas had been the most difficult task of his life. Involving them meant saving a company he'd spent a lifetime building up; saving eleven hundred jobs. Fighting them off meant obliteration by Japanese competition within two years. He owed it to his staff to make a deal. Dining with Akitō that first time, all those years ago, had been a favour to his father he felt bound to honour.

'Funny, I always thought there was something strained between you and Akitō,' Mack said. 'See much of him? Haven't seen him myself in six or seven years.'

Morton shook his head. 'You ain't missed a damn thing. Couple of months back he tried to railroad me into putting more of their guys on to the board. I won the first few rounds, then I got sick for a while. Guess it knocked a lot of the old fire out of me.' Morton sat back in the chair. 'I was designing a new database for them — all brand-new technology. I was about halfway into the project. Then one sunny morning I walked across the park to swim at the club, like I always do. I thought about fishing off Fire Island. My back was killing me and I had another lousy day ahead of me with the Japanese and I thought, damn it, Morton, life's too short, it really is. A week later I drew my first month's pension and walked. It shook the shit out of them, I can tell you.'

He got up suddenly and started to clear away the remains of the meal. 'They thought they could finish the database without me. But you know where I keep all my notes?' He tapped his forehead. 'Up here. Always did. Nashiba brought

53

in specialists to complete the work, but without my notes they were fucked.' He made a little chuckling noise. 'They either had to face starting over with an entirely new design, or coming to me on their knees.'

'Nice.'

Morton shrugged. 'They didn't come themselves, not at first – tried sending a couple of my old team down here to soften me up. Then, eventually Jap One turns up, Tatsuya Nashiba himself, standing there in my living-room. I couldn't believe it. I had no idea till then it meant so much to them.

'Anyway, I let him eat shit for an hour or two and then I said, "Okay, but on strict conditions. If I come back on the project, I come back on the board. As senior vice-president, and we start running things my way again."' He laughed. 'You should have seen his face! I don't think anyone had talked to old Tats like that in his life. A week later, I had my name back on my office door and the keys to the executive steam bath.'

'And what about the new directors they were pushing for?'

'Oh, these things don't go away. Any time now, it'll be the Alamo again.' He yawned. 'C'mon, drink up. I got an early start tomorrow.'

Mack drained his glass and headed for the door. 'Let me buy you dinner next week.'

'Sure . . .' Morton said, 'an' we'll talk bad movies.'

He clicked the door shut and slipped the chain on, slowly. 'Yeah,' he said to himself, as he turned away. 'I got a new one for you. And this one's real bad. It's called *Godzilla Versus Uncle Sam* . . .'

FOUR

'Ten minutes before landing, sir.' The voice of the air hostess filtered through the warm, comforting haze of sleep. In the hundreds of thousands of miles Akitō Nashiba had flown on business, he had become an expert passenger. He'd trained himself to sleep at will, until his mind and body were sufficiently charged to withstand the effects of whatever time change he'd encounter at his destination.

He took off his eye shades and flexed his neck and shoulders, letting the steam from the hot towel cleanse his face. Ten minutes was all he needed to marshal his thoughts before meeting Colonel Santiago – he had committed every detail of the financial reports to memory over the past few days, now he felt totally confident.

Akitō peered for a moment at the city below. Maraquilla was the last on a long list of Third-World capitals he had flown to in just over four years, it could be no different to the rest, yet the shantytowns that inevitably clung to the edge of these old colonial cities held a kind of morbid fascination. He never ceased to marvel at the ingenuity of people whose annual income was less than he'd spend on a dinner in New York, when it came to providing themselves with shelter. Whole villages made out of a multi-coloured jumble of car doors and plastic Coke crates plastered in dried mud. He'd seen one hut made from the remains of an advertising hoarding, the face of a newly-assassinated president beaming incongruously skyward.

When the Boeing taxied to a halt, Akitō was ready to be met by a member of the ground crew and deplane ahead of the other passengers. Within a minute he was aboard a Sikorsky helicopter banking steeply in the wind, heading westward towards the Cordillera Mountains.

'*Chew like Robbydumbah!*' Santiago's Major screamed over the noise of the rotor blades. '*Meester Nashiba, chew like Robbydumbah!*'

Akitō finally made the connection.

'Dumbah – Dunbar, the pop singer?'

The ugly face broke into a gap-toothed grin. '*Chew like to meet heem!*'

The question was purely rhetorical.

'*The Colonel ees weeth heem now in Artigas...*' The rest of the sentence was drowned in the mechanical hacking of the rotor blades.

Akitō had encountered Dunbar once before, in Africa, where money raised by the ageing singer's concerts and telethons had done more to put food into the bellies of the starving than the guilty donations of any Western government or charity.

'*Chew like "Hwan More Saturday Night!"*' the Major bawled out again. '*Ees good song, yes!*'

Akitō nodded amiably. It was a mistake. For the rest of the flight he was doomed to snatches of Dunbar's ten-year-old hit in Pidgin, mimicked complete with the singer's stuttering stylisation.

As the helicopter drew closer to the mountain range, Akitō could see an area of trees no more than a mile square. It was all that remained of what had been dense rain forest, kept as an oasis of shade for the village almost hidden on its edge. Below, a convoy of trucks was drawn along the single dust track that ran from the village into the mountains beyond. The Sikorsky circled once and landed.

'*Thees way please.*'

Akitō followed the Major past the column of trucks towards the ramshackle group of buildings that was Artigas. At the head of the convoy, a large crowd had gathered at an army roadblock, staring open-mouthed at the skinny foreigner who was waving his arms and shouting at the top of his voice.

'. . . Well, I didn't bring this stuff six thousand miles for this . . .'

Akitō could see the familiar head bobbing up and down. An aide was trying to reason with it:

'As the Colonel says, the problem with the Esperanza, the guerrillas here, is they have two SAM missile-launchers. It would be pointless to try to fly the grain until they've been neutralised.'

The heavy-set man in dark glasses standing next to the irate singer slowly drew his hands out of the pockets of his perfectly pressed trousers and turned towards the small group of journalists and TV crews standing by.

'I do understand how you must feel, Mr Dunbar, believe me. No one could want those people to eat more than me. All of us here are very grateful for what you have done.'

Colonel Santiago took off the dark glasses and motioned a group of soldiers forward from a nearby hut. They came, leading a line of tiny, doe-eyed children, their stomachs distended through malnutrition.

The cameras tracked the grotesque procession across the village to the gathering at the roadblock. The soldier at its head stooped down and spoke quietly to the first child. The little boy blinked a couple of times and shuffled uncertainly towards Dunbar, his arms outstretched. Santiago dropped on to one knee, embracing him and several others. He looked up at the Scotsman.

'Thanks to you, at least these children will have food today. My troops brought them out from the famine area last night. One of my best officers was killed in the operation.'

He gathered the rest of the children around him and held his hand out to Dunbar. The Scotsman glared back.

'What kind of cheap fuckin' stunt . . . ?'

The Colonel's avuncular smile never wavered. 'It's the best we can do for now, Mr Dunbar.'

The singer threw up his arms in exasperation and turned

57

to face the mountain that stood between him and the people he'd come to feed. 'Jesus Christ!'

Suddenly weary, he turned back to face the cameras and gave the Colonel's hand a perfunctory jerk. Immediately, the small crowd erupted into applause and cries of 'Viva!' Dunbar let the cameras click away for a few seconds, then stalked off towards the village, shaking his head.

The Colonel waited for the press to disperse before taking off his cap. He wiped his head with a handkerchief and walked over to where Akitō and the Major stood. Akitō extended his hand. The Colonel clasped it warmly.

'Welcome to my country, Mr Nashiba.' The slow smile showed heavily capped teeth. 'As you can see we are still not without our problems. This has always been a difficult region.' He broke off to question the Major briefly in Spanish. 'My home is an hour's flight from here. On the way I'd like to show you Lorencia. We're very proud of it.' They started to walk towards the Colonel's helicopter. 'It shows what we can achieve when we have the opportunity. Two hundred farmers have smallholdings there. They're using the latest agricultural methods to cultivate their crops. They've organised themselves into a co-operative, it's most impressive . . .'

As they walked, Akitō could see buses parked amongst the trees. Soldiers were steering the peasants who'd made up the Colonel's spontaneous gathering of well-wishers into them.

'. . . A few more Lorencias and we would not have to rely on the enterprise of the Mr Dunbars of this world. I have cold beer on board. I'm sure you could use one.'

The Casa Grande was a vast sprawling villa built on the edge of what had once been a crater lake, six thousand feet up in the Cordilleras. An earthquake in the fifth century had caused the side of an extinct volcano to collapse, leaving a crescent-shaped valley suspended above the mountain range. The villa stood at the top of a series of green terraces cut into the highest part of it.

The Romanesque entrance and balconies of the main

building had clearly been taken from something much older. Santiago's study was too. This masterpiece of pillaged treasure, with its finely carved panelling, mullioned windows and other adornments had been transported in its entirety from a fifteenth-century monastery and painstakingly reconstructed in an otherwise featureless contemporary room.

Santiago stretched himself out on a sofa, his broad, flat face in repose as he drew on a small wooden pipe; as out of place as the Jackson Pollock that hung above the high stone fireplace. *Why now, after such a long silence?* he thought. The last time he'd met Akitō had been at the enthronement of Emperor Akihito, in 1990. He was one of the many Third-World leaders in Tokyo that week who'd hoped to use the opportunity to tie down their Japanese hosts on the topic of increasing development loans. At the time, Santiago was certain he'd impressed the Nashibas with his plans for the Special Economic Zones he proposed to set up. There had even been talk of Akitō visiting Maraquilla to see for himself the progress that'd been made. But it had come to nothing, and the deals eventually struck had not reflected any great confidence in Santiago's plan for his country's economic recovery.

The Colonel had all but given up on the Nashibas when Akitō's letter arrived, suggesting that mid-July might be a good time to take up the invitation offered so long before.

Santiago drew gently on his pipe. '... In five years there will be eight more Lorencias. Each will produce enough grain to feed the people within a two-hundred-mile radius. Of course, it's only a beginning. Such schemes are enormously expensive, as you will appreciate. But the money will be found no matter what. It has become something of a personal crusade.'

The irony of these words, spoken by a man who had creamed off more than two billion dollars in aid since he'd come to power, had no cutting edge for Akitō. It was no secret that much of the aid entrusted to these Third-World despots would disappear, to turn up, often at the same banks it had come from, as part of their own deposit accounts.

Akitō kept his gaze on the view beyond the mullioned window. 'And the guerrillas?'

'An irritation. Active in a few outlying areas, like the one you saw today. We have one last leader to deal with. After that, the movement'll fall apart soon enough.'

Akitō's eyes focused on a small stained-glass panel set into the ancient framework, showing the sceptre and orb of some long-forgotten king. He turned to face a leader whose only symbols of office were the Kalashnikov and the grenade. 'If we're going to make good use of the little time we have together, Colonel, I suggest we start by being frank with one another. You and I both know that the Esperanza have control of most of the Eastern Province. The national guard have sustained heavy casualties in their attempts to contain them, and have been driven back into the mountains twice in the last month.'

'Mr Nashiba—'

'. . . I understand that only last Friday the Minister of the Interior and his family were assassinated in their home in broad daylight. With regard to the Special Economic Zones, we both know there is no money to even begin the new programme, let alone complete it. Your annual growth rate is nil; inflation is running at two thousand four hundred per cent; your country's debts are in excess of thirty-three billion dollars. The likelihood of you being able to meet the interest payments on your loans from foreign banks for more than another three months is minimal.' Akitō lowered his voice and stared into the reddening face in front of him. 'If we accept that this is the true position, then I think we can move forward. Begin to look at ways in which we might work together to improve this situation.'

Santiago's face broke into a cheerless smile and he nodded slowly. Five years he'd waited to get a Nashiba here and he'd damned himself as a fool with his first utterance. Eight years before, Santiago's military junta had seized power from a tottering democracy with a popular mandate. But the rise of the Esperanza had eroded that long ago. Farmers in the Eastern Province had been defecting to the Esperanza at the rate of hundreds a week. His régime would be fighting

60

for survival within a year, and Nashiba knew it. It'd been stupidity to believe he would come all this way without the facts at his fingertips.

'Clearly there's nothing we can do with regard to your other creditors,' Akitō continued. 'If you must default on your payments to them, then you must. As I'm sure you have discovered for yourself, there's very little the IMF will be able to do about it in practical terms. And your relationship with other banks is of no consequence to us. We are free to make whatever evaluation of your country's future we care to.'

'I don't understand.'

'We have faith in you, Colonel. Provided our consortium continues to receive repayment, on some basis or other – your titanium reserves could well prove part of the answer – I don't see any reason to let such fine programmes as these Special Economic Zones of yours collapse for want of money. Any new arrangement can remain entirely a matter between ourselves.'

Santiago stood up, walked over to the fireplace and knocked the tobacco ash out of his pipe. It was an interesting idea. Where was it written that one must deal even-handedly with one's creditors? What the other banks did not know could not hurt them. For the first time in months, he began to see a chance for the future. If the Lorencia programme could be turned into a reality he might have something to turn back the tide.

'And obviously, if we are to show such faith in you, it's important to us that we feel that confidence is reciprocated.'

So now we come to the crunch, Santiago thought. He turned to the Japanese. 'In what way?'

'By letting our bank act for you personally. You're probably unaware of all the benefits that might have. I'm sure the Farrell National does an adequate job for you in New York. But your finances there could be managed a lot more imaginatively.'

Santiago's face showed no reaction but his mind raced. There was nothing to tie him to the account at the Farrell.

How the hell . . . ? Akitō opened his attaché case, took out a leather folder and laid it on the desk. Santiago forced his attention on to his own gold-embossed name on the dossier's cover.

'This is a portfolio my staff have put together. I think you'll find it interesting. Of course it's a matter entirely for yourself.'

Santiago leafed through the document. The current balance on deposit in the Farrell National was a figure in excess of four hundred million dollars. Small beer to Nashiba, Santiago thought. He closed the file. 'This is not why you've come three thousand miles to see me, is it?'

'No,' Akitō said, at length. 'There is one other matter . . .'

The Colonel lifted the phone on his desk. 'Faustino, ' he said, 'bring in a pot of coffee, will you.'

Santiago led Akitō out through a pair of intricately worked Rajasthanian temple doors which had been thrown open to catch the cool of the early evening. There, at the centre of the highest terrace, a long wrought-iron table had been laid for dinner. Two of Santiago's senior officers snapped to attention as the Colonel and his guest came forward. He settled into a large chair at the head of the table and motioned Akitō to sit on his left.

'Allow me to introduce my wife, Rosa.' The voluptuous girl on Santiago's right looked no more than nineteen. She gave Akitō a shy smile, then spoke softly in heavily accented Spanish.

Santiago laughed at her awkward greeting. 'She says it is a pleasure to meet you. I hope you will forgive her if she stares, she has never seen an oriental before.' He waved a hand towards the astonishing view from the terrace. 'Beautiful, isn't it?'

Akitō nodded.

'Everything here is beautiful, especially the women.' Santiago grinned.

Akitō studied the faces of Santiago's family and staff. All but one – the face he wanted to look at most – were nodding and smiling in his direction. Her high cheekbones and well-defined features stood out amongst the coarse features around the table. All the time the Colonel was talking, her violet eyes never rose from her plate.

'Rosa wants to know if you like our friend Dunbar.'

Akitō made an anodyne reply. Although he spoke flawless English and German, his Spanish was minimal. And apart from the Colonel, no one else at the table seemed to speak anything else.

Santiago soon wearied of interpreting social niceties and the conversation started to flag. Akitō took his cue. He had learnt that the Santiagos of this world liked nothing better than to talk about themselves.

'Where did you learn your remarkable English?'

Santiago's face took on a satisfied air. 'I was head barman at the Queen Catherine Hotel in Maraquilla for eight years.' He paused. 'Idi Amin was once a bellhop in a hotel in Kampala. Did you know that?' Then, through a mouthful of soufflé, 'So, Mr Nashiba, next time you eat at the Washington Hilton, be nice to the waiter. He may get to be the next president!'

Uniquely pleased with this observation, Santiago translated it into Spanish for the bencfit of his guests, laughing all over again. An aide appeared at his side holding a long fax printout. Santiago skim-read it and tapped the side of his nose.

'Forgive me, Mr Nashiba, there is urgent business.' He rose slowly.

Akitō dabbed his mouth with his napkin. 'Of course.'

The Colonel kissed his wife lightly on the forehead and started towards the house. Then, almost as an afterthought, turned back to the silent brunette Akitō had been watching.

'Miss Cole, perhaps you will be so kind as to look after our guest – show him the grounds perhaps . . .'

Akitō's obvious surprise won her first smile that evening.

'Would you like to take a look at the Casa Grande now, Mr Nashiba?'

'I should be delighted.' The meal all but over, Akitō got up and followed her down the terrace steps into the flourishing garden below.

Okay, she thought, *guided tour for the goodlooking Geek.* She put her brain on automatic. 'Thousands of years ago, this was the bed of a huge lake. As you can see . . .'

'Am I to know your first name, Miss Cole?'

'Bryony.' She walked on. 'As you can see, part of the lake collapsed during an earthquake—'

'You're American. What brings you out here?'

'I'm coaching Santiago's youngest son. He's hoping to get him into St Anthony's in Connecticut.'

'Ah, I'd have thought somehow the Colonel would've picked a man for a job like that.'

Bryony shrugged. 'My father teaches at St Anthony's, that's how I heard about the job. Anyway, Paulo's only eleven, I'm more of a governess.'

'And the Spanish?'

'My mother was born in Seville. I spoke it at home.'

There was a coldness in the way she gave him the information. What was it about these creeps that made them think they had a God-given right to interrogate people?

'Still, a place like this is an unusual choice.'

'Not really; I'd just finished at Vassar and this seemed like an interesting way to spend a year. It's certainly been that.'

I bet it has! Akitō thought. *This girl must know more about what really goes on up here than any outsider alive.*

'Been here long?'

'Long enough.' Bryony walked on towards the English garden, its neat borders and clipped low hedges somehow out of harmony with the wild beauty of the valley.

'When do you finish?'

'A few days.'

'Then what?'

'Then I take Paulo back with me to sit his entrance exams, and that's it.'

'Will you teach?'

Jesus, she thought, *what is this, a Senate Committee Hearing?* 'I don't know yet,' she snapped.

Akitō probed for a gap in the wall Bryony put up against him. It wasn't racial, he was fairly sure of that. No, he was certain it was something he'd encountered before. Suppressed moral outrage was the best description for it. She would reason that this dictator, Santiago, a man who professed such concern for the plight of his people yet had no compunction in living himself in the greatest opulence, could feed his starving countrymen for a year if he cared to sell the contents of one room at the Casa Grande.

Akitō had hardened against such equations long ago. Men like Santiago were essential to the game of international money broking. To begin to question the morality of their lifestyles, or one's own morality in dealing with them, was a fruitless exercise.

A girl like Bryony would never see it that way. She would tolerate the situation and her employer long enough to take what she could from the experience. But for her, anyone tainted by association, like Akitō, would be counted among the untouchables. He decided to meet her head on.

'I was at the roadblock this morning when Robbie Dunbar's grain shipment arrived.'

'Yes, I heard about that.' Her tone was sarcastic. 'No food for the *niños famélicos*, the starving children, after all.'

They walked down a paved colonnade towards the open end of the valley. The statues that lined the way were loosely based on Greco-Roman originals. God alone knew what Santiago had paid for them but to Akitō they looked like the kind they cast in fibreglass by the dozen for Las Vegas hotels.

'With luck, if my company's deal goes through, five years from now those people won't need grain trucks. They will be self-sufficient and this country's economy will be moving again.'

Bryony turned, blazing with contempt. 'Save it, Mr Nashiba. Let me read it in *Newsweek* when you're Man of the Year.'

Akitō's change of tone was sudden and violent. 'Look, I'm not some two-bit gun-runner or drug baron. Or some crooked art dealer here to sell the boss a Matisse for the men's room! I'm a banker, I'm here to try and help and I stupidly thought that if you knew the truth, you might stop treating me like I was the Grand Wizard of the Ku Klux Klan!'

'Hey!' Bryony took a step backward in shock. 'Look, I'm sorry. It's just the Colonel doesn't invite too many people up here who are on the level. I guess I assumed you were another . . .'

'One like him?' Akitō spoke softly now, sensing a breakthrough. Winning Bryony as an informant had not been a conscious decision, that was second nature. Taking her to bed at the first opportunity had. Beauty alone had never motivated Akitō sexually. There needed to be something more. This woman had the kind of defiant energy he found attractive.

'You obviously know a lot more about the Colonel than I thought.'

Bryony looked at him. *Time to put the feline in with the wild fowl*, she thought. 'That grain you saw going to waste today, you know what happens to it now?'

Akitō shook his head.

'The bastard sells it to the Russians. So you see even the Esperanza have their uses.'

They walked on in silence to the fence that ran along the top of the cliff which formed the open end of the valley.

'Look down,' Bryony said. 'No, right down, underneath where we're standing.'

Akitō could just make out three huge gun emplacements set flush into the rock face, their missile-launchers trained on the night sky.

'Some place, huh? Santiago didn't build it. Diega, the president before him, did. Santiago doesn't have the style.' She leaned her back on one of the huge steel fencing posts. 'But he sure knows how to enjoy it. Know what his slogan was? "To free the homeland from corruption and greed." Doesn't exactly pick you up and sling you around the room, does it? But it meant a hell of a lot to the people out there. And, you know, if he was killed tomorrow, the Esperanza would rehash the same old crap, then replace him with a Santiago of their own.

'So if you really want to help this country, Mr Nashiba, you'll need a lot more than money. You'll need to have a say in the way things are done here.'

'Akitō.'

'I beg your pardon?'

'My name is Akitō.' He turned towards her. 'And I will.'

They looked out across the vast expanse of the Cordillera Mountains stretching before them and were silent for a while. Akitō watched the sun slip away, leaving a thin crescent moon in the blue-black sky.

'It is extraordinarily beautiful here.'

'Mmm.' Bryony was intrigued. There could well be some truth in what this banker had told her. But she knew well enough that official visitors only ever got to see the inside of the presidential residence in Maraquilla. This private retreat Santiago reserved for people who had something more to offer. She watched Akitō as he took in the view, studied the generous mouth, the well-defined profile. He was whispering something. She strained her ears to catch the words.

> 'Michi no beno
> Umara no ure ni
> Hafu mame no
> Karamaru kimi wo
> Wakare ka yukamu.'

'What's that?'

'A famous Japanese poem.'

'It sounds sad. What does it mean?'

Bryony listened as Akitō translated.

> 'From you with whom I am entwined
> Like the bean plant that has crept
> Over the face of the thorn bush
> That grows by the road,
> Must I now be parted, go away?'

He'd made a simple moment into a special one. He waited for his reward.

'You are an unusual man,' Bryony said, at last.

'In the East, moonlight is always bitter-sweet. It reminds us of a true love, of home.'

'Are you homesick?'

Akitō turned to walk back towards the Casa Grande, magnificent now in the floodlight from the garden. 'No, not really.'

He could not bring himself to say more during their slow climb back to the house. In two months, he would marry the girl chosen at birth for him by his parents; he would complete a contract binding the Nashibas to the Ishiharas for generations to come.

Akitō could see the tiny, pale face of Miyoko in his mind's eye. She was attractive, even pretty. But she was a trained wife. If there had once been fire in her personality, it had been bred out by now. A Japanese wife must bring harmony to the house. Above all she must be quiescent.

'You're quiet?' She broke his thoughts at the bottom of the terrace steps.

'I was wondering if you would consider meeting me in New York when you get back. I suppose it's out of the question.'

'No.' The violet eyes gave the barest hint of warmth. 'No, I'd like that.'

Akitō turned his face away from the cloud of dust blown up by the Colonel's Sikorsky helicopter as it lifted into the air above Maraquilla Airport. Inside the main terminal, the narrow concourse was jammed solid with passengers, some sitting disconsolately on their luggage, others stretched out on the dusty floor. He started to push his way through the overwhelming, sweaty mass of bodies.

'Nashiba!'

Akitō turned. 'McGowan.'

Pat McGowan had the look of a hard bastard, right down to the steel-blue eyes. He was built like a quarterback, six foot three of sinew and muscle, a sardonic smile on his lips. Akitō hated that smile. It was a smile that had sneered at

68

him from some corner of every remote airport on the planet, happy as a sewer rat in a cesspit.

'*Ohayō gozaimasu.* How ya doin', Number One Son?'

Akitō wanted to put a nice big scar down the other side of McGowan's face.

'You're getting to be quite a fixture round these bug-infested shitholes.'

'You should know.'

'Well, it looks like you're in for a long wait. "All flights cancelled till further notice."' McGowan jerked his thumb backwards. 'It's on the board.'

Akitō tried not to show his concern. At noon tomorrow, his father was meeting the representatives of the other three families in New York to evaluate the results of their Third-World campaign. To miss it would be a major personal setback.

'Seems the Esperanza blew up an army transport plane last night. Took out thirty of Santiago's best.' McGowan paused to revel in Akitō's discomfort. 'They're saying it was moulded Semtex – could've looked like anything. And there could be more. They're tearing everything in the place apart.'

The fax to Santiago last night, Akitō thought. 'So what's your guess?'

'Need to get back real bad, huh?' the journalist leered. 'Well, the *Tribune* boys are saying midnight, but I got fifty bucks on noon tomorrow.'

'And the hotels are full.'

'You got it!'

Akitō closed his eyes. McGowan stooped, let out a loud, rasping fart and picked up his bag and cameras.

'Well, if I were you I'd call your old man – maybe get him to parachute you into Times Square or something.' He laughed. 'Me, I'm going to drive across the border to Puerto Cortes, pick up a flight to Panama City and the red-eye to Kennedy.' He paused. 'If that soft tush of yours is up to six hours on the roads,' he spat into the navel of a girl in a swimwear poster, 'and you give me cash for the gas, you could ride shotgun.'

McGowan had been war correspondent for a string of

second-league papers for more than twenty years. One sniff of cordite and decaying flesh and he was there, picking his way through the ruins of people's lives till there was nothing left to shoot. Everything about the man was repugnant. But he offered the only quick escape from the place and Akitō knew it.

Two hours down the dust-track that was the only route West, they jettisoned the empty beer cans and the remnants of the stringy roast chicken that passed for lunch into the tangled vegetation that ran both sides of the road. The noon sun was beginning to bake the top of Akitō's head. The thin cotton cap he'd bought at the airport had come complete with the stencilled name of a local *vallenato* star. He pulled the peak lower to shade his eyes.

McGowan's battered jeep bounced on, leaving the occasional bus or ancient farm vehicle headed back towards the city in a cloud of dust. They were alone. Two men without a damn thing in common other than an aching need to get out of the place and more than four hours of mind-numbing driving ahead.

'You know something, Nashiba, I keep asking myself what a slick operator like you is doing in a shit-tip like this. And then this nose of mine starts twitching and I think to myself, the guy's gotta be on to some kinda scam.'

The nose in question had been thumped so many times it looked like the only thing it was still good for was picking.

'This scam, as you put it, is not exactly what you'd call hot copy,' Akitō said. 'It's legal, pro-government, non-sectarian and sadly short on female genitalia. So I don't think it'd interest your readers a whole helluva lot.

'And I tell you something else it is,' he swatted a flying beetle against the windshield with his cap, 'none of your goddamned business.'

About a hundred miles from the border, they came to a small convoy of army vehicles pulled over at the side of the

70

road – troop carriers and jeeps with machine-guns mounted on the back. McGowan swerved off the road and pulled up hard behind them.

Akitō braced himself against the dashboard. 'What are you doing?'

McGowan gathered up his cameras and took off into the dense undergrowth. 'My job.'

Akitō got out and stomped around in the road, trying to get some feeling back into his butt. Through the trees he could see a gathering of people and some huts. He went in to take a closer look.

About fifty women and children stood in a circle at the perimeter of a clearing, hemmed in by government troops. A boy in soiled white rags, his matchstick legs already smashed by rifle butts, was dragged up between two soldiers in full view of the crowd. An officer was yelling at them. Akitō recognised him as the pop-song-loving Major from his outward flight. He moved up behind McGowan. 'What's he saying?'

McGowan lowered his voice but his camera never left the action. 'Says he's one of the bunch who blew up the plane. Says they're hiding Esperanza. It's all crap. Just another reprisal.' He snapped the lens cap back on his camera and swung it over his shoulder.

'Is that it?' Akitō whispered.

'Nope. The rest's no good to me.'

The Major stopped yelling. Without another word he walked over to the kid, drew his bayonet and drove it into his stomach up to the hilt. In one movement, he slit him from sternum to crotch.

The guts came out of the kid like they were spring-loaded, ruptured, stinking offal piled out onto the dry earth. Akitō never heard the kid scream. Through a haze he saw the soldiers sling a noose around his neck and haul him up to dangle and kick in the branches of a tree, an obscene, half-butchered carcass.

Akitō felt nothing in the next few minutes, only knew that he was running. Flat, razor-edged leaves cut into his face and slashed his clothes. Twice he fell, tripped by roots

71

hidden in the rotting undergrowth, skinning his knees and elbows. Then it filtered through. He was running the wrong way. He spun on his heels in panic. Which way? His mind screamed. Which way was the jeep? Maybe McGowan had gone. Maybe . . . He poleaxed forward on to his face, his hands scrabbling at the warm mush under him. *Ants! Soldier ants on his hands and face!* He scrambled to his knees, slapping wildly. There was something dead in that mush. Something very dead. He couldn't see it but he knew it was there. The ants were eating it – eating him! He threw himself towards the widest patch of sunlight. Suddenly, he could feel air pumping into his lungs again. Through the trees, he could see McGowan sitting on the hood of the jeep, changing the film in his camera.

Akitō fought to get his breath. Then he vomited.

McGowan snapped the camera shut and climbed back into the jeep. Akitō sat silent, staring at the road ahead. The red eyes, the ashen face, told the journalist all he needed to know.

'Little bit of real life for you, Nashiba.' The cruel laugh mocked. 'Gives you the total picture, y'know what I'm saying? It's funny.' He lit a cigarette and watched the soldiers pile back into the trucks. 'Never figured on something like that getting to you. You being Japanese and all, should've been right up your street.'

FIVE

The Frobisher Club had been around almost as long as New York itself. It had been at its current address at Gramercy Park since April 1887. The rooms were large and unfriendly, the food varied from indifferent to inedible, but the waiting list for membership was longer than ever. Getting on the list meant having at least one celebrated ancestor in the Frobisher annals and a Supreme Court judge, a senator or, at the very least, a Pulitzer Prizewinner to pledge you in. Joining meant waiting for a rare resignation or the death of an existing member.

To Morton Totheroh the Frobisher was a second home. Every morning at seven-thirty, he'd walk briskly across Central Park, swim fifty lengths of the club's Italian tile swimming pool, shower and sit down to breakfast. It had taken him from mid-October 1969 to early February '70 to persuade the chef to serve his breakfast the way he liked it, to get the consistency of the scrambled eggs, the crispness of the toast and bacon and the strength of the coffee just right. Few members had his staying power.

He'd read the funny pages and sports section on the *New York Times*, then skim through the *Wall Street Journal*, cutting out pieces of special interest with the small pair of scissors that were always included in the laying-up of his table. Then he'd head for the door.

If it was raining, he'd sit inside the doorway with the Club Secretary, Willard Parkin, and enjoy their shared contempt for the administration, regardless of which party was in power, and their unshakable faith in the Mets, until the cab came to take him to the office. If it was dry he'd shout a cheery 'howyadoin' through Parkin's door and walk the nine blocks.

In the twenty-six years that Morton had been a member, he'd brought no more than a dozen guests to the club and then only to the bar or restaurant. He considered the pool his private sanctuary. The Sunday after he arrived in New York, Mack Lasky was beginning to wish it had stayed that way.

Morton was moving through the water in a steady even crawl, his head swinging rhythmically from side to side, his concentration total. Mack was a good three lengths behind and tiring fast. His mind wasn't on the game.

Mack hit lap twenty-five. He'd joined the Chicago-based conglomerate Drummond Industries at the beginning of the economic downturn of the late eighties. The Oakdene project was a vast development of luxury homes in the smart suburb of Lincolnshire. But by the time building was underway, the property business was in deep recession. Mack hit on a new marketing idea. Each house in Oakdene was being roofed using a revolutionary aluminium frame that needed minimal internal support. He figured that if the ground floor was elevated on concealed pilings, all the services could be run in later. That meant the interiors could be left as completely open spaces, the only restrictions on partitioning dictated by the position of windows and external doors. Owners could be offered the unique opportunity of creating a home that reflected their personal tastes.

Mack's 'Home Maker' kits proved to be the marketing inspiration Drummond needed. It broadened their catchment to include customers who might otherwise have opted to build from scratch. Potential buyers could move pieces of card representing interior walls and fitted units around a scale plan of a house like the one on a site they'd just viewed, giving them a real sense of having personally designed their new home. Within a year every property in Phase One was sold. Mack's star was in its ascendancy.

Lap thirty-two. *Yeah, Home Maker – Home Breaker,* Mack thought. God, he'd been so dumb. The kick Laurie'd gotten out of designing the home they'd bought together in

Phase Two of Oakdene. He could have shared it; should have shared it. But all he could think about was the next deal.

The nights he'd sat up with Jack Raskin, Drummond's market strategist, trying to figure ways of licking their electronics division back into shape. Like so many domestic manufacturers of consumer electronics, Drummond'd seen their market share decimated over the previous two decades by Japanese competition. The long-term recovery plan for the division was sound enough but what was urgently needed was a short-term source of liquidity. Again, lateral thinking proved to be the answer.

'Held up at the office, in a jam on the freeway? Missing the ball game?' the small ad in the local freesheet read. 'Set the VCR at home by phone with VideSet. One hundred and eighty dollars, including postage, packing and fitting instructions.'

It was the spring of '91. Neat idea. Mack remembered making the mental note. The ad never appeared again and VideSet faded into his subconscious. Around a year later, he and Laurie were lunching with the Raskins at a restaurant on Lake Shore Drive. Halfway through the meal, the men realised they were going to miss the beginning of the Superbowl. Raskin said he'd call his mother and get her to set her VCR. When Mack went to find out what was taking him so long, he found Raskin bellowing instructions into the pay phone. He put his hand over the mouthpiece and shot Mack a withering look. 'Tell me something, why is it that only ten-year-old school kids can set these goddamn things . . .'

It was then Mack remembered VideSet. When he traced the guy who'd invented it, the device turned out to be a box full of electronics that could be hooked into any video machine in about twenty minutes. All you had to do was plug in a phone extension and it could be set from your car or your office. The reason VideSet hadn't caught on was clear to Mack immediately. The remote control unit the user held up to the receiver was way too complicated. The thing had to be childishly simple, something that tired

75

executives on the run between meetings could use without thinking.

It took Drummond five months to iron out all the glitches and a further year to tool up. Christmas '93, VideSet was marketed direct across the country. It was the breakthrough the electronics division had been waiting for. In the same month, the value of Mack's steadily expanding investment portfolio hit seven figures.

Lap forty-three. *Thought you were so smart, didn't you?* Mack touched the pool side and turned for the next length. *The great innovator who never missed a trick. Could sit with clients in a crowded restaurant and sell 'em the Lasky Doctrine like it was your last day on the planet. And walk out with total recall of every tip on the health of the commodities market that had passed between the two dealers lunching behind. Real smart. So how come you couldn't see what was happening right under your nose?*

June of last year, had that been the first time? He'd cancelled a marketing meeting and gone to visit his mother in hospital. He got home an hour earlier than usual. Raskin and Laurie were drinking wine in the kitchen. She'd kissed Mack the way she always did and fixed him bourbon on the rocks. He never thought a damn thing about it. *If I had*, he thought, *things might be looking a hell of a lot different now . . .*

'You're out of shape, Lasky.' Morton's voice mocked him from the pool side. He was grinning as he towelled himself dry. 'What have I got, twenty-five years on you?'

'Blow it out your ass.' Mack pulled himself out of the water. 'You were breathing pretty hard at the end there, old fella. Give me a month of this and I could take you by five lengths.'

Morton moved his hands through the air like flapping wings. 'Oink, oink, oink!' It was his code for, Yeah, and pigs'll fly!

'Jesus, I'm starving,' Morton said as they walked into the club lobby. 'Let's eat.'

'Great, I always wanted to eat here.'

'That's because you didn't get to eat here yet.'

'Food no good?'

'Stinks.'

'Why don't they change the chef?'

Morton waved at Club Secretary Willard Parkin and put his weight against the heavy rotating doors. 'Because it wouldn't be the Frobisher Club any more. Washington has humid summers; Truman was a good President; the Frobisher has lousy food. These are truths. They cannot be changed.'

The delicatessen was full. The two sat up at the counter stretching their jaws to accommodate vast pastrami sandwiches.

'Know who I bumped into the other day?' Morton said. 'Max Morrisey – speaks well of you.'

Mack scowled. 'He was ballast, dead weight. He's got nothing to complain about, Drummond's saw him okay.'

'You're all heart.' Morton took another bite of his lunch and chewed it thoughtfully. 'So what happens with you now?'

'My contract with Drummond's up in three months. Then I'm out of there.'

'Good, you've let yourself get stale.'

'What do you mean?'

'Aah, executive homes, executive toys . . .' Morton swallowed hard and wiped his mouth on a paper napkin. 'You know, of the three of you, you were the one I thought was gonna take the world by the balls, go for Macro Order, you know that? I used to think Warren would make it, he's got a good head on his shoulders. But he's got no real grit, know what I mean? No judgement. He was going to over-stretch himself the first cheque he wrote.'

Mack was silent for a minute. 'What about Akitō?'

Morton sighed. 'Ah, the Nashibas've been breeding up little Akitōs for sixty generations – don't think fifteen years of his fooling around here makes a mark on that kind of history. He's out of a mould, waiting his turn till Pop lays a multi-billion-dollar corporation in his lap. He's not in the

77

equation.' Morton sipped his beer. 'No, what I'm talking about here is original thought – building from the ground up. You've been treading water at Drummond for years and you know it.'

'Listen, I've done pretty good for a guy who scraped his masters.'

'So did I. So what? It doesn't matter, Mack, not to guys like you and me. We put two and two together and make five and three quarters. We lift up stones to see what crawls out. We make mental connections the Warrens of this world'll never make in five lifetimes. It's the ability to visualise the endgame – *gestalt*, that's what counts. You can't major in that. So you made close on a million bucks last year and you got a fat portfolio. Big deal. Tell me the last time you really pushed yourself . . .'

He stared into his glass. 'I don't think too much about money any more, I tell you. Not since Betty died. I live well. That's it. That's how it becomes. If you want my honest opinion, in some ways this Chicago mess could be a blessing in disguise.' He saw Mack's mouth open to speak. 'Oh, I don't mean on a personal level, you know that. But I think it's high time you got out of Chicago and there'll never be a better time than this. You should get yourself a place here for a while, take a few soundings. Take it slow.' He looked up. 'Jesus, it's noisy in here. Eat up, we'll have coffee at my place.'

Back in Morton's study, Mack flopped into a chair and watched as the older man shuffled the papers in his hand till he found the section he was looking for. 'I don't know why I said I'd do Princeton again. I was there twice this year already. Some of those guys must've heard my whole repertoire.'

'That'll be the day.'

'The trouble with my business is you write something you think is real smart and when you look at it a year later, it's like the Dead Sea Scrolls. You never stop updating. Listen to this, it's part of my new closing section. Tell me what you think:

'. . . The computer is a tool, that's all. A boon or a curse.

It just depends on who's making the choices. In the hands of an aggressor it's the perfect weapon – an instrument whereby man can wage war without the need for military confrontation. Oh, there'll always be the Vietnams, the Gulfs, the containable bloodbaths. But global war, of the kind your fathers and grandfathers knew, is a redundant concept. National boundaries are being swept away, governments no longer take those choices. Too much power has passed into the private sector for them to have that kind of mandate any more.

'The wars of the future will be fought in the boardrooms, on the stock exchange floors; the Titans, vast multinational conglomerates. The outcome will be as devastating as any fought between the armies of great powers; the result decided by the handful of men who got their sums right. So if you never thought the expression "The pen is mightier than the sword" could have an apocalyptic ring, think again. And don't doubt that it can be so. It's happening right now, in your own backyard.'

'Is that how it ends?'

'No, I don't know where it goes from there yet. It needs a lot of thought.' Morton put the papers down, slowly. 'You know, every time I drive out to Kennedy, past Flushing Meadow Park and what's left of the '64 World's Fair, I have the same thought. All those buildings, they're just rusting away out there. You're too young to remember, but that Fair was a real big deal at the time – the showpiece of American technological might.'

Mack looked at Morton; he seemed miles away.

'I had a small exhibit there, myself, I was so proud to be a part of it. Now I find myself thinking, Jesus, look at the state of the place, it's falling apart, all choked up with weeds.' Morton snorted. 'Me, I just wish they'd fix it up or knock it down. Guess it's like a kind of statement, metaphor, if you like, for how we feel about ourselves in this country at this point. Our indifference to what's going on right under our noses. The Flushing Meadow thing doesn't belong in this speech, I know that. But it's that kind of emotion I want to get into it, somehow.'

79

'We should wake up and take control, right?'

'You got it.'

The pair fell silent for a while.

'You're right, Morton,' Mack said, suddenly. 'I should get a base here, take a look around.'

'I'll tell you what you do.' Morton put an arm around Mack's shoulder. 'Tomorrow morning, you check out my daughter's apartment, it's three blocks from here.' He took a set of keys from a rack on the wall. 'If you like it, move in, if only for a week. It'll get you out of that hotel.'

'You sure?'

'Yeah, come on. Auburn's in LA for at least a year so you won't be disturbed. I was meant to be leasing the place for her, anyhow. So if you want to hold on to it, you'll be doing me a favour.'

Mack took the keys and Morton's hand with it. 'Thanks, I appreciate it.'

Morton shrugged. 'Listen, it'll be good to have you around.'

SIX

Marco Vasari switched on the infra-red binoculars and pulled focus on the balcony of an apartment two hundred yards below him down the hill. Willow was watering her house plants as she always did at this time of the evening. She was a creature of habit. It had made his job a lot easier over the years. She checked the moisture in the soil of a small begonia, turned and went back inside. Vasari returned to his word processor. With one finger he typed in the last line of his report and started the printer. He pulled out the single sheet of typescript and checked it line by line. Satisfied, he folded it, sealed it into a white envelope and addressed it. Wherever Tatsuya Nashiba was that week, the report would be in his hand by close of business Friday. In eleven years, Vasari had never once delivered late. He knew Nashiba relied on him; that in different ways this had become an essential ritual to them both, part of the process by which they relaxed before the weekend. Vasari could not be certain, but the fact that it seemed to bring Nashiba peace gave him the satisfaction of a job well done.

Vasari had been ten before he realised he was something special, the rarest kind of Nisei: one of Japanese origins but with a Caucasian face. It was a distinction that would change his life. His Italian-American father had been part of the Allied Occupying Force that had sailed into Tokyo Bay in 1945. He'd met Marco's Japanese mother the following year. The boy's curly brown hair and chiselled features had saved him from the racial harassment that so many born of mixed blood have to endure. People simply took him to be of Italian extraction, as his name suggested.

81

His parents had been approached by Nashiba's people when he was fifteen. From then on, every summer vacation, he was flown from his home in Seattle to Tokyo for a month's stay at an exclusive boys' camp. As he grew older and the stays in Japan longer, it became the training ground that moulded his life.

At twenty-two, he was among the first of his kind to be deployed as part of the most clandestine intelligence-gathering unit in America. Controlled by the Four Families, Vasari, and a handful like him, moved unnoticed through a Western world. Going where they might not go, doing what they must not be seen to do.

At forty, Vasari was among the first to be retired from active service. He wasn't sorry. The job had changed. And if you wanted his opinion, not for the better.

It had been made clear from the beginning that retirement need not mark the end of his career with the Nashibas. He could return to Japan to help train new operatives. Or, if a position was available, he could take an administrative job with his unit in New York. Worst way, he'd end up as head of security at one of the company's premises.

Vasari hadn't been back to Japan in twenty years. Apart from a few ageing relatives, he knew no one there. Anyhow, they did things differently in the training camps these days. He'd have taken a job in administration like a shot, but it didn't look like anything was going to open up there for a while. If he was going to be stuck behind a security desk for the rest of his working life, he figured he might as well do it where the Frascati was cheap and he could spend Sundays in the Gardens of the Villa d'Este – in his beloved Italy.

Vasari's passion for Italy began at his grandfather's knee. Night after night the old man, born and raised in Rome, would fill the boy's head with lurid tales of mad Emperors and carnal Popes; of blood, lust and conspiracy. He was in his mid-twenties when he finally got to see the country for himself. It seemed to him, then, that the rolling hills of olive groves, the paintings of Caravaggio and Raphael, and most of all the people, had simply been waiting for him to discover them. To live now among so much that he loved seemed the most natural thing in the world. But the person-nel manager of Nashiba International in Rome showed little enthusiasm for employing a New Yorker with an imperfect grasp of the language on security.

Vasari had never married. He'd been careful with his money. He resolved to draw his pension, cash in his savings and take his chances in Rome on his own.

Exactly what happened to change all that, he would never know, but forty-eight hours before he was due to leave he got a call from his section head telling him that a member of the main board wanted him to stop by for an informal talk.

Vasari had been saving the new white suit for the flight to Rome. It symbolised a new beginning, a clean break. But the afternoon of the meeting, he opened his closet and took it from its hanger, determined to look his best. He sat in reception, on the seventieth floor of the Nashiba Building, lifting the coffee cup with care so as not to mark the pristine white trousers. In eighteen years with the company he'd never been to the executive offices. The nature of his work required him to stay within designated areas.

An attractive woman he'd noticed earlier crossed the polished wood floor.

'If you'd be good enough to come this way.'

He followed her to a private elevator. Moments later, he was standing in a large open plan office. The room was lit on all four sides by windows. In each corner, ancient cast bronze figures from a Buddhist shrine stood like sentinels around the elderly Japanese who sat reading at a desk at its centre. In that moment Vasari knew his meeting was with Tatsuya Nashiba.

The old man stood up and bowed stiffly. 'Mr Vasari, I do not believe we have met before.' Vasari responded with a low bow and Nashiba motioned him to sit. 'I was concerned to see that a man who has given my family such excellent service for so many years is to leave us now with no clear plans for the future.'

There was a long pause while Vasari collected his

thoughts. 'I am not dissatisfied, *Shacho*. I was given options . . .'

'I understand you were hoping for a posting to the Rome office.'

'*Hai, Shacho.*' Yes, Mr President.

'I've had our head of personnel look into staffing arrangements there.' He turned the pages of what Vasari now realised was his own company file. 'It would suit me very well if you would agree to take the post of Assistant Head of Security, starting immediately.'

Vasari blinked.

'I think that they need a different calibre of man to take over that division, one with more broadly based experience than they had in mind.'

'I . . . I don't know what to say.'

'I've explained to them that your hours will be rather more flexible than those of your predecessor.' There was the merest hint of tension in his voice. 'You see, Mr Vasari, I wish to continue to make use of your experience as a field operative. Not on the scale you're accustomed to. Just one assignment.'

His head came up slowly. He looked Vasari full in the face. 'A surveillance assignment very important to me personally. In this, too, you will be replacing another man. One who has served me well but wishes to be relieved, now, on medical grounds.' He took a faded file from a drawer in the desk. 'This assignment has already lasted for seventeen years. It can be yours until you wish otherwise or the subject dies or leaves Rome.'

Vasari returned to the binoculars. Willow was locking up for the night. He caught a last glimpse of her as she closed the shutters behind her. She was fifty-two now, tall and slim, as her Japanese nickname suggested. The round, attractive face had aged in the last five years. The ebony hair had turned iron grey. Small wonder, Vasari thought as he rubbed the eyeglass on his silk shirt. Late one Saturday night, her husband had been driving the family back from a day trip to Milan when half a dozen drunken English football fans on rented motorbikes pulled out of a turning on the wrong side of the road. He'd swerved to avoid them. Hit a concrete lamp-post. Didn't stand a chance. He and the kid had been killed instantly. She'd spent four months in the St Ignatius Hospital with multiple injuries. Another six undergoing psychiatric counselling. Then she returned to her job at Rome University as senior lecturer in Japanese studies.

For months afterwards, Vasari would fine-tune the short-wave receiver he'd set up in his guest bedroom to the bugs set into the plasterwork of her apartment to hear her sobbing her heart out. More than once he'd asked himself what possible threat this broken woman could be to anyone.

It wasn't his business. Any of it. Every week he'd make out his report and have it sent to Nashiba in the overnight pouch from the Rome building. Every month he'd bank the cheque for four thousand dollars.

Gradually, he watched Willow build a new life for herself. Her students became her family. Christmas and Easter she'd go to Milan to stay with her sister-in-law. Every summer some physics professor from the university and his wife would invite her to their place in Nice. Wherever she went, Vasari had her covered. A chef at the university supplied copies of her weekly roster and kept an eye on her when she was on campus. In Nice, she was watched by a security man from the Paris office.

Then, in the summer of 1994, with Willow safely in Nice and the responsibility of the French operative, Vasari decided to take a short vacation. He often spent a week at the exclusive resort hotel on Mount Argentario, it was his way of pampering himself. As always, he sat in the terrace restaurant behind the floodlit seventeenth-century villa and watched the waiters in their crisp white jackets serve the immaculately groomed couples that filled the tables. He looked over the menu one last time and tried to catch the head waiter's eye. The man seemed to be involved in an argument with a guest a couple of tables away.

'. . . I don't wish to come to the manager's office to discuss anything. I wish to sit here and finish my dinner in peace.' The speaker was a man in his early twenties, handsome in a petulant kind of way. And a lot the worse for drink, judging by his diction and the pitch of his voice. The tanned, very pretty blonde sitting to his left whispered something into his ear. 'And you can shut the fuck up as well!' the slurred voice bellowed.

The waiter was saying something about the young man lowering his voice. It was a mistake. He hit him so hard in the mouth that he was thrown backwards across a table occupied by an elderly couple, to land sprawling on his back amongst the ice buckets and soup tureens of the tables beyond. The blonde burst into tears and tried to get up to leave. The man grabbed her roughly by the arm and slapped her hard across the face. She let out a scream and tried to pull away. He raised his hand to hit her again.

Vasari had seen enough. He slid from his chair, moved two paces across the restaurant and slammed the edge of his hand into the man's kidneys. The calluses built up over a lifetime had softened long ago, but skills learned young are never forgotten. The effect was good enough. The man arched back. The mouth jerked open in a soundless cry, his arms flying upwards in pain. Vasari clamped one arm around his throat and used the other to force him into a vice-like armlock. He ran him across the narrow lawn and booted him into the swimming pool. There was total silence for a second and then a burst of applause from most of the tables. Vasari, his role as bouncer over for the night, walked back to his table.

The following morning, the incident forgotten, he settled back on a sun lounger to read the dog-eared paperback he'd found in the hotel's small library.

'I just wanted to say how sorry I am about last night.'

Vasari looked up. Troublemaker's girlfriend was standing in front of him, her firm breasts and tiny waist highlighted by the one-piece bathing suit. Dark glasses and a layer of make-up partly hid a red weal across the side of her face. He put down the book.

'I should be the one doing the apologising. I hear I made quite a mess of your boyfriend.'

'He deserved it. And anyway, he's not my boyfriend. Not any more.' She pulled up a chair and sat down. 'This has been coming for a long time. Hermano's lost everything building racing cars, and a lot more borrowed from his father. He's been getting worse and worse. Drinking and fighting . . .' She looked out towards the sea. 'In a way you did me a favour.'

'And where's Hermano now?'

'In prison, I hope,' she pouted. 'Why do beautiful men have to be so infantile, so utterly hateful.' She took a compact from her purse and looked at the weal on her face. 'Bastard! I can't go back to Rome looking like this.'

Vasari took the check and signed. 'You shouldn't put make-up on it. Just sea water, it contains iodine. It'll heal up a lot quicker.'

Whether Isobel saw him as the mature, caring friend she seemed to need or simply the means to a couple more nights at one of the most exclusive hotels in Italy, all expenses paid, Vasari neither knew nor cared, but suddenly she said, 'If you don't have an objection to being seen in public with a scarlet woman, with a scarlet face, perhaps we could have lunch together.'

At that moment she looked very vulnerable. It was not a look he would see often. But at fifty-one, Marco Vasari was certain that he had fallen in love for the first time. It was an infatuation that would change many lives before it was over.

For the next eight months he and Isobel were seldom apart. But their affair was never easy. She was vain, spoilt and mercurial. She could also be charming and wickedly funny. And sometimes very late, after they'd made love, even warm and caring. Then the following morning she'd sit at her dressing-table, comb out her thick blonde hair, paint up her full lips and return to the self she'd spent so long perfecting. Glacial, brittle, beautiful. And above all, expensive. Vasari watched, almost with an air of detachment, as his deposit account shrank and told himself it was the price a man of his age paid for having a twenty-six-year-old lover.

Then one night she announced, 'Franco Rossi's taking over the Saint Francis Hotel in Revello next weekend.' Vasari looked blank.

'Franco Rossi! You know, the textile millionaire. Imagine, a house party for three hundred people. Of course, I told his secretary we'd go.'

She couldn't have chosen a worse weekend to want to leave Rome. Vasari sat in his spare bedroom surrounded by surveillance equipment. On the shelf above him was a long line of desk diaries, one for each year of the Willow Assignment: sixteen compiled by his predecessor, eleven by himself. He looked at his notepad. 'The May Day Holiday Weekend', he'd written. Beneath he'd listed precisely what Willow had done that weekend for the last five years. The result of the exercise was clear enough. There was a better-than-evens chance that she would fly to Nice. Every hour of every day for twenty-seven years, Nashiba had lived in certain knowledge of where the woman was. Vasari wasn't going to risk blowing that now. Not even for Isobel. But he could already see how the conversation with her would go: 'Fine. If you don't want to take me, I'll go on my own.' Sure. He could imagine how long she'd stay unattached on that kind of weekend.

He switched on the short-wave receiver. Suddenly the sound of classical music mixed with the chatter of a sewing machine filled the room. The liquid crystal display on the directional heat sensor, a long alloy tube mounted on a tripod, monitored a body moving round the room. Vasari picked up the diary and wrote in the space for Friday: '9.40 p.m. Subject at home sewing.' He wondered for how long.

He walked to the window, and trained the infra-red

binoculars on Willow's living-room as he had the night before. The venetian blinds remained closed. *What are you thinking, lady?* He drummed his fingers irritably on the window ledge. *What are your plans?* There was only one solution. The chef. He was a man of limited intelligence, but he was reliable. And, like most compulsive gamblers, he never turned up his nose at the prospect of a little extra cash. He'd covered for Vasari before and it had gone smoothly enough. Vasari ran his finger down the list of numbers where the man could be reached, lifted the phone and dialled.

For once Isobel had not exaggerated. The St Francis Hotel was superb. It'd been blasted into the cliff face near the mountain village of Revello, known as The Rooftop of the World.

Vasari lay back against the balcony rail and surveyed the company. Tanned girls with braying voices; earnest looking young men who reeked of cologne. *Apart from me, there isn't a soul in this room a day over twenty-eight,* Vasari thought. The dying rays of the sun were making him screw up his eyes. He moved into the shadows, where the light was kinder. *What am I doing here? I don't have a damn thing to say to these people. I'm not part of this world. I should be in Rome, taking care of business.* His stomach started to churn. *What if the chef isn't there when I call?* he thought as he made his way across the lobby to the phone booth.

'Relax, Vasari, she's home. Ain't going anywhere tonight. Car's in the usual place.'

'What's she been doing?'

'You really want to hear? You must know the routine backwards.' He sighed. 'She vacuums the living-room, unloads the dishwasher, does a bit of sewing, takes a shower. All fascinating stuff. She should be in therapy, that's all I can say.'

'Why? What do you mean?'

'This person has serious behavioural problems, that's why.'

'What do you know about it?'

'I know normal people don't take a shower and vacuum the living-room three times in six hours.'

Vasari's body jerked like he'd been hit by high-velocity rifle fire. Tape. The chef was listening to a tape loop, had to be.

'Vasari? You there?'

Across the lobby a four-piece rock band began to play — the noise was deafening. Vasari never heard a note.

Fumiko Nashiba knelt in a shady corner of the rooftop garden. Every oval leaf of the gardenia jasmin methodically checked for aphids, she ran her slender fingers along the sculpted boughs and tiny gnarled trunk of the century-old Bonsai. There were no signs of disease. She placed the shallow blue ceramic dish back on the wooden plank in front of her and moved on to the miniature cypress.

'Mother!'

She gave a little gasp of delight as she turned to greet her son. He was almost beside her before she could get up and bow. Akitō was forced by convention to stop in his tracks and bow in return. He wanted to embrace her but this Western affectation was forbidden him. Instead, he took her hand, the translucent, paper-thin skin the only sign of age.

'You look tired,' she said, noticing the faint rings under his eyes.

'It's been a long week.'

'Come, I will have some green tea brought up.'

They sat until the light faded, looking out over the Manhattan skyline. Akitō was mostly silent, breathing in the calm. The aesthetic symmetry of the garden, the precise delicacy with which his mother served him, gradually soothed his raw nerve-ends like a warm poultice.

'Let me bring you *sushi*.' Fumiko rose and turned towards the French doors leading into the penthouse.

'I'm not hungry, really.' Akitō saw the disappointment flash across his mother's face. 'Oh . . . yes, do. I should like that.' He closed his eyes and slipped into a relaxed sleep for the first time in four days.

'*Gaki! Gaki-chan, Mama ga iru yo!*'

The bleeding offal spilling out behind Akitō's eyes kaleidoscoped into the deep red of his mother's blouse. She was cradling him. The silk felt cool against his sweating forehead.

Gaki-chan. His mother hadn't called him by his baby name since he was four. Hungry Demon. Like every Japanese mother, she called him an ugly name to stop the evil spirits from stealing her child's life away. Suddenly he realised he must have cried out.

'I'm sorry, sorry . . . It's all right, I'm all right.' He knew she would not ask him to explain. But she would worry if he said nothing.

'I've done so much travelling these last few months,' he said, at last. 'I'm afraid I don't sleep very well.'

'You could . . . You could try acupuncture,' she started, a little nervously. 'It has helped me in many ways.'

Akitō sat up, his head still pounding. He was ready to try anything that would rid him of the image of that boy.

Seventy-two hours to deadline. Morton wiped over the screen of the computer on his workbench with an anti-static cloth. If AmTronics got the final okay Monday morning, production of G250 would be on schedule. Commercial distribution would begin next spring. It was a long run-up but that's the way it worked. For one more weekend, it was his baby. And it wasn't going out into the world without its shoes polished and its necktie straight.

It was around ten-fifteen Saturday night and kit inspection was still far from complete when the phone on his study desk rang.

'Hi, Mack,' Morton grunted. 'Where the hell have you been?'

'I'm in Chicago. There's been a lot of stuff to figure out ... had to spend some time with my attorney, y'know. This is a big step for me. Listen, Auburn's apartment's just fine. I'm back tomorrow, figured I'd go straight there, if that's okay.'

'Sure, stay as long as you like, I told you.'

'Well, I thought maybe I'd camp out there till the fall at least.'

'Six months, a year, whatever,' Morton yawned. 'There's an inventory somewhere, but I'm damned if I know where Auburn put it. Still, I don't suppose you'll steal the cutlery. Just make yourself comfortable, okay?'

'Thanks, Morton. Get some sleep, yeah?'

Mack hung up. Morton leaned back in his chair and tried to get the knots out of his spine. *Jesus, this job fucks your eyes, your neck, your back.* The painkillers that had kept the dull ache of a thirty-year-old football injury at bay were starting to wear off again. He weighed up the pleasures of a hot bath and a pastrami sandwich against running up his software one more time.

The phone rang again.

'This'd better be good.'

The reedy voice of Bill Pasternak, the company head of PR, was barely discernible above the background hubbub. He was obviously calling from a pay-phone in a bar.

'I need to see you, Morton, tonight.' There was an urgency in his voice Totheroh had never heard before.

'What the hell's up?'

'I'll be with you in ten minutes, okay?' The line went dead.

Morton had never liked Pasternak. He'd been with the company almost from the beginning. He was good at his job, no question about that. But he was a brown-noser, you never could get a straight answer out of the guy.

Pasternak stood in the doorway, the rain still running down his fawn trench coat, his lined face creased into a frown. Behind him stood a balding man with a blunt, humourless face.

'Morton, this is Ben Karsh, he's a freelance with *Computer World*. I thought you should hear what he just told me.'

Morton cleared a lunch tray and other debris off the two armchairs in his study and they all sat down. Pasternak started to peel the foil cap-wrapping off a bottle of cognac.

'What are we celebrating?'

'Not a damn thing.' Pasternak held out the bottle. 'Take a slug, Morton. We're both gonna need one.' Morton took the bottle and waited for the bombshell to hit.

'The fact is, IBM have beaten us to the post.'

'What?'

'I'm sorry, Morton, sorry for all of us.'

The blunt-faced man took a sheet of typescript from his breast pocket. 'They're marketing a two-point-five-gigabyte computer this fall. It'll retail for almost a thousand dollars less than yours.'

Morton stared at the G250 on his workbench. 'That can't be right. Can't be. How come we didn't hear about this?' He was going to say, 'C'mon, they must be bluffing.' But when he looked back at the guy, he could see there was no point. He took a good hard slug of cognac.

The man started to read out the press release but Morton wasn't listening. He was looking at Pasternak. The frown had gone. There was a look of relief on his face. The problem wasn't his alone now, he'd off-loaded most of it on to his boss. No, wait a minute, that wasn't it . . . The thin, lined face registered something else.

A new wave of tiredness overwhelmed him. *Jesus,* Morton thought, *I'm too old for this game.* He watched Pasternak's face sub-divide into two dilute blurred images.

Morton closed his eyes. There was a rushing in his ears, like a deluge of water bursting through a tunnel. The deluge lifted him up for a moment . . . way up. Then somehow he was lying on his stomach, the pile of the study carpet pressed into his nose. An ashtray was spinning on its edge in slow motion an inch from his face.

There was the vaguest sensation of his pants and under-shorts being pulled down and then a jab, the jab of a needle in the back of his scrotum. He wanted to shout, fight, any-thing. Nothing would come.

The next feeling was familiar, the warm glow of the pain-killer kicking in. No, this was different . . . it was stronger . . . much stronger. It was squeezing like a vice, crushing him from the inside, crushing the life out of him.

Bluntface stood up, replaced the hypodermic in its plastic cover and dropped it into his jacket pocket. He stooped to inspect the tiny purple mark at the back of Morton's scro-tum. The wrinkled flesh was already starting to lose its warmth. He looked satisfied. No pathologist on the planet'd find that! He started to redress the still-breathing body. Where the hell was Pasternak? All he had to do was walk half a block to the car, get the boxes and come back.

Bluntface didn't like this job, didn't like working with an outsider. The scrawny American made him edgy. He put the bottle of drugged cognac in his briefcase and broke the seal on a pair of surgical gloves. He pulled them on, took out a bottle of the same brand of cognac with about an eighth of its contents gone and rubbed the glass rim along Morton's lips before pressing the limp hand several times around the label and leaving the bottle on the desk.

Pasternak appeared in the doorway, breathing hard. He held two large plastic carrying-cases. The two men worked systematically, removing tray after tray of Morton's software disks from his home filing system and swapping them with the identically arranged duplicates brought from his company office. Bluntface went over the apartment with a fine tooth comb. Pasternak pushed Morton's personal filofax software into the running computer. Yup, there it was, the name and telephone number of the company doc-tor. He left it up on the screen then grabbed the carrying-cases and made for the elevator.

Bluntface had found the wall safe behind Betty's portrait in the living-room. He tapped in the combination. Nothing in there he needed. He scanned the apartment one more time, then, certain that everything looked exactly as it had when he'd arrived, he walked back to the study. One final check – yeah, the pulse was barely detectable now, though the eyes were still flickering. He let himself noiselessly out of the apartment.

Morton's gaze was riveted on the corridor leading to the kitchen. Betty, her hair as deep red as the day he'd married her, was fixing dinner and singing that song she liked from *West Side Story*. He smiled inside. She never did get that part of the tune right. He'd kind of got used to it her way. A man came out of the living-room and stood a few feet from where he lay. It was his father, the way he'd seen him look in a thousand nightmares: pale, skeletal, a knotted cloth around his loins.

Betty'd stopped singing. Pity, she had a pretty voice. He never did get to tell her.

SEVEN

The vast warehouses that had once faced on to the bustling harbour area of South Street, Manhattan, had long ago been divided up into lofts and sold and leased out for office space, apartments, rehearsal rooms, film studios and artists' workshops. The offices of Aid Watch International occupied the second floor of a building at the junction of St Peck Slip, a block south of the Brooklyn Bridge. Despite the fact that it was Sunday, the highly-publicised launch of the organisation the following day meant that life continued here at its usual frenetic pace. One corner of the loft had been recently partitioned into a small reception area and its decoration was still incomplete. Bryony Cole pressed herself into a space normally occupied only by an undernourished palm tree and tried to keep out of the way as large, mounted displays were moved out through the battered wooden doors by a small army of young volunteers.

Her original intention had been to take the information she had straight to the Federal authorities the minute she was out of Colonel Santiago's reach. But the small write-up on Aid Watch that she'd seen in *Newsweek*, days before leaving the Cordilleras, had changed her mind. Her motives were not entirely unselfish. The misuse of aid was a subject she felt passionately about. But the more she read about this organisation and its aims, the more she started to see a future role for herself. Few people with her qualifications could claim to have her breadth of information and personal experience of life inside a corrupt Third-World autocracy. She could put all that to maximum use, here.

For now, that plan could wait. What she had to tell Hans Rienderhoff, the Dutch-American originator of Aid Watch, could not. He appeared at last, a tall, awkward-looking man who stooped as though his height had been a lifelong source of embarrassment. She followed him down the cluttered corridor to his office and arranged her notes neatly on the corner of the refectory table that doubled as his desk.

'It's good of you to see me at such short notice.'

Rienderhoff stretched out his long legs and studied her through his spectacles. 'Our real work has to go on. All this nonsense you see around you today is just a media exercise. I'm afraid the truth is, no publicity, no funds. And we're running on a shoestring here, as it is. So, you were with that devil Santiago for a year?'

Bryony took a styrofoam pellet out of her purse and handed it to him. 'Exhibit A,' she said. 'I'm sure you've seen these before.'

Rienderhoff turned it through his fingers. 'Used in packaging, aren't they?'

'Yes, but this type is very special,' Bryony said. 'The first time I saw one of these was about four months ago. It was lying in the bottom of the john.'

Rienderhoff raised an eyebrow and waited for the explanation.

'Santiago's wife had taken off for Paris, like she did every few months. While she was away, he had his favourite mistress flown up to the house in the Cordilleras. One night, I went into the ladies' room opposite the formal reception hall just as she walked out. One of these pellets was in the john, another lay in an ashtray, all broken up.'

Rienderhoff cut the pellet in half with a paper-knife. It was hollow.

'Took me a couple of weeks to find out what it was all about. Paulo's parents were in Maraquilla and the kid was left in the care of his grandmother. I was off duty in my room when suddenly there was all this screaming and shouting from downstairs. Paulo was lying in a pool of blood in his father's study. Seemed he'd been watching some real violent video and decided to play out some version of it

97

himself. He dislodged an old sabre while trying to get one of the antique guns down off the wall, and it severed an artery in his arm. All hell broke lose. Santiago's batman radioed for the surgeon to fly in from the city. Paulo was half crazy with fear and losing a lot of blood. I tried to keep him still while the doctor tourniqueted the arm and gave him a sedative.

'When they heard that the surgeon was on his way, they carried the kid into an elevator. I went with him. The thing went down about five levels, into Santiago's personal Führer Bunker. I never even knew it existed. There was a freezer room the size of Bloomingdale's and enough weaponry and supplies to survive a siege into the next century.'

Rienderhoff took up a pen and started to make notes. Bryony paused until he nodded.

'Eventually we got to the medical unit. It had a full-size operating theatre and a pharmacy. The doctor gave Paulo a tetanus shot but he was obviously in a lot of pain. By now, there was absolute pandemonium. Seemed I was the only one not having hysterics. So the doctor turned to me, and said, "The boy needs morphine. The keys to the cabinet are in the Colonel's desk."

'It was while I was going through the drawers in the desk that I came across a load more of these pellets. I figured Santiago wouldn't miss a couple, so I stuffed some down my bra to examine later. When I cracked them open they were filled with what looked to me to be cocaine. I can't say I was surprised to find out that Santiago did drugs, but I couldn't figure out why he'd bother to keep them in these pellets – until I realised they were packaging pellets.'

Rienderhoff leaned forward, listening intently as Bryony went on.

'I found out after I struck up a relationship with the surgeon who'd fixed up Paulo, on one of my trips to Maraquilla. I'd only known Roberto a couple of months. Then one afternoon, I walked in to find him unpacking a Red Cross container with some of his staff. There were antibiotics, anaesthetics, swabs, dressings and surgical equipment, the usual stuff, you know. But it was all packed in these styrofoam pellets. Roberto told me that the massive shipments of medical supplies brought in by the Red Cross were the only thing that kept the hospital functioning. And the only reason St Theresa's got their share was because Santiago endowed the place himself. The other eighty per cent of the stuff shipped into the country was either sold off or slung into the sea and the containers sent back to the US.

'I finally came up with the sixty-four-thousand-dollar answer to the whole thing when a guy I knew at the American Embassy told me that the Red Cross containers didn't go back to the US entirely empty. After the supplies had been unloaded, the styrofoam pellets were put back so they could be reused. Seems the containers are about the only things that aren't systematically searched by customs officials. They're taken direct from Miami dock to the Red Cross's own warehouses because they have some kind of special status.'

Bryony's eyes fixed on the Dutchman's. 'What I'm saying, Mr Rienderhoff, is that Santiago is not only wasting American aid or profiting from it personally, but I believe that he's using styrofoam packing to smuggle cocaine into this country.'

Rienderhoff got up, walked to the door and shouted down the corridor.

'Carl, get in here, will you? I think we finally caught your favourite boy with his hand in the cookie jar.'

Akitō sat stiffly in a chair in his New York apartment. The electronic device gave another buzz.

'Ahh!' The middle-aged Japanese woman standing beside him consulted the life-size tortoiseshell ear in her palm. 'Mmm.' She peered at the tiny hieroglyphics burnt into its surface.

'Large intestine – are you feeling any discomfort in the lower bowel?'

Akitō had paid little attention to the occasional twinge

of pain he'd been getting in his left side recently, but now it was mentioned . . . He nodded.

The small, rod-shaped sensor that the acupuncturist was holding continued to explore his right ear. Each time the device registered a continuous signal, she picked up her tweezers and took a tiny square of transparent tape from the silver dish on the table. Each square contained a metal ball the size of a pinhead. By the time her treatment was complete, she had pressed five into place in the recess of Akitō's outer ear.

'It is important that these stay in day and night until I re-examine you in three days' time,' she said. 'You could comb your hair a little further forward, over your ears, so no one will notice them.' She replaced the tools of her trade in their leather pouch. 'Put gentle pressure on them with your finger whenever you remember. You will sleep deeply from tonight.'

Akitō walked out of the living-room and through to the bathroom. He checked himself out in the mirror. The acupuncturist's work was barely visible. He went through to his bedroom, slipped off his robe and opened the closet door. What to wear? He leafed through the coathangers for something casual. He settled for fawn pants, a cream silk shirt and a pale check sports jacket before heading for the elevator.

'Morning, sir.' The security man held the door open.

'Morning, Max.'

'No car today, sir?'

'Nope. Sunday's stay-in-shape day.' Akitō patted his stomach. 'Getting soft, you know how it is.'

The security man smiled. 'Have a nice day.'

'You too.' Akitō stepped out on to the sidewalk, turned right and headed uptown.

The Yum Thai Restaurant on Columbus Avenue was filled with the usual Sunday-lunchtime crowd. Actors, staff and writers, who during the week occupied the ABC Television Studios almost opposite, mixed with account executives,

100

publicists and others whose incomes could withstand the extravagance of living a stone's throw from Central Park.

The Bryony Cole that sat opposite Akitō now was very different to the one he'd encountered a week before in Colonel Santiago's mountain retreat. The air of irritation was gone. She seemed relaxed, yet at the same time, charged with excitement. Above all, she was clearly glad to be home. Akitō was feeling pleased with himself. He'd given a lot of thought to his tactics on this one and it was going well. He hadn't met a woman yet who didn't like the idea of a man baring his emotions to her. The large violet eyes were getting wider as he spoke.

'. . . I found my way back to McGowan's jeep eventually. He was sitting on the hood grinning like a cat. "Little bit of real life there for you, Nashiba. To give you the total picture." The total picture. On the drive to Puerto Cortes, I did a lot of thinking. I'd always avoided seeing the worst of those places. Just wanted to fly in, take care of business and fly out as fast as I could. For four years, I'd let Santiago and others like him lead me from one set of carefully choreographed set-pieces to another, knowing that each was designed to give me the right impression and no more. It wasn't until that afternoon that I faced up to the reality. McGowan was right about that much. Perhaps the truth is I was happy with it that way.'

Akitō twirled a satay stick between his fingers. 'McGowan said something else I could have lived without, too. He didn't think my seeing the boy butchered like that would get to me so badly, me being "Japanese and all". Remarks like that don't usually upset me, but that day . . . It was like he was saying "Well, all Japanese love a good bloodletting, don't they?" I mean, what kind of people does he think we are – does the world think we are? Savages lopping off people's heads outside the McDonald's on the Ginza!' Akitō lowered his voice. 'I guess it slipped his mind that Changi Jail was torn down twenty years before I was born.' He glanced up; Bryony was looking straight at him. She stretched her hand across the table and took his. He knew he was on the home straight. 'The most violence I'd seen till then was two Irish drunks beating the crap out of each other on the corner of Forty-sixth and Seventh.' Akitō paused for effect. 'You know, before Puerto Cortes, I'd never really questioned the family line on business policy on anything very much. I guess that sounds kind of dumb to you, Bryony, but it is the Japanese way. It's part of the culture we're brought up in.'

'Believe me, the Japanese don't own the patent on that one.' She dabbed her mouth with the napkin and sat back in her chair. 'Look at me. I trained as a teacher because my father and grandfather taught in school. Some reason! I needed that time in the Cordilleras to think, to figure out how I was going to spend my life.'

'And?'

'Now I've decided. And it feels good.'

'It looks good.' Akitō smiled. At that moment he couldn't remember having seen a prettier woman. 'How on earth did the job with the Colonel come up in the first place?'

'Fluke. I heard my predecessor was picked from a short-list of six. But after two months stuck up there on Fantasy Mountain he started zapping the bourbon and the chambermaids in whatever order they came to hand first. Santiago kicked his butt all over the Casa Grande when he found out. After that, he turned to St Anthony's direct for a tutor. And they recommended me.'

She grinned. 'You should have seen Santiago's face when I walked into his office in Maraquilla! I think he was expecting some crusty old governess with her hair pinned up in a bun. He gave me a month's trial, anyhow. I think his initial view was if he couldn't jump me within the four weeks, he'd stick me on the first plane back to Panama City. But I made sure he kept his hands to himself. His wife was watching him like a hawk. Married to a man like that, I could understand why she felt threatened. Anyway, I thought she'd make a good ally, talked to her about fashion, movie stars, anything else her brain could take in. After a while I stopped being the Witch of Endor and we started talking to each other like regular human beings.

102

'At the end of the month Santiago took Paulo up to his office and checked out his progress. Much to everyone's astonishment I was hired for the year.' She took a sip of wine. 'You should have seen the contract he had his American attorneys draw up. There was this confidentiality clause in it where I had to swear on everything but *Moby Dick* to keep stumm about his private life. Still, it suited me. Without that I'd never have persuaded him to let me spend my weekends in Maraquilla. And that was the key to the deal from my end. I'd already found out for myself it wasn't a place a girl could walk around on her own. He'd have me flown in on a Friday night and a driver assigned to me for the weekend. He felt he could keep an eye on me that way and I felt a whole lot safer, so everyone was happy.

'That's when I started to find out what made the whole Santiago régime tick.' She leaned back so the waiter could clear away the dishes.

'Have you heard of an organisation called Aid Watch?'

Akitō looked up. 'Yeah, I think I read about it in the *Times*.'

'I just spent the morning up at their offices. After a year around Santiago and other leaders he had up there as guests, I thought I might have quite a lot to offer them. So do they.' She waited for a reaction.

'You're going to work for them?'

'Don't know – they haven't offered me anything yet but . . .' Bryony smiled. 'They will.'

'What do you say we take a walk?' Akitō settled the check and stepped out with Bryony into the bright sunlight to join the crowd strolling through to the flea market in a schoolyard off Columbus Avenue. Moving from stall to stall, Bryony immediately attracted attention. Female heads turned as well as male to watch her pass by. Something in the swivel of her hips fascinated the men and infuriated the women at the same time. She stopped by a rack of leather jackets and tried one on. It was made of light buckskin, padded at the shoulder, tapering from a wide 'V' neck to cling to the hip.

'You never saw the markets in Maraquilla, did you? Some of the worked leather stuff they do there is beautiful.' She fastened the single button, pulling the jacket tightly in to her narrow waist. 'Trouble is they don't have any cutters there, anyone with the first idea about style.'

'That looks real nice on you, lady,' the stall-owner tried.

The cut of the blouse spoilt the line of the jacket. She tucked the collar inside, undid a couple of buttons and tucked the cotton fabric behind the leather. It was an unconscious act, simply intended to give a better idea of how the jacket might look, but the swell of her bust was visible as she turned to show Akitō. He silently slipped the stall-owner a roll of dollar bills.

'No, no, please don't.' Bryony had spotted the move. She unbuttoned the jacket and tried to hang it back on the rack.

'Too late,' Akitō said, taking it from her hand and making her put it back on. 'Anyway, I'd look awful in it.'

Bryony stuck out her chin. 'I don't take presents from strange men.'

Akitō laughed at her. 'What's so strange about me?'

'Everything.' Bryony skipped ahead to the next stall, picked up a pair of garish ceramic earrings and hung them up to her ears, peering at herself in a small mirror. 'That's what I like about you. At least there's someone in there worth finding out about.'

'Well thanks!'

'I mean, you don't prejudge everything.'

Akitō turned over what he had in mind next. *Don't be so sure*, he thought.

'I've been prejudged all my life.' She stuck her tongue out at her reflection. 'I could use a little pragmatism right now.'

Akitō's attention drifted to a middle-aged Japanese woman. He'd noticed her before, looking at Bryony. She was still studying her from across the street. Bryony left Akitō's side and moved on to sift through the 'antiques' on the stall ahead. Few of the items offered for sale seemed to have seen active service much earlier than the mid-seventies. Akitō looked back to the Japanese woman. Her gaze hadn't shifted. It was *him* she was staring at. Had been all along. Their eyes connected for a full five seconds before she looked away. Akitō was certain he'd never seen her before. But she obviously recognised him. He began to feel uncomfortable.

He grabbed Bryony's hand. 'Come on, let's get ice-cream.' But he couldn't help himself looking back. The woman was still in tow. She appeared to be looking through a selection of silk scarves now, but Akitō felt certain she was following him.

Suddenly he took Bryony's arm, turned off sharp left and walked briskly down Seventy-sixth Street towards Broadway.

'Hey, what's the big hurry?' The remains of Bryony's rum and raisin toppled from its cone and slopped on to the sidewalk. She looked back forlornly at it as he hurried her along.

'I want to ravish you and I can't wait any longer.'

'Ah.'

The only part of Akitō's New York apartment that owed anything to his Japanese heritage was a small area of tatami matting set around a low black lacquer table. On the table, in a flat rectangular dish, was an exquisite miniature landscape. Bryony moved closer to look at the dwarf trees which flourished on a cliff-like piece of rock.

'Ah! Shoes off please!' Akitō said. Bryony obediently slipped off her brogues.

'That's beautiful.' She peered at the tiny china house with low, sweeping eaves which was placed under the 'cliff' looking out over the surrounding water in the dish.

'It is a *saikei*,' Akitō explained. 'Of course, a true *saikei* landscape should only contain natural elements: plants, soil, rocks and water. But I thought the house looked rather charming.'

'You made this yourself?'

'Oh yes.' Akitō smiled. 'In Japan, men are as interested as women in Bonsai. But I admit I had some help. I stole the trees from my mother's collection . . . Please, sit down.'

Bryony sat on the tatami mats, staring fascinated, first at the *saikei*, then at the small Shinto shrine on the wall behind, then at the old lacquer cabinet which stood below it.

Akitō brought a brass portable furnace forward; a three-legged iron stand was already in place at its centre. He bowed politely. 'Allow me to invite you to the *Cha-No-Yu*, the tea ceremony.'

'You kidding?' Bryony said, but looking up, she could see it was a serious matter.

'Please.' Akitō motioned a hand indicating that she should kneel. 'There must be complete silence.' He laid a paper mat beside the furnace and went back into the kitchen, returning with a wooden box and an ornate cast-iron kettle. He put the kettle carefully on to the paper mat before turning to the lacquer cabinet. On top of the cabinet to one side, was a vase containing a single azalea branch in full bloom. At the other side stood a porcelain incense burner. Bryony watched while Akitō solemnly lit the incense, then opened the cabinet, taking out a small earthenware tea caddy and a silk brocade bag. He knelt down by the furnace. Opening the wooden box, he spooned charcoal into the bottom. When he was satisfied, he lit the charcoal, sat on his heels and waited.

As Akitō knelt there, motionless, Bryony was studying his face. It was the essence of total calm. Here was a tranquillity that seemed to belie the energetic nature of the man. But then, she thought, she hardly knew him. Perhaps, beneath the tenacity and outward self-possession, there was a softness, after all.

The charcoal turned white-hot. Akitō lifted the kettle and set it on the tripod. He opened the brocade bag, taking out a round, porcelain cup and a red silk napkin. He creased the napkin through his hands and wiped the cup. Each move was made with infinite care, infinite control; balanced,

106

beautiful, balletic. When the kettle boiled, Akitō opened the tea caddy, took up a bamboo spoon and placed a small quantity of the dried green leaves into the cup. Next, he poured on the water and beat the tea with a little bamboo whisk. He added a spoonful of cool water from a bowl, bowed and offered the cup to Bryony.

Bryony took the cup carefully from his fingers and found herself inclining her head in response. She sipped the hot green liquid. When she had finished, she lifted the empty cup towards him, not knowing what should come next. Akitō took the cup, followed the same elaborate procedure and drank some tea himself before starting afresh and offering Bryony another cup.

They shared six cups in this way. With each, the mesmeric quality of the ceremony lulled Bryony's senses. She had never felt so perfectly relaxed. The *Cha-No-Yu* complete, Akitō came and knelt beside her. She let her hands rest on his, at peace. A light was beginning to show through the steel gate that guarded her vulnerability. Something was slipping away. It was like drifting into sleep. She closed her eyes and let her fingers push through his, enjoying the implicit eroticism. She was breathing deeply, slowly, as if in meditation, sinking into the sweet sensation of sleep. She put her head on his chest, like a child, absorbed in his serenity. Yet she felt curiously detached and dreamlike; wanting to be close but keeping herself apart. She stretched a hand upwards, feeling for his neck, tilting her face towards him, then parted her lips slightly for the kiss she knew must come. She let her whole mouth be taken into his, melting into this first unity.

Soundlessly, they undressed each other, the familiarity of experience guiding the hands and lips. She pulled herself up close to him, letting her breasts press against his chest. He unfastened her skirt, caressing her waist, feeling for the curve of her buttocks beneath her French knickers. She continued to kiss him, loosening his belt. Now she could feel his erect penis against the soft skin of her belly. She ran her fingers lightly over it. When his hand found her,

107

she stiffened, waiting. The split-second hesitation told him it was his move. His hands left her for a moment while he slid off her pants, then returned. Her legs were wider now, she started pushing softly, almost involuntarily, into his palm. His fingertips felt for her gently, unobtrusively, waiting for her to release the desire for penetration.

All the time she was dreamy, distracted, rubbing his penis between her hand and her stomach, letting it butt gently into her navel. She could feel his slight wetness on her skin as he took her shoulders and guided her to the floor. Akitō had determined to take his time. For several minutes he moved his hands and mouth over her body, slowly, rhythmically, with a care and precision of movement befitting a sacred rite. He went into her with the same slow sensuality. She moaned and brought her knees up, willing him to go in deeper, intent on her own satisfaction.

Akitō changed pace. He knew she was only responding in part. Women either had orgasms or faked them. This one was somewhere in between. He could feel her clasping on him but he fought the impulse to come. He was watching her reactions. She was completely caught up in the act but it was pure reflex. She was lost to herself not to him. He gripped her hips and thrust in hard. Her eyes snapped open as she connected with reality, releasing her muscles to cope with his sudden aggression. He thrust once more and withdrew without finishing. For some reason, he'd been trying to make love to her. But if she just wanted to fuck . . . He knelt up and turned her over, pulling her buttocks up level with his waist. He parted her with both hands, exposing everything, holding her in place until he was ready. Then he went in, drawing her on to him, pushing down into her until he touched the neck of her womb. She cried out. He was hurting her. Hurting her, damn it. She wanted to fight him but he held her fast, impelling her beyond the mental barrier that denied his identity. A spontaneous yell escaped her as she came, then came again. She was panting from exertion but he would not leave her. He was wearing down her resistance, making her ache for her own end and his.

When she climaxed again she knew it was over. There was no fight left. He withdrew and lay her down, covering her body with his, almost protectively. He entered her gently, now, kissing her all the time, and she opened to him willingly, opened until she wanted him to fill her whole being. In the moment of her release she felt him come into her at last, the relief of it bringing her to tears.

In Rome, Marco Vasari's Sunday had been an experience to forget.

EIGHT

It was 3.15 a.m. when Vasari let himself into his apartment in Tivoli. The whole place stank of stale cigarette smoke. Judging by the number of bottles on the table in the living-room, the chef had made quite a dent in his wine store. The man was stretched out on the sofa, snoring loudly. Vasari kicked the sofa leg.

'Wake up! What the hell do you think you're doing?'

The chef, a small, swarthy man, shook himself like a dog. 'Aah, it's been silent as the grave over there for hours.'

They went over to the closet where the surveillance equipment was set up. 'I did like you said, put everything I was getting on to cassette.' They listened to the playback. There was the sound of a vacuum cleaner and classical music playing on a portable radio. The chef spooled on; the clink of dishes, different classical music; later, the sewing machine, then the sound of the shower being used.

Vasari yawned. 'Spool on.'

The chef pressed fast-forward. 'Okay, this is about two hours later, it's the same sequence of sounds again, just different music. I timed the lapse between each sound. That too was identical. I was getting body movement on the heat sensor till about eleven. Then nothing.'

Vasari rubbed his chest with his hand, his breath was coming in short, painful bursts. He sprang up and switched on the binoculars. The blinds were closed, the apartment in darkness. He'd have to go in there.

*

110

Willow's Fiat was parked in the alley, to the left of the building, as it always was at night. Vasari took the pass-key out of his pocket. He'd used it once at the start of his mission ten years before when he'd positioned the bugs in the living-room and bedroom, and again three years later, when he replaced them with upgrades. He turned the key in the lock and pushed the door; the ease with which the door swung open made him sick in the gut. She'd gone for sure. The security chain was off.

He checked the bedroom and kitchen first then turned on the centre light in her living-room. Laid out neatly on the coffee-table was a cassette recorder, a portable radio and a spotlight. He snapped open the recorder and took out the cassette. It was the continuous play, loop type, used for the canned music they play in restaurants and eleva-tors. The two indentations at the back of the cassette, put in by the manufacturers to stop the tape being erased, had been covered over with transparent tape. The printed label read: 'Tape 6: Neapolitan Love Songs'. Vasari didn't need to play it to know what was on it now.

Across the front of the room was what had been her son's electric train set, an oval of 'O' gauge track, a locomotive and flat wagon. He walked over to take a look. An electric kettle with a variable thermostat fixed into the top had been placed on top of the wagon. The leads from the kettle and the train set had been fed under the track. He followed the leads to the wall. There in a quad rack of sockets were four automatic random time switches. He went back over to the train. The kettle was now empty, the water evapor-ated. The temperature on the thermostat was set at just under 37 degrees centigrade, 98.6 Fahrenheit. Normal body heat, near as damn it. So much for the heat sensor.

Vasari shook his head. The woman couldn't have figured out how to rig this lot up on her own. Then it clicked: the physics professor with the place in Nice. It must have taken him all of fifteen minutes to work out. Clever. Thousands of dollars' worth of state-of-the-art equipment duped by a collection of junk and a few dollars' worth of cable. Even if he'd run the sounds he'd picked up through the graphic equalizer to check for tape noise, the noise on the classical recordings on the radio would have masked it.

He knew now that everything monitored over the last two nights was garbage. Probably the last three. Willow was long gone.

Vasari poured himself a large vodka, took the letter that had lain undisturbed in his filing cabinet for eleven years and read. 'In the event of the subject making an unforeseen departure, contact Tokyo, 0081 3-71796044. He picked up the phone and dialled.

'Operative 29. Priority 771.'

'Please hold.'

He listened to the static on the line. *So she knew I was there all the time*, he thought. *She was laughing at me. She knew she could take off whenever she wanted and I'd be too fucking dumb to notice.*

'We've identified you, Mr Vasari. You are cleared for Priority 771, but unfortunately Mr Nashiba just boarded a flight at Kennedy Airport. He's due here in Tokyo at 6.00 a.m. Monday morning, our time. The earliest he can be reached is 8.00 a.m. on his private number. Shall I get it for you?'

'I have it. Is there no way you can get a message to him?'

'Not on a matter of this nature, sir.'

Vasari hung up and looked at his watch. 4.00 a.m. He made a quick calculation. Nashiba wouldn't know for another seventeen hours. Willow would have been gone for four days. Whatever damage it was she could do Nashiba, could well be done before he even knew she'd left Rome.

Mack put the key in the door. This time he took a good look around Auburn Totheroh's apartment. It was well ordered and clean but it had a warmth, an ambience, it wore the owner's stamp. He fingered a tiny watercolour by the bathroom door. She was an artist, he knew that, but . . . Funny, in all these years, he'd never given Morton's daughter much thought. She was a fact, that was all. But here she was, on the walls, in the furniture, the colour of the drapes. Yeah, he could get to like this place.

Still, it was strange settling down in her bed that night. As he turned over to switch off the light, he picked up a silver photo frame from the side table. It held a picture of a much younger Morton hugging a little girl, her wispy curls bright as a new copper penny under an outsized baseball cap. He closed his eyes and tried to build a woman's face out of the childish features. The transformation was incomplete when sleep came.

At four o'clock, Mack woke up in a cold sweat. A few seconds went by before he realised that the pounding in his chest was no nightmare. His nervous system was telling him that he wasn't alone. His heart was almost leaping out of his throat as he slipped on his robe. He strained his ears. The slightest sound of drawers being opened and closed was coming from the spare bedroom. He picked up a bronze horse head from the table in the hallway and turned it till the mane sat firmly in his palm. Then he took a deep breath and burst through the door.

He was halfway across the room before it hit him. A scream that could syringe your ears out stunned his senses. His jaw fell open. A naked woman stood at an easel, with a brush in one hand and a paint palette in the other.

'Back off, bastard!' She grabbed for a large craft knife.

'Hey, it's okay, I'm . . .'

She lunged for his throat. He caught her wrist as the knife came straight at his larynx. Next thing he knew he was on the floor.

'Jesus, lady, burglars don't wear bathrobes. I'm Mack Lasky, Mack Lasky, dammit, your father's friend!'

'What the hell are you doing in my apartment?' she shrieked.

Mack rolled over with a groan, nursing his bruised manhood. 'He said you were in Los Angeles for the year, said I could use the place as a temporary base.'

If it hadn't been for the exquisite pain between his legs Mack could have enjoyed what he was looking at. Auburn

113

Totheroh had a great body. A guy getting the view he'd got now could be forgiven if his first appraisal didn't extend as far as her face, the strong, attractive features and emerald green eyes framed by a mass of Titian curls.

'I called four days ago and left a message on his answering machine. How come he didn't let me know you were staying here?' She was still yelling.

'Maybe he was too busy with the G250,' Mack yelled back.

'Maybe.' She'd placed the name now. 'Well, you sure don't cut it as a burglar. Okay, if you're Lasky . . . what's your nickname for my father?'

'Orson.'

'Correct.' She put down the knife and took a couple of deep breaths to steady her nerves. 'Jesus, Pop just gets worse. It's like there's a wall between him and the world when he's playing around with all that electronic junk. Hell, you're here now and it's five in the morning so I guess I can't throw you on the sidewalk. You stay where you are and I'll sleep in here for tonight. Let's figure the rest out in the morning.' She walked into her bedroom, opened a closet and took out a robe. Mack finally focused on her figure. Ten plus. She came back in.

'You're gawping like a clam, Sam. Show's over.'

'Coffee, juice and toast?' Auburn was calling from the kitchen. 'That's what's in the fridge, so I take it that's what you have.'

Mack put his knee against the brown leather valise, snapped down the locks and carried it out into the kitchen.

'You didn't have to fix breakfast for me, you know.'

Auburn was wearing paint-spattered denim dungarees; her hair was tied back off her face with a piece of green ribbon. She looked up.

'You look a lot better in clothes.'

'Well thanks . . . I guess.' *I'd be a liar if I said the same about you*, he thought.

114

'Look. It's not your fault I've got a dingbat for an old man. How long you here for?'

'Depends on how tight my schedule gets. Maybe till the weekend.'

'Well, look, if you don't mind sleeping with the smell of paint, you're welcome to stay while you're here.' She held up three-quarters of a German *Blutwurst*. 'I take it you want some of this foul-looking stuff on your toast.'

Mack took the sausage from her. 'It's all right, I'll do it. It tastes okay, just looks gross ... Yeah, well, thanks for the offer. Let's see how it goes, can we? I'd certainly like to leave my bag here.'

She poured him a coffee. 'Jesus, what a screw-up. I still can't figure out why Dad didn't call. I left another two messages for him at his apartment and I tried to page him at his club. He swims there most mornings, but they say he hasn't been in. Guess I'll catch him at the office later.'

Auburn wiped a dab of strawberry jam off her forefinger and carried her toast over to the table where Mack was sitting. His mobile phone rang. He reached inside his jacket and switched it off.

'So, you got a heavy day, huh?'

'Could say that. I'm in the middle of changing jobs ...' Mack started at the sound of the doorbell. Auburn got up, took her plate and walked towards the sink.

'Monday. It'll be the cleaner,' she called. 'Can you let her in?'

The man in the dark blue suit was holding a police badge.

'Detective Irvine, Twentieth Precinct. Miss Auburn Totheroh here?'

'She is, but ... can I help you?'

The mouth set. 'I'm afraid I'll need to speak to her personally. But it'd be a good idea if you stuck around.'

Auburn's head appeared around the kitchen door. 'I'm Auburn Totheroh. Is there a problem?'

Mack moved aside to let the officer pass.

'I'm afraid you're going to have to brace yourself for a shock, Miss Totheroh. It might be better if you sat down.'

Auburn's face drained of colour. 'It's my father, isn't it?

115

Something's happened to him.' Mack pushed a chair towards her. Her hand shot out. 'I don't want to sit!'

'He was found dead at his apartment this morning. I'm sorry to be the one to have to tell you.' Auburn took a shuddering intake of breath, her head fell into her hands and she sank into the chair. 'He was found early this morning by a . . .' the policeman consulted his notes, '. . . Mrs Vaphiadis. That's his cleaner I believe.'

'How . . . did it happen?' Mack started.

'It's too soon to be certain of that. But all the signs point to suicide.'

The face, tipped slightly back on the gurney, seemed to belong more to a battered waxwork than Morton Totheroh. The skin was blotched with purple bruises, the flesh round the once-firm jawline hung slackly against the hard edge of the white sheet. Mack had tried to prepare Auburn for the worst – once, in some magazine, he'd seen a close-up of Marilyn Monroe, unlovely in death, after the pathologist had done his work. He'd had to steel himself to break the silence of the cab ride down, but he told himself that if it was going to save the woman from further pain it was worth being cruel to be kind. No highly-paid mortician was going to hastily remake the face of the man she'd so loved, here at a city morgue.

The sound that broke from Auburn's lips when the sheet was rolled back was low and from the stomach, a primeval sound.

Mack walked her slowly back to the entrance to sign the identification papers, then out on to the sidewalk. Half a block down was a coffee shop. Mack sat down at a window table while Auburn straightened herself up in the ladies' room. Morton was dead. Shock had descended like a blanket around him and there was no reality to the thought. He scanned every word that had passed between them in the last ten days. There'd been no hint. The man had grabbed at every chunk of his life with the same zest he had a decade ago. He'd talked of tomorrow, of a time far into the future.

116

This was not a man contemplating self-murder.

Or was there a darker side to Morton that he'd never let Mack see? A side where wry humour and self-mockery didn't belong. Where there were only stark truths to be faced head-on, alone?

The three-thirty meeting with the company doctor was to provide part of the answer.

'Blood cancer?' Mack was stunned.

'Chronic granulocytic leukaemia.' Doctor Harman patted his recent hair transplant carefully. 'It showed up in a blood test taken in a company medical ten days ago. It was in its malignant stage. There were massively increased numbers of white cells in his blood.'

'Why wasn't this diagnosed years ago?' Auburn said, her voice rising in pitch.

Harman softened his tone. 'If your father'd showed up for the medicals he was booked in for, Miss Totheroh, I'm certain it would have been.'

'When was he told?' Mack asked.

'Last Saturday.'

'I spoke to him around eight-thirty, Saturday night. He sounded fine. Tired, sure, but not hours away from suicide.'

'He was due to come in here Monday, Mr Lasky. He seemed to have an idea what the prognosis was gonna be, because he called me at home around nine and said that I should stop pussyfooting around and tell him what the bottom line was, there and then.'

That at least sounds like my father, Auburn thought.

'I told him I'd drive into the city and meet with him Sunday morning. I tried to quieten him down . . .' Harman touched his hair once more, as though checking to see whether it was really there. 'He started to get very upset. And I . . . pretty much levelled with him. I had no other choice at that point. I told him that at best he had two months to live.'

'You tell a man he's dying over the phone?' Auburn's voice cracked.

'We've never met, Miss Totheroh, but I have known your father ten years. He was a very forceful personality, not a

117

man to play games with. I did what I felt was right in the circumstances. In fact I thought he sounded relieved to know the truth.'

Yeah, and then I bet you went back to your bridge game, Mack thought. 'So relieved he killed himself two hours later,' he said.

The doctor didn't flinch. 'And what do you suggest was the alternative?'

'Well it might have been a neat idea to check someone was with him.'

Harman put his hands together. 'I did, Mr Lasky. He told me you were. Your first name is Mack, isn't it?'

Auburn took Mack's hand as the cab pulled up outside Morton's apartment building. 'Look, I have about a hundred people I have to call and a load of other stuff to take care of. You've been wonderful, I don't know what I'd have done without you. But you've got your own life to take care of. Please stay at my place tonight, I'll be fine here.'

Mack studied her face. 'I've got nothing that won't wait. I think it's kind of soon to be up there on your own. If you want to be alone, you'd be better off at your place, for tonight at least. I'll stay at a hotel.'

'I don't really want to be on my own . . .' Auburn said, suddenly. 'Come up and be bartender for a while. Let's get wasted.'

Alcohol seemed to make little impact on Auburn's nervous energy. She moved restlessly from task to task, completing nothing, smoking and talking incessantly, sometimes calm; occasionally full of self-reproach, on the edge of hysteria. Then she remembered her father's will, searched for that and called the family attorney for the fourth time that night.

'. . . It's very sweet of you, Jack. I have a friend here, I'm fine, believe me. Let me get through tonight and I'll see you tomorrow.' She hung up and the phone rang instantly. It was Morton's sister in Baltimore. Auburn carefully wrote down her flight details for the following day. For a moment

118

she was at a loss to know what to do next. *Inactivity. Time to think. Not now, not yet.* She rallied herself and hurried into the study. 'Look, I'm going to be staying here for the foreseeable, it's where I want to be. There's not a reason on earth for you to move out of my place any more, so please stay. I'll give you our attorney's number, you can figure all the details out with him.'

'Well, if it's not going to be a problem, thanks.' Mack drained his glass and returned to his own blurred thoughts. *I don't buy it. There's got to be more to it than that doctor was telling us. I swam fifty lengths with Morton a week ago. He beat the shit out of me. How can that have been a man dying of anything?*

'That's strange.' Auburn's voice intruded from the office.
'What?'
'The inventory for my apartment's missing.'

Mack walked through carrying what approximated to a 'Long, Comfortable Screw Up Against the Wall' and handed it to her.

'The disk's gone.'
'Disk?'
'Yeah, I wrote it out on Dad's word processor, saved it to a new disk and stuck it right there,' she said, pointing to a place in a filing cabinet.

'Morton thought it was lying around on a pad of paper or something.'

'What?' She took a gulp of the drink.

'When I spoke to him Saturday night, he said he'd been looking for it.'

'Well, I don't understand his filing system, never did. So I stuck it there, in the "April '95" section, right at the front. A/A – "Auburn's Apartment", so if he needed it while I was in LA I could tell him where it was.'

'Well, it doesn't matter for now,' Mack said. He closed the filing cabinet and led Auburn back towards the living-room. 'Look, it's three-thirty, I think we should call it a day.'

'The room's going round, so I guess you're right.' Auburn slipped down on to the couch.

'You okay?'

She nodded. 'Nothing a couple of paracetamol won't put right.'

Mack watched her lift her head from her hands, her eyes focusing slowly on a painting of her mother which hung on the opposite wall.

'If you don't want to be on your own tonight, I'll stay in the back bedroom.'

'Mom and Dad are in every inch of this place,' she said, quietly, 'I won't be on my own.'

NINE

To the Nashibas, anonymity was an art form. The one question Presidents of Nashiba International's American affiliates could count on being asked at least once a week was: 'So what's old Tatsuya really like?'

'Like Howard Hughes, but without the laughs.' 'Like Santa Claus — comes by my neck of the woods once a year, been and gone before you know it. Most of my people don't even believe he exists.' 'The old man? . . . Deep, devious. Cross him in business and he's deadly.'

You could take your pick. Good or bad, it fed the legend. In fifty-five years of business life, Tatsuya Nashiba had never once given an interview to the media. He'd only been photographed seven times. The most recent was a long shot taken in 1958. No more than thirty of his thousands of employees in the US knew for certain what he looked like. The open-plan design of Nashiba's offices, built on the Japanese model, helped him retain this anonymity. He could see at a glance how every member of his staff was occupying their time. He could pass amongst his employees, check out their performance at close quarters and disappear again without ruffling one executive tailfeather.

Akitō had been well schooled in the same practice and his appointment to Senior Vice-President of Nashiba International was characteristically low-key. The day his father was due to leave for a month's stay in Tokyo, senior department heads received a confidential two-line memo informing them of the new appointment. Akitō had spent his first two years with the company moving from department to department to get a feel of how the whole operation worked. Senior executives were instructed to avoid using his family name in front of other employees so that he could enjoy the desired degree of anonymity. For the four years that followed, Akitō had been occupied with the Third-World Project. Now, with most of the pieces of that in place, he officially took over the role he'd been trained for his whole life – heir to the Nashiba empire.

Monday morning at six-forty-five, Akitō moved into his newly refurbished office in New York and began his first day as Acting Chief Executive. His first move was to familiarise himself with the executive staff who'd been appointed during his absence abroad. Michio Wada was the third department head to take the private elevator to his office that morning and wait in the simply furnished reception area outside.

Akitō cradled the phone between his jaw and his right shoulder and leafed through the man's file. 'If you will forgive me, Mr President, I do not think we fully understand each other on this point. Of course, my company has the greatest faith in the future of your country. We wouldn't be prepared to make this kind of commitment if that were not the case. But I'm sure you appreciate that that faith is based largely on your personal qualities, the belief that your vision and energy will bring your country out of the difficulties it has faced for so long.'

Three and a half thousand miles away at the other end of the line, the man garbled his thanks in fractured English.

Hook baited, Akitō thought.

'Of course, if the relationship is to work we must feel that our faith in you is reciprocated.'

Mr President was effusive.

Line cast.

'Then you will see why we ask that you show that faith by letting our bank act for you.'

Mr President was moving carefully. His personal deposit account at Southwestern Banking, one of seven he held at different banks around the world, stood at something near six hundred million dollars.

Bite, you bastard. '. . . Yes I understand that. After so

122

many years it's natural that you should feel you have that kind of relationship with them.'

Trouble is, Akitō thought, this boy's too scared of being deposed, ending up living in exile and not being able to get his hands on his cash. It was time to break out the landing net. Nashiba's fees were lower than any Western banks' because their shareholders were less concerned with profits, he said. And Japanese banks were more creditworthy than their Western counterparts, according to Moody's and Standard & Poor, the world's leading credit-rating agencies. The President was, of course, well aware of the deepening crisis in the US banking system. In such uncertain times . . .

The voice of the interpreter following the call was interrupted by the President's own response.

Fish for dinner.

Akitō and the President said their goodbyes. Akitō hung up and buzzed through to his secretary. He was now ready to see Michio Wada.

Wada bowed stiffly as he came in.

'Please, sit down.' Akitō motioned towards one of the polished wooden chairs opposite his desk.

'Can I offer you some coffee?'

'Thank you, Nashiba-san.'

Akitō touched a button on the intercom in front of him. 'As you may have heard, I have taken over the reins from my father for a few weeks. I think you joined us while I was in North Africa.' Akitō's hands were folded on top of Wada's employee file. He was already familiar with the contents. 'I've seen you in the building of course, but I thought it was time we had an hour together. How are you finding New York? Your daughters must find it very different from Tokyo.'

'It's very considerate of you to ask, Nashiba-san. They're fast becoming young Americans – they spend all weekend shopping on Fifth Avenue.' He laughed, relaxed by Akitō's easy manner. 'And my wife is delighted with the apartment, it's about three times the size of the one we had at home.'

Akitō's secretary entered silently and placed coffee cups in front of the two men.

123

'How about you?'

'It is a great honour and challenge to be put in charge of such important work.'

Akitō effected a warm smile. *And you'd better get it right, Wada,* he thought, *'cos there's plenty in Tokyo ready to step into your shoes.*

The phone on Akitō's desk rang.

'Excuse me ... Yes?'

'I'm sorry to interrupt your meeting, Nashiba-san,' his secretary said, 'but Hirata Otozo-san from the AmTronics Division just called ... Morton Totheroh has been found dead at his apartment.'

Akitō put down his coffee cup. 'What?'

'It seems he took a drug overdose, sir. Hirata-san said the cleaner found Mr Totheroh's body this morning, but he may have been dead since Friday night.'

'Was there a note? Anything?'

'No, but Hirata-san said that the police are talking to the company doctor at the moment, apparently his number was on the screen of Mr Totheroh's computer. It seems that the doctor diagnosed leukaemia after his last medical.'

Morton, dead. The nights Akitō had spent with Morton, Mack, and Warren had been amongst the most enjoyable of his life. '... Don't be just a trained monkey, look behind the issues ...' '... Learn to analyse, to take things apart with your eye, your ear, your hand, even your taste buds until the process becomes second nature ...' How many times over the years had he quoted Morton's words to others, no older than he'd been then?

Wada was getting nervous. He shifted in his seat. Perhaps he had been too familiar, burdened his boss with too much personal detail. He assumed a higher level of polite Japanese. 'Would you like me to leave?'

Akitō's eyes focused on the anxious-looking man in front of him. 'No ... no, you were saying about your wife ...'

The Harvard nights seemed half a lifetime ago now. How undemanding he had been of life then, how easily fulfilled. He was part of a different world now, a different order. But he had been moulded by those years. They had left an indelible imprint on him. Morton had been key to that process. Prophetic, profane, intensely likeable and yet somehow distant, at least as far as he was concerned. Distant. Was that the word for it? Had there really been some kind of wall between him and Morton or had he merely imagined it? He had longed, many times, to slap the old ox round the shoulders like the others, the way men in the Western world did, shamelessly, but he always held back, fearing he'd feel him pull away.

Morton had been the most complete man he'd ever known. Now he was dead.

Akitō had regretted the promise to go to the Aid Watch launch the minute he'd made it. Now he felt even less like going. But there was no reply to Bryony's number. She'd already left. And he couldn't just not show up. Akitō dreaded large gatherings, it meant 'pressing the flesh', making small talk with purple-haired ladies on subjects about which he knew nothing and cared less. It meant stepping out from behind his protective shield.

'If you could just wait here till this speaker's finished, I'd be happy to seat you.' The man with the Aid Watch identity badge pinned to his lapel peered around the door of the ballroom of the Plaza Hotel. Akitō could hear a man with what sounded like a Zimbabwean accent make a closing address, followed by a round of applause.

'I'll take you in now, sir.' Akitō followed the man down an aisle, through about five hundred people seated in small fake bamboo chairs. The large set facing them was dominated by the Aid Watch logo: the thin arm of a child raised upwards, the hand reaching out; above two muscular folded arms and a head turned away. The brutish profile reminded Akitō of Mussolini. At a distance the whole thing took on the form of a twisted cross. Written above it, in dark red letters, was 'To The Mouths Of The Underfed – Not The Pockets Of The Overfed'.

The final speaker was Robbie Dunbar. Instantly recognising him, the audience rose to its feet and gave him a

125

spontaneous ovation. His rhetoric was as uncompromising as ever.

'What the hell's the good of people like me, of people like you, busting our butts to raise tens of millions of dollars to help feed people – who have as much right to a life on this planet as we do, for God's sake – if most of it ends up feathering the nests of a bunch of brutal fascist gangsters?'

The room came alive, in the way it does only when a man with true passion and the power to communicate it speaks.

'In 1946, in Nuremberg, we hanged men who committed genocide. But now we buy men like them palaces, Rolls-Royces and Renoirs! I had some lard-assed senator say to me yesterday, "We don't need Aid Watch." He's right. *We* don't.' He threw up his arm to the screen above him. Images of the world he'd devoted the last decade of his life to flashed on to the screen. 'THESE are the people who need Aid Watch!' He continued shouting through the applause. '. . . As I've seen them in the places I've been. Here they are, the good, the bad and the hungry.'

Taken by someone less involved, the photographs might have merged in the minds of Dunbar's audience with those they'd seen on the subject a hundred times before. But his stood out, the ghastly and the bizarre mixed with the hopeful and the touching. They struck a note in the room that even he seemed unprepared for.

The memory of the boy Akitō had seen butchered was revived more clearly with every gaunt face shown on the screen. All that had happened near Maraquilla had seemed a world away from his own. But confronted again with these stark images, on his home-ground, the reality of his own role in the lives of Santiago and his like began to gnaw at him.

Suddenly, there was the Major. '. . . *Hwan More Saturday Night. Ees good song, Yes? . . .*' He was posing in a group shot with Santiago and a group of children. Akitō's stomach started to churn. The photograph must have been taken only hours before he arrived there. One day later, the bastard had gutted that kid like a rabbit.

Then suddenly it was over, everyone was standing, applauding. The doors were thrown open and Akitō could feel a rush of air from the street. He took a long, deep breath. Bryony pushed her way through the crowd. 'There you are! I thought you'd stood me up.' Her face was flushed with excitement. 'Well, what did you think?'

'Extremely effective, especially Dunbar. He brought the problems right here into the room for everyone to understand. I think the media interest will be enormous.'

'Good. If I had anything to do with it, I'd say they need a different mix of speakers for the LA launch. Too many of these covered the same ground while many other points were missed completely.'

'You're right.'

'I just have to convince Rienderhoff I have a contribution to make . . .'

Akitō felt his blood run cold. A few feet away, in the crowd behind Bryony, was the Japanese woman he was certain had been watching him the day before. A journalist, she had to be; the place was full of them. But hardly anyone knew his face, even in Tokyo. That picture of him in the *Far Eastern Economic Review* less than a month before, that was it! She must have put the face to the name. She'd recognised him in the flea market, seen him with Bryony. Maybe she was going to confront them here. A piece in the Japanese press about him being seen openly in New York with a beautiful young woman was all he needed. His father was really going to appreciate that, not to mention his future father-in-law.

'What's wrong?' Bryony slipped her arm through his.

'Nothing . . . Look, I've got a couple of calls to make. Why don't you have another try at making your mark with Rienderhoff? I'll meet you in the bar here in twenty minutes.'

She tipped her head to one side. 'Are you okay?'

'I will be.'

*

Akitō drained back the last of the Scotch and called for the check. From his corner seat in the hotel bar he could see Bryony standing in the lobby. She was saying goodbye to Rienderhoff.

The waiter laid a small silver-plated tray on the table in front of him. Beside the check was a sealed envelope bearing his name.

'Who gave you this?'

The waiter shrugged. 'A Japanese lady. About fifty. Didn't give a name.'

Akitō opened the envelope and took out a folded sheet of notepaper. Pinned to it was a strip of computer printout. Two wide parallel bars of graded grey. He'd seen that pattern of data before, years ago at university. It was a DNA graph – a genetic fingerprint – plotting the unique mix of characteristics an individual inherits from his or her parents.

The note, in Japanese script, read: 'For my son. I will contact you in seven days. Willow.'

It was late Sunday afternoon when Vasari woke, his head screaming from the bottle of vodka he'd killed single-handed in the morning gloom. He was almost grateful for the pain. It took his mind off the previous night. He looked at his watch. He should call Isobel, tell her to take the train back to Rome. Maybe she could drive back.

Then he remembered. The Mercedes was at Naples Airport. He'd driven it up from Revello and taken the shuttle to Rome. He wouldn't trust Isobel with a '61 Skoda on a tow rope. He'd have to get down there and bring her back himself.

Once the paracetamol kicked in, the full significance of his position hit him again. Throughout the journey to Naples he was in a world of his own, his state of mind alternating between utter turmoil and stunned indifference.

It was all Isobel's fault, self-centred little bitch! No. It was his own. He'd known the risks, he shouldn't have gone to Revello. It was as simple as that. He'd screwed up a gift of a job and now he was fucked.

At 11.15 p.m., he called Isobel in Revello from a pay-phone in Naples Airport. She sounded drunk.

'. . . I'm not checking up on you. I just wanted to see if you were still there and whether you needed me to drive you back.'

'I can get back,' she said stiffly.

'I'll come for you.'

'Okay. If you want.'

The earliest he'd be able to try Nashiba again would be 2.00 a.m. As long as he was at the St Francis by then.

The parking lot at the St Francis was full. Vasari pulled past the hotel entrance and followed the narrow coast road. Half a mile beyond there was a layby. He'd have to leave the Merc there. Vasari glanced out at the carpet of tiny lights below that was Revello. Even at night, it was breathtaking up here. His headlights picked out a mud-spattered Nissan Patrol. Behind it, on a trailer, was a production sports racing car. The name of the owner was handpainted on the side: Hermano Mauro.

Vasari stood in the phone booth listening to the number in Tokyo ring. Then the phone was picked up.

'Yes?'

'Mr Nashiba? It's Marco Vasari in . . . in Rome. Did you get the message I called?'

'I've just seen it. What's the problem?'

Vasari ground his knuckles into his forehead. 'Willow's gone, Mr Nashiba, three, could be four days ago. I have no idea where. I searched her apartment, there was nothing.' He was having difficulty getting the words out. '. . . She gave me the slip . . . there's no excuse . . . I've let you down, I'm sorry . . .'

There was a long pause.

'Goodbye, Mr Vasari.'

Tatsuya Nashiba put down the phone and leaned back in the chair. In the beginning, she had been nothing more than another pretty, long-legged girl. Her conversation entertaining enough for an enjoyable dinner, her body promising enough to make the chase worthwhile. And he was willing to take his time. This, the daughter of his most respected adversary, would be no easy case. She was bright, well-bred and schooled in the old traditions but he knew, over time, the age difference would play to his advantage.

The thrill of discovering her that first time was still fresh in his mind after thirty years. Her lush hair, her skin tone, her symmetry. Above all, her wonderful symmetry. He thought of it now as he had so often in the past. Hers was the template by which the standards of all other women were set and in his frequent disappointment, she had been his secret stimulation.

He was smiling to himself. How easy it had seemed to take what he wanted of her and believe she held no part of him. In his scheme of things, what she felt was of no consequence. She was young and malleable. But within a year she'd become his favourite mistress. Within two, the only one. He began to enjoy her mind as much as her sexuality. A geisha could entertain him with wit or indulge his fantasies but she had more. She had a passion to equal his.

And then . . . then he blotted her out of his life. His obsession with his own destiny overshadowed all other emotions. And when she was gone he knew the sacrifice. Down the years he had denied the memory. Refused to acknowledge a need that went beyond desire. He sat back in the chair and faced it squarely now. There were three secrets, he thought, the secret you tell no one, the secret you do not tell yourself. And the third secret was the truth. Now he saw that nothing had or ever could replace her.

He leaned forward, picked up the phone and dialled.

Vasari sat in the hotel bar, still in a trance. There had been a finality in that goodbye Vasari knew would echo through the rest of his life. He had been enmeshed with the Nashibas since he was fifteen. In a remote way he'd felt part of them. Now, he was alone, as completely as if he'd been cast adrift on an open raft. There would be no more monthly cheques. His pension would be forfeit, he'd seen it happen to others.

130

It was the way the Japanese did things. And Isobel?

He needed another drink.

Vasari leaned on the reception desk. 'Is a Signor Hermano Mauro a guest in the hotel?'

The desk clerk ran his finger down the card index in front of him.

'No, I'm afraid not, sir.'

Well, the sonofabitch's sleeping up here somewhere, Vasari thought. He finished the rest of his vodka in one gulp. *No prizes for guessing where.*

Waiters were wheeling breakfast trolleys along the corridor when Vasari let himself into the room. Isobel would pull her full virgin queen act in due course. But he'd know.

The room was in semi-darkness, her blonde hair visible above the sheets. He looked around him, not, now, as the woman's lover, but as an intelligence agent with thirty years' experience behind him. Isobel had obviously remade the bed, the edges of the sheets were turned untidily; chambermaids did hospital corners. And there were thumbprints on the mirror. Someone had recently lifted it down. She loved to watch herself fuck in the mirror, Vasari thought, it was almost an obsession.

He crossed into the bathroom. The pint of vodka he'd put away in the bar was starting to weigh on his bladder. He lifted the lid of the lavatory and looked into the water. Bubbles. The acid test. It was an old catch but a good one. When a man urinated immediately after sex and pulled the flush, the mix of seminal fluid, water and air produced tiny bubbles around the edge of the clean water left behind. Nothing else did it the same way. In some men, the test was inconclusive, nobody knew why. Hermano Mauro wasn't one of those guys.

Vasari let up the blinds with a clatter.

'Wake up, will you. Get your clothes on. I want to get started. We got a long way to go.'

Isobel sat up and rubbed her eyes. 'Jesus, what's your problem?'

She didn't like the look on his face.

*

131

'Just what the hell is your problem?' Isobel was inspecting her face in the compact mirror. 'Am I going to get the big freeze-out all the way back to Rome?' Vasari manoeuvred the Merc carefully around the steep bends of the narrow mountain road as they made their descent to Revello. He hadn't uttered one word to Isobel since he'd woken her. Every minute of his existence since he'd walked into Willow's living-room hung now like a lead weight round his neck.

Still there was silence.

'Oh, I know what this is all about. You think I've been screwing around. That's it, isn't it?'

'I don't think, I know.'

The silence now was for her to digest that little gem.

'So what if I have? What the fuck's it to do with you anyway? Let's face it, Vasari, you're not exactly love's young dream, are you?'

The mask was down at last. The carbon-steel slut he knew must live behind it spoke for the first time.

'I mean a girl needs some firm flesh against her ass once in a while, you know what I'm saying. So don't give me a hard time, old man. As long as you're getting your share, what's it matter?'

She was right. What did any of it matter?

The bend ahead looked much the same as the rest. It was usually kind of smart to start turning the wheel about now. But Vasari wasn't feeling smart. He wasn't feeling anything. He looked out at the unbroken aquamarine of sea blending into sky. It seemed like a good place to be.

The car left the road so fast that for a split second it was airborne. Then it fell like a stone. Isobel tried to get out a scream but the air was sucked out of her lungs before she could draw the breath. When the Merc hit the rocks fifteen hundred feet below, the impact drove the engine clean through it, taking a sizeable chunk of Vasari and the girl with it.

TEN

The man in the fawn raincoat knelt down and gently lifted the dead lilies from the vase set into the front of the gravestone and wrapped them in newspaper. He took each fresh white rose, crushed the end of its stem with a small stone to help it absorb moisture and arranged it amongst the others as best he could. Finally he topped up the vase with water from a plastic bottle.

> Rozanne Kirkland:
> Beloved Wife and Mother
> 1908 – 1993
> Safe in the arms of Jesus

Carved into the corner of the headstone was the figure of a seraph in prayer. Two New York winters had already started to pit the surface of the stone and discolour it. A pity, it was fine work, the man thought. He opened his Bible.

> 'Behold you are beautiful, my love,
> Your hair is like a flock of goats,
> Moving down the slopes of Gilead.
> Your teeth are like flocks of shorn ewes
> That have come up from the washing.'

He looked up. *'The Song of Solomon.' Hmm. That's one that won't make Top Forty.*

The mourners at the grave the other side of the cemetery were starting to move towards the cars now.

''Bye Rosie, whoever you are. Keep thinking positive, know what I mean?'

The man stood up and brushed the dust off his knees. It

133

wasn't often he got to see a job through to the end.

The Nisei who killed Morton Totheroh was one of the new breed. The type that Marco Vasari could never have been. Devoid of humanity. This Nisei worked alone, lived alone, allowing himself neither expansive dreams nor moments of introspection. He had a blunt, unextraordinary face, the kind that was easy to forget. The long upper lip might have looked better for a moustache, but it would have been a fragment of individuality. Someone might remember 'a man with a moustache'. His short mousey hair grew naturally more to the red, but the small amount of dye he applied to it allowed him to blend more easily into the crowd.

The Nisei scanned the mourners one last time. He'd worked for Tatsuya Nashiba directly before, but never at such short notice or on an assignment that was as close to home as this. There was his man. The only Japanese face in the crowd. Akitō.

Mack walked towards the cars, his eyes fixed on Auburn, ahead of him amongst her relatives. Warren lumbered along beside him, glad to be away from the graveside at last.

'Jesus, look at all these people. When I go it'll probably be just Jackie, the kids and the guy from the liquor store.' He was panting hard in the effort to keep up. 'Ol' Mort must've been rotating listening to that guy who read the eulogy. I mean, I guess he said all the right things but, I don't know, sure didn't seem like the Morton I knew.'

'We just thought we knew him better than the rest because we spent time together having a few laughs. Under it all, he was a serious guy.'

Warren stopped. 'So tell me, why did he keep the cancer thing to himself?'

'Maybe he was hoping it would go away. That if he didn't talk about it, it wasn't so.'

'Doesn't sound like Morton to me.'

Mack shook his head. 'Me either. He sure didn't look like a guy who only had months to live . . . And you know what I keep thinking? Last time I saw him all I did was whine on about myself, never once asked him about his problems. Maybe if I had . . .'

The procession came to a halt as those at the front started to file through the narrow gateway. Mack followed Warren's gaze. Akitō was standing a short distance off, talking to some AmTronics people. He and Warren hadn't seen Akitō since a 'Class of '84' reunion. Now they were in his direct line of vision but he seemed not to see them.

Warren sniffed. 'Does asshole pretty well these days, doesn't he?'

'Could be he's thinking the same thing about us. Come on.'

'You going to go over?'

Mack thought for a moment. 'Nah.'

The two moved forward to help Auburn and some elderly relatives into one of the black funeral cars.

'Miss Totheroh.' She turned to see a tall Japanese. 'My name is Akitō Nashiba. I don't believe we ever met.'

'No.' She shook the offered hand.

'I just wanted to say how very sorry I am. Your father was a remarkable man.' He looked up at Mack and Warren, acknowledging their presence at last, with the tilt of his head. 'I know all of us here had the greatest respect for him. The company will always be indebted to him for his unique contribution. If there's anything I can do to help, I hope you'll let me know.'

'Thank you.'

The car moved off, leaving the three men standing awkwardly alone.

'Hi,' Warren offered.

'Hi.'

'Hell of a way to meet.'

'Yes.'

'This whole thing feels pretty unreal to me.'

'Totally. It's hard to think that someone as vital as Morton is gone for good.'

'Guess in different ways he made his mark on us all,' Mack said.

The three stood in silence.

135

'So where have you been for the last six years?' Warren asked.

Akitō shrugged. 'Turning a buck. You know how it is.'

'Yup.' *Must be having a real tough time*, Mack thought. 'We should get together more.'

'Give me a call.' Akitō handed Mack his card.

'You got it.'

'Right.' Warren nodded.

'Goodbye.' Akitō moved off towards his car. 'Good to see you both again.'

'Good to see you.'

'What is it with him?' Warren asked as the car pulled away.

'Sealed unit.'

Mack caught Auburn for a moment alone as the last of those who'd come back to Morton's apartment for drinks and refreshments began to leave.

'Warren and I are going to go out and get wasted . . . we think you should come too.'

Auburn looked exhausted, beyond emotion. 'I'd like to, but I can't. My aunt's staying over. She's old and she doesn't understand what's happened. I think I should stay with her. Tell you what, have a few for me, will you?'

'I'll call you tomorrow, maybe we can have lunch.'

'I'm going to the house on Fire Island, there's some stuff of Dad's I want to bring back.'

'Come on, give yourself a break. Aren't you asking too much of yourself?'

She shrugged. 'Don't think so. Can't be any worse than sticking around here. Anyhow, I could do with a top-up on happier times.' She could see he wasn't convinced. 'Look, it's only an hour's drive from here. Why don't you come up for lunch on Sunday?'

'I've got a better idea. Why don't I drive you tomorrow and come back after dinner?'

She smiled. 'Okay.'

*

Alfredo's hadn't changed much in nine years. The paint-work had been freshened, a few more battered musical instruments added to the collection on the wall, but other-wise it looked the same as it had that first of the many nights Mack, Warren, Akitō and Morton had dined there.

Mack and Warren sat at the Club's old table, very drunk. In front of them, buried under table napkins, lay an empty bottle of Hine VSOP Cognac, a cross of breadsticks at its head. An upturned wine glass stood at the place setting where Morton should have been.

'This soldier having given of his best ... will be buried with full military honours ...' Morton's traditional speech sounded strange coming from Mack's mouth. He stopped mid-sentence. It was over. The Club was gone for ever. Laurie, Warren and now Morton. In different ways he'd lost them all. He put his head in his hands.

'Oh Morton, you old bear, what happened? Why?'

Auburn stood at the ferry rail and took a good long breath.

'Wow ... real oxygen. Will you get a load of this! The air out here's like wine.'

Mack watched the mass of wavy hair bounce back in the soft breeze and began to think more clearly. He'd seen her every day for the last week but he was only just starting to know her. The journey upstate had given him the chance. She'd begun to unwind a little. There'd been no time for either of them to really think in the past few days. They'd been so caught up in the shock of Morton's death, the inquest, the funeral ... It was hardly a conventional start to a relationship. A relationship. Was that what either of them were looking for? They were just total strangers thrown together in sharing a massive loss.

God, Mack thought, she was so much like Morton. He'd got a taste of it before she found out her father was dead. The approach was just as on the nose, the caustic wit as fast.

The long row of clapboard houses alongside the Fire

137

Island jetty were becoming clearer across the water, the whitewash and pretty pastel pinks glinting in the afternoon sun. He picked up Auburn's two tote bags and walked over to the rail. It wasn't hard to imagine Morton fishing off the wharf here, the small blue eyes searching the water's surface for sudden movement, jerking his catch into the air with a short grunt of satisfaction.

The fifteen-minute walk to Morton's holiday home was taken in silence. The houses each side of the boardwalk were pleasant, if unremarkable. Each stood on a small patch of land. There'd been just enough room outside Morton's place for the wooden swing he'd built for his little girl. Mack waited while Auburn looked for the key. He was glad he'd come. If he was in her shoes right now, he wouldn't want to face all those memories alone. The door swung open as she tried to put the key in.

She stepped inside. 'Oh my God . . .'

Mack saw her knees give way. She folded up on the floor. He rushed to her and held her as she sobbed uncontrollably amongst the smashed crockery and overturned chairs. He just sat there, stroking her hair, letting her spill out the pain in awful, racking waves against his chest.

'It's so unfair,' she gulped. 'Why this? Why now?' She got up abruptly and walked over to the small, light oak bureau that stood against one wall, its drawers gaping open, the contents half spilled on to the Mexican rug.

'Oh, no, grandpa's silver inkstand's gone . . . pen too.' She bent down and picked up a crayoned picture that lay loose on the floor. It showed two smiling matchstick people with large round faces, gangly limbs and ridiculous, outsized shoes. Underneath a childish hand had written 'Mom and Dad'.

'I didn't know this was in here . . .' She laid it lovingly on the bureau's tooled leather top. 'Must be twenty years old.'

She walked aimlessly over to the fireplace. The thick wooden beam that served as a mantelpiece had been swept bare, the ornaments and photographs that had brightened it, that had made the house a home, lay scattered below.

'Don't tell me . . .' She held two pieces of what had been a salt dough teddy bear in her hand, tried for a moment to put it back together, then gave up, shaking her head. 'The hours she spent helping me make this on the kitchen table . . .'

'Come on,' Mack said gently, 'leave this for now.'

'No, I . . . Oh, poor old Boris!' Auburn fingered a shattered frame, turning over the photograph of a golden retriever it had once contained. 'Dad gave him to me on my tenth birthday, this is the only picture I had of him.' She looked around. 'Makes me sick to think that some creep's been through all our things . . .'

Mack took her hand. 'I'll call the police.'

'For what?' She snatched the hand away. 'What are they going to tell me? "Looks like you've been burglarised, Miss Totheroh." Big deal, I can figure that for myself.'

'Okay, okay.'

'Anyway, this could have happened last night, or any night over the last three weeks. Who can tell? What does it matter? It's too late now.'

Mack left Auburn to wander around the open-plan living-room/diner and the two bedrooms above. Each room held some new hurt; another memory destroyed or taken. They would never be replaced now, Mack thought. All she could do was remember.

It was already growing dark by the time she came back downstairs.

'I don't understand. There was nothing of any real value here, just stuff that mattered to us.' She took a long breath. 'Well, guess that's it. Shall we straighten up or eat?'

'I say we eat.'

Auburn picked her way through the cans, flour and rice that littered the kitchen floor and opened the freeze box. 'Jesus, they could have left us a pizza.' She wiped her damp eyes on the back of her hand. 'Looks like tuna, sauerkraut and barbecue sauce. Oh, and there's some dill pickle, if you can face it.'

'Are there any candles?'

'So candles and dill pickle . . .'

139

Mack put his head round the kitchen door. 'Christ! . . . No, the lights are all smashed.'

They rummaged in the cupboard under the stairs and found a couple of candles and a box of matches, put a candle on a saucer and sat down on the carpet with some opened cans and a couple of forks.

'Not much of a dinner party,' Auburn said. 'Still, it's the company that counts.' She sat cross-legged on the floor and forced a smile.

There was silence for a while as they ate. 'So come on,' Mack said. 'Tell me about LA.'

'Told you on the way up,' she said through a mouthful of tuna, 'I needed money. I wasn't making it as a portrait painter so I took a course in computer graphics.'

'And joined Cohn and Jameson.'

'Yeah, drove me stir crazy. Week after week stuck in front of a VDU. I just ached to pick up a brush and splash paint on a canvas again. Create something that looked like a living, breathing human being had something to do with it.'

'That portrait of your mother, at your Dad's place, did you do that?'

'Yeah.'

'You're good.'

'What d'you know?'

'I know talent when I see it.'

'Bull,' she said, but she was smiling. He let a few moments go by.

'So what before LA, I mean, what about you?'

'Men, you mean? Okay: men.' She stretched out her legs and thought. 'I had a few relationships that didn't add up to much. It's difficult, you know, Dad was such a big guy. Not just his size I mean, his personality. When the passion wore off I always found myself comparing people to him. And, you know, Mom and Dad . . . they had such a special relationship. Shared everything. They were real soulmates. It's a hard act to follow. You get to thinking, who am I ever going to find to make it work for me like that?' She ran her long fingers through her hair like a comb. 'I thought I had for a while. It started as an affair. I just saw the guy a few

140

times a month when he came through on business. It took a couple of years to really turn into something. Then one day he said he was going to leave his wife, we could set up together in LA and take it from there.'

'Aah, so that's why you went to Cohn's.'

She nodded. 'We leased an apartment and things were really nice for a while. Then . . . well, he was eating his heart out for his kids, in the end he went home. So I worked out my contract with Cohn's and . . . here I am.' She pulled herself closer to Mack and looked up at him. He slipped an arm round her. 'So are you under contract or just resting between engagements?'

'Dumped at the last audition.'

'Oh? What went wrong?'

'Nothing original.' Mack thought for a while. 'You know Bedford Park in Chicago?' She shook her head. 'There's not much park, it's all blue-collar housing. It's where I grew up. Planes coming in to land at Midway roar overhead; all the shit from the industrial estate blows into your yard . . . every day's another day you can't wait to get out.

'My Uncle Marty, he got out. Wasn't really my uncle, my mother just liked me to call him that. She started seeing him a couple of years after my Dad got killed in the Phnom Penh offensive.'

'Did it bother you?'

'No. I was like any other kid, I guess, just happy that she was happy. It was like she was a different person, you know? She'd take hours dressing, doing her make-up. She used to ask me what she should wear, that kind of stuff. No, I liked it when Uncle Marty called. He talked to me like an adult, really seemed to care about what I thought. In a way, he was the nearest thing to a father I knew.'

Mack shifted position. 'I remember him standing in our living-room, lookin' at my Ma's crappy little Woolworth prints of "Works of the Italian Masters", telling her how he was going to take her to Florence to see the real things some day soon. Then he'd talk about this big place he was going to buy. But after a while, the good times got to him, he started to relax, get sloppy. One minute, the biggest worry

141

in his life was whether he was going to get bruising if he had the bags under his eyes done; the next, he was flat – a handful of bad deals wiped him out.

'He had a stroke a couple of months later – was completely paralysed down one side. Everybody felt sorry for him at the time, but not me. I thought he was a dumb bastard. Busted his ass to make something of himself and then let it just slip away. I learnt a lot from that, learnt to take care of business; first, last, always.'

Auburn looked at his face. It was cool, serious. Yet, still, somehow, a thin mask over what he was really feeling. 'Sounds kind of tough,' she said, softly, '. . . on yourself, I mean.'

'Everyone else, too, I guess.'

There was silence for a long time. The two leaned together, lost in private grief, until the first birdsong.

'It's almost morning.' Mack pulled Auburn closer as her tiredness gave way to a shudder of cold. Gently, he turned her chin towards him and kissed her cheek.

She looked at him for a moment. 'Could I have a real one of those?'

The kiss was long but light; more fragile than passionate. Without a word, they linked hands and walked slowly to the bedroom.

Next morning, Mack squinted into the early morning sunlight streaming through the bedroom window through what would have been decent drapes if they hadn't been partly torn down. He tried to extract one very numb arm from under Auburn's neck. She stirred but didn't wake. He looked at her sleeping face. Her eyes were still swollen from crying but she looked serene. He eased himself off the bed and dressed quietly, thinking of going down to the general store to get some breakfast. But he couldn't risk her waking up while he was gone. He walked into the living-room and started to clear up. Around an hour later she wandered in to find him arranging documents, photographs and ornaments in neat piles on the sofa. She smiled, grimly.

'Thanks, that's thoughtful.' She kissed him lightly and knelt down to examine them. She began laying out the photographs alongside the frames they had belonged to. *Thank God, they haven't been torn,* she thought, *that would have been worse.*

'It's so pointless,' she started. Mack looked up. 'I mean, why smash things up? Why not just take what you want and leave the rest be?'

'Who knows?' Mack could see she was getting upset again. 'Come on, let's walk down to the jetty and buy something to eat. We can finish this later.'

The bar near the jetty was almost deserted. They ordered a couple of Cokes and wandered out to sit on the wharf. The first ferry of the day was making its way across the water towards them.

'Mack, can I talk to you about something without you thinking I've flipped out?'

'Sure.'

'You know I said I couldn't find the disk with the inventory for my apartment on it in Dad's computer file?' He nodded. 'Well there's another disk missing too. You know you said that when you talked with Dad on the phone that last time, last Saturday, he couldn't find the inventory and thought it was written out somewhere on paper? Well, I forgot to tell him that I wrote it to disk. He didn't know that it was in his file, so he couldn't have moved it. And if he didn't move it, I started to wonder who the hell had.'

'Wait a minute here —'

'No, let me finish. I'd put the thought out of my head, but you know that piece of verse Zack Latimer read at the funeral?'

'Yes, I'd heard it somewhere before.'

'Probably from Dad. It was his favourite. Well, the day before the funeral, Zack phoned to ask if I could let him have a copy of the poem. He wanted to include it in his speech about Dad because it seemed to say so much about the kind of person he was. I knew there was a copy of it in Dad's lecture file so I said I'd print it up for him. But after I put the phone down I couldn't find it. I must have gone

143

through the file a dozen times but the disk just wasn't there.

'Now it *had* to be in there, Mack, because I put it there myself. See, last April Dad was looking for the poem so as he could read it at Zack's daughter's wedding. It was pretty obscure – written by a guy called John Caulfield who died in the Civil War – and he'd let someone borrow his only copy of Caulfield's *Collected Poems*. He called me, thinking I had it. Then he realised he'd lent it to a friend who'd moved to Louisville. Well, Dad didn't have time to deal with it so he asked me to have this friend read the poem over the phone then put it on his word processor. So I did. I saved it to a new disk and put it in the "C" section of his lecture file, in case he ever needed it again.

'So, like I said, when Zack asked for the poem, I searched Dad's lecture file and I couldn't find the disk. Finally, I found a copy of the damn thing folded up inside the Order of Service Dad'd kept from Zack's daughter's wedding. Still, I couldn't leave off wondering what had happened to the disk; couldn't help thinking that wherever it'd gone the inventory disk had gone too.

'Now, tell me I'm nuts, but why should two disks that were of absolutely no value to anyone but my family both disappear and why's it become a regular obsession with me?'

'Because of the burglary. Because you can't accept Morton's death.'

'Can you?' She looked him square in the face.

'No.'

'So where do we go from here?'

'Well, let's look at the possibilities.' Mack scratched his head. 'Apart from you, did anyone else have keys to your father's place?'

'Yes, his secretary at the office did. Dad was for ever leaving his keys somewhere and calling up to have one of us let him in.'

'Well, maybe she or someone else from the office called to pick up some disks and took yours with them by mistake.'

'No way. Dad wouldn't have allowed it, he always handled the disks himself.'

144

'What if he did allow it, just that once?'

'It's not possible, my two disks were in completely un-related filing cabinets at different ends of the room, you couldn't take them both by mistake – not unless you were taking out hundreds of disk files, and that wouldn't ever be necessary.'

A door opened in Mack's mind. 'Auburn, did Morton have data in his files that only he knew about – stuff he kept to himself?'

'God knows. Could well have done. What do you mean?'

'I mean, could he have had information that the company was sensitive about?'

'It wouldn't surprise me if he had a few things tucked away for future reference – there was no love lost between him and the Nashibas after they took a chunk of AmTron-ics, I can tell you that . . . Wait a minute, are you saying someone could've been through his files to find out if he'd been behaving himself?'

Maybe that was it, Mack thought. *How had the conver-sation gone? He'd been sitting with Morton in his office. 'You know where I keep my notes? Up here.'* He'd tapped his forehead. Had there been more to it than that? Mack had had the feeling that Morton'd wanted to tell him more. Had he kept more in his head than his working notes?

'Mack?'

'Well I don't know, but if people from the office thought Morton had something he shouldn't have, maybe they took some files away without telling anyone to have a look in private.'

'There must be ten thousand disks in that study, they wouldn't know what was where. It'd take weeks to check them all. Anyway there aren't any gaps in the filing cabinets 'cos I already checked.'

'They could've taken the lot.'

'How?'

'I'm just thinking. You know you said Morton kept an identical set of disk files in his office?'

'Yes – he was absolutely meticulous, backed up every-thing he did, sometimes in triplicate.'

145

'Did that include backups of his personal files?'

'Yeah, the lot.' She paused. 'Everything except the two that I made, that is. I mean, I never took a backup of a disk in my life, and Dad didn't know they were there to backup.'

'Well, there is one solution.'

'Which is?'

'Which is maybe they swapped the entire office file with the one in his study. That'd explain why you can't find the two disks you used because whoever did the swap wouldn't have known to leave them behind. After all, if Morton didn't know those disks were there, they sure as hell didn't.'

Auburn gasped. 'When? I mean, how could they? He'd have noticed straight away if the files had been switched.'

There was silence while the two came to the same conclusion.

'They did it after he was dead . . .' she said, finally. 'That's really gross.'

'Come on.' Mack squeezed her arm. 'This is worth talking through. Look, we know that your father died on Saturday night, right?'

She nodded.

'And you found the disk missing around the same time Monday.'

'Right. Hey, Nashiba knew Dad was dead Monday morning. Maybe they were in there while we were at the morgue or with the doctor . . .'

'It's possible . . . Kind of risky though. The police had been all over the place and we could have walked in at any time.'

'Which leaves Sunday. But then they risked running into Dad, for all they knew.'

All the doubts Mack had felt from the beginning about Morton's suicide surfaced with a rush.

'What's the matter? Mack?'

'Unless . . . unless they already knew he was dead.'

Auburn looked out over the water and took a slow, deep breath. 'You don't really believe he committed suicide.'

'No.'

146

'Neither do I. Not because it's an ugly idea and not because I don't think he was capable of it. I just don't believe he'd have chosen to do it now. It doesn't add up, Mack. He hadn't finished with the G250 and I know he wouldn't have given up on that. He spent half his life thinking about it, building it, making it work.'

'I know.'

'You don't believe they went in there Sunday, do you? You think they were in there Saturday night and . . . and . . .' She stopped.

'Auburn, I don't know. I don't know what they thought was in your father's files, or how far they'd have gone to get at that information. But one thing's for sure, whatever it was they were looking for they didn't find it.'

She looked up. 'What makes you say that?'

'The burglary here. Something struck me this morning, when you were talking about the photographs being taken out of the frames? Well, that's just it, some of the frames had been prised open. The little frames had been smashed, but the bigger ones had been forced open. Now what kind of burglar looks for things behind family photos? The one thing you *could* hide in a large photo frame is a computer disk. And if there was a disk hidden in the house, I'd say whoever wanted it has got it by now.'

'Maybe, maybe not. Dad didn't come out here often enough to keep anything here that really mattered work-wise. That's what worries me.' Auburn got up and started off down the wharf. 'Come on, let's take a walk.'

Mack followed her along the narrow tarmac stretch that separated the wharfside houses from the water. He started to go over everything they'd said. Could be they were clutching at straws to make some sense out of Morton's death. Could be they were right. She'd stopped a few paces ahead of him to watch some guy teaching his son to dive off one of the wooden jetties. When Mack got alongside her, she was toying with a bunch of keys.

'You know, when Dad went away and left me the keys to his place, I used to know which was the right one for the front door 'cos it was next to this little guy here.' She picked out a small flat key with no markings. 'Couldn't figure out what it was for. But I've just remembered, the Frobisher Club, he practically lived in the place. Know what? I reckon this is his locker key.'

ELEVEN

Akitō put in his contact lenses and peered into the bath-room mirror. The dark smudges beneath his eyes had almost gone. When he moved his head a little to the left he could see the reflection of the bedroom behind him. Bryony lay on her side, her face scrubbed of make-up, her dark wavy hair spread out across the pillow. He'd never seen her look more beautiful. So many of the women he'd known looked lustreless once they'd taken off their make-up, younger and more innocent perhaps, but drained of sexuality. Sleep creased their faces and puffed their eyes like any man and made them somehow ordinary, devoid of mystery. But Bryony was different. Nothing seemed to detract from the perfection of her face. For a moment, when she opened her eyes in the morning she seemed defenceless and in those moments, Akitō felt an intensity of emotion for her he'd felt for no one in his life before.

The phone. He ran through to the living-room to silence the one bell he'd forgotten to turn down the night before.

'Mr Nashiba? It's Chuck Mackray, CLM Laboratories in Houston. Sorry to call so early.'

For a second Akitō's mind couldn't connect the name.

'Mr Mackray, yes, I'm sorry. Thanks for getting back to me so soon.'

'Well, I just hope we've come up with what you want. We made up a DNA profile from the Donor A samples, the blood and the saliva. That was easy enough. But Donor B was a real bitch. Hair samples are never the best to work with. Like I told you, body fluids or living tissue give the

149

best profile. It's not too easy separating saliva from lipstick and food particles on a table napkin.'

Akitō shook his head and tried to bring his mind to bear on what was being said. 'I'm sorry, Mr Mackray, that's all I could get.'

'Well, my report isn't as full as I'd like, but I can tell you this. There's no evidence of the donors being connected genetically. None. Chances of there being an error is about one in seventy-five thousand.'

Akitō's mind was already in free-fall as Mackray continued to explain.

'Now the woman, profiled in the printout you sent me, she was a different story. Her link to Donor A is solid as rock. I checked it through thoroughly, but you can see it at a glance. She's Donor A's mother all right. I'll send you the report straight away so you can see for yourself, Mr Nashiba . . . Mr Nashiba?'

The Nisei drained his third cup of coffee and looked at his watch. Akitō Nashiba had left the apartment almost two hours before, but until that bony brunette shifted her tuccus he'd have to sit tight. From his table at the back of the café he had a clear view of the lobby of the Trump Plaza and the exit from the parking lot. The fire exit was out of his line of vision, but he could see straight down the narrow passage that led from it. Unless she planned on abseiling down the back of the building, there was no other way out.

'Will sir be having lunch?' The slim-hipped waiter had felt the Nisei watching him, undressing him in his mind, almost from the minute he walked in. Now their eyes connected.

The Nisei tipped back in his seat. The waiter went on. 'See, from midday we only serve beverages with food.'

The Nisei took a long, meaningful look at the well-developed pectorals. 'Is that right?'

'Uhuh.' The waiter passed him a menu from a rack on the wall. There was something scary about this guy, something cold and menacing about the way he smiled. The waiter felt a shiver go down his back, couldn't tell whether it was fear or excitement. A guy like him could hurt you real bad if he wanted to. Well, it made a change from the flakes that looked like they'd fold into the foetal position if you so much as moved their cell-phones. He pouted archly as he waited for the order.

'Okay, give me a corned beef and mustard on rye, potato salad on the side. It's fattening, but what the hell.'

'Yeah, what the hell, live a little. That's what I say.'

'Put it on, burn it off.'

The waiter shrugged. 'Depends on your metabolism. See, I'm lucky. A good work-out, it's all gone.' He slapped his tight stomach muscles. 'Strenuous exercise.'

The Nisei's heavy-lidded eyes surveyed the Plaza lobby and focused back on the waiter. 'Yeah, work up a good hot sweat. Good, hard, rhythmic body movement. Does it every time.'

'Well, now if we're talking adult intimacy here, it's a fact that . . .' The waiter was enjoying the chase. The Nisei wasn't listening. A yellow cab had pulled up on the other side of the road. Bryony Cole walked past the high concrete waterfall playing on the Plaza forecourt and climbed in.

The Nisei picked up his black attaché case and stood up. 'Tell you what, I'll take a rain-check on the corned beef, maybe catch you tomorrow.'

The waiter's green eyes betrayed his disappointment. 'I'll be here, I'm always here . . .' The Nisei stuck a five-dollar bill in the top of the waiter's tee-shirt and walked slowly towards the door.

'. . . Except Wednesdays,' he called after him. 'I work out Wednesdays.'

The urgent, high-pitched alarm signal sounded immediately the door to Akitō's apartment was opened. The Nisei went to the broom closet, punched a four-digit code into the plastic control panel on the wall inside and the signal cut. It kind of gave you a head start when the subject of the assignment was your boss's son and he owns the apartment

151

building, the Nisei thought as he walked through to the master bedroom.

He rolled on a pair of surgical gloves and slid back the wide closet doors. The guy must have forty pairs of shoes. It'd take a good minute to fix a micro transmitter into the front of the heel of each left shoe and check it. He looked at his watch. The cleaner was due at two-thirty, he'd have to work fast.

'Do you mind if I take that?'

The red light visible through the glass wall of the squash court flashed, indicating a phone call for one of the players. Takuro Hamada dropped on to his haunches and lay back against the wall.

'Akitō, please! Anything. If it's going to put your mind on the game, go! I've never known you play so badly. It's like I'm here on my own.'

Hamada was Akitō's cousin. They'd been close friends through childhood, until the young Nashiba had been sent to America to be educated at the age of twelve. Now, as adults, living in the same city again, they met once a week to take the only proper exercise either of them ever got.

'I'm sorry, Takuro, forgive me. Just give me ten minutes, will you.'

'Mr Nashiba? I got someone called Willow on the line asking for you.'

'Put her through.' Akitō sat down in the phone booth and took a deep breath.

'Akitō?' The woman's voice was deep and mellow, almost a whisper. 'Willow.'

'Who are you? What do you want from me?'

'You must know who I am by now.'

'How do I know that DNA profile is even yours?' Akitō's voice was cold.

'If I can't convince you in one hour, I'll never bother you again.'

'If you're looking for some kind of pay-off —'

'Let me talk with you, that's all I want, I swear.' The voice was close to tears.

'All right, I'll meet you in the bar of the Park Lane Hotel tomorrow at noon.'

'No, I cannot leave where I am. You must come to me. There's a public pay-phone on the corner of Twenty-first Street and Astoria Boulevard, in Queens. Be there at exactly noon tomorrow and I'll call you. I'm five minutes' drive from there.'

Akitō had decided to meet with the woman hours ago. There was no point in playing games now. 'All right.'

'Akitō, be very clear about one thing. If you're followed I shall be killed, do you understand?'

Akitō put down the phone and thought hard. Along with the Rockefeller Center, Times Square, the Empire State Building and a few billion dollars' worth of other real estate in Manhattan, the Japanese owned four out of the six biggest department stores. Two of them had been acquired in controversial takeover bids by Takuro Hamada's family. He had been in charge of both stores for almost three years.

When Akitō walked back to the squash court, Takuro was standing by the Coke machine massaging his arm.

'Elbow's playing me up again.' He looked up. 'What's the matter, Akitō? You look terrible.'

'I'll be fine.' He took the offered can of iced Coke. 'I need a couple of favours from you, Cousin.'

'Ask away.' He grimaced, still rubbing his arm. 'I swear that osteopath made it worse.'

'Well, for a start, I need a crash course in state-of-the-art surveillance techniques.'

'Why ask me? You're the one with all the connections.'

'No, it has to be someone outside of Nashiba.'

Hamada thought for a moment. 'Well, we do have one guy, a real technocrat. I could put you together with him, I guess. What else?'

Once someone was electronically 'tagged', the continuous signal given out by the transmitter was picked up by a

153

network of UHF receivers set up across New York and relayed to a central computer under the Nashiba Building. The information was then plotted on to a ground plan stored in the data bank, giving a positive fix on the subject to an accuracy of four feet. The Nisei waited for more relevant data to be relayed by the voice synthesiser through his scrambler.

'Subject on Sixty-sixth turning west on to Third,' the androgenous speaker announced into the deaf-aid in the Nisei's left ear. A few seconds later it informed him that there was no change in position but the subject vehicle had decreased speed to eight miles an hour. The Nisei made the turn. He could see the Mitsuda limo twenty yards ahead. The chauffeur indicated right and the car pulled over to the kerb outside a department store. Akitō Nashiba stepped quickly over the sidewalk.

The Nisei rolled down the window of the blue Ford and spat his gum into the gutter. Department stores were a pain in the ass; too many floors, too many exits. He checked Akitō's schedule. He was already late for a ten-thirty meeting across town, he couldn't hang out here long. The Nisei spoke into the mike pinned to the inside of his lapel. 'Compute likely purchase.'

There was silence while the computer reviewed everything it had on the subject.

'Does not compute,' came the synthesised voice. 'Subject has no regular business with this retail outlet. Suggest: gift for non-family member or small personal item.'

The Nisei hit the dashboard. Twenty million bucks' worth of technology they'd got up there and apart from maybe a lawn-mower the guy could be buying anything, in any part of the store!

He moved past the limo, turned off right and pulled over. Reaching behind him, he took a metal light box from under the seat, plugged the lead from it into the cigarette-lighter socket and placed it against the windshield. Then he took a small black shoulder-bag from the glove compartment and hurried towards the side entrance of the store, looking back over his shoulder to check the light was flashing: 'Doctor On Emergency Call.'

Once inside the store, the Nisei reached into the bag and activated his own tag signal. Within a second, the receivers had identified him, placed him on the ground plan and calculated his exact position in relationship to Akitō's.

'Distance: thirty yards at 2:15. Signal quality substandard,' the voice synth droned.

Yeah, but what floor, Peckerhead, you can't tell me that, can you? This is all I need. The Nisei started to sweat. He worked his way through the crowd, diagonally across the store. Akitō was sitting in Men's Sportswear. He'd never seen him so casually dressed. He wore pale blue pants, a sweater and grey shoes. The Nisei pushed on purposefully, like he had somewhere to be, and circling round some display cabinets, positioned himself at a counter selling golfing accessories. Through the jungle of golf carts he could get a clear view of his man.

A sales assistant was kneeling in front of Akitō easing a training shoe on to his right foot. The Nisei blinked in disbelief as Akitō tried on the other trainer, stood up and walked around in them.

He's on to me! The Nisei swung the shoulder-bag round until the rifle mike built into it was trained on Akitō. Now he was giving the assistant cash, holding up his hand as if to say 'Keep the change, I insist.' Whatever the tip was, it looked like the man was going to be talking about it for a week. The Nisei fumbled for the mike monitor, he just caught '. . . Third Avenue entrance . . .', before two men speaking some Asian language moved into range and masked Akitō's conversation. The assistant put Akitō's handmade grey shoes into a carrier bag, thanked his customer once more and hurried off. Akitō looked at his watch and walked quickly across the store in the opposite direction.

The Nisei switched off the rifle mike. He was on his own now. He tracked his quarry like a cat, walking rhythmically on the balls of his feet.

Akitō walked towards a rostrum that held two dummies

155

dressed in scuba-diving equipment, veered to the left and stopped at a small elevator marked 'Staff Only'. He punched a code into the panel on the wall. Seconds later he was gone.

There's only one way this goes, the Nisei thought. *He's going to cross the store on a different floor, come back down and take off from a staff exit.* He reached down to the radio clipped to his belt and switched channels.

'Operative Thirty-seven, Assignment Two-twenty-one. Give me backup!'

On the roof of the building Akitō stepped out of the elevator, pushed through a set of glass doors and braced himself against the wind. He lowered his head and walked across to where Takuro Hamada's personal helicopter stood. The rotors were already spinning.

'Good afternoon, Mr Nashiba.' The pilot checked his clipboard. 'To Newark Airport, yeah?' Akitō gave him the thumbs-up.

Eighty-five storeys below, the Nisei was chasing around the outside of the building like a chicken with its head off. There was still a chance Akitō would double back to his car. Suddenly he heard a hacking sound above him. He looked up just in time to see the helicopter disappear across the narrow strip of sky above him.

'Afternoon, Mr Nashiba.' The heavy-set man pushed his thinning fair hair off his forehead.

'Mr Dempsey.'

'So, what are we heading into here?'

'Right now, we're just heading for a pay-phone in Queens, Mr Dempsey, then we'll take it from there.'

The two walked hurriedly through the air terminal's domestic lobby to a black Mercedes.

Yoshi looked at her watch and once more at the street below her. The derelict had picked through the last of the trashcans and moved off to the next block. She felt an immediate sense of relief; they hadn't found her yet. She leaned against

156

the window frame, looking out into the light morning drizzle. He would be here soon, here, in this sad little room. But would he listen to what she had to say? The voice on the phone had been cool, professional. It was no more than she'd expected. How must he feel, after all? She could only know in part. He was a stranger now. Her fingers followed the rain tracks down the window. What manner of a man was he? Who had he become? She drifted deeper into thought. The day he was born had been just like this, the bright sunshine broken up by showers of fine spring rain. She remembered it well.

There were fifteen close family members, Nashibas, Kugas and Tosas, gathered at the gate of Maruyama Park that day, all waiting to witness the child's abandonment. It was a ritual rarely used in modern Shinto; Yoshi had certainly never heard of it being done in her lifetime. But she was not excited because of that, she couldn't wait for Tatsuya to arrive, for the chance to see the son born of their love. When the limousine drew up, she could hardly stop herself craning her neck to get a better view of the tiny, silent bundle, being lifted by his father from the nurse's arms. Tatsuya looked at no one, he nodded a formal greeting to the onlookers and strode purposefully into the park. Some minutes later, he came out alone and walked away to wait in the Kiyomizu Temple.

'Be quick, Matsushiro,' Yoshi's aunt hissed, 'it's starting to rain again – the child will catch a chill!'

Yoshi watched her cousin go into the park. She shivered with fright. What if some stray dog had already carried him off? What if . . . ? She strained her ears. No, thank heaven, there it was, an unmistakable, mewing cry. Everyone smiled as Matsushiro came back into sight.

'He's a fine one, all right!' Matsushiro laughed at the furious, howling infant. 'Nine hours old and he's already making his presence felt.' He looked over to the nurse.

'Oh, may I hold him, just for a moment?' Yoshi could have bitten her tongue. She mustn't give herself away – yet how could she resist this chance?

'Very well. I will go and fetch Tatsuya.'

157

Suddenly the squalling baby was there in her arms. She cuddled him awkwardly.

'Hold him firmly, dear, then he'll feel secure.' Yoshi's old aunt adjusted her crooked arm and pushed aside the shawl to see the baby's face. 'Ah! He hardly looks newborn. His head is so well shaped, his face so smooth.' She peered more closely. 'All the father! Just as I said.'

Yoshi took out a handkerchief and dabbed the child's forehead and cheeks. Tears and rain softly dried away. He'd stopped crying now. The dark brown eyes were fixed intently on hers. She rocked him gently, murmuring a lullaby. Of course his face was smooth. He'd been born by Caesarean section. She was one of only four people who would ever know.

'Take the child home immediately, it's too cold here!' Tatsuya's harsh tone made her start. The nurse walked quickly towards Yoshi but she made no move. Tatsuya's violent glare had her frozen. The baby was being lifted from her limp hands, was being hustled away, his helpless cry stinging her nerves. The small party moved off to the waiting cars and away to the celebration at the Nashiba family home.

Tears and rain. Yoshi stood bareheaded, letting water drip down her face from the heavy cascades of cherry blossom. She was still watching the low cloud creep across Mount Fuji when Matsushiro came up.

'Yoshi, come on, we will be late.'

'With your permission, I will go home, cousin, I feel rather unwell.'

A rush of noise like a storm at sea filled her head as the limousine pulled out of Maruyama Park and on to the Tokyo road. She sat huddled in the corner, curled up in shock, grateful for the smoked-glass screen that hid her from the chauffeur's gaze. The sudden cruelty she'd seen in Tatsuya's face had overwhelmed the other, new sensation she had felt in holding the child. It was a cruelty she'd somehow been aware of but never been shown so openly before. She had come to know his volatile nature well enough to avoid confrontation in their two-year-long affair.

But there had been times when that cold, almost murderous look had entered his eyes – only his eyes – without a flicker of change on his face.

Once, when they'd arranged to meet, the heavens had opened and there wasn't a cab to be found in the whole of Tokyo. She'd arrived almost an hour late, drenched through. To most men, that would have been explanation enough. She expected him to laugh, be sympathetic. But he was not like other men. His time had been wasted. His precious, expensive time. He unleashed his whole fury on her. That look had been there then, that awful, freezing stare. Then too, she'd gone home weeping. He was so unfair, so hard. It was as if their affair counted for nothing, had collapsed in seconds like a house of cards. Never before had she felt she knew him so little. Then, in her hurt, she wished she'd never known him at all.

It was to be a full two years before she returned to Maru-yama Park. It was a kind of pilgrimage, a bookend. It had started here; she returned to close a chapter of her life. On that last day, she'd taken the 300-mile trip from Tokyo with a sense of grim determination. Tatsuya might stop her from having her child, but he couldn't stop her from looking at him. His terrible threats had chilled her. He was capable of great savagery as well as great passion. She had taken every precaution she could to ensure she was not followed as she got down from the Bullet Train and walked out of Kyoto station.

It was 5 May, a day of celebration for boys all over Japan. This was their special fête day and the streets of the old capital were bright with gigantic paper carps. As the carp swims upriver against the current, the tradition ran, so will a sturdy boy overcome all obstacles to make his way in the world and rise to fame and fortune. Every park was full of small boys flying their colourful fish-shaped kites or playing chase under the damp branches of the ginko trees. And there, in the garden at the ancient imperial palace, she'd found Akitō, his baby face wreathed with smiles as his own kite finally went aloft. His governess and a bodyguard stood by, clapping with glee.

159

She stooped to touch the ground at the shrine of Inari, running her fingers over the wet grass where her son had been abandoned, then looked back to where he played now with his paper kite, unaware that she even existed.

A wave of anger washed over her. Tatsuya had used her all along, swayed her with his deceit and empty promises. Made her beg, plead, and finally fight for the right to see her child. This child he'd said he would be proud of because of her. This son he'd said would be the proof of their love. The last confrontation had been the worst. But she was no longer afraid of his anger. She had grown to despise him. She stood up to him but he spared her nothing, left her nothing. In her rage, she struck him. He did not strike back, just turned his cold eyes on her and said: 'Stay away from Akitō. I warn you for the last time . . .'

She had seen the child again, now, despite him. Despite him, somehow she would reclaim him, too. *Yes, rise little kite*, she thought, *up with the wind current. Your father can secure your fame and fortune, my son, but not your love.* She stood for the last time at the foot of Mount Fuji and demanded justice from the gods.

Yoshi's pulse quickened. A black car was pulling up to the entrance of the apartment building. She moved away from the window. She did not want to see him from a distance, like before. She would wait to see him face to face. The wait seemed like an eternity. When the doorbell went, she was breathless with anxiety. She fumbled with the security chain, opening the door without checking the spy-glass. There were two men. She gasped and stepped back. The young Japanese stood in the door frame while the Caucasian took a look around. He nodded and stepped outside. The Japanese came in, closing the door behind him.

'Akitō Nashiba.' He gave a quick, perfunctory bow.

Yoshi studied his face. The forehead and cheekbones had Tatsuya's hard nobility but the mouth was soft, generous, like a woman's – like hers. She stared for several minutes trying to get used to the face, trying to fit the features of the young man over those of the chubby little boy she'd remembered.

A bolt of pain crossed her chest. She felt for a chair and sat down suddenly. The forbidden years. Too many years crushing down on the inside. Akitō's face was devoid of emotion. It wore a familiar cold look.

'What did you mean by sending me this?' Akitō had her envelope in his hand. His tone was contemptuous. 'What is this, some cheap blackmailer's trick?'

Yoshi caught her breath. 'Does a Tosa resort to blackmail?'

Tosa; the name ranked equally with that of the Nashibas among the Four Families. Akitō thought for a second.

'There is no female of the Tosa line in your generation. Takashi Tosa's only daughter died almost thirty years ago.'

'She died in his heart,' Yoshi said, quietly. 'Not in reality. When I left Japan twenty-six years ago it was as an outcast. I refused to marry the man chosen by my father. When I left, he forbade my name ever to be mentioned again.' She paused, she had her audience now, for as long as it lasted.

'Please sit down and allow me to explain, from the beginning. What I have to say will prove that I am Yoshi Tosa. That I am your mother.' She raised a hand against his indignation. 'Not the woman who gave birth to you but the woman who gave you life.

'I was a child of eight when I first met your father. I had heard about him, of course – you will know that our families have been at odds for two generations – but as relations, we were invited to your parents' marriage. I remember thinking then what a striking man he was, both in looks and presence. I was curious to know how he had become such an enemy to us. My father would tell me only that he had been responsible for my grandfather's death, because of this no Tosa would have contact with him except for business or formality's sake. From then on, I saw him only at family functions until—'

'Well?' Akitō interrupted, roughly. He had heard enough about this old feud in the past, he didn't need this woman

161

to tell him more. 'Perhaps you are a Tosa. What is that to do with me?'

'I'm trying to explain how it was between us.'

'I *know* how it was, how it is between our families.'

'No! Don't you see? I'm trying to tell you that despite it all I became . . . that I was your father's mistress.'

'Ha! One of the many, I assure you. And what right does that give you—'

'What *right*?' Yoshi's anger overcame her embarrassment. 'You have the DNA printout, you must have had it checked against your own, and you have the audacity to ask me what right I have to contact you?'

'You have a fine spirit, madam, and a lot of cheek. What makes you think I would trust this?' He waved the envelope. 'This—'

'You are here,' she said firmly. 'That says enough. In any event, I won't be bothering you much longer. I have been here for three days now, it can't take your father's hired killers more than another day to find me.'

'My father's what?' Akitō was exasperated. This woman was clearly deranged.

Yoshi looked at him for a long moment. It was so like Tatsuya to let the boy see only the side of him he wanted him to see.

'Your father has had me watched since the day you were born. When I left Japan, his men followed me to Rome. They're looking for me now. I assure you, if they find me they will kill me.'

Akitō stood up. 'I'm getting very weary of this nonsense. If my father really meant to have you killed, why didn't he take the opportunity before?'

She laughed. 'You may like to ask him that yourself.'

'Stop this idiocy!' Akitō was genuinely angry now. 'Tell me once and for all what you mean by your behaviour or leave me alone.'

'Yes, it is idiocy.' Her reply came with a deadly calm. 'But it is an idiocy I cannot change. The proof of it is in that envelope. Let me tell you about an episode in my life, that even now I'm ashamed to talk of . . .'

162

Akitō wanted to listen to what this woman was saying but again and again his attention was drawn away by the set of her eyes, her mouth, even the slight upward inflexion of her voice at the end of each sentence. All these traits struck a deep note of recognition in him. As she spoke he felt he was somehow discovering himself. Not just how he'd come to be but who he was. Things he'd never fully understood were falling into place, making sense.

'I have no excuses to offer you, except, perhaps, that I was very young. Your father was so much older than me, so much more experienced. His energy, his sheer strength of character were simply intoxicating . . .' She paused. 'I expect that much remains unchanged.'

Akitō's mind focused back on Yoshi's story. She seemed to be expecting some reply. But he had nothing to say. Almost every word out of the woman's mouth had tallied with the facts as he knew them but in a way, he had remained strangely unprepared for the worst of the truth.

She went on. 'So I agreed. I let it happen. But always I believed I would be allowed to see you. It seems stupid, now, looking back. He had obviously decided from the out-set to use me, and to cast me off when I was no longer necessary.'

Akitō felt numb. How old had he been when he'd asked his mother about the scar on her belly? Six? Seven? He'd waited until his father had left them to bathe alone in the family tub. 'You were so precious that the doctors lifted you out of me because they were afraid that you might be damaged if you were born in the normal way,' she had explained.

'But why, Mama?'

She put her face close to his and whispered. 'Shall I tell you a special secret? Your Daddy and I wanted you so much that when the rest of the world was only dreaming of such things, you were formed from his seed and mine, not in my womb, but under the eye of a surgeon in a dish, like a water lily. Once strong enough to survive you were placed back into the warmth, until you were ready to be born. Had it not been done in this way we could never have had you, or any other child.

'Remember this is our secret, Akitō, yours and mine. You must never, ever tell your father that I have told you this. Do you understand?'

He had not understood but he kept the secret. All these years he'd kept it. That was why he'd run the checks on the DNA profiles. That was why he'd seen the Tosa woman and not simply thrown her letter in the trash. Now he listened to her complete the story.

'You were born at eight in the morning on the first Wednesday in March,' Yoshi said. 'It was a particularly well-fated birth, in the year, month, day and even the hour of the Dragon. Because your parents were at ill-omened ages, your grandfather insisted you should be protected from the evil spirits through ritual abandonment.

'Your father left you beside the stone fox at the shrine of Inari in Maruyama Park. Your Uncle Matsushiro must have told you many times how he was sent to find you, how the placing was considered very auspicious . . .'

Akitō looked at the intense face in front of him, its classic beauty worn with sorrow. 'Yes,' he said at last. 'Yes. Many times.'

'It was then that I first held you. I could not know that it would be the only time.' Her voice became quieter, her tone more strained. 'Once, that once, for a few minutes while Matsushiro went to fetch your father, you were mine. You are mine, Akitō, but I can never have you.'

By the time Akitō reached his apartment his mind was in turmoil. Was he now to regard this poor, haunted woman with whom he'd spent a total of one day, as his real mother? It was unthinkable. Was he now to believe that the woman who had been the centre of his existence throughout his childhood; who had loved, comforted and reassured him his whole life, was nothing more than some kind of vessel whose only reason for being in his world at all was that she had been selected by the Nashibas to be his father's wife?

She was the one who he'd missed so terribly through those first lonely years in America; she was the one who still went to extraordinary lengths to ensure his comfort and peace of mind. Over the years, they had shared many secrets, they had forged a unique bond.

Often in the past he had looked at his mother's face or studied her mannerisms and wondered why he seemed to have inherited so little of her character. 'You have the best of your father in your face,' she used to say. 'But your love of poetry and literature comes from my side, from my mother . . .' Now there was another explanation. It had occurred to him long before that there could be a twist in the story that his mother had told him about his conception. And he was never more certain who was responsible for it. But there could be no doubt that she believed her version to be true.

So what was he to make of his father now? If life is an emotional trade-off, Akitō thought, and you get out what you put in, then Tatsuya Nashiba had now simply what he'd worked for – his son's respect. Yes, there'd been times when he thought that he loved him. But he was not an easy man to show love for. He came from a generation who found it difficult, if not impossible, to demonstrate physical affection. Even when Akitō was a child he'd been unable to throw his arms around the boy. Somehow he found such displays of emotion embarrassing, unmanly, almost an admission of weakness.

Akitō had come to question many things about his father in these early years of his manhood. What son didn't? For weeks he'd asked himself how his father could associate with a man like Colonel Santiago. A man who sanctioned the butchery of children. How could any deal be worth such a misguided alliance? What Yoshi had said was true, his father was capable of great cruelty.

He'd never pretended to understand his parents' relationship, but he knew that part of the reason he'd been shipped off to America so young was to distance him from the joyless atmosphere that so often pervaded the family home. His father was always outwardly respectful, courteous, sometimes even indulgent towards his mother but behind closed doors he knew there was a different truth. He'd always known it, perhaps was only now admitting it to himself openly.

He could understand it up to a point. His father, he was sure, felt himself trapped in loveless marriage to a woman with a fraction of his intellect who was, for him, as unaesthetic to look at as she was uninspiring to know. How ironic that in his turn, he was totally committed to condemning his son to an identical fate! Because it was the Japanese way. Because it had been the practice since the beginning of time.

Had his very existence really owed itself to his father's fanatical need to have a son, a son who could marry an Ishihara, Akitō wondered, or was there some other reason, something darker, something only a man with the basest of motives could have conceived? Was it contempt for his wife that had driven him to reject her genes for those of his mistress? If not, why had he purposely destroyed the eggs taken from her womb and had her implanted with one of those taken from Yoshi? Had it all been done out of love for an intelligent, beautiful woman, or had it been done to forge a secret alliance with the Tosas, the one Family who spurned close ties with the Nashibas at every turn?

Akitō walked through to the living-room and poured himself a stiff Scotch.

It was possible. He was capable of such an act. Akitō was chilled that he could believe such a thing of his father so readily. He drained the glass and sat down.

No wonder the Tosa woman had been so frightened. There would be no bounds to his father's anger when he knew they had met. But that he could stoop to murder, that he could have his own son followed, to be used as bait in the trap, was inconceivable. Or was it?

On the coffee-table in front of him were the notes he'd taken during his conversation with the security expert Takuro Hamada had put him on to. He picked them up. One line caught his eye.

'Wear new shoes till your own can be checked. Shoes

known to be yours can be electronically tagged.'

He stood up suddenly, strode over to the bedroom closet and slid back the door. There had been no time before, but now there was all the time in the world. He picked up each handmade leather shoe and examined it carefully. He was on the fourth pair when he found something. Akitō switched on the bedside light and held the heel up close to the bulb. Protruding from the layers of leather was a minute metal nib. He hurried to the bathroom drawer to find a pair of tweezers. If he just pulled on it, it might break. He forced a pair of nail scissors between the layers of leather and twisted them, working on the nib with the tweezers until it became loose. A minute later it lay on the palm of his hand. A tiny bulb of metal. A 'Tag' transmitter.

He flicked it across the room like a dead cockroach.

You are safe in Tokyo, my father. But if you were here now . . .

TWELVE

Back in 1969, Frobisher Club Secretary Willard Parkin had been one of the many opposed to the motion that ladies be admitted as members. A quarter of a century later, he still thought the garish clothing and shrill voices of women were out of place in a gentlemen's establishment that had counted three presidents and Thomas Edison amongst its membership. But he took to Auburn Totheroh the minute she walked into his office. Her clothes were tasteful, her voice pleasantly modulated, and privately, he'd counted her father as a friend. He would help her in any way he could.

'Thank you for your kind letter. And for the wreath,' Auburn said softly.

'I meant everything I said. Your father is greatly missed here. His table just doesn't look right with someone else sitting at it.' His thin finger rose to his lips. 'Oh, I hope I'm not upsetting you.'

'No, you're very sweet.' Auburn took her father's keys from her purse. 'I'd like to collect Dad's things from his locker. I have his key but there's no number on it.'

Parkin sprang up. 'Don't worry, I can find out for you.'

He hurried out to the reception desk, lifted a large leather-bound volume from a shelf below and brought it back into his office. He turned several pages.

'Here we are, 605, that's by the gym. If Mr Lasky here would like to come with me . . .'

'Oh, I'm sure I can find the way.' Mack started towards the stairs.

168

'I'm afraid I'll have to take you, sir. Non-members are not normally welcome upstairs.'

The lockers were made of worn dark oak, as old as the building itself. Morton's stood at the end of the long corridor that led to the gym. Inside, overweight businessmen were grunting as they sweated it out.

'Damn thing's stuck.' Parkin turned the key on Morton's ring until it started to bend but the lever on the lock refused to shift.

'Well, I don't understand that.' He straightened up, thought for a while, then reached into his pocket for his own key ring. 'Well, if the master key doesn't open it we'll have to call a locksmith.'

It did. Inside was a crumpled tee-shirt, shorts and a recent edition of a magazine called *Collectables*, designed for enthusiasts of small antiques. Mack held up the shorts. They were made for a guy weighing about three hundred pounds.

Parkin looked puzzled. '605. This is definitely the one.'

'Would you give me a minute here?' Mack asked.

'Certainly. Good to meet you, Mr Lasky. If I can be of any further assistance, you know where I am.' They shook hands and Parkin headed back to his office.

Mack took another look at the locker. The door was probably no more battered and worn than the rest but there did seem to be more than the normal amount of damage around the lock area. Mack ran his hand carefully around the inside of the locker and then underneath the dividing shelf. No disk. And he didn't need Auburn to tell him the stuff in the locker was not Morton's.

'I was so certain we would find something, maybe one answer. All we know is that Dad lent his locker to some lard-assed antiquarian.' Auburn flopped on to her sofa, letting her head hang over the arm. She glanced across at Mack. 'Will you stop walking around the place with that stupid thing? What a waste of six hundred dollars.'

'I have to be sure.' Mack continued moving round the

169

room, scanning object after object with the radio frequency detector. His eyes stayed fixed on the detector's bar graph display. So far, all it'd picked up was transmissions from taxi cabs passing outside.

'You really think someone's eavesdropping on us?'

Mack shrugged. 'Well, if I was searching for a vital piece of Morton's data, I'd be keeping a close eye on us right now.'

Auburn lifted her head. 'You still believe there is a disk, then?'

'Don't know. Just a feeling.'

She sat up, suddenly. 'You think this place'll be the next to get turned over?'

'I didn't say that.'

'You didn't have to. Well, to hell with them. Screw 'em, whoever they are! This is *my* home. They're not getting me out of here. No way.' Auburn pushed herself violently off the sofa.

Mack touched her arm. 'Hey, it's okay.' He held up the detector. 'According to this we're "bug" free – for the time being, anyhow.'

Auburn sat slowly back on the sofa. 'You think I'm crazy?'

'No.' Mack slipped the hand-sized black device into his pocket and thought for a while. When he'd gone swimming with Morton, he'd certainly put his clothes somewhere. Maybe . . .

'What d'you say?'

'I said no, you're not crazy.' Mack walked over to his attaché case, took out his phone book and crossed to the desk.

'What're you doing now?'

'Calling an old friend. There's still one thing I want to check out. And I'm going to need some expert help.'

The recorded message on the answering machine was pure Bodecker: 'I'm busy. Speak.'

'Jay, it's Mack. Call me on 212 580 5601. And don't transfer the charges, you cheap gink.' Mack hung up.

'Friend?'

'My oldest. He probably won't call back, we'll have to try him later. He's worth waiting for, believe me.'

The Prime Minister's residence, Nagata-cho, took its name from the district of Tokyo in which it stood. It was conveniently placed across the street from the National Diet Building, home of the Japanese parliament. Designed in a style reminiscent of Frank Lloyd Wright, the two-storey reinforced concrete building was partly hidden behind a forbidding wall. It would have made an imposing impression, were it not for the fact that the exterior had been allowed to deteriorate steadily since its completion in November 1928. On the first floor at the back was the Prime Minister's private office. Leading off from this was a small ante-room, sparsely furnished with upholstered chairs. Itaro Ishihara sat in one of them, gazing out at the small formal garden while the hairdresser worked. Minute tufts of greying black hair fell on to a green sheet spread out beneath him.

Ishihara did not need to have his hair cut once a week. Although it was still thick it had always grown slowly. But the previous two Prime Ministers had had their hairdressers visit them every Thursday without fail and he saw no reason to change the arrangement. The hour it took to cut, wash and dry his hair was the one time in the working week he got to himself. A rare chance to be alone with his thoughts.

He listened morosely to the sound of caterers preparing the largest of the reception rooms above for the dinner that evening that would celebrate the start of his third year in office. What would there be to celebrate this time next year? He had a powerful mandate in the Diet, and the respect if not the actual affection of enough of the electorate to ensure at least one more term in office. But what would it all add up to in the light of everything he now knew?

As a rising member of the House of Representatives he had been more than content to be appointed to a minor cabinet post in the summer of 1989. But, a little more than

171

a year later, he had been totally unprepared for events as they unfolded. It was a mild autumn day. He had been sitting with his father and uncle in the garden of the Ishihara family home in Osaka as he had a hundred times before. Only that day there was a special guest at the table, a man he'd met once, briefly, at his grandfather's funeral.

'Your uncle and I have been told in the strictest confidence,' Tatsuya Nashiba started slowly, 'that the Prime Minister will resign his office before the year is out. He is much sicker than even the newspapers would have us believe. The question of his successor has yet to be discussed openly.' He put his thumbs together. 'But it is our intention to put forward your name.'

Events moved so fast over the next eighteen months that, as Ishihara looked back on them now, much of it seemed a blur. Endless rounds of dinners, fund-raisers and interviews. A birthday celebration in the morning, a wedding reception at noon, an anniversary in the evening. At each one he would make the expected gift in cash, knowing that when the time came, the family of the recipient could be counted on to respond by helping to bring him a little closer to power.

Kenkin, the gift system, had existed in Japan as long as there had been politicians. Ishihara had never stopped to calculate the kind of money that changed hands in his campaign, but he knew it could be counted in billions of Yen — the gift fund that had been set up for him was like a bottomless pit, replenished from seemingly limitless reserves. Neither had he conceived of the breadth of influence the Four Families commanded across Japan. Yet at one time or another, the head of each clan would emerge from the shadows to cast a hand over events, to smooth the way, to open a door that had seemed until that moment steadfastly closed.

And constant through it all was Nashiba. Ishihara had been Prime Minister for a little more than six months when he came to dine with him at Nagata-cho. After the meal, when the servants had withdrawn, Nashiba sat back and lit a cigar.

'When you were three years old,' he said, 'my father, Hiromi Tosa and I stood in this room with General Tojo. He was so drunk we could barely understand what he was saying. He shouted that we should fight to the last man for the honour of Japan. Soon after, Hiroshima and Nagasaki were reduced to charred wastelands. For all we knew, those bombings were just a foretaste of things to come. We knew then that the war was lost. Tosa called the Families together to discuss the future . . .'

Nashiba had talked long into the night. As day broke, Ishihara became the first Premier to know of the existence of the Single Day, or *Tsumi* as it had come to be called – Japanese for Checkmate. From then on, his life would never be the same.

'Your administration will take us through into the greatest era in Japan's history,' Nashiba had said that night. And what high hopes Ishihara had cherished for himself as part of Nashiba's grand plan. Hopes he'd seen eroded bit by bit over the past two years.

Ishihara shifted irritably in his seat. The hairdresser winced as the scissor-points drew blood at the back of the Premier's neck. But Ishihara felt no pain.

'Oh, sir!'

'It's all right, it was my fault.' Ishihara waved a hand. 'Don't make a fuss.'

The Premier settled back into his thoughts while the hairdresser dabbed the wound. At the outset, it had all seemed to be as Nashiba had promised. But gradually, a series of events set Ishihara's mind working on a different course.

Once, in a moment alone with the head of the Kuga family, he had outlined some ideas of his own on how aspects of *Tsumi* might be refined.

Kuga's response was vicious. 'Do not presume to tell us our business in this matter, Ishihara.' It was as though he was addressing filth off the street, not the Prime Minister of Japan.

It soon became clear that in matters of special interest to the Families, too, Ishihara was expected to toe the line.

173

Twice he was forced to make embarrassing public 'U' turns on policies that he had formulated, to avoid coming into direct conflict with the very men who'd assured his path to power.

The difficulty of his position, the limits to his authority and freedom of action took a long time to accept. The Families had what they wanted: their own man in Nagata-cho, an efficient, respected Prime Minister with all the power and influence of those that had gone before him – except when they decreed otherwise. Ishihara seemed to have little choice but to live with the situation and make the best of it.

Making Isao Tamazaki Minister of Defence had been the one ministerial appointment that he'd insisted on making without interference. Tamazaki was the one trusted friend in whom Ishihara could confide – and he often proved to be an invaluable source of intelligence.

The day it had all begun, Tamazaki had sat in his office sipping tea.

'There's talk amongst the Nashibas that the old man intends to hand over the running of the company to Akitō after *Tsumi*,' he said. 'That he will create a new position for him – a reward for the *Shō* that the boy has paid him.'

Tamazaki paused to take another sip of the fragrant liquid. 'They say he will head some new council of the Families, that he will be Chief Executive West.'

'On whose authority will he be that?' Ishihara looked up from the stack of letters brought for his signature. 'I thought all the Families spoke with an equal voice in this matter.'

'Well, to hear the Nashibas tell it, *Tsumi* was forged in their camp. They are the architects of the plan. To them it is their due.' The Minister could only guess at the reaction the next statement would provoke. He delivered it carefully. 'When the appointment is made the other Families would simply be openly accepting a supremacy that has existed since the beginning.'

Ishihara put down his pen. 'How reliable is your source?'

Tamazaki could already see where the conversation was

headed. 'Not reliable enough for you to pass this on without further investigation.'

Night after night, Ishihara lay awake, tortured with doubt and fear. Were the Nashibas planning some kind of coup after *Tsumi*? The alliance between the Families had lasted almost five decades, would it still have a purpose if they succeeded? And what was planned for his family . . . for him?

As the weeks passed, the questions gnawed at him until he knew he would have to take action on his own.

'*Dōmo.*'

The hairdresser placed a mirror in Ishihara's hand and held up another to reflect the back of his head. The Prime Minister nodded. The green cloth placed around his shoulders was carefully removed and a few remaining pieces of hair brushed from his neck. He put on his jacket, walked into his office and lifted the phone.

'Are the gentlemen here?'

On each anniversary of the start of Ishihara's administration, his Chief Cabinet Secretary and three other senior ministers would gather in his office to drink and exchange gifts before dinner. He was not particularly relishing the tradition on this occasion. As Ishihara unwrapped his first gift, his mind was still preoccupied with Akitō Nashiba.

'It is exquisite,' he said at last, admiring the contents of the package. It was a carved jade figure of a scholar, the tiny hands and face fashioned with infinite delicacy.

'It is from the latter Han period,' offered Defence Minister Tamazaki, 'my wife chose it. She's so much more discerning than I am about these things.'

'I'm so glad that she is out and about at last,' said Ishihara holding the figure carefully up to the light. 'My wife and I have thought of her often in the weeks since her operation.'

'Thank you, she is much improved.'

Ishihara's secretary appeared in the doorway carrying a large flat parcel marked 'Federal Express'.

'I'm sorry to interrupt you, Prime Minister, but you asked me to bring you this the moment it arrived.'

Ishihara placed the jade figure carefully on the window

ledge, took the parcel and opened it with a paper-knife. He glanced at its contents.

'Gentlemen, will you forgive me for a moment?'

Alone again in his ante-room, Ishihara studied the letter from his private investigators in New York. A smile gradually filtered across his face. For months even the most sophisticated surveillance techniques had failed to penetrate the Nashibas' security screen. The one breakthrough had been bringing in an acupuncturist to replace the one Nashiba's wife had used for years. She'd been able, during each treatment, to implant a Mita Microbug in place of one of the tiny pins used on the pressure points in the ear. No one really expected Nashiba to discuss business with his wife. But monitoring their conversations had at least given Ishihara's New York agents a clue to Nashiba's future movements and had made tracking him that much easier. The fact that their operative had actually been able to implant Akitō's ear as well, had been a stroke of extraordinary good fortune. For eleven precious days they had been able to monitor every second of Akitō's life. Then he had ceased the treatment.

Details of the Nashiba boy's affair with the American girl were not unuseful. He was contracted to marry Ishihara's niece in less than six weeks. The family could be guaranteed to disapprove. But what filled Ishihara with delight were the transcripts of the conversation between Yoshi and Akitō. If the Tosas were to find out about Tatsuya's little genetic experiment they would start a blood feud against the Nashibas that would last generations.

Ishihara was well satisfied. This single piece of information would ensure the rise and ultimate supremacy of his family after *Tsumi* and suppress Nashiba's ambition for ever.

By 11.00 p.m. only a hard core of the ministers, close relatives and friends that had made up Ishihara's guest list, still remained. Raucous male laughter filtered through the ceiling to where Ishihara again sat scanning the agent's report. His first reaction had been to send the complete package to Takashi Tosa, Yoshi's father. Then there were the Kugas to consider. Their eldest daughter was Nashiba's wife.

As he weighed the implications of such actions, one against the other, he began to see the irreversible chain of events he would set in motion. A revelation of this scale would tear the Families apart, perhaps forever. *Tsumi* would evaporate as though it had never existed. His own position might be threatened.

There was another way. One by which he and his family would prosper. No one in Japan need ever know of Akitō's true parentage but he and Nashiba.

He took a sheet of notepaper from his desk drawer and began to write.

Jay Bodecker hadn't returned a phone call in three days. He couldn't afford to let anything break his concentration. He'd spent the morning trying to formulate the entry code into the company computer at Unique Cars on State Street. His client was Prestige Motors on Michigan Avenue. Had to be. Collecting classic cars was a select business, catering only for the mega-rich. Who else in the area would want to know?

Jay had been a computer hacker ever since, at the age of eleven, he'd accidentally stumbled on to the password into the data base at Chicago City Hall, using a beaten-up IBM his father had bought on hire purchase. Just for the hell of it, he'd given a couple of minor employees with unpronounceable names, who were probably janitors, a ten-million-dollar rise each and left it at that. These days he played for real, and it paid well.

Jay lived in the Cicero district of Chicago above what had been his grandfather's secondhand electrical store on Pershing Road. A potential customer had to be pretty persistent to find the place open. If Jay shifted a toaster and a vacuum cleaner, it was a big week. The centre of his life was his two-roomed apartment. Half the living-room was taken up by a partially dismantled '58 Harley Davidson Electroglide, empty beer crates and stacks of porno magazines. Every inch of the area between this and his beloved computer work-station was knee-deep in cigarette ends, soiled socks and underwear and the mouldering remains of take-out meals. Jay had gotten used to the smell long ago. Once it had built up to a certain level, it didn't seem to get a whole lot worse. The last person to clean the place out thoroughly was his mother, and she'd been dead seven years.

The work-station area looked like it belonged to a different person. Here Jay would sit for days at a time, searching for the word or number that would take him into a spreadsheet, a data base. Or a hundred other places he had no business being. From here each morning, he would phone his list of potential informers, disaffected employees who might be finessed into supplying him with the pass codes that would get him through corporate security systems.

Jay was a prince of thieves. He'd been sticking his nose into other people's business for the better part of ten years without being caught. He'd break into the computer systems of big spenders who went to lengths to keep their buying behaviour to themselves. Establishing what gifts they sent, what wines they drank, where they took their holidays – information that was hard to pick up in detail from other sources, was invaluable in rounding out geo-demographic profiles sold on to the direct marketing industry. Thanks to Jay, the nation's high-rollers could rely on a little more junk mail to toss in the trash each morning.

Supplying information to data bureaux kept him in beer and burritos. But what kept him in Havana cigars was industrial espionage – snooping for one client through the computer files of a rival. When Jay put his mind to it, no marketing campaign, corporate strategy, design, plan or patent was safe from his prying eye.

The phone on his desk rang.

'Jay? It's Mack.'

'Hi, Lasky, how you doin'? Still chopping out hearts?'

'Yeah, blood on the streets, business as usual. How's Pig Palace?'

Jay sniffed the air, held his nose and talked through it, in the Betty Boop voice of the weather girl on WAMQ, Chicago. 'The air quality in Cicero today will be unhealthful . . .'

Jay and Mack had known each other since childhood. Jay had processed and printed Mack's used-car sheet and mail-order catalogues on his faithful IBM. As adults, Mack had used Jay's talents a dozen times to check the bona fides of the companies he was planning to do business with.

'Is this line safe?'

Jay yawned. 'No. Carry on.'

'I want you to take a look at a couple of subscription lists for me. A magazine called *Collectables*. Offices at 1607, Lexington Avenue, New York, and the Frobisher Club, Gramercy Park. I want you to make a list of any names you find on both. Just the men . . .'

Jay rubbed his hands with glee. Piece of cake. He picked up the elderly kitchen timer on his desk and set it to one hour.

'Okay, Bodecker, beat the clock.'

It took three minutes to get through to the TRW data bureau in St Louis. They owed him a few. Half an hour later, he had what he wanted. He jerked the middle finger of his right hand at the kitchen timer.

'Congratulations, Mr Bodecker, you got a weekend in Poughkeepsie for two.' He started dialling New York.

'Mack? I got five names for you. One of these guys ain't paid subs to anyone in a while. He's probably stiffed out. I'll give you his name anyway.'

Mack wrote them down carefully. 'You're a jewel, Bodecker.'

Jay chewed on his nicotine-stained moustache. 'Ain't I just.'

Willard Parkin was surprised to see Auburn back at the Frobisher Club so soon. He, the hall porter and the Maître d' sat awkwardly in his office as she went through her little presentation. Everyone's attention was directed towards three cut-glass decanters on the desk.

'I wanted to deal with these particular bequests myself. I think my father would have wanted it that way. The decanter in the middle, Mr Parkin, is said to have belonged to Thomas Jefferson. That's the one he said you should have.'

Parkin reached forward and lifted the decanter with great solemnity. 'Your father was a very thoughtful man. But then of course you know that. I'm very touched.'

'Very touched,' echoed the Maître d', dabbing his eye with a handkerchief. 'I was only saying to the Secretary here, yesterday, we should have a silver plaque put up to him in the dining-room, by his table.'

'A portrait!' announced the porter, turning to Parkin. 'You might bring it up at the next committee meeting.'

Parkin nodded thoughtfully. 'Well . . . I'll certainly discuss it with some of the members.'

While the little charade played out in the Secretary's office, Mack used the opportunity to go through the leather-bound register at the unmanned reception desk. Three of the four members whose names Jay had given him had lockers assigned to them.

By the time Auburn emerged from Parkin's office, Mack was already on the second floor of the building and had checked out the first two lockers. Morton's key wouldn't open either of them. The third locker was on the top floor at the end of a corridor. The key turned in it so easily, Mack gave a shudder of surprise. He was right. He had to be. Inside was a towel, a three-week-old edition of the *Wall Street Journal* with a piece cut out of the front and what looked like Morton's wristwatch. Mack ran his hand carefully around all the inside surfaces. It didn't make sense. There was nothing there.

Mack had worked the thing backwards a dozen times in his mind. This locker originally belonged to the guy whose outsized tee-shirt and shorts they'd found the day before. Fat Boy must've come to the club to work out in the gym. He couldn't have been too thrilled when they gave him a locker two floors above it, on the other side of the building.

It was one hell of a way to lug all that blubber. He must have jumped at the opportunity of swapping lockers with Morton when he suggested it; his was right by the gym.

But why did Morton make the offer? He wasn't doing himself any favours. There was only one reason he'd choose to take a hike out this far. He had something to hide. The swap would give him a second line of defence. Put Fat Boy between him and anyone who came sniffing around.

Mack was certain now that whoever had picked over Morton's apartment and the Fire Island house had also been here. They'd forced the locker by the gym, found nothing and crossed the Frobisher Club off their list.

So where the hell was the disk? Mack squatted down and rocked back on his haunches.

'Can I help you, sir?'

Mack looked up to see a man dressed in white glaring down. He was built like a Buick. Probably a masseur.

'I'm ... I'm Morton Totheroh's son-in-law. You may have heard he died recently. I've come to collect his stuff ...'

The newspaper and the towel hardly looked worth collecting. Mack made a big display of the wristwatch. Buick's fingers started to drum on his wide leather belt.

'... Mr Parkin has been very helpful, brought me up here himself ...'

The menacing look on the face faded a little.

'I'm sorry, sir, I just hadn't seen you up here before. Very sad about Mr Totheroh.' They started to walk towards the wide, sweeping staircase. 'He was one hell of a swimmer. Must have really been something when he was young.'

'Yes, narrowly missed selection for the 1960 Olympic Team.' Mack was starting to worry. If the masseur followed him much further down the stairs, they'd run into Parkin again in the lobby. It might lead to some awkward questions. He started to adjust his story to fit with what Parkin knew.

'Seems Morton put his back out playing football the week before. As a matter of fact this watch was a gift from his grandfather at the time, kind of consolation prize I guess.'

The lobby was now in view. 'My wife was anxious to get it back.'

'I can relate to that.'

Parkin was standing with his back to the stairs, talking to a man in a tuxedo.

'Mr Parkin tried to find it for us yesterday,' Mack rattled on, 'but we had the wrong locker or . . . or the wrong key.'

'Aah, they're a pain in the buns these lockers. Came from some ritzy boy's school in Boston about a hundred years ago. You'd never believe some of the stuff we find in the boader drawers.'

Mack stopped on the stairs. 'The what?'

'The boader drawers. For boaders.' The masseur pronounced the 't' as a 'd', what he meant was 'boaters'. 'You know, those wimpy straw hats they used to make those guys wear. Each locker has a drawer for one at the top, to keep it out of the damp or from getting crushed.'

'Is that so? Well, what do y'know?' Mack gave the top of Parkin's head one more glance. 'Maybe I should take another look, I might have missed something.' He pressed a twenty-dollar bill into Buick's palm. It didn't look much sitting in that big hand.

'Thank you, you've been most helpful.'

Buick nodded, looked at his watch and strode off to pound the crap out of somebody else. Mack breathed a sigh of relief and turned back to Morton's locker. He opened the door again. He couldn't see a drawer. He reached up and felt the top of the frame. The front cross-strut slid forward and dropped slowly down, opening up a gap about six inches deep. Mack put in his hand.

There was no 'boader' inside. Just an AmTronics computer disk.

Mack sat at Morton's G250 trying to make sense of the unintelligible series of computer commands on the screen in front of him. He shook his head. 'Well, whatever this is, it sure meant a lot to your father.'

Auburn looked pale and nervous. 'And to whoever . . .'

'. . . To whoever else was looking for it. Come on, let's just take this one step at a time.'

'Looks like we're caught up in something, now, whether we like it or not.'

'Let me do the worrying, will you? Do you know how to make copies on this thing?'

'Same as any other computer, I guess.'

'Good, make half a dozen. Give me a couple and stick the rest in safe deposit boxes around the city.'

'Why, you going somewhere?'

'Yup. Pig Palace.'

THIRTEEN

Akitō banged his fork down on the table. 'I thought you said you checked this place out.'

Warren scanned the restaurant, anxiously looking for the Maitre d'. 'I did, it's been well reviewed everywhere.'

'Well, are you going to eat this?'

Mack was already damn certain he wasn't. He looked at his plate. Game pie. He'd always been wary of game, avoided ordering it unless he knew how long it had been hanging around. Some places, they left it till it dropped. He shook his head. It was that smell that was getting to him most. That terrible stench.

He picked up his knife and separated the pie-crust from the small earthenware dish in front of him with the knife and lifted it off. The dish was alive with insects. Maggots, ants and silverfish slithered under and over one another to get to whatever was beneath. He felt the gorge rise in his throat. What was wrong with the others? Couldn't they see what was happening?

Morton stared blankly ahead, his eyes flat. The insects in his dish had established a bridgehead along his fork to his hand. Mack watched as those that had found their way into his clothing through his sleeve started appearing from the collar of his shirt. Now they were moving under the flesh of Morton's face and neck, distorting his features until they were unrecognisable . . .

Mack was suddenly awake. He rolled over and opened his eyes. Garbage. Everywhere. He was lying in a garbage tip and his head hurt like hell.

'How you feeling?'

Mack's eyes slowly pulled the back of Jay Bodecker's head into focus.

'Why the fuck don't you get this place cleaned up, Bodecker? Jesus, it stinks in here!'

Jay turned from his computer terminal and sniffed the air. A look of genuine surprise filtered across his long, bony face. 'Guess it does.' He threw Mack a tube of large white tablets. 'Here, chew on a couple of these.'

Mack struggled up from the mattress and fell down again, his head in his hands. 'What are these?'

'Peppermints, strong as hell. Can't smell fish fanny through 'em.'

'What time is it?'

'A quarter of four. It'll be light soon.' Jay turned back to his work. 'Too much Dermot's Special, that's your problem.'

'Eh?'

'That stuff you were knocking back last night – moonshine, 'bout a hundred and twenty proof. Well, they call it moonshine, but it's Irish Potcheen.' Jay was grinning like a Cheshire cat. 'The vintage stuff. Could be a week old, even two.'

Mack stood up. The peppermints were starting to work. He picked a path through the debris to what passed as Jay's bathroom.

'Never met Morton Totheroh,' Jay shouted above the sound of running water. 'Read a hell of a lot about him though. Sure was one smart ol' dude . . .'

Mack peered round the door, his face covered in shaving foam. 'Figured out what's on that thing yet?'

Jay kept punching buttons on the computer keyboard and chewing at his moustache. 'I know what I think it is. But we'll have to wait and see.'

'Well, one thing's for sure – he went to a lot of trouble to hide that disk.' Mack went back to his shaving. 'And I'm pretty certain that someone's itching to get a hold of it. The same someone who turned over Morton's home in Fire Island.'

Jay let out a long, low whistle. 'Wow, this stuff ain't cool, it's positively hypothermic!'

Mack came out of the bathroom with a bloody piece of toilet paper tissue stuck to his neck. He glanced at the jumble of data on the computer screen and shook his head. 'It is?'

'This guy's in a league of his own.'

Mack sat down at the computer and dabbed his face with a towel.

'See, this is a batchfile. It gives the computer instructions. It's basically a list, a long list of commands that take you through an application program to the place you want to be. Saves you having to type in every line at the keyboard yourself.' He prodded the screen. 'It's kind of like having a map with the route marked out on it and every one of these lines is a signpost that speeds up the trip.'

'Yeah, right through Nashiba Country.'

'What?'

'They have a major stake in AmTronics. There was no love lost between Morton and the Japanese. My guess is he was caught poking around somewhere he shouldn't have been and . . . you might as well know . . . his daughter and I think they had him killed.'

Jay pushed his chair back from his desk. The half smile that seemed to be a permanent feature of his face faded. 'Oh, I wondered why you were in such a big hurry to get up here, all of a sudden.' He took out the disk and put it in the fan file on his work-station. 'So what do you think we're gonna find with this thing?'

'I dunno.'

'Well look, this here batchfile's serious shit. It's going to take a while to follow every path to the end.' Jay took another chew on his moustache and thought hard. 'D'you remember when we were kids we went to see that picture *Land of the Pharaohs?*'

'Vaguely. Turkey?'

'Turkey. But it had a couple of good things in it.'

'Wait a minute, wasn't that the one with all that stuff about building a pyramid? With all those incredible

186

contraptions to seal the passages after the Pharaoh croaks, to keep out grave-robbers?'

'You got it. Well, remember the last reel, when they give Jack Hawkins the Tutankhamen treatment? His stiff, his servants and his treasure are about to be walled up into the thing for all time.'

'Yeah.'

'Then the architect says, "Okay, set the machinery in motion, seal up the vault! Thanks a million boys and, if you don't mind, I'll get back to the wife . . ."'

Mack froze. '. . . And the High Priest says, "Sorry fella, you're the only one who knows how to get back into this baby. Pharaoh's instructions: You die with the project."'

'Exactly. Only old Morton covered himself for that day. See, if he wrote the database, he could've built what's called a "trap door" into it — a way for him to get in and out without being detected. And I reckon what we got here's the key to that door.' Jay thumped the arms of his chair. 'Sweet Jesus, Mack, if it's a key that was worth murdering someone like Morton Totheroh for, it's got to open up one hell of a box of tricks!'

'Yeah. No prizes for guessing who the box belongs to,' Mack said, half under his breath.

'Morton was keeping an eye on Nashiba?'

'You could say that. Listen, can you hook up to their database?'

'You bet.'

'How long before you'd know if the stuff on the disk is related?'

'First I got to see if it gets me past the dragon on the gate — access control, to greenhorns like you.'

'And if it does?'

Jay shrugged. 'Give me a couple of days; if I haven't got anywhere by then, I probably never will.'

Auburn lifted another suit out of the wardrobe and laid it on the bed. Maybe she should get them cleaned, give them to charity. Couldn't just throw them away. She sighed. *Now*

187

I know how it must've been for him after Mom.

She looked around. The empty room seemed even colder than it had a few minutes before. She gave Mack's mobile phone number another try.

'Lasky.'

'Hi, it's me,' she said, flatly.

'Oh, hi. Sorry I didn't call you sooner. Trying to get free of Drummond's taking more time than I thought.'

'That's okay. Did you hear from Jay yet?'

'Called about ten minutes ago, I'm heading over to his place as soon as I'm finished here. Listen, I'll be back in New York at the weekend . . .'

'Fine. Catch you then sometime.' She hung up and slumped down on the bed. 'You're a schmuck, Auburn Totheroh,' she said to herself. 'So he's nice to you in your hour of need; gives you a half-decent bang . . .'

She left sorting the suits and wandered back into her father's office. *Three days I don't hear from the guy . . . well two can play at that game.*

She smoothed a hand over the G250's beige plastic case. 'The power of pure logic. Sometimes I wish I were like you. Switch on, switch off – click! Simple.' She reached for the power switch, then stopped. 'Ah, enough for one day. Sorry, computer, I'm going home.'

The penthouse above the Nashiba Building in Kabuto-cho, Tokyo's financial district, was Tatsuya's favourite. It had been the first and was still the finest of the nine he owned, scattered across the globe.

At 6.00 a.m. Wednesday, 2 August, he sat down as he did every morning to a breakfast of *sashimi*, the best cuts of raw tuna taken from a whole fish that had been flown in specially from Okaido. Laid out in front of him on the polished table in neat rows was every newspaper, business periodical and fact sheet that had been published in Japan's principal cities since midnight. One headline in particular caught his eye.

'Yamagata Wins Tank Contract' . . . 'The minister of

defence announced yesterday . . .' Nashiba did not bother to read on. He put down his tea and sighed. Six-ten and already the harmony of his breakfast was spoiled.

Yamagata owned a multinational conglomerate as big as any controlled by the Four Families. They had tried a hundred times to gain a foothold in its structure, to seize enough of its stock to get a measure of control and force Yamagata into their camp. But no matter how they disguised their identity, no matter how many nominee companies were placed between them and their quarry, Yamagata would sniff them out and fend them off.

Yamagata had come from the streets, built up his company from nothing. He loathed the Families. Loathed their high-handedness, their aristocratic pretensions, their fanatical need to have a voice in every Japanese institution. And the Families loathed him with an equal intensity. But they needed him. He serviced an enviable chunk of the armaments industry and Japan now had the second-largest and best-equipped armed forces in the world. The Kugas and the Tosas held key contracts to supply a whole range of military hardware to all three services. Nashiba's factories supplied them with most of the electronic components, as they had in the war years. But the profits from just the missile guidance system Yamagata had developed dwarfed those of both of the families combined.

In the photographic industry, too, Yamagata was the watchword for excellence. And the little man had the unerring knack of cornering expanding markets. From cameras for the film industry to camcorders for the man-in-the-street, from flat-bed scanners for the computer industry to security systems for the home, Yamagata never missed an opportunity. His slice of the American market, with his hundreds of domestic plants there, was equal to any one of the Families'.

Nashiba shook his head. Yamagata's participation in *Tsumi* was much to be desired but it was a dream he had all but given up on. The old man did not notice his manservant move up to his side and refill his cup before laying a small white envelope beside his plate.

'This came for you a few minutes ago, *danna sama*.'

Toichi's voice drew Nashiba's attention to the letter. The perfectly executed characters on the envelope had a familiar look. Nashiba nodded. Toichi moved silently towards the door. The *danna sama* had made a very poor showing with his breakfast this morning. Perhaps the satsumas he'd bought from the market an hour before would tempt his palate. He turned back to ask if he should serve these but the look on the old man's face stopped him dead in his tracks. He seemed drained of blood. Beads of sweat glistened on his forehead. Toichi hurried to his side.

'*Danna sama*, are you unwell?'

Nashiba rose without speaking, picked up the letter and walked out into the hallway to his private elevator.

Jiro Matsuno had been planning on getting to work early that morning anyway. Nashiba's call to him at six-thirty had simply meant him finishing his breakfast in the car as he moved fender to fender through Tokyo's rush-hour traffic. Matsuno had been Nashiba's chief communications expert for nearly eight years. He'd taken over the job on his father's retirement and was well satisfied with his lot. Computers were his greatest passion, he'd been obsessed with them since childhood. He was rewiring motherboards when many of his contemporaries were still gluing model aircraft kits together.

He felt a sudden rush of excitement as he made his way to Nashiba's office. An urgent call from the *Shacho* was certain to mean that he was going to be busy; that his ingenuity was going to be stretched to the limit.

Nashiba was sitting calmly in his large leather chair. He motioned Matsuno forward.

'On many occasions over the last eight years, I have had to ask for your complete discretion.' Nashiba folded his hands. 'The matter before us now is of a delicacy that goes beyond anything I have entrusted you with before.'

Matsuno bowed his head. 'You do me the greatest honour as always.'

190

'I suggest you call your wife and tell her you will not be returning home until tomorrow. I can have a change of clothes brought over for you, if you wish.'

Nashiba walked over to his safe and took a small plastic card from a shelf inside. He sat down in front of the computer. Matsuno watched as he placed an eye against the tiny built-in camera. The screen flickered. The security camera had accepted the individuality that could only be found at the back of the designated user's retina. Nashiba slotted a plastic Smart Card into the computer console. The screen flickered again: 'Enter your password.' Asterisks appeared to mask each of the six digits entered. Finally a menu of directories appeared. Nashiba positioned the cursor and pressed Enter.

'In these files are over a thousand bank codes and passwords. They are continually updated using information from employees at the banks themselves.' Nashiba pushed the chair back and consulted his notes. 'The one highlighted on the screen accesses a Yamagata reserve account at the Kaida Bank in Osaka. Make a transfer from it to this account number at the Freidler Bank in Zürich.' He handed Matsuno a slip of paper. 'And backdate the transaction ten days.'

Matsuno looked at his boss. The old man was serious. He pulled a chair up to the screen. 'How much do I transfer?'

Nashiba scratched his chin. 'Oh, eight hundred million Yen.'

'Shacho?'

'Is there a problem with that?'

Matsuno could think of quite a few. He swallowed hard. 'Well, it depends on how vigilant Yamagata's accountants are and how often they check the Kaida deposit.'

'Not often enough.' Nashiba's voice betrayed a sense of triumph. 'Ask yourself how long it would take us to pick up something like this if it were one of our little rainy day accounts? One week, two? The transfer only need stay in place undetected for forty-eight hours at the most.'

'Well, if the passwords are up to date, I can certainly do it.'

'They are.' Nashiba got up, stretched himself and crossed to the door. 'When you've done that, go through the Freidler account statements from the time it was opened in the spring of '91. I want all the telegraphic transfers to the account changed to cash deposits – all except the one that you are about to make. And give me a printout of everything.'

When Nashiba returned at two that afternoon the steady hum of the laser printer confirmed Matsuno's success. Sheet after sheet of bank statements were stacked up in the out tray. Nashiba placed the large plate of *sushi* he was carrying under the communications chief's nose.

'Here, I had my chef make these for you.'

Matsuno was hungry. He reached out, stuffed several delicacies in his mouth and carried on tapping at the computer keyboard.

'You'll notice that all debits against the Freidler account are transfers to an account at the Hanaya Bank here in Kabuto-cho,' Nashiba said. 'As soon as you're ready, access that account and call me in the penthouse.'

At four that morning Nashiba sat at the huge bureau that dominated his penthouse study. Toichi appeared in the open doorway carrying a steaming-hot towel on a silver platter.

'May I bring you something else, *danna sama*?'

'No, thank you, I will sit for a while. Please sleep now.'

Nashiba pressed the lightly-scented towel on to his face and let the heat sink in until the desperate desire to sleep subsided. Trusting Ishihara with details of the *Tsumi* had been a mistake. Not his alone, but a near-fatal mistake for all that. He had calculated that Ishihara would prove that much more malleable in the run up to *Tsumi* if he knew how much he stood to benefit from it. But this of all secrets should have been kept between the handful of those that unquestionably needed to know.

Nashiba fingered the white envelope in front of him. Why? What had rocked Ishihara's confidence, shaken his belief that he would be fairly dealt with? Whatever it was, it had made him feel threatened enough to resort to blackmail. The struggle for hegemony amongst the Families was often bitter; there was certain to be something to find. But never, even in the conceit of his wildest ambitions, could Ishihara have expected to discover something of this magnitude.

The old man smiled grimly to himself. Had the roles been reversed, he would certainly have considered using this information for his own gain. So what were his options now? He could comply. He could give Ishihara the financial guarantees he demanded in return for the damaging evidence he held. But one could never be certain that the man hadn't made copies of the tapes and transcripts as a fail-safe. And, in any event, his mouth would always be weapon enough. He could confront Ishihara head on, matching threat with threat. But Ishihara was a weak character, he might break under the pressure, decide there was so little to lose that he may as well tell what he knew.

Perhaps there was a middle course. A way of applying enough pressure to restrain and disarm Ishihara while offering a promising enough future to ensure his silence. But he would clearly have to be removed from government. The Families had spent billions of Yen over the past five years putting together a hand-picked political team to take the Japanese nation into the New Era. Ishihara could not now be left as its leader. Nashiba pondered the thought for a moment. Saburo Tanaka commanded enough respect in the cabinet to replace Ishihara. He could also keep the party united if it came to a vote of no confidence on the Diet floor. The Kugas were closer to him. They should make the approach.

Nashiba let his hands relax on the desk top. So, for now, the middle course was the option. But Ishihara would not yield easily. The ringing phone broke his concentration.

'I am ready, *Shacho*.' Matsuno's voice sounded weary. Nashiba got up at once, and, still wearing the silk bathrobe he'd had made for him in London's Savile Row, took the

193

elevator to his office. Each stage of the plan was set in his mind.

Matsuno started scrolling through the Hanaya Bank account displayed on the screen in front of him. 'It seems to be funded solely from the Freidler account in Switzerland.'

'That is correct. Take a look at the withdrawals – I think we'll find they're all in cash.'

Matsuno's fingers moved over the keyboard for a moment. 'Yes.'

'Good. Now, let us see who the lucky recipients of all this money have been.'

Matsuno's fingers moved over the keyboard for a moment. The names of the account's two signatories came up on the screen. He stared in disbelief; Itaro Ishihara and Isao Tamazaki, who for the last year had been Defence Minister. When he'd changed all the telegraphic transfers to the Freidler account into cash deposits, he'd noticed that all the money had come from a numbered bank account in Geneva, which he knew from previous transactions belonged to Nashiba. Now that link was erased. The only traceable credit was from Yamagata's slush fund. He let out an involuntary gasp.

Nashiba patted his shoulder. 'Young man, you've just earned yourself a fifty million Yen bonus.'

'Prime Minister!'

Ishihara rolled over, his face pressing into his wife's back.

'Prime Minister!'

Slowly the voice penetrated his semi-conscious mind. He sat up, felt for his glasses and squinted over the quilt. His valet stood in the doorway.

'I'm so sorry to disturb you, Prime Minister. Isao Tamazaki is on the phone. He says he must speak to you with the utmost urgency.'

'What time is it?'

'A little after five-thirty, sir. I took the liberty of making you some tea.'

Ishihara eased himself as quietly as he could from his

194

futon and struggled into his robe. He left the Nagata-cho apartment and passed into his private office. The voice at the other end of the line was barely recognisable.

'What in God's name have you been up to?'

'What're you talking about, Isao?'

'Haven't you seen the papers?'

'Papers?'

'The newspapers!' his Defence Secretary screamed. 'Haven't you seen them? The *Yomiuri Shimbun*'s saying we took bribes from Yamagata – that that's how they got the tank contract! The others are bound to follow and the TV people will be on to the story next. It'll be all over the fucking country by lunchtime!' The man at the other end of the line was starting to come apart. 'I didn't take any bribes. Just what have you been doing behind my back? They're saying we used the money as campaign funds . . . Don't you see? It's that damn Gift Fund of yours. They say it was Yamagata money . . .'

Ishihara spun round to his valet. 'Where are the newspapers?'

The valet started with surprise. He checked his watch. 'Why, they'll just have arrived, Prime Minister.'

'Bring them to me. Now.'

The voice on the phone had degenerated into sobs. Ishihara was impervious. His wits were at full gallop. What on earth could the *Yomiuri Shimbun* have got hold of? Some poisonous gossip from the opposition? No, no idle story would be strong enough to make the front page. Yamagata money? He'd never had so much as a Sen from Yamagata. The bank statements would prove that.

Bank statements.

His heart kicked so hard he felt like someone had applied an electric charge to his ribcage. His face twisted into a grimace as his stomach muscles cramped. Nashiba!

Ishihara sat in his chair, staring out at the same garden as he had seventy-two hours before, only now it was a make-up man who held up a mirror for him to inspect his work, not the hairdresser. No make-up could hide the strain and exhaustion on the gaunt face.

The Prime Minister closed his eyes and took several long deep breaths in an attempt to steady his nerves against the tramp of feet in the reception room above. This time, there were no caterers setting tables for a celebration. Just TV crews waiting to record the climax of the greatest reversal in contemporary Japanese politics since the Recruit Scandal of the eighties. Well, if they were hoping for an impassioned resignation speech, they were going to be disappointed, Ishihara thought. 'Keep it short. One simple statement,' his lawyers had counselled. That was exactly what they were going to get.

'*Dōmo.*' Ishihara waved away the make-up man at last. His secretary was already waiting in the doorway, Ishihara could see pale-faced members of his cabinet in the hallway behind.

'They'll be ready for you in ten minutes, Prime Minister.' He paused, wondering whether to go on. 'By the way, Nashiba Tatsuya-san phoned. He said he was certain you would wish to return his call.'

When Ishihara finally emerged from Nagata-cho that night he was a solitary, broken figure. The chauffeur and bodyguard, who had been at his side almost every day for three years, were shocked at the change in his appearance. He stooped as he walked, his head seemed to have shrunk into his shoulders. He managed a thin smile as he bent to climb into the black limousine.

Fifteen minutes later the car pulled into the forecourt of the Imperial Hotel. Ishihara lowered the glass partition between him and the two men.

'I'm sorry to spring this on you,' he said, 'but I'm going into the hotel on my own. I know this goes against every directive you've been given, but we all know that your responsibility for my safety ends at midnight tonight.' He glanced at his watch. 'It's eleven-forty. You can let me go now and get home to your wives a little earlier or we can all sit here like idiots for twenty minutes and then I'll leave alone anyway.'

The two men got out of the car and talked nervously for a moment while Ishihara waited in the back. Then his bodyguard opened the door and helped him out.

'Go quickly, Prime Minister. You don't want to be pestered . . .'

Ishihara thanked the men for their years of service, pulled on a battered felt hat, and hurried across the forecourt to the hotel. As soon as the limousine had moved off, he hailed a cab and headed west to the address Nashiba had given him.

The taxi drew up. If the driver recognised his passenger as he hastily paid his fare, he gave no indication. He eased the car into gear and pulled away.

The only part of the building visible from the road was the wide, low entrance to the garage. The steel door had been lifted. Isami Koto waited inside. This was the Prime Minister? he thought. Ishihara was smaller, older than Koto had imagined. The face he'd seen so many times on television seemed distorted now, as though an inner turmoil had in some way altered its very structure.

Koto had been Nashiba's aide for almost fifteen years. That he was an indispensable member of his personal staff had been demonstrated more times than the man cared count in the thoughtfulness and generosity that had been shown to him and his family over the years. His bond with his employer was an unusually strong one. In all the time he'd worked for Nashiba, Koto had never seen him look so distracted and preoccupied as he had in the last few days. The fact troubled Koto. However irrational the feeling, it seemed to him that in some way he was failing his *Shacho*.

He led Ishihara to the elevator. They descended three floors and stepped out into a corridor where Goro, the custodian of the building, took charge. He steered the *Shacho's* guest towards a set of high doors, put his weight against them and ushered Ishihara in.

A vast gallery, perhaps two hundred feet long, opened out before him, the walls lined with dark silk, the floor covered with tatami matting. Ishihara stooped and took off his shoes as custom dictated. The paintings on the ancient *Fusama* screens which were mounted at intervals along the walls showed scenes from legends dating back to Japan's earliest history. Nashiba legends, telling of a time when the dynasty were feudal warlords, Samurai warriors, Ronin outlaws. The lights above these screens provided the room with its only illumination, the areas between were shrouded in semi-darkness. Beneath each screen, rare ceramics were arranged on long, narrow tables, each priceless object turned to a precise angle, catching the light to its best advantage.

Beyond the screens were large, faded maps showing the boundaries of the Nashiba Daimiate at different periods in its history. Further on still, towering reliefs showed their massive network of banks, industrial complexes and real estate developments across the globe. As he walked slowly past them, Ishihara was certain that no eyes looked upon all this unless Nashiba himself had sanctioned it. And he was equally sure that the sanction was given to very few.

The Ishiharas, too, had their history, their legends, their empire but somehow, as he stood faced with the full might of the Nashibas, theirs seemed small, puny. It had been madness to challenge this man so openly, he thought. Here was power on a scale beyond anything he'd imagined. He knew his only hope now was to put himself entirely in Nashiba's hands. Perhaps for the good of the Families, the old man would find some way to turn the clock back a little, find some small part for him in the historic events ahead. Surely he had been punished enough.

His eyes had accustomed to the dimness of the light. Now, as Ishihara drew closer, he could see Nashiba sitting cross-legged at the far end of the room. He wore a dark blue kimono, its wide sleeves rhythmically sweeping the matting as he wrote. Ishihara stood a few feet off, waiting for acknowledgement. The minutes ticked by. Still the only sound was the whisper of brush on paper.

Suddenly Nashiba thrust his left arm forward, the palm of his hand outstretched. The action hit Ishihara like a smack in the face. For the first time in his adult life a man did not stand for him, did not allow him the opportunity to make a proper greeting. A new fear gripped him. To Nashiba he was a man without a face, a non-person. There was to be no forgiveness, just ignominy and obliteration.

His trembling hand placed a bundle of buff-coloured envelopes in Nashiba's upturned palm. Nashiba put down his brush to scan the contents: tapes and transcripts of Akitō's conversations with anyone of consequence during an eleven-day period earlier that month along with covering letters from Ishihara's New York agents. He turned the pages of the transcripts until he came to the section he wanted – the meeting between Yoshi and his son. The details of its location were inexact: 'Subjects met at 1170, Steinway Street, Astoria, Queens, NYC, New York . . .' He read on. Directional surveillance equipment placed them on the south side of the eighteenth floor. It was close enough. If she was still there, the Nisei would find her.

'I have instructed the agents in New York to send me all original tapes immediately.' Ishihara shifted nervously from foot to foot. 'They too will be forwarded to you, you have my word of honour.'

Nashiba's eyes locked with Ishihara's at last. The impassive look seemed to say, 'And how much is that worth now?' 'I shall do all I can to repair the damage that has been done, not for your sake but for the good of the Families and the alliance between them. Most of all, I will do it for your own family, upon whose name has been brought so much dishonour.'

There was some hope. Ishihara wiped the sweat from his palm on his trouser leg.

Nashiba's eyes returned to the transcripts. 'My car will take you to wherever you're staying tonight.'

The custodian had appeared in the doorway. Ishihara moved back over the tatami and into the elevator. As the doors closed, Isami Koto slipped into the gallery, removed his shoes and hurried to within a few feet of his employer. He kneeled down, bowed and waited. In the stillness of the room he watched Nashiba complete each Japanese character with infinite care. When he had finished, he put down his brush and sighed.

'Listen, Isami. Silence.' Nashiba closed his eyes as if he

199

could drink it in. 'It is such an elusive quality.'

Koto looked at his *Shacho*'s face. The normally smooth countenance was creased with wrinkles, the cheeks under the eyes smudged with black.

'And now, *Shacho*?'

Nashiba gave a shrug of indifference, a quick gesture of the hand that seemed to say, 'It is no concern of mine'. He made a short stiff bow. He had no more to say. Koto stood, bowed in return and withdrew. He was certain, now, who was responsible for his *Shacho*'s anxiety. By the time he stepped out of the elevator at ground level, his mind was made up.

Ishihara pushed his back into the plush seating of Nashiba's limousine and rubbed his face with his hands. For the first time that day he felt something like relief. Perhaps Nashiba would find a way of disentangling him from this mess, after all. He had what he wanted now. Perhaps . . .

A second before the door of the limousine closed, he heard the dull metallic clunk. Immediately his nose filled with a stinging, acrid smell. His eyes snapped open. A stainless steel canister the size of a Coke can lay inches from his feet, pouring out a cloud of gas. He threw himself against the car door. The handle thumped downwards, disconnected from the lock. Panic seized him. Through the glass he could see the face of Nashiba's aide, his features becoming indistinct as the gas overcame him.

A sudden jolt brought Ishihara out of a dreamless sleep. Above him the night sky blazed with starlight. There was the sensation of cold, the stink of rotting seaweed. He knew he was somehow naked, that three men were carrying him between them. He felt himself being lifted and thrown violently forward; the impact of hitting water. He tried to kick and strike out with his arms but his muscles wouldn't move. Again and again his brain sent commands to his spinal cord but his limbs failed to react. His still buoyant body broke the surface once. Koto watched dispassionately from the jetty. *Not so elusive, my* Shacho, he thought.

Ishihara's descent was so fast, little water seem to enter his lungs. *Not this way!* his mind screamed. *Not like this!*

Then his feet struck the stony bottom of Tokyo bay and the long business of dying by drowning began.

Saburo Tanaka's twenty-five-minute statement to a packed House of Representatives at the Diet Building had been interrupted by continual heckling.

'... And I can assure the House that any improper dealings between the Yamagata Corporation and the government were strictly limited to those of my late predecessor.' He continued over the noise. 'Although his decision to take his own life must leave some questions unanswered, there is no evidence to the contrary.'

The heckling grew louder. 'In conclusion,' he went on between the Speaker's pleas for order, 'in conclusion, I repeat that the recently announced Katana Tank Contract has been cancelled and all earlier deals made with the Yamagata Corporation are under review by an all-party committee ...'

'On one point at least, we are all agreed,' Nashiba noted in his diary that night, 'this Prime Minister must know nothing of *Tsumi* until the last move on the board has been played.' He laid down his pen with satisfaction. And now, he thought, we have Yamagata.

FOURTEEN

The gun-metal grey limousine was already waiting. Akitō pushed through the crowds spilling out of the Metropolitan Opera House to open the door.

'Come on, you two!'

Takuro Hamada took Bryony's arm, guiding her through the crush on the sidewalk and into the back seat of the car.

'The dancing was magnificent, of course, but the music's quite unremarkable.' Akitō opened the cocktail cabinet as the limousine pulled away. He poured everyone champagne. 'It always surprises me that *Giselle* has survived the test of time the way it has.'

Bryony sipped her drink. 'I enjoyed the music.'

'Well, as far as I'm concerned, Adolphe Adam fails the Harp-and-Oboe Test.'

'The what?' Hamada took off his glasses and looked at his cousin.

'Imagine a harp playing a rolling arpeggiated figure,' Akitō said. 'Behind it, barely audible, there's a blanket of muted strings. Then high above them, you hear the pure sound of an oboe, just hanging in the air. To me, it's one of the most emotive sounds an orchestra can make. But I know that if the composer fails to move me in the few bars that follow, then he never will. I hit that point twice tonight. Each time I thought, here it comes, that melody I'd forgotten was even from *Giselle*, the one that'll suddenly dissolve into something exquisite. Twice I was left feeling deflated, disappointed.'

'You're a hard man to please, Akitō.' Hamada poured himself more champagne.

'Perhaps Adam was striving for a purely textural effect,' Bryony offered.

'Oh you mean he could have passed the Harp-and-Oboe Test if he'd wanted to. There's proof of that in another work perhaps?'

Bryony paused for thought. 'Well, at this moment I can't think of any . . .'

'Aah!' Akitō was enjoying himself. 'And I'll tell you why. Nothing else of Adam's is played today. Apart from *Giselle*, he's forgotten. QED.'

The conversation continued as they were shown to their table at the Italian restaurant.

'Tchaikovsky can transport you six, seven times in the course of every ballet he wrote,' Akitō said.

'I'm always too busy watching the dancing to concentrate properly on the music.' Bryony sat down and unfolded her napkin. 'I had no idea you knew so much about music.'

'I don't. Not really. I play the piano a little.' Akitō was silent for a moment. He toyed with the breadstick in his fingers, watched the waiter pour the Frascati. Distant echoes.

'Excuse me a minute.' Hamada left the table and headed towards the men's room at the back of the restaurant.

'I listen to music in different ways,' Akitō went on. 'I might concentrate on the way the melody in the violins moves against the harmony in the violas and cellos; or the way a darting figure in the reeds adds excitement to the brass. A thousand ways. I like to understand what makes a piece of music work.'

They sat watching the other diners. 'What are you thinking?' Akitō said at last.

'Oh, that we've been out maybe a dozen times in the last three weeks. And that, apart from that first time, never on our own.'

'Takuro's family are in Tokyo,' Akitō said. 'He knows very few people here in New York. I just felt —'

'Can I ask you something?'

'Sure.'

Bryony's face showed the hint of a smile but there was

no amusement in her voice. 'Is Takuro a beard?'

'A what?'

Akitō's English was so immaculate that Bryony often forgot that it was not his first language. 'A beard: a man another man brings along on a date to make it look like the girl's not with him.'

'Ah.' Akitō put his hands together and studied the large violet eyes. 'You think I'm married, is that it?'

'I really have no idea.'

To tell Bryony that he was due to marry Miyoko Ishihara in less than six weeks' time was to end their relationship here and now. To lie was only to delay the same moment. But Akitō was not ready to let her go, yet.

'Well, I'm not,' he said, truthfully. 'Tomorrow night we'll go out to dinner, just you and me, I promise.'

She kissed him and immediately seemed to relax.

'Believe me, if I was going to employ the services of . . . a beard, I'd choose someone a little more discreet than Takuro,' Akitō said casually, making a mental note not to underestimate her again.

The Maître d' began reciting a detailed description of that evening's specials. But Akitō's mind was far away. It seemed an age since the April trip he'd made back to Tokyo to visit Miyoko. He'd spent 'Golden Week' – a period packed with public holidays – with her and her family. For the first four days he'd stayed at the Ishiharas' estate in Nagoya, discussing every detail of the forthcoming marriage. For the next six, he and Miyoko had scoured the four main islands of Japan, travelling from one plot of land owned by his family to another owned by hers, in search of the perfect site for their first country home together. They'd decided on building a property in Karuizawa and had spent the last week together in meetings with architects and landscapers. Akitō had been glad of the activity; the pace of events had denied him time to think. Work on the house had begun within a week of his return to New York in mid-May. Since then, Miyoko had called him almost daily with progress reports and queries regarding future work. Twice there had been talk of her flying in to spend some time with him, but the house was soon occupying her so completely that it had come to nothing. Secretly, Akitō had been relieved.

The Ishihara Scandal had attracted almost as much coverage in the US as it had in Japan. Itaro Ishihara was Miyoko's uncle. Akitō had called the Ishiharas the previous night to offer his condolences. The minute he'd begun to speak with Miyoko, he found himself enquiring whether her family would now be entering a long period of mourning, whether the wedding would have to be postponed. She'd said that from the little talk there'd been on the subject, her mother's view was the family had to be seen to be standing solidly together. To delay their marriage would only lead to speculation.

So he had six weeks left. Then he would honour the contract drawn up by his parents and hers when they were children. He'd marry Miyoko in a full Shinto ceremony in front of five hundred distinguished guests. After, like most Japanese 'salary men', he'd spend his evenings dining with male colleagues, seeing his wife for an hour at most before they went to bed. Like them, too, after a time, he would probably take a geisha to amuse and entertain himself and satisfy his wider sexual curiosity. When he returned to New York, Miyoko would accompany him. Perhaps there too, he would take some additional female company.

But it couldn't be Bryony. To pretend for a moment that a woman like her would consider such an arrangement was crazy. As he watched her now, enjoying her pleasure as she tried to choose between one culinary delight and another, he sincerely wished that the meal was already over. That he could settle the check, take her straight back to his apartment and make love to her. How would he face her with the truth in six weeks? How would he face it himself? He would lock the memories of their time together away in some part of him. He had no other choice. And, whenever life, lustreless life with Miyoko became intolerable, he would bring them out, relive each of them. And remember a time when he was truly happy.

*

205

The taxi pulled away down the battered back street. Cicero. It was a real classy district. Mack shoved his change into his pocket and headed towards the electrical store. The peeling paintwork looked like he felt, world-weary and neglected. He rang the bell. One long, two short. The clatter of heels told him Jay was on the way down. When he opened the door, he looked like a man who'd just seen the face of God.

'What's happened?'

'I've found the Land of Oz.'

'You crazy?'

'Come see for yourself.'

Jay leapt into his work-station chair. 'Did you get my smokes?'

Mack handed him the cigarettes and pulled a chair up to the computer. 'Okay. Go.'

'No, wait.' The hacker's hands were shaking so much he was having trouble lighting his cigarette. He inhaled heavily, his fingers poised over the keyboard like a virtuoso pianist. He looked at Mack and giggled. It sounded like he was on helium. He lifted an arm and stabbed a button on the CD player on the shelf above him. Suddenly, the Eroica Symphony burst through the room.

'You're out of your friggin' tree, you know that?' Mack yelled above the weight of noise. Jay punched three keys and sat back. The screen in front of him went black and then filled with vertical lines of Japanese characters.

'Here it is.' Jay's voice was barely audible through the Beethoven. 'Nashiba's Holy of Holies. The inner workings, the most intimate secrets of the only trillion-dollar corporation on the planet.'

Mack switched down the music. 'You're still on line?'

'What d'you want, they should get a trace on me? You got to duck and dive to stay alive in this business. This is a little something I down-loaded earlier.'

'You going to tell me you got a doctorate in Japanese, now? How in hell do you know what this stuff is?'

'Easy.' Jay put a disk in the drive and punched at the keyboard again. Within seconds, the screen split, lines of English text came up opposite the Japanese script. Mack

206

pulled his chair closer to the computer.

'Scroll up.'

Over the next few minutes, the pages of an in-depth financial report passed across the screen.

'Slow down, can you?'

'Sure, take your time. It's all good bedtime reading.' Jay stubbed out his cigarette on a rusty ashtray that had once displayed Jayne Mansfield's cleavage. 'You want a coffee?'

'Sure.'

Jay made his way to the kitchen while Mack went over the information on the screen. By the time the coffee came, he was no further forward.

'Can you print this stuff out? Can't make head or tail of it this way.' Jay nodded. 'What else is in here?'

'What do you think I am, psychic? Have you any idea how complex hypertext is?'

'If I knew what it was, I'd maybe sympathise.'

'Look, regular databases sort information according to pre-defined fields, you'd have to know where to look to find a record, else go through them alphabetically or numerically. Hypertext works more like the human brain, it links information through thought and idea association.'

'Like how, for instance?'

'It's like I say: Abraham Lincoln, you say: Gettysburg Address, or maybe: Civil War, or maybe: emancipation of slaves: or maybe: Ford Theater, assassination, John Wilkes Booth – any of those things. In an ordinary database, you'd have to search out all those links one by one, with hypertext, if you want to find out what Abe said at Gettysburg and why, you click your mouse on "Gettysburg" and Hey, Presto, you're offered a menu of related subjects, you pick "Address" and there's the whole text. Or if you decide you want to know more about the town itself, click, you got that too. You just keep on going into a labyrinth of detail.'

'No kidding.'

'There's only one problem.'

'What's that?'

'I don't know how much detail I got. I only stayed on line to the database for an hour, didn't want to give them too long to start tracing me. If the phone system wasn't so goddamned slow, I'd have been able to get a whole lot more.'

'So whatever we have here is only part of the story.'

'You got it.'

Mack walked over to the sofa and started to leaf through the printout. Half an hour later, he threw it on the floor and put his head in his hands. Why would Morton be so interested in an economic review of Peru? It was thorough, all right. A report on the current leadership; a review of the state of the economy; forecasts on inflation, the bank rate and the value of the 'New Sol' against a basket of currencies. After that, a tally of foreign aid received over the current decade and a schedule of the country's debts to foreign banks. Most of the figures were shown in Yen but Mack could approximate them closely enough to dollars in his head to get the general picture.

'So Peru's around twenty-seven billion dollars in hock,' he muttered. 'Nothing I couldn't get out of the *Wall Street Journal*.'

He turned back a couple of pages. 'With the economy in the state it is now,' the report concluded, 'it seems inevitable that the administration will be forced to default on the interest payments on its foreign debts within the next three months.'

Bet that was one the Peruvians were hoping to keep under their hats, Mack thought. *Result: zero credit rating and international blacklisting.* He looked up. Across the room, Jay was poring over a printout of the batchfile.

'Jesus, a brain that could figure a batchfile to get to the guts of a hypertext database . . .' he murmured.

Mack groaned. *C'mon Morton,* he thought, *give me a clue. What in hell am I doing here?* There was only one way, he'd have to take it apart for himself. He got up and walked over to Jay's work-station.

'You say this hypertext thing works like thought association?'

Jay nodded.

'Can you run this stuff up again?'

'Sure.'

The Peruvian data came back on the screen.

'Okay,' Mack said. 'Let's start with Development Loans.'

Jay rolled the mouse up the desk until the arrow on the screen moved on to that heading. He clicked the button. A window of text superimposed itself over the information on the screen – a schedule of countries whose banks had made loans appeared on the screen. Japan was listed last.

'All right, click on Japan.'

The database brought up a schedule of the payments made by a syndicate of banks to Peru over the previous twelve years. The amounts, as shown in Yen, had remained more or less steady over the years. Mack shook his head.

'How do you like that? The Japs keep telling us how they're pouring more into the Third-World pot than ever before but it's still a lot less than the other major powers.' Mack tried to clean the dried ketchup off Jay's calculator. 'What was the exchange rate ten years ago?' Stupid question, he thought. He took an educated guess, converted the figures in front of him, from Yen to dollars, and compared it with the current rate. He pushed the calculator under Jay's nose. 'See what I mean? It just looks like they're giving more because of the way the Yen's risen against the dollar.'

Jay shrugged. 'Can't get hung for that.'

'Turn a few pages, keep going, let's see what else we can find . . . Wait a minute, stop, go back.' He jabbed a pen towards the screen. 'Look, according to this, they were still making payments last week.'

'I bet someone got their butt kicked for that,' Jay said. 'It's just money down the toilet now.'

'No way, José. These guys run the slickest operation on the planet. They just don't make those kind of screw-ups. They'd monitor a tinpot régime like this twenty-four hours a day. So why do the banks give them another 200 million dollars in July when they know they probably won't be getting any interest back after November?'

'You tell me.' Jay snapped his fingers on the mouse. 'Who gives anyway? Let's move out of here, we ain't getting no place.'

'No, wait. I don't believe they'd pay out another penny if

209

they really thought the country was going down the tubes – there must be more to this. Let's find out who made the payment.'

When the window came up, it showed a syndicate of Japanese banks headed by Nashiba.

'I don't get it. The Japanese were bottom of the list five minutes ago.'

Jay clicked the mouse on the word Nashiba before Mack even asked. The file on the screen detailed the bank's internal negotiations on the development aid given to Peru over the years.

'Wake me up in the spring.' Jay stifled a false yawn.

'Have faith. Just let me read this.' *December, why December? The show'll be over by then.* 'Scroll forward to December, will you . . .' Mack blinked. 'Does that say what I think it says?'

'They've made a new deal, must have. Looks like a lot of dough.'

It made no sense at all. No bank was going to go on pumping billions into a country after it'd defaulted on its debts. He made a quick calculation. 'Our Peruvian buddies've just been promised around three billion dollars by these people.'

'Geesh, when I go bankrupt, this should happen to me.' Jay lit another cigarette. 'So what do the Jap banks know that we don't?'

'Beats me. I mean, warm-hearted philanthropy doesn't make good banking practice. A cynic would say they only have the aid programme they do to take the heat off public opinion over their arms build-up.'

'So they've got to be getting more out of this than the Mother Teresa Award for Brotherly Love.'

'You bet. I'd like to see where it's going. Let's look at the development programme for this place.'

A summary mentioned a hydro-electric plant tied in with an irrigation programme and two new hospitals.

'Very nice. Still doesn't tell us what's in it for them.'

'What do we do now?' Mack slumped back. 'Let's go back to the deal.'

Jay clicked the mouse at the corner of each window of information, closing them down one by one until he reached the Nashiba screen again.

'Looks like they signed the agreement in July.'

'And look who's doing the talking – Emilio Varas, ever heard of him?'

'Can't say I have.'

'President of the Republic to you and me, let's see what they've got to say about him.'

The profile that came up on the screen seemed to cover every aspect of the President's life in the minutest detail.

'Christ!' Jay said. 'They do their homework, I'll give 'em that.'

Mack was concentrating hard. 'Now there's something I'm interested in, his investments portfolio. Bring that up, can you?'

Jay clicked the mouse. 'This boy's in everything from futures to gambling clubs.'

'Okay, let's take a look at what he's got in real estate, shall we?' Jay carried on scrolling through the pages of information.

'Jesus, this is some document!'

'Yeah. If a dozen sets of eyes in the world have had sight of this data, I'd be very surprised. Okay, let's take Liquid Assets.'

The file showed substantial funds deposited in Geneva and the Dutch Antilles. Over seven hundred million dollars were deposited in the First City Bank of Illinois.

Jay whistled. 'Whew! Rich boy. I've heard of staying liquid, but . . .'

'He's not alone. This is what happens to a whole chunk of Third-World aid. Billions and billions of dollars' worth gets syphoned off from the treasuries of these places and after a bit of creative accounting, turns up again in the personal deposit accounts of the guys at the top.

'Hey, look.' The smell was starting to get to Mack again, he slapped a handful of mints into his mouth. 'See that? Varas closed the Bank of Illinois account in June and transferred the assets to a Yen account in the Nashiba Bank in

Tokyo. Interesting timing. Wonder who else's they've picked up recently. Go back to new accounts.'

'Nothing doing.'

'Right, try Third World.'

'Still nothing.'

'Can we get into development programmes from here?'

'Ring-a-ding-ding! Another delightful customer. Stand up, Colonel Juan Santiago . . . Holy shit! Look what Laughing Boy's been creaming off!'

'Yeah, and most of it's at the Farrell National, NYC. But if I'm reading this right it's set to move to Nashiba Bank, Rome Branch. There's the account number . . . but no date.'

'Looks like that's the deal,' Jay said. 'We give you development loans, you give us your bank account.'

'Doesn't equate. This is just a deposit account, a colossal one sure, but that's all it is at the end of the day. There's a lot of money in banking, but not enough to balance what the Japs are putting in the other end. This could be part of some sort of a pay-off but there has to be a lot more to it.'

'Let's see what else is on this file.' Jay went back to the top. 'Johnathan Ngeburi . . . Bank Accounts . . . Same info on him, whoever he is.'

'Ngeburi; president of Côte d'Ivoire.'

Jay studied the file. 'Seems he's got a nice little checking account in Tokyo, too.'

'But it was in the Pacific Interstate in LA three weeks ago.'

'Same pattern.'

'Not quite,' Mack said. 'Ngeburi's a Kaida Bank customer now. So why does he turn up in a Nashiba file?'

'They're keeping an eye on the opposition. That's the name of the game, believe me I know. A lot of the outfits I work for are as interested in the customers their competitors are losing as anything else. You can look at these things two ways. Kaida catches a big fish . . .'

'. . . The Pacific Interstate loses one. Now there's a thought. The Pacific Interstate.' Mack went back over to the sofa and picked up the Peru printout.

'That's what I thought, they're shown as one of Peru's big creditors.'

'Maybe . . .'

'Hold on, I'm thinking. I don't know whether Peru's intention to default is general knowledge yet. But I mean, what does a bank do, in practical terms, when they're faced with default on that scale? And what if they lose a nice fat deposit account like Ngeburi's in the same quarter? The Pacific Interstate's as solid as a rock, as far as I know. But the principle's an interesting one. Now if the bank concerned was say . . . The Southwestern — that's been tottering for a year . . .'

'Meltdown,' Jay said. 'But that's not what we've got here.'

'Dammit Jay, Morton's brought us here for something. Somewhere in this lot is — '

'Something worth more to Nashiba than Morton's life?'

'Gimme a cigarette, will you?' Mack hadn't smoked in ten years. He held the cigarette awkwardly as he took a light.

'So far, all we've got is three loaded despots who either have moved, or are about to move their money to Japanese banks.' He flung himself on to the sofa and started exhaling smoke slowly out of his mouth. 'There's no way that's a coincidence.'

It was late evening before Mack got to his feet. He couldn't figure which he was more sick of, trying to make sense of what he'd found or laying around in the stench of Pig Palace. He walked over to the apartment's one window and put his face up to the bars. The fumes that came up from the street hit his senses like a breath of fresh air. He took a big gulp. They had to have the answer. Had to. When he turned back into the room, Jay was still leafing through the printout of Morton's batchfile. Mack walked over.

'Can you really make sense of that stuff?'

'This ain't sense, Mack, this is brilliance.'

'Give me another cigarette will you?' Mack took a light. 'Look, I know I'll never understand computers like you do, but the answer must be in there somewhere.'

'Well, if it's any help, there is one thing that's been bugging me.'

'Why didn't you say so before?'

''Cos it's somethin' and nothin'. See this?' Jay pointed to a command line. 'These three letters here probably mean it's a graphics file. The rest are for text files for sure.'

'Do we have this?'

'Should have.'

'Well get it up, damn it.'

'It's not that simple, Mack. If this is a graphics file, it could be anything from a pie chart to an architect's plan.'

'I pick the plan – go to new developments.'

Fifteen minutes later they came to a file headed: 'Multifunctional Polis No. 8. All Phases.' Pages of graphics detailed the housing, factories and offices designated for a large section of real estate. Jay shifted the data sideways, scanning across plans for a rail terminal, a freeway overpass and a shopping mall.

'This is some project,' Jay said. 'Looks like one of these Third-World watering holes is going to get its very own Brasilia.' Jay started to enlarge part of the aerial view of one of the massive housing developments. 'I mean, look at this. You could house two, three million people in a city this size.'

In the centre of the screen now was an area of parkland with a golf course and other urban amenities. Dominating the whole was an irregular-shaped patch of water.

Mack jerked forward. That outline was engraved on his mind. 'Come in closer.'

Mack gripped the desk till the veins stood out of the back of his hands. As the outline grew, he could almost feel the pain in his ears. . . . *I'm travelling at 250 knots . . . 15,000 feet up . . . in a plastic tube flown by a paranoid schizophrenic . . . 'Warren! Bring her down!!'*

'Beaver Lake!' he yelled. 'It's Beaver Lake!'

'Jesus, what's the matter with you?' Jay grabbed a bottle off his desk and thrust it towards Mack.

214

'This ain't going to be in Brazil, pal. It's going to be right here in the US of A!'

'Give me a break.'

'I'm telling you, I know this place. Can you move on the plan the equivalent of about twenty miles southeast?'

'If the plans extend that far we can go there. What are we looking for?'

'I'll tell you when we get there.'

Simmond's airfield, Mack thought. *It was just marked with a number but that's what it was. O'Connor's Steak House.*

'Come a little further east . . . stay on the highway in the centre screen and come south. That's it . . .' Mack took a deep breath. 'Now run the translation program.'

There it was. The text read: 'Cedar View Development. Phase Three.'

'Come in real close, can you?' Warren's property wasn't hard to find. It was the only one with the tennis court and the corral at the end of a long lawn. As the plan enlarged, Mack could see the house had the name of the owner written against it.

Only it wasn't 'Steadman'. It was 'Fujikawa'.

As they pulled back on the map to take in the rest of the street and gradually the whole surrounding area, Mack could see that every house was labelled with the name of a Japanese owner.

'This isn't real estate development, Jay, not on this scale. It's fucking colonisation! You know what we're looking at, here? Nashiba City, USA.'

This called for a heavier level of nicotine. Jay reached for a half-smoked cigar, lit it and inhaled. 'And this time they didn't even need to bomb Hawaii.'

'And this is number eight?' Mack paused. '. . . So where the hell are the other seven? We got to know more. We got to go back into the database.'

'Not a hope. It's too risky. You know, all the time I was on line to that baby I was thinking, how come it's so easy, how come they don't cut me off . . . how come they didn't change Morton's entry code yet?'

'What are you saying?'

'I'm saying that an operation like Nashiba has got to have a data security system that Fort Knox'd be proud of. They'd update their entry codes all the time.'

'Maybe they figured Morton's code died with him.'

'Maybe. But the thought makes me nervous.'

The Nisei had already left. He would be in Chicago by midnight, local time. Tatsuya Nashiba lifted the fax as it fed slowly into the study of his Tokyo penthouse, folded it and turned back to the report lying on the bureau in front of him. It had to be dealt with now.

Yoshi had been in New York for three days. Operatives had finally traced her to the address in Queens. Nashiba went over the options again. She had been a threat for almost thirty years. At any point in that time she could have made this journey. At any point he could have ensured her silence. But even in moments when his worst fears had kept him from sleep, even now, with so much damage done, he was unable to make that call.

He took a sheet of paper and wrote: 'Maintain surveillance.' He folded his hands over it on the desk top. How different life might have been but for the hatred of the Tosas. It had changed so much that might have been. It would change much that was to come.

Part 2

FIFTEEN

21 December 1948

The Hong-Qui limousine rounded the wide bend in the Tokyo road and made the descent towards the bay foreshore. The Tosa Compound seemed larger to Tatsuya Nashiba, in the full light of day, than it had on that last journey three years before.

For seven months, twenty-four hours a day, teams of demobilised Japanese troops, many still in their uniforms, had laboured under American supervision to repair what had been forty miles of shell-holes and diversions. Now, every third vehicle that passed over the smooth concrete of this key route west carried the colours of the occupying forces. Nashiba had grown to accept them more than most.

In 1945, General Douglas MacArthur had stripped away the echelons of the Tojo Administration, leaving what remained of the old bureaucracy to squabble for a place in the new order. In the private sector, he set about breaking up the fifteen *Zaibatsu*, the huge financial combines and the old tenant farming system, both of which had been essential to Japan's war-time economy; a move which sent shock waves through the Four Families. But for the Nashibas, whose industries were not judged instrumental in involving Japan in the war, it was less of a blow than most. And their chief concern, the bank, remained untouched. So, as America's policies turned slowly from purging a defeated Japan to rebuilding it, new and different opportunities began to present themselves. Tatsuya Nashiba made good use of this time.

'If, as Napoleon said, the British are a nation of shopkeepers,' he told executives of the family's numerous manufacturing subsidiaries, 'then Americans are a nation of customers. Get to know your customer, learn from him, earn his respect and you'll make your sale.'

In the winter of '46, Nashiba had been among the first Japanese to dine with MacArthur when he moved into his new headquarters almost opposite the Imperial Palace in Tokyo. He was young, tirelessly energetic and spoke perfect English. He'd spent the war years doing nothing more sinister than manufacture the fuel gauges, speedometers and dynamos the military needed. His Princeton education, his background in banking, coupled with a passionate belief in the reconstruction of his country for peaceful co-existence with its neighbours, made him a natural choice for the Allies as one who should have a say in the shaping of the new Japan.

For three years, Nashiba worked hard to make himself useful. There were times when he was seen to be so firmly in their camp that the fragile bond he had established with the Tosas, Kugas and Ishiharas became stretched to the limit. Yet he often used his special relationship with Mac-Arthur for the betterment of all. In time, he knew, they would come to see things in a larger perspective, they would come to see, as he did, that the sooner the Japanese economy was rebuilt and the country self-sufficient again, the sooner the Allies would be gone.

The Hong-Qui moved forward into a courtyard on the western edge of the compound. The chauffeur drew it alongside the other limousines that were parked there. Takashi Tosa had been watching anxiously for this arrival. Every minute that passed brought his father closer to death. And as much as he hated Tatsuya Nashiba, he was the only man who could save him now.

Nashiba stepped from the car. He knew well enough what Hiromi Tosa would ask of him and he already knew the reply. Tosa might be old but he had more cunning in him than all the other Clan heads put together. Nashiba would have to move with the greatest care.

*

220

'I think it's done, Sarge.'

Master Sergeant Victor Crenna walked back to the large aluminium pot boiling on the gas range and peered in.

'No, let it stew a little longer. You can't rush these things.'

'Well, so long as it don't spoil.'

'It won't.'

He walked back to the door and lit another cigarette. Through the railings he could see two small Japanese boys playing amongst the rusty wrecks of cars on the other side of the road. One was in the driver's seat of what had once been a family saloon, turning the disconnected steering-wheel frantically, an expression of deep concentration on his face. The other sat in the remnants of a vehicle which wobbled dangerously across the trunk of the first, a competitor in an unwinnable race of his own imagining.

Strange, Crenna thought, up until last week the Japanese were just the alien species he'd seen on the newsreels. Creatures who could move through the jungle unseen and unheard; who showed no fear and no mercy; who, out-flanked, would fight on to the last then stand in a hail of bullets defiantly screaming, '*Banzai!*'

Yet, in this past week, his first brush with the Japanese on their home-ground had shown them to be a people much like any other. Industriously attempting to rebuild their shattered homes, waiting patiently in line for the basic commodities of life, trying to re-find one another in body and spirit.

'It's had forty minutes now,' Rawlins called from the kitchen.

'Okay, turn it off.' Crenna stubbed out his cigarette. The boys across the road had finished their game and sat eating rice cakes on the kerbside. They reminded him of his sister's kid.

The Sergeant walked back to the cooker, took the wooden tongs from the sink and put them into the bubbling water. Rawlins held the pot steady as he lifted the end of the one-inch manila hemp rope and pulled it out across the

221

length of the kitchen, till eighteen feet of it lay on the tile floor.

'That's the last of 'em.'

When it cooled they carried it out to lie on the grass next to the six others. Crenna knelt down and turned a length of one of the dry ones through his hands. The springiness and stiffness had gone. Put it up to stretch overnight, it would do the job nicely. He'd never offed four at once before. He'd done the Pagett brothers before the war but that had been one at a time. Four and three, that's what the orders were. They didn't want a replay of the Nuremberg mess, dragging on for over two hours, each condemned man having to wait his turn. It wore on everyone's nerves. Apart from that, all the normal procedures applied. Each prisoner was to be weighed and the 'drop' calculated exactly. Too short, and he'd strangle to death, kicking and jerking for twenty minutes while the body voided itself of fluids. Too long, like the Johannson screw-up in '39, and the prisoner's head'd tear clean off his shoulders. As little as six inches could make the difference. Crenna liked to get these things right.

The top brass had given a great deal of thought to Crenna's assignment to this project. The eyes of the world had been on Japan's war crimes trial and the seven who were now set to die. Crenna was an experienced professional, he'd lost no blood relative in the war and he'd had no direct involvement with the Japanese himself. He was as impartial and dispassionate a man as could be found in what could truly be described as a dying profession.

He'd been in the country only forty-eight hours when he met his clients. After his initial briefing by the Commandant of Sugamo prison, newly renamed US Army XI Corps Stockade No. One, he'd made his way to the ugly, squat building in the centre of the prison complex where the condemned men were housed. Crenna only ever saw his clients twice; once at the 'weigh-in' and once in the death house. That day, a weighing machine had been set up in the exercise yard outside. The prisoners stood in a ragged line, eyeing the machine as though it was the gallows itself.

Crenna recognised Tojo immediately. It was hard to believe the drab, ineffectual-looking man had been overlord of the greatest empire the Japanese had ever known, that any of the seven had been the swaggering martinets who had brought devastation and terror to the peoples of the East on a scale beyond any of the great oppressors of ancient times. Dressed in their shapeless, grey prison uniforms, stripped of all that had made them mighty, they were just seven weary old men, shuffling aimlessly through the leaves with nothing more to occupy their minds than the next meal and the next game of Go.

And dying. That day, they'd really started to think about that one. You could see it in their faces. It was no longer just a distant possibility, to be faced if the worst came to the worst. Crenna took his time as he weighed them, meticulously noting the results in his book. The prison doctor was getting more irritable by the minute.

'It would be a lot quicker if I did this,' he announced. 'These men are getting cold standing here.'

Hell, we mustn't have that, Crenna thought as he slid the smallest of the chrome steel weights a notch further along the balance, *got to have 'em all bright-eyed and bushy-tailed for their big day.* He'd come up against jerks like Benchley before. To them Crenna was some kind of salaried psychopath, getting paid to do what other men got fried for.

Crenna turned to look at the thin, colourless face. He was one of those creeps whose Adam's apple went up and down when he talked. You didn't know whether to look at his puss or the stupid thing in his neck. *Okay, Bub,* Crenna thought, *if you're so big on the sanctity of life, what are you doing pitching on this team? Cry off or stay out of my hair.* All he said was, 'You do your job, Benchley, and I'll do mine.'

'I know the regulations. I was just trying to speed things up, that's all.'

So, you know the regulations, huh? We'll see. He wrote into his notebook in a clear, legible hand, 'Prisoner Number Four: a hundred and thirty pounds.' That was a drop of seven foot. Seven. He'd check it later in the manual, always did, but it was just a formality. Number Four had been putting on a good show. But really he was crapping himself, fretting away something terrible. *Cheer up, fella*, Crenna thought, *soon be dead.*

'Next!'

Hiromi Tosa was propped up in a chair against a large yellow silk cushion, his eyes closed. It seemed to Nashiba, as he entered the wide conference room, that the old man had not long since risen from his futon, had perhaps dressed just for this meeting. Nashiba took his place at the square table where his father had sat three years before and waited. The frail fingers came up to meet the face and flicked away a fly.

'As you see, Tatsuya, I am unwell ... But even if I last the week, it seems I shall outlive my son.' The eyes opened. They were watery and weak, filled with pain.

'My family were deeply shocked when we heard of the US Supreme Court Decision this morning. If they have no power to set aside these sentences, who does?' The question was purely rhetorical.

'If they believe in the Geneva Convention as much as they say, they must spare my son anyway. He is sick, Tatsuya. Not in body but ... in mind. The strain of the trial, the accusations, the waiting ... it has disturbed the balance of his mind.'

Tosa's bony finger moved along the deep furrow in his forehead. 'He has never coped well under great stress. Even as a child he would lose the ability to distinguish between the real world and an imagined one. He is fast retreating to a place in his mind where he feels safe ...'

The picture of the fragile psychotic that Tosa painted jarred with the image Nashiba had of the man. His earliest memories were of a posturing bully, barking orders at everyone in a tone usually reserved for the lowest servant. But his view of Shigeru Tosa's role in the war was, like much of his philosophy, devoid of sentiment or morality. It was, though, touched by a grim truth. At the height of the international trial of Japanese war criminals, in 1946, he'd written in his diary:

'Violence is a part of man's behaviour. It is as integral to his nature as feeding, sleeping and procreation. Used in a controlled manner, it is often effective. History has shown us only that those who take acts of violence beyond accepted boundaries, when their own history may yet be rewritten, do so at their peril.'

Shigeru Tosa, like millions of his generation, had believed that the peoples of the conquered territories were no more than sub-human waste . . . 'little stones to be kicked'. As the trial went on, the chronicles of savagery that unfolded seemed to belong more to the times of Genghis Khan than that of a civilised race existing in the twentieth century. Whole families buried alive in Manchuria; others shot, bayoneted and decapitated in their thousands. Prisoners of war starved and worked to death on the Bataan Railway. Others in New Guinea, eaten by their captors. Rape, torture and mass murder, developed almost into an art form. The catalogue of carnage consumed tens of thousands of pages of affidavits and transcripts. In modern history, only crimes committed under Hitler's Third Reich stood equal in bestiality to those perpetrated under the Tojo Administration.

Nashiba watched the trial with detached interest and noted: 'No totalitarian régime in the last hundred years has outlasted living memory; no act has been totally erased by time. There are always those left after the fall, who will be brought to book for their actions and the actions of others.'

Shigeru Tosa, he knew, was one of these. But his personal opinion of the man and his crimes was not at issue. What was at issue was the relationship between the Nashibas and Tosas, the joint architects of the alliance of Families. The question came at last.

'Time is very short now. Somehow General MacArthur must be apprised of my son's condition. Our family name has become sullied by the accusations against him, I believe any intervention on our part would be cast aside. But I'm told that you have MacArthur's ear. Therefore, I ask you . . .' the voice wavered, 'I beg of you, intercede for him.'

Nashiba paused long enough to seem to consider the request.

'I shall do whatever I can, of course. But I must warn you that it is possible that MacArthur's hands are tied on this matter.'

'This matter is of his making.' The old man's eyes blazed. *'How can it not be within his power to reverse his decision? Is he not appointed Supreme Allied Commander in Japan?'* He dug his knuckles into the table and forced himself to his feet. 'Shumei Okawa was declared unfit to stand trial, why can't my son be seen, now, by the same psychiatrists and be declared unfit to die!' His hand slammed down on to the table. *'How can he have lost that right? How can he?'*

Nashiba watched the old man. Each desperate entreaty seemed to use up some part of his very life-force.

'I have no answers to these questions, Hiromi-san,' he said gently, 'I will see General MacArthur tonight, you have my word, and I shall tell him all you have said.'

'My second son died in Singapore. My third, on Okinawa.' Tosa sat down slowly, closing his eyes again. 'Surely my family has paid price enough.'

Shigeru Tosa leaned forward and retched into the bucket in the corner of his cell. There'd been a time when he'd wondered why men found the prospect of death so terrifying. Now he knew. He'd been in Burma, on the main route north from Rangoon, when he'd first heard it, the sound of grown men, shrieking hysterically. It was a little market town called Thazi. Three hundred prisoners had been herded into the cattle pens. Two men with *katana* swords had been executing them for six hours. By the time his car stopped for refuelling, there were still a hundred or so left waiting to die. He'd got out of the car to stretch his legs. He remembered, the noise from the cattle pens had been unlike anything he'd heard in his life. Some men were throwing their arms upwards to the sky as they cried for the compassion of Heaven; some were sobbing uncontrollably, tearing at their hair; some bayed like dogs. Did they have no dignity, these men, he remembered thinking, no self-respect? They had been offered an honourable death, death by decapitation, and they were behaving like animals, creatures unworthy of pity.

'This is a disgraceful exhibition,' he'd snapped at the officer in charge. 'These men do not deserve such niceties. Dig a pit, here in the square and throw them all in. A few feet of mud will soon stop their caterwauling.'

But he was the one who could have caterwauled now. Now he knew exactly how it was to feel the minutes of your life ticking away. His would not be an honourable death. He would be hanged, strung up, like a carcass in a slaughterhouse to strangle and drip. It was a disgusting way to die.

Tosa looked at the single bare bulb in his cell. It would go out in less than an hour and his last full day of life would be over. No one would come now. He was not even sure any more he could pull it off if they did.

The shaking began again, and the cramps. He'd never known such stomach pain. Tosa climbed back on to the bed. He had no way of knowing how long he'd been staring at the grey wall opposite when he heard the sound of keys in the steel door. Standing in the doorway were the prison Commandant, the doctor and an interpreter.

They'd come. At last they'd come.

'Who are you, can I help you?' There was a curious child-like quality in Tosa's voice. The doctor moved forward and put a stethoscope inside his shirt. 'Am I to be moved now?'

The interpreter translated the question.

'Yes.'

'Hai.'

'By special order of General MacArthur?'

'Yes.'

'Hai.'

Benchley removed the stethoscope and bound the man's arm to take his blood pressure.

227

'I'm glad I'm being moved. It's too noisy here.' Tosa prattled on in as detached a way as possible. 'The guards do it on purpose, you know, to keep us awake. Did you know that?'

The interpreter made no attempt to translate.

Life, Tosa thought. *Life in a prison hospital, for the rest of my days perhaps, but life nevertheless.*

Two prison guards moved into the cell and handcuffed him between them, then the party moved out into the square. Tosa could see the gates that led to the main prison across the exercise yard. Somewhere in there was the hospital. The Commandant, the doctor and the interpreter moved on ahead.

'Is it warmer where I'm going? I hope it's warmer.'

Takashi Tosa picked up the ringing phone.

'I finally got through to MacArthur at three. He promised to come back to me within the hour.' Nashiba sounded sincere enough. 'I called his headquarters at five and the residence at seven. They say he's tied up. It could be true, either that or he's just not taking my calls. I'm afraid all I can do now is wait by the phone.'

'Thank you, Tatsuya, we'll be waiting for your call.' Takashi put down the phone. *So, my father is to die at noon tomorrow and I have to take the word of Tatsuya Nashiba that General MacArthur is too busy to consider a reprieve*, he thought. He'd seen the way Nashiba ingratiated himself with the Allies, laughing at their flat jokes, running to their beck and call. And he'd done everything possible to distance himself from the atrocities issue. The word was that Nashiba had some big deal going through with the Allies at that very moment. Was he going to jeopardise that for the life of a Tosa?

Takashi didn't trust him, never had. And now events were playing out exactly as he'd predicted they would. He'd decided on a secondary course of action days ago, and now that Nashiba's gambit seemed doomed to fail, he set it in motion. He picked up the telephone and dialled.

228

'Phil Bracken, please. It's Takashi Tosa . . . No, I'll wait. Perhaps you'll tell him I'm holding.'

There were ways to get to MacArthur. This route was messy, Takashi thought, but at least it'll take me where I need to get.

Phil Bracken had been brought in as a consultant engineer on a US-inspired project to convert one of the old Tosa tank factories into a plant to produce tractors. Takashi had never been able to establish whether he'd been picked because he spoke some Japanese or because his uncle was a senior aide to MacArthur. But he'd taken the opportunity to get to know Bracken anyway. A year later, the young American'd asked Takashi to make a few connections he needed, real bad. He'd been only too pleased to help out . . .

You had time enough to talk to me when you needed a boy and somewhere discreet to take him, Takashi thought as he waited. *Away from the military base and that thin-lipped little wife. At times like this, even discretion has its price, I'm afraid.*

'. . . You're out of your mind if you think I'd get involved in this.' The voice on the other end of the line sounded scared.

'Look, Bracken, get your uncle to take my call. Believe me, the last thing I want to do is to have to go shooting my mouth off . . . He's my last chance, don't you see?'

Within minutes of Takashi's call to the MacArthur head-quarters, Major General Bracken was on the line. Judging by the tension in the man's voice, his nephew had had to tell him a whole lot more than he'd wanted. Takashi tried to sound calm.

'Tatsuya Nashiba tells me that he has already brought this matter to the General's attention. He promised to look into it immediately but we're still waiting for his call.'

'I can assure you that no request for a psychiatric report on this prisoner has come through this office,' came the curt reply.

MacArthur had made fools of them, Takashi thought,

told Nashiba whatever he needed to hear to get him out of his office.

Or Nashiba had lied and done nothing.

'I'm sure your nephew has explained that my father's mental condition has deteriorated rapidly in the last two weeks. Time is now very short as you will appreciate, but if there is any way that you could reach General MacArthur and put the facts before him . . .'

'I can't guarantee anything. But I'll do what I can.'

'When will you call back?'

'When I've got a goddamn answer, that's when! And let's get one thing clear. Whichever way this goes, Tosa, after tonight I never want to hear of you again this side of the grave.' The line went dead.

December 22 1948 dawned cold and overcast. The shrivelled, brown leaves of the Paulownia tree that grew in the corner of Sugamo prison were blown in gusting winds across the empty courtyard that separated the prison block from the death house. The light had blazed there since early morning as Sergeant Crenna and his team checked every detail for the day's events.

At 11.00 a.m., Crenna completed his final checks. The knot for each noose was correctly tied and greased. He knew that, he'd done it himself. The drops he'd calculated when he'd weighed the prisoners had been checked against his notes and the army's Manual of Procedures for Military Executions. Each rope-end had been bound to a shackle with cord and slung on to a hook which was bolted through the crossbeam of the gallows. Each rope had been coiled until the noose hung at the correct height and held in position with button thread which would break the instant the trap was sprung. If the knot of the noose had been arranged correctly behind the prisoner's left ear, it would throw back his head and snap the cervical column in half a second. A certain amount of nervous and muscular reaction that could be mistaken for life would go on for three or four minutes

230

afterwards, but Crenna would know his clients had died quickly.

At 11.15 the trap was loaded with sandbags, tested twice and declared ready. Crenna stooped to lay four aluminium coffee-trays on the concrete floor in a neat line under the nooses. The final touch. Satisfied that everything was in order, he turned and walked out across the prison yard. The four representatives of the Far East Commission were taking their positions against the west wall. At least Mac-Arthur's ban on press photographers had cut the numbers of spectators to a minimum, Crenna thought. Across the frozen exercise yard in the hastily converted chapel, Crenna could see four men kneeling in a haze of incense while the Japanese chaplain chanted prayers. He wondered what god would bend to hear them.

Crenna could see Number Four clearly now. That's how he liked to think of them. One to Four; Five to Seven. The prisoner's face was ash-white. Crenna took a good look. Yup, just as he'd thought. Four had been fretting away something terrible. Must have lost five, maybe six pounds. Crenna walked back across the yard to the death house. The prison doctor was standing inside the door talking to the Commandant, his bony Adam's apple going up and down like a monkey on a stick. *Okay, Doctor I-Know-The-Regulations Benchley*, Crenna thought, *what about Section D, Sub-section 19. Remember that one? 'Cos when Number Four goes down, you're going to fold up like a deckchair. You just don't know it yet.*

Hiromi Tosa lay on his futon, a dark silk quilt wrapped around him. His wife held his hand gently to her chest. The sedative the doctor had given him had slowed his pulse to such a low rate, she counted each beat as it came. Takashi's brother, uncles and cousins knelt in rows at the other end of the room, swaying as they chanted the Mantra. He looked sadly at the thousand paper cranes that had been brought in to stay the forces of death. It would take more than a flock of origami birds to stop his grandfather's spirit slip-

231

ping away. Takashi took the old man's hand and pressed it to his face. He was trying to speak. Takashi bent closer.

'Whatever MacArthur decides, your father is gone from us. Through these years when we had most need of him, he will be lost in body, perhaps in spirit too.'

'There is still time, Grandfather.'

The old man sucked a breath in through his teeth in an audible hiss. 'Your uncle will take your father's place as head of the family for a time. And then it will fall to you to take charge.' There was a long pause before he spoke again.

'The alliance of the Four Families is vital to us all. You must hold it together at all costs.' He held Takashi with a steady gaze. 'I believe in this plan of Nashiba's, this *Tsumi*. Whatever your personal feelings for him, or the others you will have to work with, set them aside. When *Tsumi* is complete, there will still be many centuries left to settle old scores.'

'If it is your wish, Grandfather.'

'Remember the story of the arrows.'

Takashi squeezed the frail hand he held in his own and nodded. The story had been repeated to him often in his childhood. In ancient times, it ran, a feudal lord called his three sons together and asked each of them to break an arrow. They did so easily. But when he gave each three arrows and asked them to break them all at once, none could do it. 'A single arrow breaks without much effort but three arrows at once will not,' the feudal lord said. 'The same is true of human beings. You three must join together to preserve the Family.'

Takashi's wife appeared in the doorway and signalled him to come. When he looked down again, the old man's eyes were closed.

'I will, Grandfather,' he whispered. 'I will.' He got to his feet and crept out to join her.

'There is a phone call for you,' she said, 'a Major General Bracken . . .'

Takashi moved so fast he almost tripped over the little

girl who had rushed up to clasp his knees. He pushed her gently away.

'Not now, Yanagi darling. Go back to Mama, Willow, there's a good girl.'

The three prisoners stood in position on the trap, their arms and ankles pinioned with leather straps. They fought to keep their composure as Crenna strapped up his last prisoner.

Number Four: General Shigeru Tosa. *The fretter*, Crenna thought. *Tosa was chicken-shit. Knew that the first day. Funny, he'd been a real big noise too. You could just imagine him, strutting up and down on his little bandy legs handing out the crap.*

Crenna pulled Tosa's arms in nice and tight. The man was shaking so much he could hardly close the buckle on the strap.

I mean one word from Chicken-Shit here and heads rolled. They'd rolled in the dust right across China and Indo-China, right to the borders of India itself. So the indictment said.

Crenna marched his prisoner up the scaffold's thirteen steps and stood him on the end of the trap, in front of rope four. He bent to strap up Tosa's ankles. Hell, this was the boy who came up with the idea for reprisals after the Battle of Midway. Twenty POWs, picked from a score of camps at random, marched out into the compound and beheaded. Whack. No waiting. He knew. His sister's husband, Eddie, had been one of those four hundred. They still hadn't found what was left of him. Probably never would.

Crenna pulled the strap tight. *Shake away, Chicken-Shit,* he thought, *I'd take an evens bet that Eileen's sitting up in bed, right now, sobbing her heart out. Her boy'll never know his Daddy thanks to you.*

Crenna could feel Number Four's ribs as he re-positioned him. *But you know what? Everyone gets lucky once. An' I got lucky. 'Cos I got you.*

He put the noose over the prisoner's head and pulled the

233

knot up tight under his left ear. *I can't dance on your grave, you fucking bastard,* he thought, *so you're going to dance on your own.*

The split second before he stepped back, Crenna shot a glance towards Benchley. *Section D, Sub-section 19,* he thought. *'It is the doctor's responsibility to notify the officer charged with the execution of the order, of any change in the prisoner's bodyweight which should occur prior to the date of execution.' That's what it says, Benchley. What it doesn't say is that if the prisoner isn't eating, it's kind of smart to have him reweighed before the hanging. But you ain't smart, Benchley. And I'm clean as a whistle. Everything by the book.*

The prisoners were ready. Crenna put his hands to the steel lever that extended from the floor and waited for the order. His eyes never left Number Four. When the Commandant's command came he was good and ready. He pulled hard.

Here's lookin' at you, kid.

SIXTEEN

7 August 1995

Another night at Pig Palace was too much to face. Mack left Jay still picking through the Nashiba data late Friday night, took a cab to the Chicago Hilton and slept undisturbed. He spent most of Saturday with his accountant and his attorney, reshaping his life. Laurie had moved Raskin into the Oakdene house. Accepting his offer to buy out Mack's equity in the place would cut the umbilical cord that held him to Chicago.

That night, Mack dined with his mother at the apartment that had been his home until he was seventeen. They ate early, as they always had, and went for a drink. Cassidy's on State Street played Sinatra, Andy Williams and the occasional restrained Presley classic on continuous loop tapes. It was his mother's sort of place. So they sat punctuating the embarrassed silence between them with small talk. Mack looked at his mother's glass. She was still nursing the same gin and tonic he'd bought when they first walked in. Any time now she'd be ready to go home. He couldn't say he was sorry.

At ten, Mack walked his mother home and went back to the bar for a nightcap. He'd had a basinful of the past. He was certain now. The Chicago chapter of his life was over for good.

When the flight from O'Hare taxied down the runway late Sunday afternoon, Mack found himself counting off the seconds till it lifted into the air and headed east towards Kennedy. Looking out of the window into the unblemished blue above the clouds, he thought about Auburn in clear terms for the first time. She was very much her own woman. Yet under it all there was a vulnerability that touched off something special in him – the protectiveness that for him, at least, had occasionally led to something meaningful. Auburn could have been the first woman after Laurie or the fortieth, but the fact that she touched that vital part of him was not to be discounted or cast aside lightly.

Mack hurried down the travelator that led out of the domestic air terminal clutching his mobile phone. Auburn was out. He pushed it back in his pocket; should have called her before he left. As he stepped into a cab, he realised that in the back of his mind, he hoped she'd be waiting.

Auburn's apartment was bathed in bright sunlight. Mack flung down his attaché case, glad to be back.

'Want a Coke?' The voice from the kitchen took him by surprise.

'You're here.' Mack walked through to the kitchen. 'I tried to call you from the airport but there was no reply.'

'I was washing my hair.' She offered him a drink with an ironic smile.

'I take it I'm in trouble,' he said and pulled up a chair.

'You bet.' Auburn took a gulp of her Coke. She stood for a second before putting her glass down on the table. Then she stooped and gave him a long, warm kiss. Suddenly, she slid to her knees and kissed him again, moving her hands down over his hips, opening his pants and caressing him gently. Mack leaned back. Her lips left his and closed around his erection, her mouth soft and warm. He was filled with a delicious excitement. He reached down and stroked her hair, the texture of her wild curls heightening his enjoyment.

When she was ready, Auburn moved away and stood up again. Mack made to push his pants off. She waited a second, then straddled him, lifting her wide, red skirt provocatively as she did so. Then he saw why. Under the skirt, she was completely naked. The thrill of her nudity melted seamlessly into the sensation of her slow descent. Mack watched her slip the tight, white top over her head, then

236

the skirt. He kissed her breasts as she stripped away his shirt, grasping her waist, pulling her closer.

Their bodies locked in an ecstasy of motion; all thought shut out, all time obliterated, until, complete, they clung to each other, silent.

Monday breakfast was more of a brunch. Mack took a bite out of his bagel and tried to concentrate on the half-year report that the headhunter acting for NBS Television had sent him. If he was going to meet their Senior Vice-President this morning, he'd better make it look good. And Saul Leibersen was something of a legend. He'd run NBS for a quarter of a century. Worked his way up from floor manager to producer in the mid-fifties. Within a decade, he'd helped change the whole shape and direction of net-worked television. And, if the half-year report was anything to go by, he was still holding his own.

Auburn walked in from the kitchen with a fresh pot of coffee. 'D'you remember Zack Latimer, the guy who gave Dad's eulogy?'

'Sure.'

'Well, he knows the owner of the Sheldon Gallery. He's bringing him over this afternoon to take a look at my work.'

'That's great.'

'Only if he buys something.' Auburn looked serious. 'At least Zack's given me a commission. He wants me to paint his new racehorse.'

Mack brushed the breadcrumbs off his suit pants, stood up and put on his jacket. 'Well, I'm going to go see if I can't get working again too.'

'Oh? Anything special?'

'The dazzling world of television.' Mack bent to kiss her, letting a hand wander over her thigh.

'Hold it, handsome,' she grinned. 'They're still working on the damage down there.'

*

237

Saul Leibersen re-read the first few lines of the CV that lay on his desk.

'I think Drummond were lucky to hold on to you as long as they did, Mack.'

'I like to see something through to the end, Saul, it screws up a lot of options.'

Leibersen opened a drawer in his desk and took out a VideSet. 'I like the way this was marketed. Very smart, good short-term move.' He put the black box on the table in front of him. 'It's Leibe, by the way. What I got here, Mack, is long-term, HDTV. The networks are fighting for their lives these days, I'm sure I don't have to tell you that. But the technology for the high definition system is still out of the ball park, financially, for anyone else. This is their big opportunity to build a new audience.'

'I don't think the heightened picture definition is the only turn-on for consumers,' Mack said. 'The aspect of it that catches the imagination is in the wide screen ratio. The idea of being able to watch a seventy millimetre feature in your own home, in movie theatre quality, without a quarter of the frame being lost at each end. Though, I guess with sets retailing at around six thousand dollars, some folks are going to have a long wait.' Mack took a breath. 'The initial market has got to be in VCR and home video. The FCC plan to choose a "simulcast" system for transmissions, utilising currently unusable channels. You're looking at the options right now because you intend to be the first off the mark with a limited service of programming starting in ninety-eight.'

Leibersen's smile faded. 'How the hell did you know that?'

'I didn't. You just told me.' Mack shrugged. 'Why else would you be talking about HDTV to someone like me? The date was just a guess. It's the earliest anyone could have the technology in place in this country.'

Leibersen smiled. 'I'm looking for a market strategist and they send me a smart ass.'

'Second City smart ass.'

'Well, you check out every which way, Mr Lasky, so maybe that's what I need.'

Leibersen opened a fat file on his desk. 'Next year we're shooting two mini-series, five feature-length subjects, three prime-time series and three documentaries in the new system. The year after, double. By 1998 we'll be able to offer six hours of continuous transmission, nightly.'

'You're going to have one hell of a job pacing media growth rate to sales of the hardware.'

'That's exactly why we want this thing packaged and marketed properly. We need an awareness campaign aimed at all the groups involved, not just the public. The media, the manufacturer, the retailer, even the reactionary elements inside the network itself.

'This isn't just about television, not in the end. It's about communication, getting disparate groups to work together smoothly and efficiently, stroking people with wrong ideas the right way; getting into the marketplace with a strong pitch. It's going to be damned hard work. That's why I want you to get together with Marin Ashby. She's the project director on this. If you've got time, I thought I'd take you down to meet her now and you two can make your own arrangements to take this further. Have you been up here before?' Mack shook his head. 'Let me show you around.'

The last stop before Marin Ashby's office was the newsroom. 'This is my favourite place in the building,' Leibersen said as they walked down the lines of computer terminals staffed by reporters and researchers. 'It's a lot quieter than it used to be, now they have all this junk, but it's still the hub of the building to me.'

They crossed the corridor to the control room. The familiar face of the network's lunchtime anchorman filled three screens. On another, a foreign correspondent stood in Red Square, framed against the floodlit onion towers of Saint Basil's patiently waiting for his cue. Two remaining screens showed a business news presenter shuffling papers.

The director checked the time. 'We'll go to Gary next.' The anchorman read the cue.

'Now, for the business news, we go to Gary Sherman.'

The presenter launched into his report: 'Well, Ed, it's not surprising that in a society like ours, where you are what you drive, the state of the auto industry should be used to gauge the health of the economy. And the official word on that today is "sick". There's been a steep decline in auto sales in the last month, and there's a lot of unsold cars rusting up on manufacturers' back lots.'

'How's Wall Street reacting?'

'There are a lotta grim faces down here, Ed. This news is being taken together with a Commerce Department report published today, showing a seven-point-nine-billion-dollar deficit on our international trade in July. That's forty per cent worse than had been expected. Analysts are claiming Japanese trade barriers and a lack of US-made substitutes for Japanese products sold here, are the principal cause. US Under Secretary of the ITA, Robert Galbraith, has just announced that talks with his opposite number in Japan are to be brought forward and he's expected to leave for Tokyo in the next few days.'

'Do we have any reason to believe the Japanese are gonna be any more flexible on the subject of import quotas than they have in the past?'

'Unfortunately, whatever the outcome of the talks, Ed, it could prove too little too late. The dollar has already fallen steeply against most currencies and this, amid renewed fears of increased taxes, rising inflation and a further climb in interest rates gives little cause for merriment on Wall Street this Monday noon . . .'

'Hi, I'm Marin Ashby.' The casually-dressed woman with the intense face caught Mack and Leibersen unawares. She extended a hand towards Mack. 'Heard you were on your way up, so I thought I'd come and meet you.'

The closing credits of the network news were rolling as they left the newsroom. 'I'll tell you this, Leibe,' she said. 'I'm damn glad we're not trying to market this thing right now.'

'Ah, it'll blow over.' Leibersen turned to Mack. 'Let me give you my card. My home numbers are on the back.'

It was a little after six when Mack got back to Auburn's apartment. Her paintings were propped up all around the living-room and the windows had been opened to clear the smell of cigarette smoke. The bicycle she kept in the utility room was gone. He made himself coffee and checked the answering machine.

Jackie Steadman's voice sounded shaky. '. . . Please call as soon as you can, Mack.'

He dialled Warren's number straight away.

'Oh, I'm so glad it's you, Mack.' Jackie sounded close to tears.

'What's the problem?'

'Warren's in a terrible state. We're losing the house, everything.'

'You're kidding.'

'No. They say we've got to be out within the month.' Mack could hear her take a deep breath to steady herself. 'And as if that wasn't bad enough, I've just found out that Warren's . . . he's a morphine addict, Mack.'

'What?'

'It was those pills he was taking for his back. I didn't realise they were morphine-based – he's been popping them like candy for a year. If the company doctor hadn't changed his medication, I'd never have known.'

'How did you find out?'

'Well, Warren'd been going through these terrible mood changes, shaking, sweating, completely falling apart. The company doctor said it was clinical depression. That's when he changed his medication. But the new drugs made him a lot worse, he just wanted the old pills all the time. I decided we needed a second opinion, so I took him to my own doctor. He said it looked like Warren was suffering from withdrawal symptoms. When I showed him all the stuff the other guy'd been prescribing, he'd never seen the original pills before. Said he'd have to check them out. They turn out to be some new thing developed by Western Pacific Pharmaceuticals.'

'What did the company man have to say about the morphine?'

'Sherrard? He said Warren had had a minor spinal injury when he'd first come to him, a displaced vertebra or something. I remember him saying at the time that it was a common enough thing in people with sedentary jobs. They tend to develop bad posture. And if they drink a lot, sharp crystals can build up in the muscle tissue and cause pain.

'Anyway, Sherrard sent him to an osteopath and put him on the pills. He seemed to relax a lot more after that so Sherrard gave him a repeat prescription. After six months, Warren went to get another repeat because he said he was still having problems. Now he tells me that the backache had cleared up and he just went back because the pills made him feel good.'

'And what's Sherrard's excuse?'

'He says it's nothing to do with him. He had no way of knowing that Warren was lying about his back and, anyway, the dosage was clearly marked on the pill bottles. If Warren had ignored it, it wasn't his responsibility. So Sherrard's clean as a whistle and I've got a husband with a morphine habit.'

'Terrific. It sounds like the sooner you get him into drug rehabilitation the better.'

'It's going to take more than that to cure our problems now.'

'Don't worry, we'll fix it somehow. Is Warren there?'

'Sure.'

'Put him on, will you?'

Warren sounded dopey. 'Well, it's finally happened, Mack. Mitsuda are calling in their credit. They're throwing us out and moving in some Japanese executive. Doesn't that about say it all?'

Mack started. The name shown next to Warren's house, on the computer plan of Cedar View. Fujikawa, that was it, Mr Fujikawa. Whatever the Nashiba scheme was, it was starting to play out in front of his eyes.

'They finally got what they wanted, they didn't need me any more.'

'Why? What happened?'

'You don't want to hear, believe me.'

'You're wrong. Tell me about it.'

There was silence for a moment while Warren tried to pull his thoughts together. 'Remember when DMC bought Emerson Electric, a couple of years back?'

'Yeah, I remember that.'

'Well Emerson supplied all the hardware for our on-board computers. They're developing a navigation system for us too.'

'The navigation system sucks, doesn't it? Too many glitches, I heard.'

'Same with the other stuff. Great ideas but development costs were crippling them. DMC took the chance to get an exclusive on what they saw as the technology of the future at a bargain basement price and made a bid. Took a massive loan from the Pacific Interstate to fund the acquisition. Course, things were looking good then. But now we're having real problems making the interest payments. You know how it is in the motor industry right now.

'Anyhow, it all came home to roost at a board meeting a couple of weeks ago. We got to bite the bullet, I say, trim down and cut the losses. Sell off Emerson and get some cash flow.'

'Makes sense.'

'Yeah, well wait till I tell you this. The Mitsuda boys dug their heels in real good. Did a lot of shouting about short-term thinking. I guess Fleming, the Chairman, thought, let 'em, what's two directors against the rest of us?

'. . . Jesus, if I'd have known I was going to get trashed, I'd never have done it, but they were all yelling at each other and I got to thinking, hell, I'm in hock up to my eyebrows with the Mitsuda bunch, got a wife and kids to think about too . . .'

'What are you saying?'

'I'm saying I voted with the Japs, damn it. Had to, don't you understand? At that moment, I couldn't see how it would make a lot of difference, the way things were stacked against them. One of the other guys – he's in the same kind of mess I'm in – he votes with Mitsuda too. But Gustaffson! He was a bolt out of the blue. Turns out he's a principal shareholder of Mitsuda through a family trust, or something. Anyway, next thing you know, the Emerson sell-off's blocked.'

Mack thought for a while. 'Why would the Japs want DMC in financial schtuck, when they got a thirty-five per cent stake in it?'

'I don't know . . . ask them! Anyway, Fleming goes crazy. I haven't seen a guy get that mad in a long time. He calls an extraordinary meeting of the shareholders for this morning to get us "collaborators", as he called us, kicked off the board. Mentally, I'd already cleared out my desk. But then, you know, the damnedest thing happened? It went to the vote and Fleming got creamed. I couldn't believe it. And you know how Mitsuda did it? Only by joining forces with the guys from Nabaki, their biggest competitor!'

'I'm not following you.'

'One of DMC's major shareholders is the LTC Group. Nabaki's had a stake in them for about five years. It never seemed to be an issue before – guess no one expected two rival Japanese companies to gang together. But Nabaki'd obviously put the pressure on LTC, the same way Mitsuda put it on DMC.

'So I still got my seat on the board, Mack. Because the Japs want me there, that's the only reason. And now they don't have to pussyfoot around any more. They know they can do what they like with me. I got this letter a couple of hours ago: "Out of the house, Fat Boy, we're calling in our credit".'

'That's bad.'

'You want to know how bad it is?' Warren was beginning to crack up. 'Bad enough to have Jackie in tears all day. Bad enough to take Tyler out of school and send him and little Maggie to their Grandma Steadman's till we're through with the whole damn thing.'

'How are you for cash?'

'Screwed. What d'you think?'

'How much do you need to hold things together?'

'. . . I don't want your money, Mack. Listen, you're a sweet guy but you can't—'

'Would a hundred K help?'

244

'Sure, but—'

'Listen, take it for now.'

Warren went quiet.

'You'll have it by ten tomorrow. Come on, Warren, you'll come through. Hell, I'm going to make you!'

'Thanks Mack, thanks a lot. I didn't call for money, I swear.'

'I know that. Take care of yourself, good buddy, I'll speak with you tomorrow.'

Mack sat for a long time staring at the phone. So, Nashiba City was already taking shape. Warren moved out, Mr Fujikawa moved in. How many other Warrens were there in Cedar View? In Detroit? What was any of it to do with Japanese investment in the Third World?

It'd taken Mack until two in the morning to tell Auburn what he and Jay had dug out of the Nashiba database. Talking it through with her focused a lot of his doubts. In the end, it didn't add up to much. Just a bunch of schedules and projections. There was no firm proof that anything untoward was going on. But now he knew Mr Fujikawa was coming to town, Mack was even more certain that what he'd got was part of a much greater whole.

'Hi!' Auburn dragged her bicycle in through the apartment door. 'How was NBS?'

'Scalp City.'

'No kidding. You going to take the job?'

'Who knows? We're talking.'

She walked over and dropped down on to the sofa. 'Something wrong?'

'I'm worried about Warren. The company's taking the house back.'

'That's terrible.'

'It gets worse. Seems the pills he's been throwing down all this while were morphine-based and now he's got a drug habit.'

Auburn stared into space. 'Morphine . . . funny, that's what they said Dad OD'd on . . . found the pill bottle right by his side.'

245

Mack caught her hand. 'The pills, what did he take them for? Back injury wasn't it?'

Auburn nodded. Mack flew to the phone and started dialling.

'This may be complete coincidence but that's what Warren was taking them for too. Company doctor prescribed them.' Mack held up a hand as Auburn opened her mouth to speak. He'd got Jay's answering machine.

'I'm busy . . . Speak!'

'I know you're there, Jay . . . Lift up the phone, this is important.' Jay came on the line.

'Listen, I need you to go through the Nashiba stuff again.'

Jay's mind was on the outer edge of the hacker zone. 'What am I looking for?'

'For a start, anything on Western Pacific Pharmaceuticals. And employees' personal files, medical histories, anything like that. If you can get anything that leads to a Dr Sherrard or a Dr Harman, all the better.'

Bodecker snorted. 'Okay, I'll kick it around. But it's going to take time.' He hung up.

The early morning dockside was deserted. Akitō checked his watch. Seven-twenty-eight. She should be there by now. He kicked idly at a tin can that was lying in the gutter. Was it pity or plain curiosity that had brought him here? He wasn't responsible for the past. He couldn't change it. One meeting wasn't going to make up for all the years she'd lost. And it wasn't going to commit him to anything either. He'd done a lot of thinking. Had a lot of mixed emotions. Still he couldn't be sure what he felt. Not exactly more for her. Not exactly less for the woman he called mother. But somehow he couldn't help wanting to know her better, wanting to find a measure of himself in that knowledge. He glanced upwards at the sound of footfalls on the sidewalk. Seven-thirty – precisely.

'Beautiful day!'

'Isn't it.'

The smile that greeted him was the first happiness he'd

seen on her face. It made quite a difference. The air of tension had lifted enough to let some warmth shine through. He offered her an arm.

'Shall we take a walk?'

'I'd rather take a trip.'

'What? To Staten Island?'

'You know what us tourists are like.'

A sudden rush of city workers heading for downtown Manhattan jostled past as Akitō bought tickets and they pushed through the turnstile to board the ferry.

'It's the perfect time of day for this view.' Akitō leaned on the rail, looking back towards the twin towers of the World Trade Center. 'Another hour and it'll be hot enough to bring the mist off the water.'

'Extraordinary, I never expected the sky to look so blue above such a big city. It's quite breathtaking.' Yoshi turned towards him. She could feel his slight embarrassment. 'Call me Willow. It's been my nickname since childhood.'

'It's a pretty name.'

They stood silent in the fresh breeze, neither knowing how or where to begin.

'Tell me something . . . about yourself,' Yoshi said. 'I know it sounds lame but I have imagined so much over the years.'

'There's nothing you couldn't guess,' he said. 'I was sent to school here when I was twelve, followed the usual pattern to Harvard – I'm what they call a regular Ivy-Leaguer!'

'No, I mean tell me about you, about who you are, how you feel, the things that you love.'

'I thought I had the answers to those questions, or some of them, until last week.' The words came out before Akitō could stop them but they had the ring of truth. What he thought he knew about himself owed less to the arrogance of youth than the conditioning of a received identity. He had never been invited to consider his real emotions before. He had not enjoyed the experience.

'And what do you think now?'

'I'm uncertain.' He stared down at the handrail for a

moment. 'How did you keep it to yourself all these years? How could you bear it?'

'I suppose I found an inner strength – part defiance, part determination. I had to go on, make a life for myself that wasn't dependent on the whims of pedantic males.'

'Our culture has a lot to answer for.'

'I was born to be a rebel, anyway, culture or no. But yes, you're right. I found it unconscionable that I should be forced into an arranged marriage – doubly so, since I was very much a sixties teenager. Emancipation seemed to come to everyone but the Japanese woman.'

'*Teishukampaku* – the little tyranny,' Akitō smiled. 'Yes, the accepted chauvinism of the average Japanese marriage is unfair on women. But don't you think that Japanese men are just as constrained by their culture? In different ways, perhaps, but bound nevertheless.'

'As a girl I used to curse myself for being born female. My brothers seemed to be treated like demigods whereas I was, I don't know, not unloved or unwanted, just somehow second class. It irritated me beyond telling. I thought it must be wonderful to be a man. It took me years to realise that they would grow up to be subject to much greater expectations. They would have to be brave, strong, successful . . .' Yoshi laughed, suddenly. 'All I had to do was marry the right man and I couldn't even get that right.'

'Because you didn't love him?'

'Because I could never have loved him.' She paused for thought. 'No, to be fair, I'm sure I would have accepted fondness for love if I had never known . . .'

If you'd never known something better existed, Akitō thought. He turned his back to the rail and the distant gleam of the Manhattan skyline. A week before, he wouldn't have identified with that emotion. You could do a lot of reassessing in a week.

'. . . It's difficult to stay within given boundaries once you know that other choices are possible.' Yoshi finished the sentence while Akitō was still considering it. 'Living in Italy, I began to see that that was as true of countries and cultures as it is of relationships.'

'Does Italy really mean that much to you? Don't you ever long to go home?'

Yoshi looked into the water foaming up from the stern of the boat. 'For what? For whom?'

'Your father, Takashi, is old. His health is failing. Surely your brothers will not continue to hold this old feud against you after his death.'

'You know the duty we owe to our ancestors. My father's right to *Shō* will be even greater after his death. As head of the house of Tosa, Hidezo will have no choice but to honour my father's wishes.'

Yoshi turned around. 'Ah! There she is . . .'

'Liberty.'

'Very majestic.' Yoshi wrinkled up her nose. 'But she looks rather less sympathetic close up.'

'She must have seemed like the guardian of the gates of Heaven to the thousands of immigrants who passed through here.'

Yoshi watched the great, grey-green statue come closer. 'No. I have no desire to return. If my ancestors have forgotten me, I have forgotten them. In the whole of Japan, there is only one person I would like to see again. My younger brother, Zentaro. You asked me how I have borne so much for so long. Alone.' She turned back to face Akitō. 'When I left Japan, Zentaro was twelve. He was the one person in my family I could talk to. Even he only knows that I had a lover, a much older man. He was too young for me to tell him any more. We have stayed in contact over the years. I have seen him a number of times. The last time was in Nice, three years ago. He arrives here in a week. I hope to see him again then.'

'I've met him,' Akitō said. 'At meetings of the Families. He always seems to avoid me.'

'You're wrong. He is not as influenced by the old feud as the others are. After all, Shigeru Tosa had been in his grave ten years when Zentaro was born. He has mentioned you from time to time in his letters. It was the only news of you I ever got. Judging by his tone, I think he felt as much rebuffed by you.' A light breeze swept Yoshi's greying hair

249

off her forehead. She lifted her hand quickly to keep it in place. 'He's only ten years older than you, Akitō. Almost your contemporary. He's very aware that in time, you will both take your place as head of your families. And that you should at least be able to talk with one another directly.'

Until that minute, it had never occurred to Akitō that a relationship of any kind was possible between him and a member of the Tosa clan.

'He's here in a week, you say?'

'Yes. I'm certain I could arrange for you to meet him if you wished.'

SEVENTEEN

The Nisei switched off the heat sensor. It was no use. The hacker hadn't budged. He glared at the receding reflection of Bodecker Electric in his rear-view mirror and turned the dark blue Audi on to Laramie Avenue. Left to him, the job'd have been finished the first day. He could have softened up the hacker in five minutes without leaving a mark, had him begging to show where every last piece of data was hidden. The guy probably broke into ten systems a day, he'd have had no way of pinning down who his assailant was. The risk to security was minimal. But no. Orders were to keep a low profile. Three days now he'd been waiting to get into this toilet and all for one lousy disk that looked like any other. What a waste of life.

The Nisei headed back to his hotel. The hacker wouldn't be going anywhere for a while. He'd made his morning trip to the supermarket, he'd sit at that computer terminal the rest of the day and most of the night, too. He'd sleep for about six hours and then start again. Same pattern as before. There was time for a good, hot bath and a light meal before coming out and checking the place over again.

The coffee was cold. Mack put down Tuesday's edition of the *Wall Street Journal* and crossed into Auburn's kitchen, deep in thought. The previous day, described by the NBS business news presenter as holding 'little cause for merriment', had ended as the worst day's trading for three years. The Dow Jones had fallen 109 points to 2,247, a loss of 4.6

per cent for the day. It had wiped out almost 150 billion dollars in stock value.

Mack poured himself fresh coffee and turned to Don 'Doom' Toomey. Like most Wall Street watchers, he made a point of following the Princeton Professor's regular articles. Toomey had the uncanny knack of gauging the mood of the market right. He'd predicted more than seven shifts from Bull to Bear market in twenty years. But it was the crash of '87 that had earned him his nickname. He'd forecast Black Monday and Terrible Tuesday so accurately that his name passed with them into broking history. And every judgement he'd made since was taken as seriously as the writing on the wall at Belshazzar's Feast. This morning, 'Doom' Toomey was shooting from the hip. Quoting a sign some wise ass had hung on an exit at the Stock Exchange Building in '87, he entitled his piece: 'To the Life Boats!'

Whether it was how the runes fell, a shadow in the tea leaves or unaccountable feelings in his water that shaped his visions of future events, no one knew. To what extent his pronouncements actually influenced investors' thinking remained a subject of much debate. But Mack was certain Wall Street would be battening down the hatches for another day of ill winds and shattered fortunes.

He folded the newspaper and slung it in the trash. Better put in a call to Stan Kopyc at Lowenstein's, get him to offload the Hardacre stock, he thought. He made a mental note to check through his whole investment portfolio.

The phone rang. It had to be Jay calling from Chicago.

'So, do you want the good news or the bad news?'

Mack took up his note pad. 'The bad news.'

'There's nothing on Western Pacific Pharmaceuticals in what we captured to disk. Likewise anything on Doctors Harman and Sherrard.'

'Great. So what's the good news?'

'I've found some kind of employees list. There's about five or six hundred names on it. And one of them's Morton Totheroh.'

'Who else?'

'No one I've heard of.'

'Any indication of where these people work, departments, branches?'

'No. They're just numbered.'

'Fax me a printout, will you?'

'Sure. Listen, Mack?'

'Uh?'

'I can probably raise the lowdown on anyone you're interested in through the data bureaux I deal with.'

'Let me get back to you.'

Mack hung up. A low humming noise struck up from the centre of the room and paper started to spill out of the portable fax machine. He tore it into sheets and ran his eye down the columns of names. On the second page was the name 'Zack Latimer'. Latimer and Morton had started AmTronics in the fifties. It had been he who had given Auburn the commission to paint his racehorse. She was with him now, taking photographs and making preliminary sketches. Further on, he found 'William Pasternak'. Wasn't he the AmTronics PR man Morton always referred to as Brown Nose Bill? And then there was Morton, listed right after him. Mack didn't recognise the other name in the section but it seemed probable he was a director of AmTronics too. He read on. On the next page another name caught his eye. Only this one was nothing to do with AmTronics: Paul Morrisey. He was on the board of Century Twenty-one Communications. Had been for years. Mack went over the final page. Eugene Gradinski: the new Chief Executive of Compton Services? There'd been a picture of him in yesterday's *Times*, announcing . . . what the hell was it?

He went to the garbage can in the kitchen. The picture was smeared with sweet-and-sour sauce but the caption was clear enough: 'Eugene Gradinski Ties the Knot with Amatsu's Senjuro Taka . . . "This is a natural marriage for us," says Compton boss . . .' Mack rammed the paper back in the bin.

What Jay'd sent him wasn't a list of Nashiba employees. It was a list of the directors of a hundred and fifty, maybe two hundred major corporations. Two of the ones he'd identified were in the Fortune 500. And there was something

253

they had in common: all had Japanese participants.

Another fax was coming through. Mack watched the paper curl out of the machine. More names. One stood out before the transmission was even complete. Three sections before the end, plain as day, he could see 'Warren Josef Steadman'.

Morton and Warren on the same list. A list in the Nashiba database. What was Warren to Nashiba? DMC too had a Japanese associate. That fits with the rest on the list. So? Why would Warren's name be singled out? Why were any of these guys singled out? What else connected Morton and Warren? Both were on morphine-based medication: there was no evidence at this point to suggest that was any more than coincidence. Morton and Warren had both been directors of corporations that'd had the squeeze put on them by their Japanese associates: that was more to the point. Maybe that was what was in store for the other corporations on the list. What else did they have in common? Warren was in hock up to his neck with Mitsuda; Morton was too smart for that one. But both men had been disposed of when they were of no further use.

The phone rang. It was Jay.

'Hi, Mack. So, any good?'

'Could be. Look Jay, this isn't a Nashiba employees list. Truth is, I don't know what it is, but I'm going to fax it back to you with a lot of stuff written in: the corporations a lot of these guys work for, their positions on the board, a few home addresses. I want anything you can get on them. Their credit rating, buying behaviour, medical records. Anything personal. Should be right up your street.'

'Yeah? Well, it's going to take time.'

'Okay, okay. Listen, do you still have this data on screen?'

'Yeah.'

'Did it come up like this . . . in English, I mean?'

'Yeah, why?'

'I'd like to know what that Japanese character is. Looks like the same one . . . on the bottom of each page. Can you run the translation program on it?'

'Can I finish my lunch first?'

'No.'

Jay took a large bite out of the cold, carry-out pizza and slung the rest across the room. He reached for his desk-top disk file. 'Wait a minute.' He wiped his hands on his jeans and loaded the program.

'Well, it doesn't look like it's the sort of word that easily translates.'

'What do you mean?'

'Well these programs aren't perfect, y'know. The translations can come up a bit literal or a bit vague. It's not as good as a human interpreter.'

'What's it say, damn it!'

Jay squinted at the screen. '"Neutral – Plural. Suggest: Neutrals."'

'That's it?'

'That's it. I'll fax you the stuff as I get it. Ciao.'

Mack pulled up a chair. Neutrals. Five hundred and sixty-three of them. Including Morton and Warren. What made them ... neutrals? There was no way the Japanese could be planning to offload all of them. They had to have a collective use.

He picked up his pen and wrote. *All directors, all Japanese associates, all neutrals.* He studied the words. How would Morton have played this? 'Put two and two together and make five-and-three-quarters.' Gestalt, that was what counted, the capacity to see the larger issue, the endgame. But what in hell was the endgame?

By early evening, more faxes from Jay had started piling on to the living-room floor. Soon Mack's head ached with the strain of mental leaps in the dark. He switched on the NBS evening news. The shock waves that'd rocked Wall Street on Monday had continued through a second day's trading. From the first hour, rumours had swept the market that the Federal Reserve was going to up its interest rate on loans to member banks. Meaning the banks, in their turn, would raise interest rates on their loans to businesses and consumers. The Dow Jones average had tumbled until noon, when the Treasury Secretary and Presidential chief economist had met with reporters in an effort to calm fears and the market had rallied a little.

Then the bombshell hit. Portland Financial, the third largest bank in New Hampshire, had gone down with all hands. Portland had lent aggressively during the property boom of the eighties, especially in the commercial sector. As the recession of the early nineties had bitten, a trickle of bad debts on those loans had turned to a flood. Portland Financial had been one of the many banks who'd run to man the pumps. Mack remembered reading their first quarterly report for '95. It announced that the bank's capital had been wiped out by losses of $450 million. A massive injection of funds from the Federal Deposit Insurance Corporation had kept Portland Financial afloat, but rumours of a disastrous second quarter's losses had started a run on the bank's deposits early Tuesday morning. Some small depositors had panicked. One old guy'd even marched into the bank with an ancient scattergun and demanded his savings in cash.

At noon, the FDIC pulled out. Most private investors, with no more than a hundred thousand dollars on deposit it seemed, took a deep breath and crossed their fingers, in the knowledge that, if the bank collapsed, they'd be covered by insurance. While larger investors waited to know their fate, trading in Portland Financial's stock was suspended on the Exchange, resulting in a wave of panic selling. By the closing bell, the Dow Jones had spiked downwards another thirty points.

Mack's mind switched back to the boardroom clash between DMC and Mitsuda. There was only one reason Mitsuda could want to hit the motor giant's cash flow: to cut off loan repayments to the bank that was supporting them. The Pacific Interstate had been the real target. Mack looked back at the TV report. Was the PI next? He sifted through the notes in front of him. He would need a lot more information. Data that only Jay could get.

Faxes from Jay concertinaed on to the floor with barely an interruption till the early hours of Wednesday morning. Mack started to weigh the events of the last two days against the patterns that began to emerge from the data.

He was still scheduling, cross-referencing, formulating his conclusions at daybreak when Auburn let herself into the apartment.

'Hi. I thought you'd be in bed.'

'How was the horse?' Mack said without looking up.

'Answer to a maiden's prayer.'

'I thought you were staying over.'

'I've done as many preliminary sketches as I can.'

He rubbed his face in his hands. 'What time is it?'

'Seven. Want some coffee?'

He nodded. 'Please.'

She crossed to the kitchen, stepping over the heap of unrolled fax. 'So what's been happening?'

Mack got up and stretched himself. 'Let me make a phone call and then I'll tell you.'

It was more than a year since Mack had spoken to Senator Brodie. Brodie had been involving him in projects ever since he selected VideSet as one of the showpieces for the 'America The Beautiful' Exhibition in Tokyo in '93. The fair was part of the government's campaign to get the Japanese to increase their quota of US imports and help reduce the imbalance of trade between the two countries. Organisers had scoured the States for anything that was exciting and original in the hope of tempting Japanese consumers. VideSet fitted the bill perfectly. And through it, Mack had been able to impress Brodie with his marketing ideas. But how would he react to him on something like this?

Mack tensed as he waited for his call to be answered. He checked his watch: 7.10. Brodie was an early riser, it was a good time to catch him. *If this isn't macro order, Morton, I don't know what is,* he thought.

'Hi. Can I speak with Senator Brodie please?'

'If I can take your name, sir.'

'Lasky, Mack Lasky. Is this his service?'

'Yes it is. The Senator is taking no calls at this time but if you'd care to leave a message I'll see that he gets it.' The androgynous voice might as well have been a recording.

'Will you ask him to call me back urgently.' That's not enough, Mack thought. 'Say that I have some important

257

information for him, that it's a matter of the highest priority that I speak with him personally.'

'I'll see that he gets that message, sir.' The line went dead.

Auburn appeared with the coffee. 'So am I going to get the lowdown or what?'

'Sure. What's your problem?'

'Just that I'm kind of tired of playing chief cook and bottle-washer while you're out there being Captain Incredible.'

'What is this? I'm doing it for all of us.'

'All of who?' Auburn turned. 'You're not doing this for me, or Warren, you're not even doing it for Morton. You're doing it for yourself, Mack, that's the truth.'

'Look, I've been up all night working on this, don't give me a hard time.' Mack re-ordered the sheets of fax paper in front of him and checked his notes. 'Do you want to know what's been happening or not?'

Auburn looked at him for a moment. 'Why won't you ever talk?'

'Read my lips – what do you think I'm trying to do here?'

'I mean *talk*, talk. I mean, let me in.'

Mack let out an irritable sigh.

'Okay, that does it,' she said, suddenly. 'I've been thinking this over for a long while. Now's as good a time as any to tell you what I really feel.'

'Wait a minute—'

'No, you wait. You listen for a change. You were great to me in Fire Island, Mack, and I don't know what I'd have done without you. Whether going to bed together meant anything to you or not, I won't believe the way you came across that night wasn't a you that exists somewhere inside, somewhere under that six-inch-thick mahogany veneer you give the world. I liked that guy, liked him a lot and I keep hoping he's going to turn up again sometime. But all I keep getting is this other fella, this guy who's locked away, closed off. I've been on the outside looking in before, Mack, this lonely I can be on my own.'

He put down the papers, slowly. 'So you want me to leave, is that it?'

'Go or stay, that's not what's important. What *is* important is that you should recognise that you can't be an emotional hitch-hiker all your life. You can't just give or take as the mood pleases you. Other people need input if they're going to stick with you, whether it's me, now, or some other woman, down the line.'

Mack stared at his hands for a long time. 'I'm sorry,' he said, at last. 'I didn't mean to take you for granted.' He reached out for her. 'It's hard for me . . . just give me a little time, okay?'

Auburn thought for a while then squeezed his hand. 'It's a deal.' She sat down on the floor between the rolls of fax paper. 'So, tell me, what's all this mean?'

'Well, we'll never know what went on in Morton's mind in the last year of his life but I think we've got some of the answers here. You know that Nashiba had him design a new database for them.'

'Yeah.'

'Well, he must have known his way around it better than anyone else. I'm sure now he was keeping an eye on Nashiba. My guess is that while he was checking them out, he came across data that he wasn't meant to see – that no outsider was meant to see. Secrets that only a selected handful were meant to know. I think that whatever it was he stumbled on, the conclusions he drew from that data were so momentous, so beyond anything he'd encountered before, that he went to great lengths to hide what he had and to cover his tracks while he decided what to do next.'

'The disk.'

'That's it. Now, my guess is that he felt he had only part of the story, so he decided to keep monitoring data updates, and nosing around to see what else he couldn't find. You know, in a way, I think he was trying to tell me something of what he thought was going down, that last Sunday. He read me a piece he'd written for a lecture he was giving at Princeton. It wasn't about an actual event but a hypothetical one.'

Mack fought to remember the words. 'The essence of what he had to say was that the computer was just a tool, a good or bad thing according to who was making the choices. In the hands of an aggressor, he said, it could be the perfect weapon, an instrument whereby man could wage war without . . . how did he put it? . . . "the need for military confrontation".

'See, he kept the whole thing hypothetical because he still didn't have all the answers, because he had an idea what was happening but he couldn't prove it. The data that was on the disk we found took us part way to the truth. I began to figure the rest after I spoke to Warren.'

'Warren? What's he know?'

'Nothing about all this. But what he told me about his last weeks at DMC filled in a lot of blanks. There was more in that speech of Morton's, he said that the wars of the future would be fights between vast multinational conglomerates, that the battleground would be the boardroom and the stock exchange floor. I've been turning over what we found for days now and I'm convinced that whatever's going on here doesn't just involve Nashiba. Other big Japanese corporations are tied into this thing.'

'So? What's it to us if they want to get into a slugfest?'

'There's no fight between them, Auburn. This is between them and us. Dozens of corporations are involved. Perhaps hundreds.' Mack tapped the fax sheets in front of him. 'They seem to have a number of complex strategies in place, all designed to fit together. All set to trigger at the same time.'

Auburn frowned. 'And achieve what?'

Mack thought for a moment. 'The conclusion I've come to is that it's some sort of economic coup.'

'When . . . when's it going to happen?'

'I don't know. And that's my biggest problem right now. I just know it's going to happen. I tell you this, it's made me look at everything Japanese in a whole new way. Everywhere you read how people in the West are starting to understand the Japanese, appreciate the subtleties of the Eastern mind. I think that's bullshit. We only know what they want us to know, what they want us to believe. We just take it for granted that these Japanese corporations who keep us all in videos, TVs, washing machines, cars and computers, lead in their markets because they turn out a better, more efficient product for the money than their Western counterparts. And that the only serious competiton they have is with each other. That's what they want us to think. But the truth is something else. I think that when it suits them and there's an advantage to be gained, a handful of corporations group together and work as a unit – for a day, an hour, or however long it takes to achieve an objective against a targeted American corporation. Then they separate again without leaving so much as a ripple on the pond. I'm starting to wonder if there isn't some controlling group, some body of men that they all listen to. I'm starting to wonder if there isn't a hell of a lot more to our Japanese friends than we've ever believed.'

'This is the final call for American Airlines Flight 4946 to Washington National now boarding from Gate Nine.' Mack picked up his attaché case and joined the line for Executive Class. Brodie's call had come through in time for him to catch the late afternoon flight.

How do I convince Brodie that what I have to say is twenty-four carat? Mack thought. *Isn't all I have just a pile of circumstantial evidence? Maybe I'm pitching way out of my league.*

The over-made-up face of the stewardess in the gangway of the plane broke into a smile, revealing several thousands of dollars in cosmetic dentistry, and muttered a welcome. Mack ignored her and pushed slowly forward down the cabin. Why did grown men take so long to stow a couple of pieces of hand luggage, for Chrissake? He checked his boarding pass. Aisle seat, he thought irritably, that meant getting rammed by the drinks trolley at least twice. God, he needed to sleep. He stowed his attaché case in the overhead storage, sat down and fastened his seat belt. Kennedy to Washington National. Even Winston Churchill couldn't have slept on a flight this short! He closed his eyes and tried to block out the searing light and the mindless synthesised music. Two guys in the row in front were arguing over who'd been assigned the window seat. Mack turned to try

261

and find a more comfortable position.

'Can I offer you a paper or a magazine, sir?'

He opened his eyes. The masterpiece of dentistry blazed at him again. 'No. Thank you.'

The stewardess moved on. The guy across the aisle had asked for *Newsweek*. The cover caught Mack's attention. Said something about Japan. He leaned over to take a closer look. His eyes locked on the colourised photograph of Emperor Hirohito recording a speech. Below it, the headline ran: 'Japan Surrenders – Fifty Years On.'

Mack slid slowly up, his eyes fixed on the magazine. It was that simple. A sudden rush of fear and elation swept his senses. Over and over he'd asked himself, when? Why? Now there could be no doubt. He took his diary from his pocket and wrote: 'Seven days.'

The Boeing 737 lifted into the air and Laurie, Raskin, Drummond were swallowed up into the darkness. He was ready for Brodie now.

Macro order.

The dark blue Audi slowed to ten miles an hour. The Nisei lifted the heat sensor to the offside window. The hacker had moved down to the ground floor of the building. The Nisei pulled over two blocks down and adjusted the wing mirror till he got a clear view. The street door to the left of the electrical store was the only way in. He'd checked the building the first night. The back door was bricked up and the shop entrance was protected by half-inch steel mesh. He switched on the directional rifle mike and turned up the amplifier. Heavy shoes or boots were moving towards the passageway. At last . . .

The door swung open. The hacker stepped out into the street and walked towards the rusty Dodge pick-up parked out front. *What in hell do you think you look like?* the Nisei thought as he strained to see in the failing light. *Jesus, I really get the good ones.*

He watched the truck move off westward towards Laramie Avenue. *Goodbye, Mr Smart-ass Hacker,* the

Nisei thought. *You think you're one cool dude, but I got news for you. We were on to you the second you went on line. Nashiba'd been waiting for that user number to show up for a month. You clevered yourself right up your own butt this time.*

The High Chaparral Saloon stood on a block by itself. It had been purpose-built in the late fifties and the punishment it'd taken from almost five decades of the faithful gave it an authenticity that added greatly to its appeal. Jay Bodecker lifted himself out of the Dodge pick-up, taking care not to scratch his silver toecaps, and headed towards the door. He was all dressed up with everywhere to go. Apart from hacking, country music was his only enduring passion. He'd inherited it at full strength from his old man. Bodecker Senior had been obsessed with everything Western since the day an eighty-year-old Wyatt Earp had turned up as a passenger in the taxi he'd driven during the Depression.

And so it was that the right-hand end of the closet of Jay's bedroom was always kept pristine. The cupboard was mostly just a dump for soiled clothing. When something reached the point where even Jay found it unacceptable, he'd simply throw it on to the heap, ram it down and go out and buy something new. The only clothes that saw the inside of a dry-cleaner were the hand-worked Western-style leather jacket, checked shirts and immaculate Levi's that hung in a plastic suit-bag on the end of the chromium rail. On the shelf above stood the leather boots with the silver heels and toecaps Jay'd bought from Nudie's in LA, and a white cardboard box that protected a spotless Stetson hat. Wednesdays and Saturdays, Jay'd take a shower, wash his hair, shave and be transformed into Jay Bodecker – Urban Cowboy. Tonight was one of those nights.

Jay crossed to the Chaparral bar, enjoying the snap of his heels on the pitted wooden floor. He got up on a stool and grinned at the bartender. Bern Tasker kept his elbows on the heavy oak counter.

'You look like you just won the Silver Buckle.'

'You know, Bern, I'd be a liar if I told you this hasn't been a damn fine week.' Jay's grin broadened. He pushed away the beer glass Bern put down in front of him. 'Tonight it's gonna be IBDs all the way.'

The cocktail was the house special. Bern called it 'Instant Brain Damage'. It was a mixture of God-knew-what over a base of Irish Potcheen. And it was aptly named.

Cherry Sullivan sat at the other end of the room, at a table near the wall. Jay knew she was there all right, he'd come over in his own good time. But tonight she could see that that was likely to be longer than she felt like waiting. She crossed the half-empty bar. Over the past ten years, the looks she attracted had dropped off in direct proportion to the number of pounds that'd gone on between the leather jacket and the skirt. But she was still somewhere in the Twilight Zone between faded sex appeal and outright blowsiness. She sat up next to Jay, watched Bern shake the cocktail and set a vodka and orange in front of her.

Cherry'd decided that she was going to have Jay tonight, no matter what. Trouble was, you had to catch him just right. Too little booze and he'd sit up all night singing Hank Williams songs in his dumb-assed way, too much and he'd lay on the bed hard as a rock, snoring loud enough to set the windows rattling. Tonight, she wanted Jay's mind on the game. That meant getting him off the IBDs.

Jay kissed her. 'I got something for you.'

'Yeah?'

'One more for the collection.' Jay reached inside his jacket and slid her a condom packet. She could feel the hardness of the disk hidden inside as she took it from Jay's hand and put it in her bag. 'Thanks for nothing. I wouldn't mind so much if I got to help you empty these things.'

'You got 'em somewhere safe, yeah?'

'Very. In my lingerie drawer.'

'Gee, Bern, don't you just love the way her lips move when she says "lingerie"?'

Jay looked at his watch. Time to try Mack again.

'Order me another drink, Angel, I'll be back.'

Cherry watched him disappear through the swelling crowd. Her hopes began to fade. If he was making a call, his mind was on business. She was starting to get a bad feeling about tonight.

'Is Mack Lasky there, please?'

'Who's this?'

'Are you . . . Auburn Totheroh?' Jay was cautious.

'Yeah, why?'

'This is Jay Bodecker.'

'Sure. All right, tell me what Mack calls your place.'

'Pig Palace. Now where's the big fella?'

'He's in Washington.'

'Shit.'

'If it's important, you'd better tell me.' There was a pause. 'Is this a private club you've got going between the pair of you? I do have a right to know what's going on.'

'All right. The translation program's thrown up this word, it was on the bottom of one of the files.'

'Like "Neutrals"?'

'Yeah.' Jay started to loosen up. 'See, all the other files have title names like you'd imagine: "Paraguay, President; Profile of." That kind of thing. But this one's real off the wall. The closest I can get to it in English is Checkmate. Now in my line of work, you spend your life trying to figure out passwords. After a while, you get a feel for it, for why people choose the words they do. Y'know, their favourite football team, make of car. I'm telling you, Auburn, this "Checkmate" or *Tsumi* – I don't know how you pronounce it – is a password.'

'Does it access anything?'

'May never know. I can't get back into the Nashiba database. But . . . well, I'm trying to relax here, and the word keeps bugging me and . . . I meant to tell Mack earlier but I forgot.'

'Okay. As soon as he calls, I'll tell him what you said.'

Jay walked slowly back towards Cherry. He'd trimmed his moustache too short to chew on it, he needed another drink. The cocktail glass was gone. In its place stood a beer. His eyes swivelled up to hers. 'If I'd wanted a goddamned beer, I'd have asked for one.' He tried to catch Bern's attention.

Cherry's face reddened. 'I was just thinking about your guts, that's all, hon.' She reached over to take his hand. 'Hey, come on, don't get sore at me. I've been thinking about you all week.'

Jay gave a knowing grin. 'Well, is that so?'

A high-pitched signal sounded inches from Cherry's face. She put her fingers to her ears. 'What in hell's that?'

Jay reached into his shirt pocket, took out an electronic pager and switched it off. 'That, sweetness, means some sonofabitch is breakin' into my shop.'

Jay'd realised long ago that if he was going to keep his precious equipment, he'd have to look after it himself. A regular burglar alarm wouldn't scare off a sparrow in Cicero. Anyhow, no cop in his right mind was coming down that part of town after dark just for a break-in. So Jay rigged up a short-wave pager system to a pressure pad in his living-room and carried the bleeper around with him. This was the first time it'd gone off in almost five years.

The Dodge pick-up pulled up two blocks south of Pig Palace. Jay took off his hat, carefully folded his jacket and laid both on the passenger seat. Then he reached down and pulled out a rolled-up blanket. Inside was the Ruger pump-action shotgun he'd bought mail order three years before. He'd taken the gun up to the lakes once when he'd first got it and blasted off at a few wild birds. Since then, it'd stayed in its hiding place, ready for a time like this. Jay'd kept it clean and oiled just in case. Night after night he'd lain awake figuring out just how he'd play it. Jay felt his adrenalin rise. If the cops'd wanted to search his place, they'd have hit him with a warrant. No legitimate law enforcement agency was going to break in unless they could catch him in the middle of an illegal hack. So whoever was nosing around his stuff had to be fair game. He jerked back the gun stock, forcing the first cartridge into the chamber. *Duck Season.* He slid out of the truck and reached underneath, pulling the Saturday Night Special from where it was taped to the clutch housing and shoved it into his belt. And if the sonofabitch wasn't armed, he sure as hell would be when the police found him.

The Nisei pressed a little more petroleum jelly into his nostrils to stifle the stink and went back to work. There was no rush. Nobody got themselves all dressed up like that to go for one beer. Mr Hacker was gone for the evening. He picked through the soiled socks and underwear piled at the bottom of Jay's closet and shuddered, glad of the rubber gloves. There wasn't a lot that got to him. The few sensitivities he'd been born with had been trained out half a lifetime ago. But filth, that was different. It was anathema to anyone brought up Japanese. He threw the few computer disks he'd found into a tote bag with the rest.

Keys in the front door. He moved out of the light that shone in through the barred windows from the street. So. It was going to be direct action after all. He crept forward to the stairs and checked that the piano wire that he'd stretched across the bottom of the doorway was taut. *I got everything I need*, he thought. *I can still be in New York by one o'clock.*

There was the sound of body movement from the passage-way below. The Nisei strained to hear. And singing. It was barely audible. But that's what it was.

> 'Good night ol' buddy,
> Hate to see you go,
> Hate to see you lyin'
> Down there on Body Bag Row . . .'

The Nisei closed his eyes. *The guy's a fruitcake!*

> 'Bad break, ol' buddy,
> Gonna miss you so,
> All shot up and bleedin',
> Down there on Body Bag Row.'

267

The cassette machine in the passageway could have been louder, Jay thought. Still, the effect was good enough. He was fifteen feet from it now, squatting barefoot, three steps from the top of the stairs.

Whoever's in there, will be one side of the door, he thought, *they'll try and shove past me as I come through. So, which are you going to go for, Bodecker? Left feels good. You got to get up pretty early in the morning to catch Jay D. Bodecker.* He stood and slung himself forward.

Jay came down so hard over the wire that the impact broke his nose. The Nisei was over him and down the stairs before he could figure out what'd happened.

Jesus Christ! He sat up and shook the blood out of his eyes. *God, that hurts ... I cracked my fuckin' ribs too.*

He searched for the gun. Had to find the gun. *Take it easy, Bodecker. Don't rush. The guy's not goin' any place.*

The Nisei reached the street door and pulled it open. His exit was blocked by a wall of rusty metal. The hacker had backed his truck hard up against the entrance. Must've let off the brake and rolled it down the hill, then crawled through the tight gap between its roof and the top of the doorway.

The Nisei jammed his foot high into the door frame and levered himself up. With his head hard over to the left, he could make it.

The noise of the shotgun in the narrow passage was deafening. The Nisei hung frozen in the air, clinging to the side of the truck with his left hand, as though pausing for thought. He ran his free hand round behind his ear. There was a soggy mess where the back of his cranium should have been. In what was left of his consciousness, he realised he was touching his own brain. The second shot took off most of the head above the ear lobes. He slid soundlessly back into the passage, wedged between the doorway and the truck.

The body was almost erect, the muscle tissue in tension. The lower jaw, having nothing left to hold it in place, hung slackly against the neck. The arms stood away from the torso, vibrating, as though expecting further instructions from the cerebellum. None came. Somewhere inside the Nisei, a light went out. The body pitched forward, slamming against the floor like a sack of beets.

EIGHTEEN

L e Lion d'Or Restaurant on Washington's Connecticut Avenue had successfully weathered the changing culinary tastes of folk from Capitol Hill for more than thirty years. Its classic cuisine and elegant décor lent the atmosphere a rare mix of tranquillity and prosperity. But that's where the old-fashioned niceties stopped. The hushed conversations that took place daily around these tastefully arranged tables could make or break political ambition. Never so much as the one Senator Stanton Brodie was about to begin in the restaurant's upper room.

Brodie took off his half-rim glasses and set them down on the table top. He smoothed his grey, wavy hair and looked up at Mack Lasky.

'I'm not going to tell you there aren't factions in Japan who'd like nothing more than to pull off something like this, Mack. And they're more than capable of putting it together. If you want my private view, the Japanese are as imperialistic now as they ever were in the thirties, so something like this wouldn't go down too badly in a lot of circles. But in practical terms . . .' He turned back to the last page of Mack's report. '. . . The repercussions of something like this are unimaginable. The backlash would turn the global economy upside down. I can't believe they'd risk that.'

'Which is exactly why this whole thing's been set as it has. In each of these scenarios the Japanese are just figures in the background. The only visible participants are the directors and shareholders of the various US corporations and the premiers and governments of the countries receiv-

270

ing aid. They're the ones that'll be calling the shots, or will appear to be. That's precisely the value of these documents. Without them, there'd be no link between the various elements at all. They're the key to everything.'

Brodie was nodding. Mack went with his next point. 'I also think the scale of the operation is deceptive. It's probably been developed on a contingency basis. If conventional military strategy is about establishing bases everywhere you might ever need them, knowing that in any likely confrontation you'll only ever have to draw on a small part of that capability, why should a plan like this be any different? See, I don't think the Japanese can know till the very last minute just which combination of elements they'll need to trigger the mechanism, so they've covered their asses every which way. The less they need to deploy, the less visible their own involvement becomes. And that's the way they want it.'

'Well, I'll tell you one thing, if Nashiba is involved in this, it's hard to believe half the *Keidanren* hasn't got a toe in the water.'

'I thought the council only advised the Japanese government.'

'You kidding? The men who make up the *Keidanren* are some of the most powerful bankers and industrialists in the country. They say jump, the Japanese government jumps! After all, they have the weight of 900 enterprises and industrial associations behind them, that represents a fair chunk of the big business community.' Brodie paused. 'I've spent a lifetime studying the way these Japanese corporations work. Ever heard of the *Keiretsu?*'

Mack shook his head.

'It's a financial clique reincarnated from the four big prewar *Zaibatsu*. You see, Nashiba is one of seven giant multinationals. It'll own maybe twenty or more other companies in different spheres. Like the spokes of a wheel, arms extend out in every direction to those related and dependent companies from the central hub – the bank.

'But as you've seen for yourself now, the connections go much deeper than they appear on the surface. The major

271

shareholders of each company belonging to a particular *Keiretsu* are also group members. This type of interlocked cross-shareholding, or beneficial shareholding, if you like, is characteristic of *Keiretsu* groupings and insulates each company from outside control.'

Mack thought for a while. 'Then Nashiba International's *Keiretsu* grouping has a hell of a voice in the *Keidanren*?'

'All seven *Keiretsu* do. The original four have figured strongly since the war, of course. I tell you, Hirohito's kid, they enthroned five years ago, is Emperor of diddlysquat. These are the real boys, industrial czars on a scale it's hard for us to imagine. You never read a word about them. But they're there all right.'

All those years at Harvard with Akitō, Mack thought, *and I never saw his father once, not even at graduation. Akitō . . . an Emperor in waiting?*

'. . . of course, some of the key movers are pretty old now. Tosa must be in his seventies: his father was hanged with Tojo and a bunch of others in 1948 for war crimes. Kuga in his late sixties: most of the factories his family owned that survived the war were taken apart and sent as reparations to Korea and Indo-China. Quite a lot of these boys have got an axe to grind . . .' As Brodie spoke, Mack could sense he was chewing over the report, point at a time. Weighing the conclusions he'd been presented with, against what he himself knew to be true.

'You know the biggest difference between us and the Japanese, Mack? They can wait. I don't mean years. I mean decades. Centuries, if need be. Your date of August fifteenth is an interesting one. The signing of the surrender, September second, is the day most Americans remember. But for the Japanese of Nashiba's generation, it's August fifteenth – that's when Hirohito broadcast to the people, told them it was all over. It was the first time they'd ever heard his voice. There was a weeping and wailing that day, none of those old boys have ever forgotten.'

'The fifteenth's a week from now.'

'Well, if you're right about all this . . .' Brodie held up his

272

hand, '. . . and I'm not saying that you are. That's the date we should be tying this to.'

'Okay.'

'Look, I know this is a damn fool question, but I have to ask it. How did you come by this stuff?'

Mack had been waiting for that one for almost an hour. 'It was bequeathed by a close friend. If you're asking whether Nashiba mailed it to me as a press release, the answer is no. I doubt whether there are more than a few dozen Japanese who have seen this, let alone anyone else.'

'And I take it the "close friend" wasn't one of them?'

'Right.'

'Well, you know the position on this as well as I do. If this data was obtained illegally, it's really going to tie our hands. I don't doubt these documents are what you say they are, but, well, on the crassest level, they're not on company paper, they're not signed by Nashiba personnel. All I can do is pass on my belief in their authenticity to whoever sees them next.'

To whoever sees them next. Brodie was buying it.

'The second problem is, of course, we can't use this stuff at an official level. I guess we can quote from it, purely off the record. If pushed, we could say it was leaked to us, make a lot of noise about having to protect our sources. But that's about as far as it goes.' Brodie summoned a waiter from the doorway and ordered fresh drinks. 'The one thing we must do is keep the lid on this,' he said almost to himself. After a moment's deliberation he looked up at Mack. 'In all the circumstances, I think the right person to hit with this is Robert Galbraith.'

'The Under Secretary of the International Trade Association?'

'If we've got to rely on behind-the-scenes diplomacy, he is the right man. He's in Tokyo now, sabre-rattling on import restrictions again.'

'Wasn't he our ambassador in Japan a while back?'

'For eight years. He did four in South Korea before that. He's got links into the Diet that go back a long way. He understands how the *Keidanren* works, Mack. I think we should drop this in his lap and see which way he jumps. I could get your report and some kind of covering letter to him in a diplomatic pouch overnight.'

'If he decides to check a few things out, he's in the right town to do it, I guess.'

'Exactly. And if this . . . *"Tsumi"* of yours is set to kick in in seven days we don't have too much time.'

The black bulletproof Rolls Camargue turned on to Broadway at Twenty-eighth Street and headed downtown. General Juan Santiago lit a Havana cigar and lowered one of the smoked-glass windows an inch to allow the smoke to join the other fumes that soured the Manhattan air. This rare trip to New York had been carefully timed. An almighty killing was planned, of that he was certain. Why else would Nashiba have been so inflexible on his dates? Being born into a tiny, backward community in the Cordillera Mountains didn't automatically make you a fool, he thought as he drew on the cigar. He knew very well that what he could contribute to the Nashibas was as great in its way as anything they could offer him. If the Yen was going to rise into the stratosphere in the next week, his fortunes could go with it.

Santiago had never had any illusions about the strength of his position. To stay on top you had to think ahead. From the first week of his presidency he'd begun to plan against the day it might end. He had no intention of winding up like Diega, the president he'd deposed, waking up one morning to find the barrel of a Kalashnikov shoved up his nose – not to die against a wall, by firing squad, as the papers had reported but to bleed to death, trussed up on a cell floor with his private parts rammed down his throat. No. He'd put a set of options into place so that if the time ever came when they were needed, he could make a clean getaway and live in comfort, in a place of his own choosing with some certainty of enjoying a peaceful old age.

Amin, Marcos, Noriega and Ramone had all had contingency plans and seen them evaporate before their eyes. San-

274

tiago had no intention, either, of being passed round from country to country until a government could be induced to take him in. And global history was being re-written too fast these days to rely on any one promise of safe haven. So Santiago had prepared seats for his government in exile in no less than four locations. A tiny island off Antigua was the preferred sanctuary. It'd been bought in the year he came to power, a large complex completed and readied for immediate occupation, if necessary. An island near Zákinthos in the Ionian Sea provided a second option, and bolt-holes in Mexico and Madagascar were in the development stage.

His personal finances had received no less detailed attention. Much had been soundly invested. But liquidity was the key to keeping one's options open. Until a year ago, Santiago had believed that the deposit account he kept at the Farrell National Bank in New York, together with nine others he had around the world, would buy him as many options as he would ever need.

But in the last decade, many who'd held power by the gun had seen American benevolence turn to hostility and betrayal when their usefulness was outlived. The US-backed coup that had toppled Carlos Ramone in the fall of '94 and resulted in the freezing of his US assets, had again caused Santiago to question the wisdom of maintaining an account in the US.

Nashiba offered a package no US bank could come close to matching. But Santiago was certain that what had been offered him had been offered others, that there was a much greater pay-off for the Nashibas than they'd ever hinted at. That pay-off had to come this week and Santiago was damn sure he was going to be in at the kill.

The Camargue was slowing down. Before it came to a halt, two burly, armed bodyguards swung out, one each side of the car, to check out the corner of Wall Street and Broadway. Four back-up operatives had been placed strategically at vantage points around the junction two hours before. When they radioed in their final 'all clears', Santiago slid swiftly from his seat and, flanked by his human shield, hurried into the side entrance of the Farrell National Bank Building.

Thirty-two storeys above, Vernon Cochrane checked the boardroom one last time. The morning sun caught the colours of the Pissarro and the Courbet at the west side of the large oak-panelled room perfectly but the jewel of the collection, the Manet above the fireplace at the south end, was lost in shadow. He turned the dimmer switch until the light above it lifted the tones of raw sienna in the woman's face and brought the painting to life. Satisfied, he walked slowly out into the reception area to wait for the elevator. Cochrane had last met Colonel Santiago in Bermuda seven months before. Once again he'd allowed the bank to cross briefly into the narrow, grey no man's land that separated legitimate dealing from the illegitimate to satisfy this man. For a customer of such importance, it was a necessary expediency. Santiago had shown his gratitude and Cochrane had slept the easier for it. At last, he was beginning to feel he could relax a little in the knowledge that the 400 million Santiago had on deposit with Farrell National was safe.

The doors of the elevator rolled back and the Colonel stepped out into reception alongside Cochrane's assistant.

'Good to see you again, Colonel.' Cochrane's thin-lipped mouth bent into a smile as he offered his hand. 'Is it still Colombian coffee and a Danish?'

Santiago shook the hand briefly and walked into the boardroom. 'Not this morning, thank you, Vernon. I'm on a very tight schedule.' He sat at one end of the table and waited while Cochrane tore open a sealed white envelope and presented him with up-to-date statements of his account. For three minutes the only sound was the ticking of the Louis Quinze clock on the mantelpiece. Then Santiago folded the document, placed it in his inside jacket pocket and took an envelope of his own from the small attaché case he'd brought in with him.

Cochrane took the envelope from the Colonel's hand and opened it. He couldn't force himself to read beyond the first paragraph. The wide shoulders drooped forward, the long chin disappeared into the neck. 'My dear Colonel, I . . . We have obviously failed you in some way ... offended you, perhaps?'

Santiago seemed to consider that for a moment. 'No.'

'Then why ...? I hope you believe that we have always done everything possible to accommodate you.' Cochrane was taking on the look of a stunned sheep. 'Nashiba is highly respected, of course. But you have a special relationship with us here, built up over many years ...'

'400 million dollars, that's what I have here, Vernon. And now I wish to bank it with Nashiba. There's really no more to it than that. I'm grateful for what you've been able to do for me in the past, as I will be to you now, if this matter can be attended to without delay.'

'I beg you to reconsider this, Colonel.' *Your whole life does not flash before your eyes when you're drowning,* Cochrane thought, *only your future.*

Santiago checked his watch. 'You'll forgive me, I hope, if we cut this short? I'm due at my embassy in fifteen minutes.' He stood up and shook Cochrane's limp hand warmly. 'Cheer up, Vernon. It's going to be a fine day, believe me.'

Somewhere in his head, Cochrane could hear the helicopter blades fading into the distance. He fumbled for the keys of his drinks cabinet. For the first time in twenty years, he poured himself a pre-noon drink. There was barely room for the ice in the hand-cut crystal whisky glass.

'I'm sorry to interrupt you, Mr Cochrane, but your next appointment is waiting. And ... well, he's getting a little agitated.' The voice of Cochrane's assistant filtered through the numb haze in his mind.

'Who is it?' Cochrane asked as his hand went back to the decanter.

'Surely you haven't forgotten?' The assistant handed him his diary. Cochrane tried hard to focus his eyes on the page. He was filled with a sudden dread.

'Bring the President straight up.' Cochrane was damp with sweat. His direct line rang as his assistant left the room.

'Hi, Vernon, it's Harvey.' The familiar voice of his opposite number at Southwestern Banking across the street sounded strained.

'Listen, can we forget squash this afternoon?'

'You got problems?'

'Problems – Sweet Jesus, if the rest of my meetings go like the last couple . . . !'

Cochrane began to turn the pages of his diary. 'Heavy, huh?'

'You could say that.'

'Harvey . . . do you have many . . . non-reschedulables this week?'

'Do I! Son of the Premier of Surinam this afternoon; the President of Gabon Thursday . . . A regular UN! . . . Why you asking?'

Special Agent-in-Charge Dean Thorensen had been trying to figure how he could get the girl in the plain fawn suit back to his condominium in Key West. She'd been sitting in his office in the Drug Enforcement Agency at the Federal Building, Miami, now for an hour and a half. He turned a single fax sheet to the failing light and carried on talking. If he was going to come on to a woman like Bryony Cole, he'd have to look like he was taking her seriously.

'. . . Okay, we managed to get a man aboard a freighter out of Puerto Cortes when it docked at Kingston two nights ago. She's called the *Sarasota*.' Thorensen watched Byrony making careful notes. 'He conducted a search of a consignment No. 7704/7; Fifty-eight empty aluminium packing cases, value: four thousand six hundred dollars; for return to the Red Cross here. He checked out the styrofoam pellets in three of the containers. What was inside was not cocaine, as you thought, but in fact raw opium.'

'Opium? From South America?'

Thorensen nodded. 'This is a very serious new development. 'So you see, your information's already been very useful.' Thorensen tried to look impressed. 'And when the *Sarasota* docks at Pier Three at six-thirty tomorrow, we'll be able to begin our operation. Here, let me show you.'

Thorensen led Bryony over to a large map of the Miami Docks which was mounted under glass on a central table. 'Customs Inspectors with sniffer dogs and rummage crews will board the craft immediately and check the cargo and the actual structure of the vessel as part of normal procedure. Even if the dogs do locate this particular shipment, it'll be left in place for offloading as though it's been cleared. All other cargo is taken to the customs bonded area, here, for thorough examination.' He pointed to a ringed rectangle on the map. 'Red Cross shipments are the only exception. They're picked up by the organisation's own trucks and taken to their main depot down here. The likelihood is that the opium is offloaded at some point after it reaches the depot and transported for purification. Nevertheless, as you can see, it's a good twenty-minute drive from the pier to the depot. Now, according to the Red Cross's warehouse manager, two of five men could be assigned to that duty. We've checked them all out on NADDIS and they seem to be clean. But we still have to cover ourselves in case the truck makes an unscheduled stop along the route. We've already tagged the truck but unfortunately the human eye is still the only satisfactory monitoring device for this kind of work, especially as far as the courts are concerned. We'll use four vehicles on a block system surveillance. In a perfect operation we should be able to keep track of this shipment from the minute it hits the wharf right through till the first stash hits the street, with all the stops along the way, maybe get ten or fifteen indictments at the end of it. But I'm afraid there are very few perfect operations in this game.'

Bryony closed her file and put away her notes. 'I can understand that. But, I must stress again that Aid Watch has a lot riding on the outcome of this operation. Our people are working with the authorities in Puerto Cortes and Maraquilla right now trying to establish exactly what happened to the medical supplies that were originally packed into those cases. Just how much, if anything, reaches the people it's intended for, what's dumped and what's sold off. We're also trying to pinpoint the stage at which the impregnated pellets get into the system and how. The risk is, Agent

279

Thorensen, that one misjudgement, this end, could alert those involved in Maraquilla and have repercussions right through everything we're doing.'

The half-smile on Thorensen's face faded. Who the hell did this woman think she was talking to? 'Listen lady, I've been told to co-operate with you fully on all aspects of this case and that's exactly what I intend to do. My own feelings in this don't count. But let's get something straight. This is one highly sophisticated outfit I'm running and I'm only interested in one thing: results. If we screw up and we do a lot more often than I'd like, it's because we're up against the smartest boys on the block. Some of them blow in a month more than this city gets as its entire federal budget for drug enforcement for a year. That kind of spending power buys anything. It buys a guy who's been working this waterfront all his life whose biggest crime till yesterday was making a "U" turn on Main Street, Tampa. My first objective is to keep this shipment and the guys who try to traffic it off the street. If I can help you too, I will. But I'll put it no stronger than that.'

'And I'm not down here for a suntan and a *piña colada*, Agent Thorensen. If it wasn't for our tip-off, you'd never have known to check out this shipment and we'd both be living our lives in blissful ignorance of each other's existence.' She shot him a dazzling smile. 'But as you say, there are very few perfect operations. I'll see you here at six tomorrow morning.'

The driver counted the aluminium containers that half filled his ten-tonne, stainless steel-panelled truck once more for luck. Fifty-eight. 'Dale McKenna', he scribbled his name quickly at the bottom of the paper on the clipboard and walked back to his cabin where the foreman stood. While the two men struggled to light cigarettes in the freshening wind, Ferris French mounted the tailboard, climbed into the back and pulled the doors to.

McKenna climbed into his cab, slid the gear shift into first and moved out along the wharf before swinging right to join traffic on Biscayne Boulevard. Two minutes later, the DEA's eyeball vehicle was in place. Two agents dressed as rock band roadies manned the brightly decorated RV. The driver moved into lane, twelve cars behind the truck. His partner spoke into the voice-activated mike that was set into the sun visor above his head.

'Target in sight, Bill, move in. 'Kay?'

'Ten-Four,' came the reply. Two avenues away, a dirty yellow Volkswagen Golf moved away from the kerb at Safeway and accelerated till it was running parallel with the target. The married couple crammed into it, with their week's shopping, were only able to make visual contact with the truck at each block intersection, but this tactic coupled with the positioning of the eyeball vehicle was an effective combination. Roadworks on Biscayne Boulevard were producing severe congestion and McKenna, as predicted, hung a left on to the slower Second Avenue.

'Target going left, left, left. 'Kay?' Thorensen radioed.

'Come out, Bill.'

'Ten-Four.'

'Move in, Don. 'Kay?'

Don acknowledged. An Aaron Courier Service motorbike and rider slid out from the gas station on Second, swung right and moved up, nine vehicles behind the target. The exact moment the traffic signals ahead changed from amber to red, McKenna changed down to second, swung hard left and right and disappeared into the narrow service road ahead.

'Target moved left, left, left. 'Kay?' radioed the motor cyclist urgently. 'Turning north on to service road at Twenty-sixth and Second.'

'Ten-Four.' The Volkswagen, the RV and a black Chevvy, driven by Thorensen, moved in to within reach of each end of the block.

McKenna heard the doors of the truck swing open and waited for the hum of the hydraulic lift. Nothing.

'Get on with it, French.' He spat through the small grille between the driver's cabin and the rear of the truck. A second later he heard the hum of the hydraulic pump.

The courier moved into view at his end of the service road. He got off his bike and started to search through his panniers. 'Target approximately five outlets down,' he whispered into his helmet mike. 'Offloading tall metal container . . . on castors.'

'Fifth retail outlet is the Chuck Wagon diner,' Thorensen, moving up fast along Second, radioed back.

'Could be a food storage unit for refrigeration,' Wex Carver, the RV driver, offered. 'That's how food's delivered to those places. Pre-cooked and sealed for microwaving.'

'Well, how in hell did it get in the back of that truck?' Thorensen shouted above the roar of the engine. 'I checked it myself at five this morning. It's not been out of our sight since.'

'Search me,' Carver said. 'But it's there now and it ain't full of pizza.'

Thorensen turned up the level on the transmitter. 'Do not interdict. Repeat: do not interdict.'

McKenna was getting edgy. *Come on French, you dumb flat-faced fuck!* He checked his mirror. The motorbike courier was still searching through his pannier. He was taking too long. Check him. McKenna reached forward for his lunch box and took out a mobile phone. The courier moved out of sight into the store on the corner. What the hell was the name of that place? Logan Brothers, that was it. The phone number of Aaron Courier Services was painted on the pannier of the bike.

'Aaron.'

'Oh, this is Logan Brothers Men's Wear,' McKenna drawled. 'I called for a bike twenty-five minutes ago. Nothing. What's the story?'

'Please hold.' There was a pause. 'I don't seem to have . . .'

Another pause. Too long.

A male voice came on the line. 'We have a computer down here, sir. Bear with us for a couple of minutes, will you?' McKenna wasn't listening, not to that voice at least. In the background he could hear another voice coming through on a radio channel. He only caught two words: 'Target vehicle.' It was enough.

The courier returned to his bike. McKenna watched him shoot a lightning glance towards the truck. He revved the engine, slung the gearbox into reverse and rammed the bike and rider at forty miles an hour, throwing them both twenty feet across the road. Then he slung the truck into second and shot forward. He braked and moved the wheel a couple of inches to the left. The truck skewed round, scraping and grinding against the buildings on either side. When it finally stopped, it was jammed horizontally across the alley. McKenna reached for the mobile phone and dialled. The answer came immediately.

'Say goodnight, Dick.' He flung down the phone, took the Magnum from his lunch box and rammed it into his belt. By the time Thorensen's Chevvy rumbled into the alley, McKenna was almost at the top of the rusty fire escape that serviced the building directly behind the truck. Thorensen screamed at him to halt, then lamely slammed off a couple of .45 shells into the coping stones and lurched after his quarry. McKenna knew he'd be clear across the next building, screened by three old chimney stacks before the DEA agent was even at roof level. He reached the end of the building. The gap across the next alley to the building opposite was no more than fourteen feet. *Easy*, he thought. *Why, when I was in tenth grade, I could clear that.*

Somewhere in mid air, it struck him that that was twenty years ago. He missed the building by almost three feet and plummeted to the railings that lined the basement stairway below.

McKenna opened his eyes. Three cast-iron spikes were protruding through his chest. He blinked. *Well, I'll be damned, now you'd have thought that would've hurt like hell.*

Then he died.

The staff of Aid Watch crammed into Hans Rienderhoff's small office. Bryony turned up the sound on the TV. CNN reporter Murray Wilson was standing in the kitchen area of the Chuck Wagon Diner, making his report in that airy way that seems to lend as much importance to a street fair as a plane crash.

'For sheer invention, the modern drug smuggler takes some beating! But beat 'em they did. The Miami DEA interdicted this shipment of opium, with a street value of over two million dollars, concealed in this alloy freezer. How did they do it?' He moved out into the service road behind to the now empty truck. 'This may look like an ordinary truck but it's been specially adapted for the Red Cross. Normally, it's a little bit of Third-World aid all on its own. It's designed to take blankets, tents, and other essential supplies across vast areas of rugged terrain to people who need them.'

Now there was a close-up of a large compartment concealed in the floor of the vehicle. 'This central section of the floor has been designed to slide back. Underneath it, as you can see, there s a compartment that can carry up to two hundred different spares – these are not good places to break down.'

He stood up, indicating a cue to the anchorman. 'Only it wasn't carrying spares at noon this morning, Steve. Instead, it was carrying a skilfully adapted food storage unit with fake packs of chilli set into the front. Police say that while the truck was in motion, twenty-four-year-old Ferris French poured thousands of drug-impregnated styrofoam pellets, from recently imported containers, into the unit and wheeled it in to stand with nine others in the freezer room of the diner. The driver – who's been identified as thirty-six-year-old Dale McKenna from Denver – died from injuries received during the bust.

'Just who was waiting to collect the haul, we may never know. The DEA says that a tip-off to the perpetrators probably means that the trail stops here. And staff of the diner are saying nothing. The Red Cross are promising a full enquiry. Now back to you, Steve.'

'Thanks, Murray. We'll have an update on that story within the hour.'

'Three thousand agents in the DEA, and we have to get Thorensen!' Bryony flung back her chair. 'They blew it, the whole thing. No pick-up, no link to Santiago.'

Hans Rienderhoff's face was flushed with anger. 'And what about Aid Watch? This was our baby. Not a word about us! We needed that recognition, goddamn it.'

The staff started to file quietly back to their desks. Rienderhoff slammed the files he was carrying down on his trestle table. 'People have to know we were part of this. Without their goodwill and donations, we'll be shutting up shop inside six months.'

'That Thorensen had schlonghead written all over him,' Bryony said. 'Should've known better than to trust him.'

Rienderhoff moved towards the door. 'Well, I'm not standing for it. You bet CNN will be back with an update on this story. Rene! Get me Joanna Golden at CNN.' He looked at Bryony. 'I'm going to him 'em so hard with our side of it, their ears'll ring. Red Cross aid used as a cover to smuggle opium into this country; the Maraquillan Connection. By the time I've finished, Special Agent Thorensen'll be the most overqualified street hygiene operative in Miami.'

The secretary shouted from the adjoining office. 'Miss Golden on two . . .'

'Right. After this, get me the Chief of Police of Dade County.' He took a breath and lifted the phone. 'Hi, Jo. Congratulations on the drama series. What do you mean, what do I mean? You've been sold a bill of goods. If you're going to do a follow-up on the Miami bust, there's a few things you should know . . . What did you miss? Only the biggest drug story since Bayer invented Aspirin. Nothing to lose any sleep over . . . Oh yeah? . . . Well, I've got the key witness sitting right here in my office . . . You've got fifteen seconds to say something stunning or I take the call from ABC . . .'

The quality-control laboratory of the Western Pacific Pharmaceutical plant was on the first floor overlooking the supply depot. All day long a steady stream of trucks rattled into the loading bays with consignments of primary drugs, used in the manufacture of WPP's products. Barrett Stubbs had been a control chemist in the lab for just two months. He wound up the magnification on the microscope and examined the cluster of blue-white grains. The molecular structure of the sepia-coloured grain to the upper left of the sample was about as different as it could be.

'Marv, take a look at this, will you?'

Marvin Krause crossed the lab and stared into the microscope, adjusting the focus to suit his increasingly defective vision. 'Yeah, we get boogas now and again.'

'Well, what is it?'

'Ah, nothin' to worry about. We had this one nailed before you joined us. Your predecessor, Gerry Kanaar, found it. Said it was eliminated in the processing.'

'Did he now,' Stubbs said irritably. 'And that was rated as a scientific conclusion? Nice to know I'm working for a real tight operation.' The chemist leaned against his workbench. 'This impurity mayn't have killed anyone so far but I'm taking no risks. C & H Chemicals are getting this batch back. Where do I get a copy of the delivery note?'

'Sig'll have one.'

Stubbs made his way to the Chief Controller's office. Sig Weaver's real name was Aubrey but he'd been dubbed Sigourney, or Sig, from his first day with the corporation. Though no one called him that to his face.

The plain, dumpy secretary was filing a broken nail when Stubbs came in. She wasn't going to put herself out. Especially not for a black. 'I'm afraid Mr Weaver is on a management course in Cincinnati till Wednesday.'

'Well we have a problem with one of our consignments ...'

'If you make out your report I'll see that he gets it.'

'Look, this delivery has to be cleared by tomorrow morning latest.' Stubbs tried to stay calm.

'Well.' She got up and slowly manoeuvred her forty-inch hips towards the door. 'I'm on my lunch break now. I'll try and reach him at his hotel later.'

God forbid that one faint spark of initiative should dis-

turb that vapid goo that passes for brain matter, Stubbs thought. He gave her a minute to get down the corridor and opened the filing cabinet. He found the invoice he needed and headed back to the lab. Then he dialled C & H Chemicals' Chief Dispatcher.

'Dimitri? It's Barrett at WPP. How you goin'?'

'Fighting the world. How's Junior?'

'Ah, still has us up four times a night. Every day you think, I can't get any tireder than this. And every day you do. Listen, Batch 88604. It's full o' shit, Dimitri.'

'Get out of here! It comes straight from processing into the bags. No way've you got boogas in there.'

'You telling me I don't know a booga when I see one? What's happening out there? You people into germ warfare now or something?'

Dimitri sighed. 'Okay, hold on, let me get the order up on the screen here . . . What number did you say?'

'88604.'

'. . . Get a little more sleep, Barrett my boy. Ain't no such batch number. As a matter of fact, says here that the last morphine you ordered from us was December second '94.'

'I'm holding the delivery note in my hand, Dimitri.'

'And I'm telling you that no such consignment was ordered from us. Have you checked this with Sig, Barrett? Barrett?'

'No,' Stubbs said at last. 'But I will. Hey, I'm sorry if I, er . . .'

'Forget it. Get some sleep, huh?'

By the end of the working day, Weaver's secretary still hadn't located him. Stubbs typed out his report. 'Morphine samples. Seven, Eleven and Twenty-one: Unidentified impurities. Inorganic material. Has reacted chemically to purification process of soaking in water followed by filtration through slaked lime and ammonium chloride. Identification impossible without control sample.'

The impurity was still bugging Stubbs when he got home.

'Start without me, hon,' his wife Gayle called back to the

kitchen from the baby's room. 'He just won't settle. The steak'll be ruined.'

Stubbs turned down the grill and lifted a steak on to a floral dinner plate. He drained the corn-cobs, forked one of them and some fries on to the space next to it and sat down at the kitchen table opposite the TV. Some grinning moron carrying about a hundred pounds of cellulite on his gut was leaping up and down in front of a garish game show set. He flicked through the channels. CNN was showing footage of Customs Inspectors and sniffer dogs boarding a freighter; Drug Enforcement Agents going over some truck. He switched up the sound. A nice-looking girl was being interviewed live in the studio. The caption below her face read: 'Bryony Cole – Aid Watch.'

'. . . It was clearly agreed with the DEA at the outset that this was to be basically a surveillance operation to enable both of our organisations to follow through a number of leads to the end. The DEA not only blew it but went public with it. In doing so, they blew weeks of our most sensitive and valuable work.'

'But Miss Cole, they netted a haul of opium with a street value of over two million dollars.'

'That may be so, but they left the smugglers free to do it all over again. Look, the men supplying these drugs are the same ones who dump and sell off billions of dollars' worth of US aid every year. They don't care that children are dying of the thousands of diseases we eradicated in this country forty years ago. And I'll tell you this, so long as the DEA allow their operations to be run by small-minded publicity seekers, that's the way it's going to stay . . .'

Stubbs chewed his steak. *Nice going lady*, he thought. *You tell 'em.*

'The DEA gets millions of dollars in Federal funding every year. Aid Watch and organisations like it have to operate on a shoestring. Sloppy operations and betrayals of trust like this threaten our very existence.'

The anchorman was enjoying himself. 'So what precisely are you saying has been lost?'

'I'll show you.' The woman held up a white pellet the

size of a peanut shell. The camera moved in for a close-up. 'Our people in Maraquilla were days away from locating the factory that turns these out. This is moulded styrofoam. The pellets are used in packing. Normally, they're solid but these are hollow.' She broke the pellet open. 'The opium is impregnated into them. It takes quite a sophisticated process to do it. Now we believe that the factory that makes these is the same one that's been burning most of the medical supplies that are sent to Maraquilla. Thanks to the DEA in Miami, that factory's probably already been turned over to manufacturing cattle-cake. The original machinery would have been removed within hours of the bust this morning.'

'Steak no good?' Gayle stood in the doorway holding a wriggling child.

Stubbs forced his attention back to his uneaten food. 'Oh no, it's fine. Listen . . . what happened to the packing the radio we bought at the weekend came in?'

Gayle sighed. 'I guess it's still out back by the trashcans.'

The cardboard packaging was ripped to shreds, but the two sections of styrofoam that had encased the radio still lay by the trashcans in the yard, where Gayle had thrown them. Stubbs snapped off a section the size of a cue ball, got into his car and set off for the lab.

The chemist screwed up his eyes against the glare of the strip lighting. He poured himself a strong black coffee and settled back to his work. He reduced an ounce sample of the styrofoam to the finest powder, divided it up into five samples which he transferred to slides, then treated each to quantities of slaked lime and solutions of ammonium chloride in varying strengths. It took a matter of seconds for the chemicals to react. He placed one of the new slides under the microscope. Next to it he set the slide with the morphine smear that contained the sepia impurity he'd found during the day.

Stubbs's vision was almost double now, his body screamed for sleep. But his mind was not ready to rest. He checked the samples through the lens of the microscope, sat back, sipped more coffee and checked again. In science, as in life, there were possibilities, likelihoods and certainties. He didn't know the answers to a thousand questions right now, but that the slide on his right contained several milligrams of morphine refined from Maraquillan opium was hardly in doubt. And WPP had been processing it into some form of medication for eight months.

Why? Stubbs thought. Legally produced morphine was readily available to the pharmaceutical industry. He shook his head; *come on, Stubbs, how long have you been in this industry? Nine years? How can you ask yourself such a question?* The Maraquillan stuff, bought in these kind of quantities, probably undercut legitimate stuff by twenty-five per cent. Hundreds of thousands of dollars. Someone here was buying through the back door, faking invoices from C & H Chemicals and banking the difference. An' that someone had to be Sig. Only he had the authority, the freedom to take those kinds of risks.

So what had these low-grade batches been used to manufacture? Something he'd felt almost unconsciously from the day he'd arrived at WPP began to take clear form in his mind. On certain issues, it'd always seemed like an invisible wall existed between his division and the manufacturing plant. Were WPP in on this?

Stubbs rubbed his stinging eyes. He needed this job. Gayle and he had been able to put down the deposit on the three-bedroomed house with the yard because of it. A bedroom for them, one for baby and one for his mother. So that once in a while she could sit the baby overnight and they could stay out till late. If he went to the DEA, it meant official enquiries, signed statements, publicity. The spotlight turned on him.

He couldn't afford the risks. He'd make no accusations, just pass on the samples he had and the scientific conclusions he'd come to. But only if he was guaranteed anonymity. Let the proper authorities do the detective work. If Sig Weaver was the boy, let them point the finger. He had a wife and family to think about.

Wait a minute, hadn't the girl from Aid Watch said that the DEA had fouled up the Miami bust, betrayed their trust?

Stubbs shivered. *No DEA. No way. Jesus, who needs that!* He thought, *I'm getting little enough sleep as it is.* He took another look at the identical sepia smears under his microscope.

The girl from Aid Watch; what was her name?

NINETEEN

Akitō re-ordered his paperwork and tapped it into a neat sheaf on the edge of his desk. Four-fifty. In ten minutes it would be 6.00 a.m. in Tokyo. Before five more minutes had passed his father would call. He looked at it sullenly. Ironic. He'd waited for years to make Senior Vice-President of Nashiba. But now it seemed like this had been the longest week of his life. Every evening, almost on the hour, from five till he left the building his father had found some reason to call. Almost always to check on the outcome of something that Akitō thought he'd been assigned to deal with. What would it be this morning? He rubbed his eyes with his forefinger and thumb. At first he'd told himself that his father was reacting to the pressure of the build-up to *Tsumi*, but most of the issues he'd phoned to discuss had had no bearing on that. The simple truth was that his father couldn't bear to let go. Of anything. To him, Nashiba International was his personal creation, and no one but he was qualified to run it.

Ah! The private line. Right on schedule.

'Everything in place for the Yamagata briefing?'

'Of course.' *I might have guessed*, Akitō thought.

'And the Santiago matter, are you on top of that?'

'I've spoken to him again. I'm not anticipating any more problems.'

'Any more on the Greenfield deal?'

'I've already faxed it all to you,' Akitō said irritably. He reached for his summary of press quotes. 'We're all over *Fortune* Magazine: "Borg Takes Greenfield in 30 Billion Dollar Buyout." *New York Times*: "Borg Corporation

292

executes thirty billion dollar leveraged buyout of frozen food giant, Greenfield. . . . the biggest corporate purchase in history . . ." You can see for yourself.'

Tatsuya was silent for a moment. There was an echo on the line from Tokyo. But he could sense the coldness in his son's voice. 'Are there . . . any other problems?'

'Nothing that will not wait until your return.'

Tatsuya caught the inference. *Give him time,* he thought. His meeting with Yoshi would have disturbed him deeply. But he was his father's son. *Tsumi* would be his finest hour.

'Let us have one thing clear between us, Nashiba-san,' Toshio Yamagata fought to keep his composure. 'I have no doubt as to who implicated us in the Ishihara business. Equally, I have no doubt that foul slanders like it will continue to damage our company's reputation unless we toe the line.' He kept his eyes off Akitō. 'My father took a back-street family business and built it into a Global Five Hundred Corporation. It took him thirty-eight years. He has earned some tranquillity and peace of mind. Whatever my personal feelings in this matter, my first consideration must be for him and the future of the company. That is why I am in your office today.'

The green tea Akitō had poured sat untouched in front of the guest. Akitō picked up his own cup and sipped, giving himself time to frame his reply. 'Yamagata-san, whatever you feel – rightly or wrongly – my family or any other has done to yours, it is none of my affair. You have my word that I have had no part in any campaign to discredit the Yamagatas. I have known the other families all my life and I'm equally certain they would stoop to nothing so low. I had hoped that we were meeting here today simply because it made sound business sense.'

'An eloquent speech,' Yamagata sneered. 'And true in every part, I'm sure. Which is why your father was so anxious that it should be you I met with.'

Akitō ignored the insult and lifted the phone. 'We have

a great deal to get through in the next few days. I suggest we make a start.'

'Yes, indeed. You can be sure that we will co-operate in every way with this *Tsumi* of yours, Nashiba-san, but when it is done, things will be as they were between us. And it is my devoted hope that we will never have the need to meet again.'

Akitō allowed himself a faint smile. 'That is a sadness.'

A few minutes later, the two men were joined by senior members of their staff. The group moved through to the conference room. Akitō sat alone in a corner and watched as the first of the series of briefings began. Toshio Yamagata was about his age. Like him, he'd been groomed from an early time to take over the empire his father had begun. He was clearly an intelligent, educated man. But how different they were. How different their beginnings had been. As a child, this man had played chase on the streets of Tokyo. Akitō had spent many of those same afternoons trying to master the intricacies of the ancient game of Go. Then there was *Tsumi*. How old had he been when his father had first introduced him to the concept? Eleven? Twelve?

Twelve. It had been the first week of the summer vacation . . .

'Where are we going?'

'I've told you; fishing.'

Tatsuya Nashiba sat stiffly, close up to the wheel. Akitō couldn't remember ever having seen his father drive before. He watched as he constantly checked his mirrors. They had been on the road for almost an hour. The traffic had been so congested through Tokyo's Shinjuku district that much of their journey had been taken at walking pace. After three months at school in America, Japan seemed a slightly alien place to Akitō now. He watched the mass of pedestrians struggling to push between the cars. Many had their faces hidden behind anti-pollution masks. Tatsuya watched too.

Last time these people had been refugees, fleeing from Allied bombers, Tatsuya Nashiba thought. Last time there

294

had been eleven battle-weary men to convince. Now there was only one twelve-year-old boy. But he was spirited, with a will of his own. The task would be no less onerous.

Twenty minutes later, he pulled off the road near a railway bridge, into a narrow parking lot. Tatsuya opened the trunk of the car and took out fishing rods, collapsible stools and other equipment.

'There's nowhere to fish around here.'

'You'll see. Come on.' Tatsuya motioned for the boy to follow him up the bank that ran parallel to the almost stationary lines of cars. Once on top Akitō could see what looked like a small reservoir beneath them. As they went down, he could see that it was divided into small squares of water by a gridwork of walkways. Sitting at each were fishermen, many in business suits, studying the tiny patch of water in front of them for sudden movement.

Akitō followed his father down to an attendant in green overalls who punched them a ticket. The man handed him a small weighing machine from the neat row that stood beside him then led the two along the walkways to one of the squares. The businessman already seated at it looked at his watch and hastily gathered up his equipment, apologising for having overrun his time.

Father and son settled on their stools and studied the water. The area of water in front of them was no more than ten feet by ten. Casting a rod in the normal way was impossible unless you wanted to catch your hook in the eye of the man seated directly behind. But if Akitō found the whole thing faintly ridiculous, he was too well-bred to show it.

'When you catch a fish, take out the hook but be careful not to damage the mouth,' his father said. 'Then weigh it.'

'Then what?'

'Throw it back of course, so the man next to us has something to catch.' Akitō nodded gravely.

'Do you know who that is?'

Akitō followed his father's eyes to where a small, balding man sat with his attaché case in front of a square of water like their own, near the railway bridge.

295

'President of Hatsuda Electric.'

The man rebaited his hook and returned it to the water. The sudden roar of a Bullet train, banking steeply as it sped towards Kyoto and Osaka, drowned out what his father said next. But Akitō gathered that the man drove for an hour every lunchtime to fish in this place for thirty minutes before driving back.

Akitō looked into the water.

'What are you thinking, Akitō? Tell me honestly. I'd like to know.'

'What did you bring me out here for?'

'To fish . . . and to learn. To learn about your country and the way things are here now. You spend so much of your time in America you could be forgiven for losing your sense of perspective. In the States you can drive out a short distance from most cities, even New York itself, and find clean air and vast unbroken waterways to fish in. As you see, this is all we have. When I was a boy, there were rivers and streams around here. Most were filled in years ago to provide more building space. Those that remain are too polluted to support life. So this is the best we can do.'

Tatsuya jerked back his line and landed a small fish. It had been caught so many times before most of its lower lip had been torn away. He unhooked it with great care. 'We are a nation of a hundred and twenty-five million people compressed into an area a fortieth the size of Texas. If we still want to live within reach of our businesses and all the facilities we've come to find so necessary to life, this is the penalty we must pay.' Tatsuya weighed the wriggling fish and entered the details on the card provided. Then he threw it back.

Akitō studied his father for a moment. 'Do you like this?'

Tatsuya put down his line, put his hands together and looked back at his son. The look of composure faded from his face. 'No, I hate it. I hate to see what has become of us. My generation raised this country from the ashes. We've lifted it to a zenith no one believed possible. There was no economic miracle as they teach you at school. Just hard work – a lifetime of it.' He gestured around him. 'Is this to be our reward? To see our people scrambling over one another like ants on a hill? The problem is bad enough now but in a time soon to come, it will become a nightmare. Did you know that we Japanese live longer now than any other race? We have solved the problem of health care for the elderly and created the even greater problem of where to put so many old people. Soon they will number more than half the population. If we stem the birthrate then we shall gradually become a nation of geriatrics! If we do not, there'll be no place left in these islands soon for anyone to live at any decent standard at all.'

'There are other countries to live in.'

'Certainly. Our family is fortunate in that. We have homes in America, Switzerland, France . . . You and I were educated in America, we understand their culture. It's almost a second home to us. And perhaps someday it could be for many Japanese.' Tatsuya thought for a moment. 'The first time I flew across the country from coast to coast it struck me that the greater part of their best land is unpopulated. You could put Japan's whole living space into that land a hundred times over and still miss it. And you know, the American is not an unnatural neighbour for us. We modelled our new society on the best of theirs. Much of our modern culture is an extension of theirs.' Tatsuya reeled in his line and put it back in its canvas cover. 'But unfortunately, it's just not a practical solution, right now. Such things are way beyond the dreams of the average middle-class Japanese family. And even the few who could afford to live elsewhere would not choose to go in isolation, to be cut off from relatives and friends. They would want to go as a unit or not at all.'

They packed up their things and began to walk back towards the attendant. On the way, Tatsuya passed a man he knew. He held up his card to show off his list of catches. Tatsuya smiled and nodded and they passed on. 'Ours is a very young economy, Akitō. Twenty-five years ago, we were struggling to even be noticed amongst the other world powers. Oh, I'm sure they teach you at school that we have limitless resources, trillions of dollars in reserves. Well, whatever they might tell you, our resources are as finite as anyone else's, believe me. All that we have will not come close to curing the living space problem as it will exist in the next century. A solution will never be found without a radical change in the balance of the First-World economies.'

'What sort of change?'

'A change to our advantage.' They started to climb the bank back towards the car. 'We are in charge of our own destiny in this life, Akitō. Nothing happens unless we make it happen. I and many others have worked half our lives for such a change. I believe that you will live to see a time when all Japanese people own a home where they can stretch out their arms without touching the walls, where they can shout, "This is my space on the planet!" without the man next door hammering on the wall for quiet.'

US Under Secretary of the International Trade Administration, Robert Galbraith, sat nervously in the waiting room at Nagata-cho. He'd never needed a breakthrough on Japanese import quotas more than now. The last agreement, signed earlier in the year, had been greeted by Wall Street with barely concealed contempt. Sure, it had eased the way for increased imports of American-built aircraft, telecommunications equipment, a wide variety of agricultural and tobacco products. But desperately needed increases to quotas on a whole range of consumer and electrical goods were no nearer than they had been five years before.

Just in this last week, he'd seen a ray of light on the horizon. The Japanese aerospace industry, developed originally with American know-how, had expanded too fast. It had not become self-reliant as the Japanese had hoped but was still highly dependent on US technology. If he could lock up substantial new orders in that field alone, Galbraith knew that Wall Street would have to sit up and take notice.

Talks had been going well. The groundwork was done. All he needed was another forty-eight hours and the new deal would be sewn up. Least it would have been. The contents of Wednesday morning's diplomatic bag suddenly threatened the whole issue. He rolled up the document he was holding and tapped it on the palm of one hand. Damn this thing! As if his week in Tokyo hadn't been difficult enough. The Ishihara Scandal had turned the Japanese administration upside down. His opposite number at the Ministry of International Trade and Industry, a man who he knew trusted and respected him, had been made Premier. And in his place was a man who, up until a week ago, had been Finance Minister. Establishing a relationship with the new minister had been tortuous enough. Now he'd got to cope with this Lasky Report. When it first arrived with Brodie's covering letter, his reaction had been to dismiss it out of hand. The US economic recession had become a breeding ground of anti-Japanese paranoia. If you put enough facts together with enough theories he could see how you would come up with the types of conclusions contained in the report. But he was certain that nothing remotely like it was actually on the cards. Nevertheless, to ignore the report completely was to run the risk of Brodie going over his head, direct to the Secretary of State.

So, now here he was in Nagata-cho, with the diplomatic mission of a lifetime to pull off. Galbraith thumbed through the report again. The situation was a comedy of errors. It should have been an advantage to be an old friend of the man who was now Prime Minister. As things stood, it was the one connection that could cost him the new trade deal. If it looked like he'd been trying to lobby the Premier over the head of the new Minister of International Trade . . .

'The Prime Minister will see you now, sir.' Saburo Tanaka's Personal Private Secretary stood in the doorway of the visitors' waiting-room. Galbraith got up. He'd have to rely on twenty years of friendship to get him through this one now.

Galbraith knew that whenever possible, Tanaka took a half-hour break at six-thirty in the evening. He'd pour himself a Scotch and sit alone and watch the news on television, until it was time to change for the evening. But instead of being shown into the Prime Minister's office as he'd expected, Galbraith was led to one of the smaller official reception rooms on the first floor. Tanaka stood at the far wall, his face half-hidden by a video camera.

'Look frightened, Bobby,' he called.

'What?'

'Look terrified, like you're about to be eaten by something huge. Come on. Move a little to the left will you?'

The Japanese were not exactly renowned for a finely developed sense of humour. Galbraith had always thought the deficiency added greatly to their difficulty in dealing with Americans, for whom laughter was an essential ingredient of life. Neither was Saburo Tanaka the Orient's answer to Steve Martin. Twenty years' work alongside him in diplomatic circles had taught Galbraith that Tanaka was iron-willed and ruthlessly efficient. But he knew too that in moments of repose, the amiable Japanese was capable of taking himself a lot less seriously than many of his peers.

Galbraith looked towards the video camera. Tanaka was waving at him to stand in front of something. Looking behind, he saw a screen of blue plastic sheeting which had been stretched out on an alloy frame.

'Come on, do something. He's moving in to get you!'

Galbraith gave in. Feeling utterly ridiculous, he gave the Japanese Prime Minister his rendering of a man trying to beat off some vast unseen menace.

'Good.' Tanaka laughed. 'Excellent, Bobby. You're a natural. A little inhibited, perhaps, but you have the makings of a fine performer. Come and see.' As Tanaka wound back the cassette in the camera, Galbraith moved over to a vast TV monitor. 'See, the camcorder's been programmed not to record that background shade of blue, so all that's on tape is you. Now . . .' He plugged a lead from the monitor into the camcorder and pressed the remote control unit that operated the set. A movie-theatre-quality image of a modern metropolis was thrown up on the screen. A towering, green lizard-like monster rose out of a river that ran through it and started to wreak havoc on the skyscrapers with its fists.

'It's computer animation of course, but it's enhanced to look like live footage. Now look.' The monster stooped at a building that was meant to be City Hall and tried to reach inside. Tanaka started the camcorder and immediately, a tiny weary-looking Galbraith appeared in the doorway feebly attempting to fight the monster off.

'Clever isn't it? It'll be on the market this Christmas. That's the Godzilla tape, he's a big favourite here again, you know. They do a science fiction feature, a pop video, a jungle adventure, or you can shoot your own animated sequences. My grandson is going to go crazy when he sees this, I tell you.'

Galbraith shook his head. 'Extraordinary.'

Tanaka studied his friend's face. 'You look like you could use a stiff drink.'

The two men walked down to the ground floor, through the Prime Minister's office and into the ante-chamber that faced on to the garden. Tanaka opened the drinks cabinet. 'Scotch on the rocks, isn't it?'

'Yes, thank you.' Galbraith sank into one of the two well-worn armchairs. Tanaka passed him his drink.

'Here's to an historic administration.' Galbraith raised the glass.

'Thank you, Bobby.' Tanaka settled down in the chair opposite. 'Thanks to Ishihara-san, it's destined to be that anyway.' He sipped at his Scotch.

'It was good of you to see me so quickly.'

Tanaka gestured that it was a pleasure.

'I've thought for hours how I should say to you what I have to say. In the end, I came to the conclusion that it was best you saw for yourself the report I've just been sent from Washington.' He handed over some papers. 'This is a translation I've had prepared.'

In fact, what Galbraith handed him was a carefully edited summary he'd spent four hours working on that day. It combined the most telling elements of Mack's report and Brodie's letter. He knew he would have, at best, half an hour with Tanaka and that the new Prime Minister spoke English a good deal more fluently than he read it. This way, Galbraith reasoned, he could hit him with something he could absorb in the time available.

Tanaka looked up at last. He took off his reading glasses and shrugged. 'Most of this data is hardly news. It's readily available to anyone who cares to contact the usual sources. The rest of it? I think I could reasonably ask for more concrete evidence than your informant supplies here before giving it credence. And as to the interpretation he puts on the whole . . . I've known you too long, Bobby, not to know that you're taking this seriously, but . . .'

'I'm not alone in this, Saburo, I assure you,' Galbraith said.

Tanaka shook his head. 'The connections your man makes are certainly an improvement on the usual "Japanese Conspiracy" theories, I'll say that. But really, this economic coup concept is plucked out of the air.' He looked hard at his friend. 'When will you Americans ever understand? We have no . . . hidden agenda. What you see is all there is and all there ever will be: a commitment to hard, competitive business.' He sighed. 'The economic outlook in your country is depressing, I can see that. It is natural that there should be . . . how do you put it . . . some raw nerve ends. But this paranoia, this . . . loathing of us . . . I've seen that television commercial you have, you know the one, "Go on buying Japanese! Make Main Street America into Banzai Boulevard!" I've seen your Senators on the news, smashing Japanese radios on the steps of the Capitol Building.' Tanaka rubbed his eyes wearily. 'This report of yours is about as rational. How long have we known each other, Bobby?'

'Twenty years.' Galbraith's face still registered concern.

'Have I ever lied to you?'

'Not that I know of.'

'Well, if it's going to make your people sleep any easier tonight, let me give you my personal assurance that no such . . . strategy or coup is planned. Or has ever been.'

'Saburo, I appreciate that. And it's what I was hoping you'd say. I think it'll smooth a lot of ruffled feathers.' Galbraith crossed his legs and tried to look relaxed. 'But, dare I say that the Secretary of State does not know you as I do. Now, please don't take this as a slight, but he has asked me to get a statement from the *Keidanren*. Your word—'

'. . . is the word of a Prime Minister who's been in power six days?'

'Not to me, old friend,' Galbraith said softly.

'But to him.' Tanaka looked at his watch and got up. 'Look, I'll speak to the principals in the *Keidanren* within the next twenty-four hours and get you a statement. Then perhaps we can have an end to this matter.'

Go for broke, Galbraith thought. 'I know I can rely on your discretion, Saburo. But once this matter is discussed outside this office . . .'

'If you're concerned about the current trade talks, Bobby, forget it.' Tanaka smiled and offered Galbraith his hand. 'What has that to do with this? You're in a difficult position, I can see that. I hope what I've been able to tell you has helped a little.'

'It's helped immeasurably. Thank you.'

The US Embassy limousine moved through the Nagata-cho checkpoint and joined the rush-hour traffic. If Saburo Tanaka knew of no coup, Galbraith told himself, then there could be none. But twenty years of behind-the-scenes diplomacy had taught him to cover his ass, every way. The statement from the *Keidanren* was to be his insurance policy. He'd call Senator Brodie in Washington, bring him up to date and tell him that he'd be reporting to the Secretary of State direct on the whole matter and that he, Brodie, need do nothing more. That would take the heat off. Then he'd wait till he had the *Keidanren*'s assurances, fax the Lasky Report and his own through the encoder to the Secretary of State's office and back it up with a phone call. *In twenty-four hours*, he thought, *this Lasky thing'll be out of my hair for good.*

Saburo Tanaka sat alone in his ante-room and considered his next move. He'd been a lot more alarmed by the Lasky Report than Galbraith could guess. Was it possible that the Four Families, whose influence on the *Keidanren* was well known, had a secret strategy of their own? One that even he, the Premier handpicked by them, knew nothing about.

It'd taken until midnight for Tatsuya Nashiba to return his call. He wished he'd been able to see the man's face as he read him extracts from the report.

'Let me call a few people first thing in the morning and come back to you, Prime Minister,' Nashiba said.

'If you think that's necessary.' Tanaka forced a laugh. 'But a flat denial from you, right now, would go a long way to resolving this matter, once and for all.'

'I'll get back to you tomorrow. Good night, Prime Minister.'

Tanaka stared out at the walled garden. The early morning light gave the small Shinto shrine at the far end a strange unearthly quality. It was the first time he'd seen it at this hour. *What if there were to be no assurances?* he thought. If something like this *Tsumi* was planned . . . What then? To give Galbraith even a hint of his concern would be seen as treachery by the *Keidanren*. To say nothing and to let it just play out, would rend apart diplomatic ties it had taken fifty years to establish, for generations to come.

Marty Kovacks had seen enough. Now he needed some air. He stood up and squeezed down the rows of seated shareholders and made for the door. The corridor outside the ballroom of the Marriott Hotel in downtown Los Angeles was crowded with guests, lunchtime diners and conventioneers. Kovacks made for the men's room. This was the first shareholders' meeting he'd attended in forty-seven years. And it would sure as hell be the last. He'd joined American Associated Pictures as a carpenter, straight from school in 1947, caught the last of the boom before the movie industry was decimated by television. He'd seen the studio go through more changes than he cared to count, but his dogged belief in the company had paid off handsomely. At the age of seventy-one he was happy in the knowledge that a modest investment in Associated stock made in 1950 had increased its value fiftyfold. He'd just begun to get to grips with the takeover by GMA Communications in '84. Now he had to contend with this Japanese outfit that had come out of nowhere and bought the whole goddamn shooting match.

He stood up to the urinal and unzipped his fly. *These Tokyo Joes seem to be able to bulldoze through any damn thing they want*, he thought. *The way things are going, they're going to screw the whole company.*

'Fucking Japs,' he muttered.

'They got us by the balls, pal,' said the heavy-set man next to him.

Kovacks acknowledged the speaker with a quick turn of his head. 'I could've sworn they'd've got their butts kicked in that last vote.'

'Birds of a feather vote together. The dice are loaded, see.' The man crossed to the washbasin. 'Half those Ivy Leaguers with their hands in the air either represented nominee companies fronting for the Japs or US corporations where the Japanese have hidden control.'

'No kidding.'

'You can think yourself lucky they didn't propose the return of the Volstead Act! We'd have been drowning our sorrows in Doctor Peppers, this time next week.'

'It's a damn shame.' Kovacks crossed to the mirror and ran a comb through his thinning hair. 'I remember this company when it was a family business. First-generation Americans sure, but as American as apple pie for all that.'

The other man shrugged. 'Before my time.'

'Hell, I remember when President Truman visited the lot. They shipped in every star signed to Associated, that day . . .'

'Signed to where?'

'American Associated . . . Pictures.'

The thickset man turned to look at him. 'What room're you in, pal?'

Kovacks looked confused. 'The ballroom.'

305

'I'm in Conference Room Three. Columbus Business Instruments.'

They stared at each other for a moment. 'Well, I'll be damned,' Kovacks said.

The traffic signals at the junction of Sixtieth and Third changed through their sequence again but the gun-metal grey limousine remained locked in Manhattan's uptown traffic. Akitō watched the chauffeur's fingers drumming on the steering-wheel.

'Don't worry, Minoru,' he said, at last. 'It's only six blocks. I'll walk from here, the exercise'll do me good.'

Akitō moved quickly along the sidewalk. His nerves were on edge. The Yamagata meeting had been merely tedious; his father's incessant calls, infuriating. But what was really eating him away was the private turmoil he'd suffered since his first meeting with Yoshi. How his father could have calculated his genesis so cold-bloodedly, how he could have ridden roughshod over so many people's emotions for the sake of a plan, was beyond comprehension. It tested his endurance, now, to talk to his father at all. Akitō could think of him with nothing but anger. At the beginning he'd actually considered flying to Tokyo and facing him with the truth. But he had no doubts as to how such a confrontation would go. First he'd be met by a wall of defiance, then a display of undisguised irritation. Finally the old anger, that had so terrified him as a child, would explode, with the exaggerated gesturing and vocal histrionics, that seemed to belong more to the world of *Noh* theatre.

It was better to wait, there were other ways. And his father would be back from Tokyo soon enough. After *Tsumi* there would be time.

Akitō turned the corner into the forecourt of the Trump Plaza. All he wanted at this minute was to be alone with Bryony. On that issue, at least, he had no doubts. He found himself being drawn to her more with every passing day. What had started out as sexual attraction had developed into something far more, and, as inconvenient and untidy as it was, he knew now that he really cared for her. The fact of her had made the frustrations of the last weeks tolerable.

As he got into the elevator, all he could think about was the evening ahead. In Japan, he would have been expected to go out and socialise with male colleagues, clients and customers at night. Girlfriends and especially wives would be left at home to find whatever pleasure they could in their own company or domesticity. Top-salary men would be expected to spend around three hours a week with their families. Akitō had lived in the West too long to identify with that kind of lifestyle. At the end of the working day, whenever possible, he put business to one side and relaxed in good company. And if that company came in the shape of a beautiful, intelligent woman, so much the better.

'Hi!' Akitō's cheerful greeting met with a stony response. Bryony was sitting on the window seat, looking out at the street below. As she turned, he could see that she'd been crying.

'Hey, what's wrong?' He made to embrace her but she pushed him away. 'What's the problem?'

'Does the name Western Pacific Pharmaceuticals mean anything to you?' Her voice was cold-edged.

'Sure,' Akitō said, wondering what was coming next. 'What about it?'

'You know I told you that Aid Watch had information about the opium smuggled into this country by Colonel Santiago?'

Akitō nodded.

'Well, it's being processed into morphine, not heroin as we thought. And not by some back-street outfit, either.' She searched his face. 'No prizes for guessing who.'

'Western Pacific. Okay, call the DEA, whack an indictment on them. It's nothing to do with you and me.'

'You're either a liar or a fool! So tell me you don't know that Nashiba International has a controlling interest in Western Pacific – oh, well behind the scenes, of course. There's so many nominee companies between the two, no judiciary in the world would think to tie them together.'

Akitō was shaken by the violence of her reply. 'Of course

I know we have an interest in them. But as for processing smuggled opium . . . You have to be kidding!'

'Don't give me this, Akitō. You're the Senior Vice-President of Nashiba, for Chrissakes. You're trying to tell me you don't know what goes on?'

Akitō held up his hand. 'Look, if you're right – and I'm sure you have every reason to believe you are, hell, I'll call the DEA myself! Now, if you'll just cool down—'

'Nice try, Mr Nashiba. But you seem to be forgetting where we met. At the home of Juan Santiago: thief, mass-murderer . . . and dope-dealer.'

'Oh now, wait a minute . . .' He walked towards her. She backed off.

'My first instincts are always the right ones. I wanted to believe you were on the level, I really did. But I couldn't figure out what you'd be doing up there at the Casa Grande, if you were. Now I know.' She pushed past him, and hurried towards the door. Akitō tried to catch her arm.

'Please . . .'

'Don't touch me!' Bryony pulled away. 'Look, I've done a lot of thinking. It's just too big a coincidence.' She moved into the corridor, turning briefly to give him one last glance. 'You're the worst kind, Akitō. We're on opposite sides now. But then, of course, we always were.'

Akitō stood frozen in the door frame, numb with the sense of unreality. He watched her walk to the elevator. How could he have explained how the last week had been? For fifteen years he'd assumed that once he was elevated to Senior Vice-President many things would change, doors that had remained closed to him would open. Too many times in the last few days, he'd discovered some new involvement the family had, some new vein, hidden below the surface that stretched out to the extremities of the Nashiba empire and gave it lifeblood. Too many times he'd been faced with a dismissive explanation that left him wondering what was concealed behind it. His father had handed him a sinecure. The Vice-Presidency was his. The price: his compliance.

The elevator doors opened. Bryony stepped inside and was gone. Akitō felt his throat tighten.

Everything. His father had ruined everything. Taken away his pride, his security ... and now he'd taken away the woman he loved. Akitō slammed his fist into the wall.

'*Bastard ... Fucking bastard!*'

Whatever it took to get Bryony back, he was ready.

TWENTY

'Y ou sound real strange.' Mack moved the phone to his other ear.

'So would you with your snoz in a splint.' Jay's voice was strained. 'Like I say, seems burglars are out of season this time of year.'

Mack swivelled his address book round on Auburn's desk. 'So where are you now?'

'Back home. I had a couple of interesting hours with the boys at Homicide. We got on so well they've asked me back. I get to keep my passport so I guess things could be worse.'

'Do you have any idea who this guy was?'

'Nope. No one does. All he had in his pockets was lint. They can't make a mug-shot 'cause he ain't got no mug. Not any more.'

'Fingerprints?'

'Nothing. I'll tell you this, Mack, he was a professional – a professional what, I don't know. Oh, I know what you're thinking – Nashiba sent him, right?'

'Could be.'

'Maybe they traced me through the phone line when I hacked into the database. Who knows? I took all the usual precautions – used a mobile phone like I always do. I buy 'em with cash across the state line under a phoney name, work with them for a month, then toss them in the trash. Till now I thought it was foolproof. Maybe this time, a month was a week too long.'

Mack tried to sound calm. 'So what're you going to do now?'

'Repaint my hallway. What else? What's the latest on the Nashiba scam?'

Mack sighed. 'Right now, not a damn thing.'

'Well, keep me posted.'

'Sure will.'

Mack put down the phone and walked back over to the coffee-table. *Akitō*, he thought. *Call Akitō. Why the hell not? He was right there on the inside looking out. He said to call him . . .*

It seemed a lifetime since Senator Brodie's call Wednesday night. According to him, Under Secretary Galbraith was taking the report seriously enough to have made an appointment to see the Japanese Prime Minister. Mack'd felt his whole nervous system throttle back. The matter seemed out of his hands. But Galbraith's meeting was scheduled for Thursday night. Even allowing for the thirteen-hour time change, the latest Mack'd expected an update was this morning. None had come. Brodie had heard no more and his further enquiries produced nothing.

Mack looked at his watch. Eleven a.m. – midnight in Tokyo. No call'll come now, he thought. The earliest Galbraith will be able to reach Brodie will be late tonight, long after everything here's closed for the weekend. *Tsumi* is Tuesday. That's too late, way too late.

A sense of impotence began to set in. Mack got up and started to pace the room. *What do I do? Stomp around here until Monday morning and wait for the roof to cave in?*

'I will call Akitō, damn it,' he said out loud. He started dialling Akitō's home number. It was answered by an operator from some central switchboard. He gave his name and was put on hold. To his surprise, he was connected immediately.

'Hi Mack, how've you been?'

'Akitō?'

'Yes. Why, who did you want?' He could tell from the quality of the connection that Akitō was speaking from a car phone.

'You. I need to see you. As soon as possible.'

311

'Great, we should get together. Maybe we should do lunch . . .'

'I need to see you now, tonight, Akitō.'

'I can't do tonight, Mack.' The voice sounded subdued, distracted. 'Maybe we could do breakfast next—'

Go for broke, Mack thought. 'You're not hearing me, pal. Look, we were good friends, once, you and I, I'm not sure what we are now, but—'

'Friends.'

'What?'

'I said friends. We're still friends.'

'I'm telling you, Akitō, if you ever cared about me, Morton or Warren you'll come tonight . . .'

Mack eased Morton's white Lincoln out of the parking lot and on to West End Avenue. It felt strange to be driving his car. Jay's call had changed a lot of things. Sure, the man who'd turned over Pig Palace could have been working for a dozen people. But Jay makes the hack of a lifetime. And forty-eight hours later some slick operator turns up looking for disks. Mack didn't like the odds. If he was sent by Nashiba, and Mack's gut told him he was, then they were getting desperate. Whatever he said about friendship, Akitō was not the same guy that he and Warren had known at Harvard. Hadn't been for a very long time. Exactly who he was and what he was capable of these days, Mack had no way of knowing, but one thing was for sure, Akitō was a Nashiba, first, last and always. That same gut feeling told Mack that meeting the man alone, now, wasn't the smartest of moves.

Mack turned on to Central Park West. Akitō'd been heading south on the New England Thruway when they spoke. He was due in Long Beach at eight. Mack'd told him to keep coming south and he'd call him back. He needed time to choose a venue. Mack looked at the clock on the dash. In forty minutes Akitō'd be in Queens; if the traffic was no worse than usual, he could be too. He was certain that if the Nashibas actually resorted to killing to keep their secrets, they did so only *in extremis*. But if they'd been monitoring him recently, God knew they had reason enough to move against him, now. Mack could feel the muscles in his neck beginning to tighten. They'd killed Morton. He was certain of it. They might have wanted to kill Jay. Mack tried to think clearly. *Right now, I'm more danger to them than anyone. Why wouldn't they try to kill me too?*

His best chance of staying alive, if it came down to it, was to meet Akitō somewhere that was as public as possible. He picked up his mobile phone. Kennedy Airport. Open concourses, crowds of people. But if he really was in danger, the less notice Akitō had of the venue, the safer he'd be. He'd leave calling him another thirty minutes.

The Friday-night rush-hour traffic slowed for roadworks just beyond La Guardia. To Mack's left, set back from the road, was Flushing Meadow Park. Amongst the trees and bushes were the rusting remains of what had once been the 1964 World Fair. Something Morton'd said that last Sunday came back into Mack's mind.

'Whenever I drive by that now, I find myself thinking, Jesus, look at the state of it, all choked with weeds and falling apart. For me, it's like a kind of statement, for how we feel about ourselves in this country these days . . .'

No, not Kennedy. Flushing Meadow.

Akitō stopped a short distance off and looked around him. 'Do you mind telling me why we had to meet here, of all places?'

Mack shrugged. 'Seemed like a good idea at the time. I wanted to talk . . . somewhere we wouldn't be disturbed.' Behind Mack, towering above him, was a vast, rusting, skeletal globe of the world.

Akitō's mobile phone buzzed. He laughed. 'Nice try. Sorry.' He switched it off and laid it on the concrete wall beside him. 'The wonders of modern living. I've wanted to talk to you, Mack. For a long time.'

'Yeah?'

'Yes. I know you and Warren have wondered why I've been such a stranger. It's hard to explain.' Akitō leaned back on the wall. 'If a Japanese spends a long time living away or as part of another culture he's expected to . . . rediscover his Japaneseness when he returns. That process began for me when I joined the corporation. That's why I cut myself off from everything I'd known before. I think that was a mistake. I've missed our friendship . . . the Club.'

There were a dozen ways Mack had figured on this conversation going. This wasn't one of them. Akitō looked bad, Mack thought. His eyes were flat, his whole face seemed to have sagged.

'Why did you say that if I'd ever cared for any of you, that I'd come tonight?'

'Because I thought that if there was anything left of the Akitō I knew, you'd come. We got a few things to talk over, you and I. See, Morton didn't commit suicide. He was murdered.'

Akitō's forehead creased into a frown. 'The police told you that?'

'No. I found out for myself.' *Did he really not know?* Mack thought. 'I believe that Morton knew he was in danger; in a way, he told me that himself. And he went to great lengths to make sure that if anything happened to him, the truth'd come out.'

'What truth?' There was no hint that Akitō felt threatened.

'He snooped around the company database. Accessed a lot of stuff he shouldn't have. Someone up there got real sore – arranged to have him OD'd and his medical records fixed.'

'Someone at AmTronics? Come on, they—'

'Not AmTronics. Nashiba.'

Akitō's face muscles tightened. There was just enough surprise there for Mack to believe that this was news to him.

'Someone at Nashiba? In New York? You can't believe that . . .'

'I don't have a choice.' Mack's voice was calm.

314

'Oh c'mon, you don't believe that I had anything to do with—'

'I'd like to think not.'

Akitō stood staring at Mack. Hadn't Yoshi said that she walked in fear of his father's hired killers? *Don't let this be so,* Akitō thought. *Not Morton.* 'I used to know you well, Mack,' he said at last. 'No one changes that much. You wouldn't say these things unless you thought you could back them up. But you have to be wrong. Why should anyone connected with Nashiba do such a thing?'

Timing now was everything, Mack told himself. Take this real slow. 'Because he found out what you're going to try and pull on Tuesday.'

'Well, if you know, perhaps you'll tell me. I'm sure I'll learn a lot.' There was no humour in Akitō's reply. But it had to be a lie. *Tilt,* Mack thought, *no points, start again. Lasky to play.* 'Well, where would you like to start? Maybe we could talk about the Neutrals.'

'Who?'

Wrong answer. You should have said 'What?' Not 'Who?' You're stonewalling, Akitō. On a good day, you could block me out, put ten feet of solid granite between us, and I'd never even know it. But not today, pal. Okay, last ball, Lasky to play. Blow this and you blow everything.

'Okay, then maybe we should talk about *Tsumi.*'

'*Tsumi?*' Akitō said softly. Dozens of people had knowledge of one small element of the plan but only a handful, maybe thirty men in total, knew what that element was a part of. Only twelve men knew the nature of, knew the word, *Tsumi.* How could Mack have learnt it?

Mack stayed on the attack. 'I know what *Tsumi* is, Akitō. I know that it's Tuesday and I know why. Whatever you're all getting out of it, I just hope it was worth Morton's life.'

'As far as I know, Tuesday will be just another day.'

He's clamming up, Mack thought, *I got to hit him real hard.* 'Don't give me that, you know the pay-off. It's a fifty-year-old vendetta that means nothing to anyone but a bunch of sick old men! What's it to you, pal?' He stared hard into Akitō's face. 'You're thirty-one years old, Akitō, you've spent most of your life in this country. Do you know something? My mother's Scots, my father was Yugoslavian, and that's about as American as you can get. Remember what Morton said. We're a nation of immigrants. The way I see it, Akitō, you're as American as I am. I know I can't stop this thing. But you could, Akitō. If not Tuesday, then afterwards – you could change what happens then. You're the future. When your father dies, you'll call the shots.'

Akitō was shaking his head.

'Tell me I'm wrong about Tuesday, Akitō. Tell me I'm wrong.'

'You're wrong, Mack,' Akitō snapped. 'You hear me? Wrong! Satisfied?' He took his mobile phone off the wall and started to walk towards his car. Whatever his feelings for his father, his loyalties lay with his family. 'You got it wrong, all wrong,' he said without looking back.

'Is that it?' Mack yelled. 'Are you so driven by your father that you can't act for yourself? What's it going to be, Akitō, your way or his?'

Akitō spun around on his heels. The skin of his face was taut. He stood looking at Mack for a full fifteen seconds. Then he said, 'Save yourself.'

Mack stared blankly.

'Save yourself, Mack. Do that. Sunday night.' He climbed into his car and moved off into the traffic. *What did he mean?* Mack thought. *Save myself, Sunday night? If I'm so wrong, what am I meant to be saving myself from?*

Suddenly it hit. He was talking about the Nikkei, had to be. Trading opened in Tokyo 10.00 a.m. Monday; 9.00 p.m. Sunday night, New York time. He had to sell everything in his portfolio on the Nikkei Sunday night. Of course, he'd been wrong! *Tsumi* wasn't Tuesday, it never had been. Akitō was trying to tell him it was Monday.

But what was the significance of Monday? What did it matter? *Tsumi* was on.

'This is one hell of a portfolio you got here, Lasky.' There was a pause while Edgar Brent, chief trader for Denton

316

Securities in Tokyo, wreathed through yards of fax. 'A lot of this stuff is not listed here. You realise that?'

'Yup.' Mack could hear the staccato vocal tones of a samurai series playing on the TV in the background.

'You know you'd do a lot better waiting till New York opens, Monday. Too long, huh?'

Mack aimed his answer where he knew it would find an easy target. 'Ex-wife trouble. I need to clean up my act real fast, Ed. This is my only hope.'

'Okay, got it.'

'So I really need you to make a market in this stuff for me Monday morning on the Nikkei, Ed. It'll give me a twelve-hour start.'

'I'll do what I can for you. Us walking wounded got to stick together. Listen, I know a great attorney if you need one. Killer.'

'If you come through for me, I won't.'

'Consider it done. You want me to call you, close of business? That's three o'clock Sunday morning, your time.'

'Yup.'

'Women; pain in the ass!'

He hung up. Mack turned on the light on Auburn's desk and leafed through the pages of his address book, putting a pencil line through all the names of friends he knew he dare not call. Brodie was right, this had to be contained. The domino effect created by word of mouth could be as dangerous as *Tsumi* itself. So far he had just four, men he'd known most of his working life, some of whom had helped him at the beginning. All of whom he felt he could trust now. He'd tell them just enough for them to save themselves and swear them to secrecy.

The last name he came to in the book was Jack Raskin. A flicker of a smile played on the corner of Mack's mouth. Well now, perhaps there was a God somewhere . . . He put a line very slowly through the name.

Daybreak Saturday, there was still no word from Brodie or Galbraith. For most of Friday night, Mack'd considered

317

handing his report, together with an update covering the recent events in Washington and Tokyo, to Saul Leibersen at NBS. But he knew he'd come to the same conclusion Brodie had: most of the assessments were based on evidence obtained by hacking. Acting on them privately was one thing; handing them over to a TV network was likely to get him three to five years in the state pen. There was only one thing he had that he could use safely: his knowledge of the Neutrals scheme. No one could block personal testimony, all he needed were statements from enough of them to convince Leibersen of the breadth and efficiency of a nationwide scam.

But why would any of the Neutrals even take his call? Mack decided to start with one who he was sure would. Warren sounded dopey, but sober. Six-fifteen in the morning was too early even for him to start drinking. Mack was gratified to find that some of the old Steadman spark was still in there.

'We been house-hunting the last two days, I'm bushed. You know, in a way I'll be glad to be out of this place. Really! All the overhead and upkeep. There's an apartment for lease above the liquor store. I've figured I could run a tube straight down into their stock room, you know, cut out the middleman.'

'Listen Warren, try to concentrate. Through Morton I was able to access highly confidential material in the Nashiba database. Amongst other things, I found a list of major US corporations, all of which have Japanese participants. Under each name were the names of one or two of their main board members, about four hundred in all. Yours was amongst them. I don't think it was for Nashiba eyes only, I think it was just their copy of it. Do they have any tie in to DMC?'

'Not that I heard of. It's strictly Mitsuda country round here.'

'Well, I wouldn't mind betting Mitsuda have a copy of this list locked away somewhere too.'

'What am I listed as being?'

'The file was headed "Neutrals". What does that say to you?'

Warren let out something between a moan and a sigh. 'Weak-minded suckers.'

'Well, I've checked out a lot of the people on the list very thoroughly. I'd say most of these guys were "crown princes": young, aggressive, with intellect and the power to question.'

'You say "were". Why, what are they now?'

'Obviously no two scenarios are the same but most of these guys have problems. A lot of them have serious money problems, that's for certain.'

'In hock up to their ears to their Japanese partners, right?' Warren's voice was starting to rise. 'Too far in to dare speak up for themselves or their corporations. Is that about it? They should rename that file Corporate Eunuchs.'

'This may not be much consolation to you, Warren, but I don't think what happened to you was entirely your fault. The truth is, you never stood a chance. You were targeted by Mitsuda as a potential troublemaker. They wanted your voting power but not your input. So they softened you up until they were sure you'd vote their way on anything that affected their control of DMC.'

There was a pause. 'They did a good job.'

'Look, I'm going to fax you this list. I've ringed the people I know personally on it. I want you to do the same and fax it back.'

'What are you planning to do?'

'Trust me, Warren.'

Minutes later, Mack's fax arrived back in Auburn's living-room with Warren's additions. As Mack tore it off, Warren was back on the line.

'So what happens now?'

'Hang on, let me read this . . .'

As Mack read he could hear Warren breathing heavily the other end of the phone and then the sound of him sipping what sounded like a hot drink. 'Pour it away, Warren. Make a fresh one . . .'

'What?'

Mack's temper snapped. 'Without the Jack Daniels in it. Get off the booze, Warren! . . . Look, I'm trying to give you a break. You're one of a whole bunch of guys who happen to be some of the best corporate brains in the country. As a voice you have to be taken seriously. . .'

'Do we? Why should what's happened to us matter to anyone else?'

It was then that Mack told him about *Tsumi*. Warren had always respected Mack, believed in him. That was why he'd helped him through Harvard. Listening to what Mack had to say now and accepting most of it at face value was a measure of that faith. At the end, he felt almost buoyed by what Mack had told him. Making a stand now did have significance.

'. . . But as you can see, Warren, we only have forty-eight hours to do anything.'

'What can we do?'

Mack decided to strike while the iron was hot.

'I'll tell you. You've ringed nineteen names on the Neutrals list. I've ringed twenty-two. We're each going to call our own. Some of the home numbers are marked in, the others you have, don't you?'

'Sure. What am I telling them?'

'You want to meet with them as soon as possible. You have problems in common. Tell them anything that'll get them to open up.'

'Wait a minute, if these guys are in the same mess I'm in, they'll have no illusions about their legal position. Jesus, they're guilty of . . . violating their fiduciary duty to act in the best interests of the company . . . failing to disclose a conflict of interests . . .'

'That fear is exactly what the Japanese are relying on. Why do you think this has stayed under wraps as long as it has? These guys have got to believe this is a nationwide thing. That we already have the sworn statements of others in their position, others who were blackmailed by their creditors into taking corporate decisions they wouldn't otherwise have taken.'

'We've got to show extortion.'

'Exactly. It's our only hope. But I'd keep the bottom line to yourself until you're face to face with them, if I were you. We need statements from as many of these guys as we can get. And any other evidence that's gonna help stand this up. And for Chrissakes, Warren, don't mention Monday.'

'If I get that far. First we got to reach some of these people.'

'Well, now's a good time to start. Most of them should be having breakfast. Let's talk again in a few hours when we know better where we stand.'

Three hours later, Mack and Warren had established the status quo: eight couldn't be reached; six hung up more or less immediately: ten prevaricated and then cried off. Seventeen agreed to meet. But only thirteen of those over the weekend.

'It isn't a lot, is it?' Warren said.

'Quality not quantity – it's who they are that matters. We got representatives of eleven key corporations here. Even if we can't get testimony from every one, we can show a clear pattern that begs serious examination.'

'There's one small problem. Two of my boys are in Detroit, two are in Chicago, one's in Cincinnati and one's in Louisville.'

'Repeat after me, Warren: "I have a decent energy level, I just need motivating . . ."' Warren started to speak. 'Shut up! ". . . I can take my pills if I have to, but I must, repeat must, stay off the liquor." Am I making myself clear?'

'Okay, okay. I'm trying here, Mack. Really I am. I'm . . . I'm . . .'

'. . . You're sick.' Mack softened his tone. 'I know that, pal. But now you see what's at stake.'

'You can rely on me, Mack, I'll do my best, I swear it. In a way this is part of the cure, isn't it?'

'Maybe.'

'I'll see the Detroit guys right away, this morning. I'll fly to Chicago this afternoon, maybe even get to one of those two, late tonight, certainly both by tomorrow noon. I should have a feel of the thing by then, so it should go faster. How I'm gonna get all this notarised on a weekend

I don't know, but I will. I'll make sure I'm in Cincinnati by late afternoon and nail that sucker.' Warren took a breath. 'I don't know about the guy in Louisville . . .'

'He's second league compared with the rest. Leave him. And don't worry about the notaries. Just have your guys sign their statements in front of a witness.'

'Okay, I'll fax you all the stuff as I get it.'

'I've got all my guys to cover – here, LA, and San Diego – in the same time scale, so it may be late Sunday before we know where we are.'

'Well, let's hope it's all worth it. You realise faxes won't be admissible as evidence?'

'They'll be good enough for what I want.'

'What are you going to do with them?'

'That depends on what we get. Take your portable fax and phone so we can stay in touch. And Warren . . .'

'I know. Stay off the booze.'

The next eighteen hours for both men were a continuous round of plane flights and soul-baring interviews prolonged by the doubt, fear and indecision of the interviewees. There were frenzied bouts of drafting and redrafting statements over snatched junk food meals in the back of taxis. But as faxes crossed and re-crossed the country, enough of a pattern started to emerge to re-energise the men sufficiently for the next round. At exactly five-thirty Sunday afternoon, Mack called Warren in the flight club lounge of Cincinnati Airport as they'd agreed. It was the seventh time they'd been in touch in two days but the first time they'd spoken. Warren sounded totally beat.

'The asshole here turned chicken on me at the last minute,' Warren said. 'The guy from CLS International, Chicago, is still holding out on me. His statement's not unuseful though, is it?'

Mack strained to hear above the noise around him in Dallas-Fort Worth's domestic air terminal. 'It's fine, Warren. You did better than I did. I drew two chickens and a no-show in my lot.'

'So that gives us nine. Nine very scared guys.'

'Ten. Do me yours, Warren, and have it ready to fax to

me when I hit New York around ten tonight, Eastern Time.'

'Sure.' He yawned. 'Can I have a drink first?'

'Have a couple, you deserve it.'

'Okay, I got to catch my flight home. Tell me something, do we have enough to show nationwide conspiracy yet?'

'I don't know. It's what we've got, it's going to have to be.'

Mack tried the second number written on the back of Saul Leibersen's card. It was his home number in Manhattan. All he got was the answering service. The third number was Leibersen's weekend home in the Hamptons. His wife told him that Leibe was still on the golf course but after some persuasion, she gave him Leibe's mobile phone number. *Well*, Mack thought, *he said he believed in me. Now we're going to find out how much.*

The lady with the blue rinse was nodding eagerly. Her friend obviously knew everything there was to tell on the subject.

'Did you know that they used to sacrifice virgins to the Sun god in these places?'

'You don't say.'

'And they call that civilisation . . .'

Yoshi smiled to herself and waited for the women to move on. It was strange to be standing in front of a complete Roman temple in the middle of New York when you'd just flown in from Italy. The sheer size of the Metropolitan Museum's exhibit was overwhelming. The room itself rose up like a cathedral. The light from its massive window fell in soft slants across the floor, spreading out over the low, formal garden that was meticulously laid out before the ancient steps. The time-worn stone lent a wonderful tranquillity to the room. How safe it felt in the aura of age. The weathered pillars seemed to speak of thousands of centuries of peace. A stark contrast with the clash and bustle of bodies in the streets outside. Yoshi stood gazing for a long time before going on to the Egyptian section. Laid out in large, humidified cases was an extraordinary array of artefacts. Jars of preserved food, rolls of linen, a vast collection of ointments and jewellery; all the necessities of everyday life that had once been intended for the long journey into death. It seemed almost sacrilegious to look upon objects that rightly belonged in their owners' tombs; sad to think that so many Pharaohs had had to travel into the underworld without them.

She bent forward to study an exquisite miniature barge. Each part had been reproduced in the greatest detail, a worthy testament to the sophistication of a culture that flourished more than three thousand years before. Yoshi pressed closer to the glass. Even the faces of the little oarsmen seemed to belong more to real men than wooden figures. Faces. Her eyes focused back to her own reflection in the glass. Next to it was another. A face that wore a familiar look. She turned round, suddenly, her shock apparent in the low gasp that broke the silence. Tatsuya Nashiba bowed respectfully. A slow, enigmatic smile warmed his face. He stood for several minutes with his expression unchanged but his eyes betrayed the merest hint of emotion. Yoshi was rooted to the spot. His face had mellowed with age but strength remained written into every feature. A strength as consuming as it was intimidating. An intensity of presence she remembered too well. Fear and longing cut her as keenly now as it had the first time she was ever alone with him. He turned and walked away without speaking a word.

Fear and longing. How many years she'd kept the two sealed up inside. Yoshi went back into the Roman temple and slumped down on a bench. Time spiralled out of significance as she sat, deep in thought. His magnetism was as dynamic as it had ever been. How stupid it'd been to think she had really learned to hate him. She could deny him no better at fifty-two than she had at nineteen. In her mind's eye, the memory flooded back. The venue had been a private suite on the fifth floor of Tokyo's Imperial Hotel. She recalled the mixture of nervousness and guilt she'd felt as she joined him for a drink. She watched him talking and moving around the room. He was perfectly calm and controlled; charming, compelling. Yet she could almost feel his temper, barely in check beneath the composure like a coiled cobra. The effect was mesmeric.

He took a few steps towards her. She wanted to get up but her limbs were leaden with apprehension. Then, suddenly, he was kneeling at her feet, staring at her trembling knees. He ran his hands lightly down her calves and slipped off her shoes. He kept his eyes on her feet as his hands extended gently up her outer leg again, under her light dress. She felt a shiver of excitement and fear wash upwards from her thighs over her whole body as he released the stockings from the suspenders and slipped them off. He knelt there for several minutes caressing her feet, then lifted them to his lips and kissed them softly. 'Come,' he said. She followed him into the bathroom, standing mutely while the jacuzzi filled, hardly aware of the rest of her clothes falling away, hardly aware of her sudden nakedness and his.

He sat cross-legged in the deep part of the tub and turned on the jets, holding out one hand to help her step over the rim and into the swirl of hot water. He drew her to him, unfolding his legs as he did so. She slid easily into his arms, between his thighs, into the wild sensation of her skin against his. Still she did not dare to kiss him. Terror and passion gripped her as fast as the hands on her hips. He kissed her and entered her in one motion. The burning pain made her yell into his mouth. He didn't flinch. The lips and hands, the pulse within her went on, willing her to yield to his strength. And she was crying a conflict of tears. The fear, the pain that gave way to an awful pleasure. He must stop and yet he must not. She was entirely possessed.

Without a word, he slipped one hand round the small of her back and the other under her buttocks. He stood and she instinctively crossed her ankles behind his waist. He stepped out of the tub and walked to the bedroom as though her weight was nothing. There, on the soft cream counterpane, he laid her back, the shock of his withdrawal almost as great as his entrance. But she lay completely still, breathing rapidly, like a trapped animal.

Tatsuya stood for a moment, looking at her. The breasts were full, the waist and hips slim, the legs surprisingly long

325

and well-shaped for a Japanese. He admired her as he might a fine sculpture. And he loved beauty. Yet her nakedness did not reveal everything. There was one curiosity left. He took her ankles and drew her to the edge of the bed. He spread her knees and ran his hands slowly up the inner thighs. Perfection. She was made to perfection. He felt her quiver as he ran a finger over the perfect shape. He kissed her carefully, tenderly, until he felt her tension slip away and he knew she was ready to accept him again.

This time there was no pain. Her desire for him was total. And as he brought her to climax, her need to be absorbed into his terrible strength made her cry in strange, rising gasps from the pit of her stomach. He was sweating, watching her face contort and release, contort and release until he was almost jealous of her sheer abandon. Physically, she was already his, but his mind wanted to have her perfection. He came into her with a shout. The consummation total.

The sudden crackle of the public address system filled the empty room. The museum was closing. Yoshi dabbed her eyes and looked up. The Roman temple dreamed on in the fading light. It was almost too perfect. The scattered pillars of Rome itself spoke more to her of reality. They had once been whole; still elegant but broken, they existed now only as an echo of unrepeatable glory.

She turned the thought over in her mind. What was there, really, to go back to? The university? Her students? There had been happy times, rewards. But in truth, nothing had or could replace the joy of a family life that had ended so suddenly in a tangle of steel and shattered glass on the road from Milan. As for Akitō, he was curious now but it was a curiosity that would soon be satisfied. And then? Then, she would still be the stranger who called herself his mother.

Yoshi stood up to leave. No, there could be no fulfilment, no peace. Only the torment of the past.

TWENTY-ONE

S aul Leibersen took off his golf shoes and massaged his
feet. His eyes lingered on the report that lay on his desk.

'The extortion angle doesn't have enough bite, Mack.
Now if you had video tape, audio material, hard evidence
of the Japanese putting the squeeze on these guys . . .'

Mack had centred the version of the report he'd given
Leibersen around the Neutrals scam. Aware of the danger
of handing him illegally accessed data, he had removed as
much of the Nashiba printout from the *Tsumi* section as
he could. Maybe that had been a mistake, Mack thought,
now. It'd weakened his hand.

'We got what we could get in forty-eight hours, Leibe.'

'It's not enough.' Leibersen stared into space for a
moment. Then he opened a drawer in his desk and took out
some sneakers. Still deep in thought, he got to his feet and
walked over to the bookcase and opened a wall safe.

Senator Brodie had been impressed enough with the
report to pass it on to the Under Secretary, Mack thought.
The summary of the ground covered at the Washington
meeting must have cut some ice.

Leibersen took a buff-coloured file out of the safe and
returned to his desk. 'See, what you have here is just part
of a story. Now, you see this?' He patted the file. 'It's part
of a story too.'

Mack turned the file round. The label read: 'Aid Watch;
Western Pacific Pharmaceuticals: An Investigation.'

'Do you know about Aid Watch?'

Mack shook his head.

'They're a new outfit. Got a few smart folk working up

327

there. They've tied raw opium, smuggled from Central America, to the same corporation you talk about – Western Pacific Pharmaceuticals. They've even got the testimony of a senior employee, a chemist, showing how it's processed into morphine.'

Leibersen was enjoying the reaction beginning to register on Mack's face. 'According to Aid Watch, the DEA had their shot at this at an earlier stage and blew it. So this time, they came to us. The story's potentially dynamite. But as it stands, I wasn't at all sure I could do anything with it. You see, the big trouble is that their investigation runs up a blind alley at the most crucial stage. They couldn't pin the morphine to any medication manufactured by WPP. It just seemed to disappear inside the plant somewhere. We needed to know how it hit the streets and in what form. It has a beginning, a middle but no end. But . . .' He put the file on top of Mack's report. 'When I put it together with yours – with the testimony of Steadman and the others – it seems to me I got the whole goddamn thing. Beginning, middle, end.'

Leibersen handed Mack the Aid Watch file. 'Take a look. They've got the dish on this Santiago too, the boy who turns up in the first section of your report.'

Mack flicked through the file, his eye falling instinctively on key points and conclusions.

'Now I'll tell you something else,' Leibersen said. 'From my own point of view, even if you're only partly right about Monday, it certainly answers a question that's been driving me wacko for the last couple of weeks. Do you remember Henry Howard?'

'The veteran Hollywood director? Sure.'

'In 1944, he and a camera crew followed MacArthur back to the Philippines and stayed on his case, right in the front line, through till VJ Day. But MacArthur despised Howard. Didn't like his attitude or his politics; thought he should've stayed in Hollywood, shooting westerns. After the war, the footage was suppressed, and later, just forgotten about. Hey, are you listening to this?'

Mack put down the Aid Watch file. 'Yes, go on.'

'Well, before he died last year, Howard took me down into his cellar and showed me thirty cans of film, asked me to take a look at it. Four months ago, I finally got around to it. It was like stumbling on buried treasure – has to be the finest footage ever taken on the subject. Howard shot it in colour, with sound and his own live commentary. I tell you, he's as good as Ed Morrow ever was. I had the best of it reprocessed and cut together into two ninety-minute documentaries. For my money it's the definitive work on the Pacific War.'

Leibersen passed Mack a script. 'The obvious scheduling date was September the second but we were already covering the official commemorations that night and it didn't pan out. So we settled for the unofficial surrender date you talk about in your report. The first half goes out on the fourteenth of August – tomorrow. The concluding half, the following night. At least this way we get the jump on the other networks.

'Three weeks ago, we had the press show. It seemed like a smart PR move to include a few Japanese. Turned out not to be such a hot idea. I think if we'd picked them off the street it might have been, but the two boys our press office settled on were big guns from the boards of corporations we're involved with. To be fair, the general feeling here at the time was: Hell, it all happened fifty years ago.'

Mack snorted. 'Tell me about it!'

'This sequence where MacArthur looks at a dead Japanese soldier and says, "That's the way I like to see 'em," really got to these guys. Then, three-quarters of the way through the showing, they just got up and walked out. But the first sign that there was gonna be real trouble was when we started to lose advertising, not just for our air date but right across the board. We realised it was a Japanese initiative when Hollywood money started drying up too. A big budget mini-series we were all set to do with Century Twenty-one suddenly got the thumbs down, and then GMA pulled the plug on two features. Oh, they came up with some pretty inventive excuses, but in the end the message was clear enough.'

329

'The Vice-President of Century Twenty-one was one of the names on the Neutrals list. The Japs paid over twelve billion for the whole group, last year, didn't they?'

'They have seventy per cent of Hollywood now. You don't hear too many anti-Japanese wisecracks in Beverly Hills these days. They even tell me a Japanese-American's running for mayor. But this was something new, Mack. What they were effectively saying to us was: Pull "Henry Howard – War in the Pacific", or we're gonna bleed you dry. I mean, where does that end? Next, they're gonna be up here re-writing the goddamn news.'

'Well if you legislate against them owning radio stations and TV channels in this country, the Hollywood connection's got to be the next best thing.'

'Not so long as I'm running this network. Anyway, your report puts all this in an entirely new context. It's not hard to see why they might be so sensitive about Monday night. Even if you're only partly right about what they're going to try and pull, if they've gone to all this trouble to keep their involvement with Monday undercover, the last thing they need is the Howard marathon going out. Enough fingers are gonna be pointed their way, anyway. It's just something like this new footage that's guaranteed to inflame old hatreds.'

Mack leafed through the Howard script. 'When did you say the Japs walked out of the showing?'

Leibe shrugged. 'Around halfway through. After the POW montage.'

Mack got up and took his report off Leibersen's desk. He flicked through it and folded it open at the summary of his meeting with Senator Brodie and handed it back. Then he read aloud from the Howard script.

'Shot One Twenty-one: detachment of US Marines captures high-ranking Japanese officers disguised as Burmese peasants on the road from Rangoon. Voice over: "These guys were once Tojo's bully-boys. No one will ever know how many died by their order. The guy on the right here, trying to avoid the camera as I speak to you now, was responsible for the deaths of thousands of POWs, boys like the ones we saw earlier."' Mack broke off. 'Run your finger down the page to the list of the principal players in the *Keidanren*, Leibe.' He went back to the script. '"He doesn't look a lot now, does he? But this here's General Shigeru Tosa, the Butcher of Malaya. Chances are, he'll die at the end of a rope. A lot quicker than his countless victims."'

There was total silence in the room for a minute. 'I think part of your problem might be right there,' Mack said at last.

Leibersen took up Mack's report. Like it or not, its conclusions had to be faced, not as distant possibilities but as palpable facts. 'Tell me,' he said. 'What exactly did you have in mind when you came up here tonight, Mack? I mean what was it you were hoping I'd do?'

'Take a risk. Interview the Neutrals who'll talk, Monday. And monitor Wall Street, Reuters, AP, the lot, from the first minute's trading, Monday morning. My guess is you won't have to wait too long to see this kick in. You've been running this network for twenty years, Leibe. After that, if I'm right, you won't need me to tell you how to play it.'

When the Tosa family acquired the Empire State Building in the fall of 1994, it caused uproar across the country. Of all the buildings bought by the Japanese in recent years, few rated so highly in the affections of the American people. It seemed that nothing was sacred. The *Washington Post* cartoon, showing realtors taking Japanese businessmen around the Statue of Liberty above the caption: 'Of course, it may need some repartitioning . . .' struck a deep chord. But, over time, the hullabaloo died down. As an essayist in *Time* magazine wrote, 'At least they can't take it home with them.'

Zentaro Tosa didn't need to. In any case, he hardly ever left Japan. Akitō was surprised that he'd chosen a suite he apparently kept at the Empire State for their meeting. As far as anyone knew, the Tosas had shown little or no personal interest in it since the acquisition. And the venue seemed high profile for such a sensitive encounter. He tried Bryony's home number in Connecticut from his car phone

one last time. Her answering machine was still on.

The underground parking lot he'd been directed to was almost three blocks from the building. From there, Akitō was taken through a tunnel, which appeared to have been created by knocking through a number of adjacent basements, to an elevator. On the eighty-fifth floor, Akitō stepped out to be confronted by Tosa himself.

He bowed deeply, greeting his guest in the highest level of polite Japanese. Akitō responded likewise, slipping easily into the deliberately obscure forms *Keigo* demanded. The two men had met no more than a dozen times before and then only in the company of other family members. Formality was to be expected. Zentaro was ten years older than Akitō but he looked younger. Spending less time outside Japan than any of his contemporaries, he had remained resolutely Japanese in thought and behaviour. Although the original thirties features of the apartment that he guided Akitō to had been retained, it was in every other way a reproduction of an apartment he might have kept in Tokyo.

Akitō slipped off his shoes and followed his host across the tatami matting. The two sat facing each other over a low cedarwood table.

'You must forgive me for insisting that we meet here,' Zentaro said, 'but I have had a fascination for this building ever since I was a child. I was very anxious that we should acquire it. I'm so seldom in this country, I can't bear to miss an opportunity to stay here. May I offer you some tea?'

'I would be delighted.'

As Zentaro busied himself with the elaborate preparations, Akitō took the opportunity to study him. His resemblance to Yoshi was quite striking.

'I have often thought,' Zentaro said at length, 'that in different circumstances you and I might have been good friends.'

'It is a great sadness that we did not have that opportunity.'

Zentaro tended the fire beneath the kettle. 'Unfortunately, we are what the past makes us.'

If his host chose not to avoid the issue that had driven a

wedge between their families for forty-seven years, making it impossible for them to meet openly, neither would Akitō. 'So much of the past lives on in our fathers,' he said.

'Indeed.' Zentaro lifted the boiling kettle and filled the porcelain cups he had set out on the table. There was silence as he waited for Akitō to taste the tea.

'I should tell you,' he said, 'that I have always regarded the events surrounding my grandfather's death, as I was told them by my father, as – how shall I put it? – open to interpretation.'

The shift from *Keigo* to a more frank tone of conversation caught Akitō unawares. 'It is inevitable that your family should feel strongly about it,' he said.

'Yes. Even after all these years, I do not air my views too often. But perceptions change over time. My brother is twelve years older than me, naturally he's more influenced by my father. But there comes a time when a man should be the master of his own destiny.'

Akitō took care not to let any emotion register on his face. He must not be tricked into showing his hand.

'Naturally, we must act in the best interests of our families,' Zentaro went on. 'From tomorrow we shall all be part of this . . . New Era. The past will play a less important role in all our lives. Each family will begin to reassess its own position, to change its attitudes towards . . . all that has been.'

So that was it, Akitō thought. *The Nashiba supremacy.* The alliance struck between the Families in 1945 had been a fragile one at best. That it had held through the schism between the Tosas and the Nashibas was a tribute to the principal players' capacity to separate business and Japan's future from personal issues. But after *Tsumi*, the alliance would be redundant, the Nashiba dominance challenged. *The Tosas may consider themselves to have as much influence as us*, Akitō thought, *but they will need the full support of the other Families to displace us. My marriage contract with the Ishiharas is insurance enough against that.* Marriage contract. Was Bryony already part of the past? Could he slough off his feelings for her so readily?

Akitō felt a numbing sense of resignation setting in.

Zentaro set his cup aside. 'My father is seventy-seven. Though it saddens us all to see his decline, I'm afraid the truth is that he's senile. He talks only of the old days now. My brother begins to listen to me more on some matters. Although, I must say, his feelings towards your father are not something I have discussed with him in recent years. But, if you will forgive me for saying so, your father is an old man too. Still with all his faculties, I've no doubt. But the time must come soon for our generation to take up the reins.'

The feuds of the past will die with our fathers, is that what he's saying? Akitō thought. *They will take the old enmity with them to the grave?*

'It would give me great pleasure, Nashiba-san, if you would accept this.' Zentaro placed an elaborately-wrapped package on the table. The paper was exquisite, a minor work of art in itself. It was immediately obvious to Akitō that the gift had been purchased and wrapped in Japan. Only there was the wrapping as important as the contents. He raised himself on one knee to accept the offering, taking it up with a low bow of his head. He set it to one side.

'Please, don't stand on ceremony. I would like you to open it now.'

It took Akitō more than a minute to peel off the many layers of paper. Inside was a long, thin box. The wood had been hand-split, in the *Masame* tradition, to give a fine straight grain that would neither shrink nor bend. He took off the lid. Whatever lay inside was wrapped in a piece of pale yellow silk. He unrolled it with great care to find two arrows bound tightly together with cord. He turned them over, wondering quite what to say.

'The legend of the arrows,' Zentaro said, quietly. 'I'm sure you are familiar with it. It was my great-grandfather's favourite. It has passed down through the generations in our family.'

'Of course, I know it well. It is a beautiful gift,' Akitō said. 'But, forgive me, were there not three arrows in the story?'

'Oh yes. Please, try to break them.'

'I'm sorry?'

Zentaro's eyes glinted. 'Try to break them, as in the legend.'

Riddles and symbols. How Japanese Zentaro was, Akitō thought. Such things seemed out of place here in New York. He moved his hands towards the ends of the arrows and tried to break them. To his surprise, he could only bend them a little. Even when he put all his strength into the task they remained intact.

Zentaro allowed himself a polite laugh. 'Extraordinary, isn't it? I couldn't do it either. When the legend was written five hundred years ago, arrows were made of wood. One needed to bind many together to withstand a man's strength. But fortunately, times change.' He took the arrows from Akitō and weighed them in his hand. 'These days they make them out of fibreglass. Surprisingly strong . . . Now, only two need be bound together.'

Mack locked Morton's car, stepped over a low wall that separated the parking lot from the sidewalk and walked down the block towards Auburn's apartment. *Still so many gaps in the information,* he thought. *If Leibersen knew just how much of this stuff was based on gut reaction . . .*

Some instinct made him look up. At the far end of the street, a man sat on the railings, his foot tapping to the sound of the rock music pounding in his headphones. An emotion Mack hadn't felt in a long time caught him in the pit of the stomach. *Dead Man's Pass.* He hadn't consciously strung those three words together in his mind since teenage. He could almost hear the rumble of the el-train above him, smell the stench of rotting trash that came up from the alleys flanking Chicago's Arnold Canal. Dead Man's Pass – the oldest set-up in the world. This wasn't an alley. But roadworks cordoned off with fencing had reduced the street to a narrow single lane. It amounted to the same thing.

Don't look back! he thought. *If I'm right, another man'll have already moved into position at the other end to close*

335

my retreat. They'll roll me for my watch and cash. If I'm lucky.

He moved on at an even gait, straining to hear. The sound of footfalls came from some distance behind him; the rhythmic slap of rubber soles on the sidewalk. Could be anyone; could be that waiter he saw locking up for the night at the diner two blocks down. Could be . . .

Don't react! It's your only hope. Don't let them know you know.

To Mack's right there was a solid line of apartment buildings. *Press a bell*, he told himself. *Get someone to let you into a lobby . . . Sure. New York! Two-fifteen in the morning! Some hope.* To his left was the fencing. There was no escape.

Mack could see the man ahead of him clearly now. You could pass a hundred like him on the street in a ten-minute walk down Seventh Avenue. Mid-twenties; denims; soiled trainers and a black tee-shirt with the skull motif of a heavy metal band on the front. The dark hair was cropped short. Hispanic? Greek? It was hard to say. Mack was fifteen feet from him. If he didn't make his move in the next five seconds, he never would.

The steady slap of feet behind him broke into a run. *Make him come to you*, Mack's mind screamed. *Make him come to you.*

He never saw the knife. The sudden thrusting movement of the man's arm, the jerk of his body, said all he needed to know. As Heavy Metal swung out, Mack's posture transformed. He rammed his attaché case forwards to meet the thrust of the blade. There was a sharp thwack as it embedded into the black fibre shell.

Ten seconds till the other guy connects. Mack spun the case in his hands like the wheel of a car, then wrenched it backwards. *Let go you sonofabitch!*

Heavy Metal kept on coming, like the handle of the knife was welded to his palm. Mack swung his leg into his stomach and threw every ounce of his hundred-and-sixty pounds into the kick. The guy fell back against the railings, choking his gum into Mack's face. Mack turned. The man

336

behind him was shorter, heavier built. He slammed him in the side of the head with the case with such force that it disintegrated in his hands. He tried to run, ducking left as Heavy Metal made a dive for him.

Mack lost his balance and fell into the fencing that shielded the roadworks. It gave instantly. Next thing he knew, he was sprawling on his back in broken tarmac and earth. Heavy Metal lurched forward. Mack's hands flailed wildly, searching for something to cling to. Then his right hand locked on to one of the steel uprights that had supported the fencing. He jerked it from the earth and swung it between himself and his attacker. The guy took the upright's three metal feet full in the chest. Thrown back, he was too mad now to feel the pain. He struggled with something inside his jacket.

Shoulder holster, Mack thought. *The force of the kick'd knocked it back under his arm.*

The hand fumbled. It was a mistake. Mack heaved the iron bar forward in a wide arc, driving one of the feet into the top of the man's head, like a rivet. It fell with a clatter on to the sidewalk as Mack wrenched it free. He saw Heavy Metal's eyes roll up as a line of dark blood fountained from a wide hole below his hairline. Then he sagged at the knees and went down.

Mack looked round. The man behind him was on his feet again and closing fast. *Run!* Mack half tripped over the inert form beneath him and made off down the street. He darted left as a .38 shell punctured a car windscreen ahead of him. Mack kept on running. The entrance to Auburn's apartment was only twenty yards away but he knew there could be no refuge there. He dipped low and right, stealing a glance at his pursuer. The attaché case had cut the guy up pretty good; the left side of his face was a real mess.

Suddenly something smashed into Mack's right knee knocking all the breath out of him. If someone had sheared his lower leg off with a chainsaw, it couldn't have hurt more. But there'd been no gunshot this time. Almost as soon as he stumbled forward over the cast-iron fire hydrant and fell into the gutter, Mack was trying to scramble to his feet. His chest ached as he fought for breath. He forced himself up on to one elbow. The man moved out to the centre of the road twenty feet behind him, breathing hard. He held the gun steady with both hands and spread his legs slightly apart.

Nice try, Mack thought. *Nearly made it, too.* He gritted his teeth and waited for the .38 slug to tear out his insides.

The yellow cab swung a right off West End Avenue, at close to forty. You could hear the suspension creaking, straining with the force of the turn. It took the man in the small of the back with a dull crunch. For a split second he was pushed along, then he was dragged under the wheels. There was a screeching of brakes as the cab juddered and skidded. Mack saw the man's arm shoot out near the rear wheel. Then came a sound like a watermelon bursting.

The driver changed down, swung right and was gone.

Mack sat on the closed seat of the lavatory and pressed the steaming towel to his knee, his eyes never leaving the tiny oil painting on the wall in front of him.

'You must call the police, Mack, you have to.' Auburn came through the bathroom door with a large glass of brandy.

He shrugged. 'They're no use to any of us, now.'

Auburn stared at the grazed, ashen face. 'At least let me call a doctor.'

Muggers steam you for cash, Mack thought. *Beat up on you if you give 'em trouble. But these guys . . . these guys were trying to kill me.*

'I fell over a hydrant, that's all,' he said. 'It's just bruising. Nothing's broken. Look, I can stand on it.' He forced himself to his feet and staggered painfully around the bathroom.

So if they weren't muggers, who were they? Men sent by Nashiba? . . . Jesus, this whole thing's really getting to me.

Mack tried to shake away the thought but something still nagged at the corner of his mind. He looked at Auburn. She was frightened enough already. He took a gulp of the brandy and forced a smile. *When I fell over that first guy, my face was a foot from his. There was something. Something my subconscious registered . . . not his face: his hand.* Mack took another gulp and shook his head. Nothing.

It was four in the morning before he asked himself what mugger had manicured nails.

TWENTY-TWO

The morning of Monday, the fourteenth of August dawned unusually cool for the time of year. Yoshi put down the book she had been reading since first light and walked to the window. She lifted the blind a fraction to look down on to the street below. It was as cold and ugly as the room in which she stood; a sudden wrench from the beauty of the poetry she had been reading a moment before. She shivered and moved back to the table. On it, beside her book, lay a writing case. Inside, her unfinished letter to Akitō. Yoshi fingered the hand-tooled cover of the Paulownia-wood case. This, her graduation gift from her father, had been her companion in many lonely hours. She opened the case, took out a sheet of paper and smoothed it out on the table before securing it with a metal paperweight. She looked at it for a moment. The mood must be right to start; there would never be a better time. Her eyes went back to the case. The gold-embossed inkstick was already half used but there was enough to complete the task. She lifted it out along with a small, flat grinding stone. On this, she dropped a little water. Then, gripping the inkstick firmly, she started to rub it in a precise, circular motion on the stone. When the consistency of the ink was good, she took up a brush and wrote:

Koishiki ni
Inochi wo kauru
Mono naraba
Shini wa yasuku zo
Aru-bekari-keru!

340

The letter complete, she wrapped the single sheet of paper in another sheet of plain paper and placed it in an envelope. She marked the envelope, simply, 'Mr Akitō Nashiba, The Trump Plaza' and placed it in the inside pocket of her jacket.

There was one more letter to write. Taking out another piece of paper, Yoshi picked up her brush. In swift, deft strokes she wrote: '*Shō* is repaid.' Again, she wrapped the single sheet of paper in a plain sheet and placed it in an envelope. She paused for a second, transfixed by the thought of forming the characters of her father's name after so long. She finished quickly and placed the letter next to the one for Akitō.

So, she thought, *it's done at last.* Yoshi laid the writing tools back in the case and closed the box. She got up and walked back to the window. The morning rush-hour traffic was pushing relentlessly north along Grand Central Park Way. How small and insignificant the cars seemed. Now she raised the blinds. She snapped off the latch and slid up the window until the sound of motors and horns was a deafening roar. She couldn't tell how many minutes passed as she stood there watching, her mind intent on the words of the poem. They were fitting words she thought.

> 'If it were possible
> To give away my life in exchange
> For (your) love
> How easy Death would be!'

In an instant she stepped out on to the parapet and flung herself down.

Under Secretary Galbraith's weekend had started well. He'd spent Friday with the US–Japan Working Group on the Structural Impediments Initiative, refining the text that would form the basis of their Joint Report. If there were no unforeseen hitches, the agreement could be signed Monday night. That'd mean a better week on Wall Street. And God knew, it needed one. Although not exactly elated, Galbraith had felt a glow of satisfaction for a difficult job well done. All thoughts of the Lasky Report and the promised assurances from the *Keidanren* were put aside.

The deadline's barely up yet, Galbraith thought, as he prepared to go to bed Friday night. *If I know Tanaka, his will be the first call of the day.*

But no call came. By noon of Sunday, the Trade Secretary was deeply concerned. The Premier would have had to call no more than four members of the *Keidanren* at most to get what he needed. What could possibly be taking him so long? The official bulletin from Nagata-cho stated only that the Prime Minister was attending a private engagement in Kobe and would return to the official residence late that night. For three days now, Galbraith had told himself that Tanaka, having committed himself on the topic, probably felt that the heat had been taken out of the situation and viewed a corroborative statement as no more than a formality. But now he was starting to panic. What if he was wrong? What if Tanaka had lied? It was unthinkable. What could he possibly gain? Except time. Galbraith was certain that couldn't be it. What if Tanaka had called members of the *Keidanren* and been told a different story? That the issue was none of his business? Did the *Keidanren* have such power? Certainly some of the families did. Especially if they were the same ones who'd greased Tanaka's road to power.

On Monday morning, the few staff at the US Embassy in Tokyo to be given access to Galbraith noticed he was red-eyed and irritable. At times, he showed signs of hysteria. The instruction to the chief telephonist on the switchboard was simple enough: 'Hold all calls; try Nagata-cho every half hour until you get the Prime Minister on the line.'

It was now 4.30 p.m. Galbraith had been closeted in his office for over two hours, he'd seen and talked to no one. He sat hunched at the large mahogany desk at the front of the building and completed his second hand-written note to Tanaka in six hours. He looked at his rough draft. '. . . If you ever counted me as a friend, I ask you . . .' Wrong approach. It showed weakness. The Japanese deplored that. As he struggled with closing platitudes, his hand began to shake uncontrollably. He looked at the phone for the hundredth time. *Ring, you sonofabitch!*

Maybe I should call the President, Galbraith thought. Yeah, and say what? 'I've had this report predicting a Japanese economic coup on Tuesday, sitting on my desk for four days. I didn't pass it on because the Premier said it was bullshit.' Political suicide. It'd be like writing your own obituary. No, better to wait and pray there was a reasonable explanation for the whole thing.

There were still thirty hours to go. Time enough.

Suddenly, outside, he could hear a succession of car doors slamming. Galbraith hurried to the window. As he crossed the room, the phone on the desk rang. He grabbed at the extension by the window.

'I have Glen Mishon here again, Mr Secretary,' his assistant said nervously. 'I know your instructions, but he says it's vital he speaks with you.'

'Okay,' Galbraith said, at last. 'Show him in.'

Press Secretary Glen Mishon appeared in the doorway. 'What's going on out there?' Galbraith asked, trying to keep his voice steady.

'It's the press, Mr Secretary. For the signing.'

Galbraith sighed. 'Yes, of course. Are any of the Japanese contingent here yet?'

'Not so far as I know, sir.' Mishon looked at the desk. The latest stock market reports lay exactly where he'd left them earlier. The television was still off. And the Secretary'd taken no calls. *He still doesn't know*, Mishon thought.

'I'm afraid we could be in for a rough ride, Mr Secretary.'

Galbraith spun around. 'Why?'

'Well, I was told not to disturb you, but it's all here on your desk. The Nikkei just closed more than six hundred and fifty points down. In the last hour's trading, investors started dumping US Treasury Bonds . . .'

'Dumping Treasury Bonds?' That was like saying they're pulling the carpet out from under the whole US national debt! Galbraith picked up the neatly folded ticker-tape and

343

moved it through his hands like a film editor checking his footage. He caught his breath. 'Why are they bailing out now?'

'They're saying it's a kneejerk reaction to last Friday on Wall Street,' Mishon said. 'They obviously think we're going to take another pounding today.'

Today. It's going to be today, not Tuesday, Galbraith thought. *I don't have thirty hours, I have five. Less than five!* He fought to hold his thoughts together. Were the Families behind the move to dump the bonds? Not if Lasky was right. If they were trying to keep a low profile, it was the last thing they'd do. It could be a genuine market reaction. Or the beginning.

Galbraith grabbed the dog-eared copy of Mack Lasky's report which lay on the desk. He turned again to the concluding statement: 'That this plan was developed over years, undetected and unchecked in our own backyard, says as much about our own complacency as it does about Japanese ambition.'

'With respect, Mr Secretary,' Mishon said, 'I think that under the circumstances, the sooner we talk to these press boys the better.'

Galbraith looked at his watch. In a few hours, the New York Stock Exchange would be hit by a crash that would make the losses of '29 look like loose change.

'Screw 'em,' he said.

A loud crack resonated in Mack's left ear. His head came up with a jerk. A score of nameless fears pitched through his mind before he realised that the noise'd come from the bottle of sparkling mineral water he'd put out the night before. *Fucking plastic had to choose now to snap back into shape,* he thought. Felt like his heart was pulsing at the top of his throat. He rolled on to his back, trying not to disturb Auburn, and flexed his legs. God, his knee hurt. He stretched a hand down to the swollen joint. Better put some ice on it. *Hell, I'm awake now, anyway,* he thought as he felt for his robe and made for the kitchen. The ice-maker was down. Mack propped himself on a stool and leaned miserably against the breakfast bar clutching a pack of frozen fish fillets to his leg. He watched the digital clock on the cooker console click off the minutes. 4.10, 4.11, 4.12 . . .

Monday, it's Monday. His brain started to register more than pain. *The countdown's already started. 4.15, 4.16 . . . c'mon Lasky, for Chrissake, do something.*

He limped back into the bedroom. Auburn was still asleep, most of her face hidden in the quilt, her bright curls spread out over the pillow. He scribbled a note, put it on her bedside table, then took his clothes from the closet and slipped out.

When the cab drew away from the corner of Broadway and Wall Street, Mack wasn't certain of anything but the crazy notion that just being there could somehow change things. He started towards the Exchange building, his footsteps echoing down the canyon of high-rise towers from the empty sidewalk. This day would start like any other, he thought. In a few hours' time, clerks, tellers, secretaries and office boys would pour in from subways, ferries and elevated trains. Bankers and brokers would arrive in chauffeured limousines or at the ramp at the foot of Wall Street in planes. And the financial heart of the nation would start to beat again.

Mack leaned his back against the grey stone of the Manhattan Company building and blinked up into the rising sun. Across the street, the sculptured pediment of the Stock Exchange was thrown into relief. It would happen quickly. So fast that even the most vigilant would be caught unawares. The Exchange's high-speed computer network zipped electronic orders from member companies direct from their traders' computers to the Exchange floor, at the rate of over two hundred a second, without any human intervention. Billions of dollars in financial paper could be sold within minutes. Nashiba would use that speed.

Mack bent to rub his aching knee. By the time the bell in the Great Hall rang and the morning began for New York's traders, most of the world would've been on its feet for a full day. What might the Japanese have achieved by then?

A wave of tiredness sent a cold shiver through Mack's frame. He turned into Broad Street. Two blocks down, limping badly, he finally found what he was looking for. A deli that'd just opened up. He sat down gratefully at a window table and ordered coffee and bagels. Looked like it was going to be a real pretty day. The waiter sweeping the sidewalk outside took off his vest and went on working in his shirtsleeves. Mack watched him for a while. Then he noticed the sign on the wall opposite. Beaver Street.

Well, what d'you know, he thought, Warren, Beaver Lake . . . That's where this whole damn thing started . . . an' I still don't know where it's headed.

Leibersen. Leibersen's the only hope. I got to stay on his case.

Specialist Market Maker Liam O'Connor had still been a wealthy man when he'd driven to work that morning. Now he sat in the third cubicle of the men's room in the Exchange building, trying to come to grips with the prospect of putting his home in New Haven on the market to stay afloat. He took another gulp of the Bushmills that'd come into the building in his attaché case, and wiped his mouth on his sleeve. Given the fall on the Nikkei, no one was surprised when prices opened well below their Friday close. But within minutes, pension funds and insurance companies started dumping stocks. Soon, O'Connor had stocks waiting for takers at almost every trading post on the floor. The Dow Jones Industrial Average plunged almost fifty points in the first half-hour's trading and although circuit breakers in the computer system kicked in automatically to slow the rate of selling, the Dow continued to plummet.

By 10.00 a.m., O'Connor was sweating blood. The Reuters newsflash had sent him scurrying to the only comfort left. The bottle.

Reuters had given the statement from the Peruvian

Embassy in full. O'Connor smoothed out the printout and brooded on the last paragraph: '. . . So it is with the greatest regret that we must declare that we are unable to meet interest repayments on these debts until there has been an improvement in our overall economic position. Our many friends around the world have believed in us, supported us and shown us the greatest generosity over the years. Now we must ask them, too, for their forbearance.'

He screwed the paper up viciously and threw it down the john. Peru owed close on twenty-seven billion dollars. Shareholders of the US banks servicing the loan had showed their forbearance just as long as it took for them to reach for the phone and call their brokers. Blue-chip stock prices were sure to fall again. All he could do was hope that the rash of selling would level off.

Great way to start a week, he thought as he pulled the flush and walked back on to the floor. He had no way of knowing it was the last day of his life.

'Read 'em and weep!' Fellow specialist Frank Gotz stared up at the market information screens on the wall ahead.

O'Connor's eyes focused slowly on the latest Reuters report, a statement from Côte d'Ivoire. The wording was different, the reasons for defaulting more artfully expressed, but the message was the same as Peru's.

O'Connor watched powerless as the deluge of sell orders poured in. Figures on the NASDAQ screen, logging transactions, scrolled like a railroad station indicator board. By 10.15 a.m., three hundred and seventy million shares had been traded – more than the normal rate in any one day. O'Connor's portfolio was getting thinner than a comb-across with every minute that passed.

Lines to the Exchange jammed solid with orders to sell as the list of defaulting countries increased. By 11.00 a.m., dealers who'd spent the last hour snapping up stocks at bargain-basement prices were hard pressed to find the cash to carry on trading. And worried banks were refusing to give more credit. Liam O'Connor was one of the unhappy band who offered their portfolios as collateral for further loans, only to be turned down as stocks continued to tumble. By

11.15, the Dow had shed 250 points and trading was halted for sixty minutes.

Frank Gotz turned his thin pale face to O'Connor as the announcement was made. 'Things'll cool down now, you'll see.'

O'Connor snorted. 'In a pig's eye, they will.'

'Santiago!' Saul Leibersen stared in disbelief at the screen in front of him. A man with Hispanic features was making a statement to reporters from the reception room of an embassy. 'Jesus, this is like watching goddamn synchronised swimming!'

'What can I tell you, Leibe?' Mack's voice was subdued. 'Welcome to Meltdown Monday.'

Karen Kaufman, executive producer of the news division, glanced up at the computer-animated credits that announced the lunchtime newscast. She waved a piece of paper towards Leibersen. 'Well, do we run with this or what?'

Leibersen turned. 'Are we certain of the source of the leak?'

'Bank employee. There's no doubt about its authenticity.'

Leibersen read the report again. 'Well, if we don't run with it, someone else will.' He looked up at Mack. 'I thought the Farrell National was solid as rock.'

'So did everyone else. That's the whole point.' Mack took the report from Leibersen's hand and scanned the text. *'Almost two billion in losses will be announced in the second quarter's financial report due to massive arrears on corporate loans.'*

He looked up. 'Usual story – loans on leverage deals gone bad, takeovers and acquisitions draining cash flow . . . But I honestly think if that was the Farrell's only problem, right now, they'd weather the storm. It's all this Third-World default that's really caning them . . .'

Mack scanned the bank of TV screens ahead of him. Most news channels were running flash reports of events on Wall Street. Some, like NBS itself, had already shipped in analysts and commentators to give their reactions. He looked back from the screens to the faces in the room, lit eerily by the moving coloured images. A couple of hours back, they'd been uncomprehending, detached, now they showed a new sense of urgency.

'Looks like we got an epidemic.' Economics editor Paul Costello grabbed at an urgent report from the newsroom. 'Another leak – the Pacific Interstate's in trouble.'

'Can I see that?' Mack took the report. A minute later, he passed it over to Leibersen. 'Three point two billion in losses this quarter . . . largely in private accounts.'

'Jesus! That's a lot of nervous depositors.'

'Or just a few very rich ones. Remember? Varas, Ngeburi . . .'

'. . . And your pal Santiago again?'

Mack shrugged. 'Could be. Either way, the Farrell and the Pacific Interstate are going to take it right in the shorts.' Mack turned back to the screen displaying stock values. 'And, if I've judged Nashiba right, these two are just for openers.'

Karen Kaufman opened her second pack of cigarettes that morning. 'I don't get it.'

'Makes perfect sense,' Mack said. 'Key banks are already struggling under the weight of corporate defaults; if you pull their biggest depositors and hit them with a rash of defaults on their Third-World loans at the same time, they're dead in the water.'

'I can see why Japanese banks would want to skim off major depositors but why would they want Third-World defaults? I mean, haven't they got massive investments in these countries themselves? Aren't they gonna get reamed along with everyone else?'

'The countries that have been defaulting owe most to Western banks. That's why they were targeted in the first place.'

'Otherwise they'd have gone for somewhere like Brazil or Mexico,' Costello broke in, 'and zapped the market in one swipe.'

Mack nodded. 'That's it. Anyway, the Japs aren't stupid.

They're going to get paid off through the back door some way or other, believe me.'

Kaufman waved a hand to disperse the cloud of smoke that hid her face. 'So what happens with these defaulting countries as far as their other creditors are concerned?'

'They get blacklisted by the IMF,' Costello said. 'Their international credit rating's zeroed.'

'That's it?'

'Well, over time, the world community tries to starve 'em down economically.'

Over time. Mack rubbed at his swollen knee. *Over time. First they give 'em time to reconsider their actions,* he thought. *Months. How would it really affect what was happening right now, if one of these defaulting countries, say in two or three months, decided they'd over-reacted – that some level of repayment was now possible? What if a whole bunch of them did, either because of pressure from the IMF or because the promised aid from the Japanese suddenly evaporated? Or some combination of both. The reasons were irrelevant for the purposes of the proposition. No one outside of the key elements involved in this plan could see into the future. As far as the scam went, what Wall Street thought right now was all that mattered.*

'My God, Leibe, I know what's going down here.' Mack ran out into the corridor. When he reached Leibersen's office, he picked up his notes and threw himself into a chair.

'I'm an idiot. I'm a goddamned idiot.' He looked up as Leibersen came through the door. 'Don't you see? I took all this shit at face value. But what we're looking at here is just a vast smokescreen. Well, that's all it has to be. Everyone's choking, running around the place screaming "Fire!" but no one stopped to check what's behind it: an inferno or a clear blue sky! Oh, some of what we're seeing is real enough, in time we'll find out what. But most of it, most of what's to come, can be a load of bullshit. Doesn't matter whether it stays in place a year, a month, or a week, so long as it's a recognisable quantity right now, this minute. All they're counting on is holding this in place for one day's trading.'

*

Tatsuya Nashiba had been awake for almost twenty hours. It was now 2.30 p.m., but he still felt fresh. As the hundreds of elements of *Tsumi* fell into place, up-to-the-minute bulletins were brought to him in his penthouse study by members of staff. In the background, soundless television monitors flickered with emergency newscasts of events on Wall Street. Figures on a computer screen which showed the day's share values were changing so fast they looked like drums spinning on a fruit machine. The first stages had gone well.

Tatsuya picked up a cup of hot *sake* and turned to his personal computer. Numbers were falling down the screen into a meaningless jumble. He smiled in grudging admiration of Morton Totheroh. The same fine mind that had devised the ultimate database had devised its ultimate destruction – a virus that would wipe the software and sabotage this day of days. But Nashiba was ahead of the game. Taking over AmTronics had been a two-pronged decision. He'd needed Totheroh as much for his work on hypertext as his team's progress on the market's first 2.5-gigabyte computer. Totheroh was to be the architect of a database that would take Nashiba International into the twenty-first century. He would create the new software, reprocess the data it would control and then retire.

Allowing Totheroh to view the data had always been a risk. As soon as the hypertext shell was finished, Nashiba had had the most sensitive information fed in by a trusted, handpicked team of his own experts. When Totheroh left the project prematurely of his own volition, Nashiba heaved a private sigh of relief. But then the team started to run into problems. Totheroh had kept few formal notes, much of the design for the database was carried in his head. Fearing that it would not be completed in time for *Tsumi*, Nashiba was forced to bring him back on the job.

From that point on, he had little peace of mind. Suspicion grew into paranoia. Totheroh knew how to access every piece of data in the system. Even though, in reality, he'd have to spend a lifetime searching the thousands of files to find anything condemning, he was a massive security risk.

351

Nashiba saw to it that his every move was monitored.

When technicians identified a 'Logic Bomb' virus in the system, panic set in. The virus was hidden at the end of a minor accounts package and although it was an impossible task to identify who'd planted it, Nashiba had no doubts. Totheroh had become a threat that must be eliminated. Reluctantly, Nashiba gave his orders. When Totheroh was dead, his files were to be removed and searched for any clue to the virus. No one could tell when the Logic Bomb was programmed to go off, but when it hit, it would delete every file on the system. Disassembling the virus was top priority.

With *Tsumi* two weeks off, operatives were still unable to find the virus disk Nashiba was certain Totheroh had made. All data on the corporation's primary and secondary mainframe computers were wiped and experts worked round the clock to write and reprogram virgin software. The job was finished, within hours of *Tsumi* beginning.

Nashiba poured himself more *sake*. He'd been unable to resist leaving the corporation's third mainframe computer contaminated so that he could watch the intended sabotage play out. The screen in front of him jerked like the last twitch of a corpse and was still. Nashiba raised his cup in silent memory of Morton.

The old man's thoughts went back to his plan. He reached for the draft press release which lay on the desk in front of him. He had always known the final wording would have to wait till the last, until the exact shape of the whole was known. Now was that time. But where was Akitō? He should have been helping with this. The wording of the press release was vital. Its tone had to imply that the decisions that had been taken at the board meeting that morning were the unavoidable action of responsible men. Nashiba tried again to concentrate on the matter at hand but he was in no doubt that a great divide had opened up between himself and his son. The dawn conference he'd called, where decisions that would reshape global economy for the next twenty years had been discussed, was the first time the two men had stood in the same room together in five weeks. Akitō had been solicitous, even respectful, but there was an icy coldness in his dealings with his father. It had drawn no comment, passed unnoticed. But Nashiba had known that there were difficult times to be faced between them. He was equally certain that Akitō would never allow a matter of personal conflict to have a bearing on a matter of family duty. The capacity to separate such issues had been imprinted on him from earliest childhood; it was part of his matrix.

So where was he now? It was unforgivable that he should behave in this way. Akitō had been created, tutored and groomed all his life to take his place at his father's side, on the summit of the mountain that now rose remorselessly beneath them. In time, the boy would stand alone, above his peers, *Shacho* of an industrial empire beyond the scale of anything ever dreamed of. Akitō's empire would not be a charred wasteland strewn with the dead and the dying, with only lines of twisted steel and blasted stone to mark where great cities once stood. His legacy was to be an unblemished jewel, a vast continent of matchless beauty. Tens of thousands of square miles of commercial enterprise, the best of it now owned, controlled, or in some measure obeisant to the Four Families . . .

Nashiba read the press release one last time. Satisfied, with meticulous care he inscribed the characters of his name and lay back in his chair.

. . . Hundreds of thousands of acres of land, prime real estate . . . waiting. For the New Americans. In a single day, with barely a hand raised against him, he had gained the means to secure for his people that which they had come to value most – *Lebensraum* – living space in which the Japanese could grow, in which to enjoy their families and the fruits of their labours, for generations to come.

With luck, he would live to see the first five million relocated. By the time Akitō was himself an old man . . . who knew how many tens of millions of ordinary Japanese would call America *Jitaku* – home.

TWENTY-THREE

Saul Leibersen stood in a huddle with four of NBS's senior executives in the narrow corridor that ran from the main control room. Wes Tyrell, head of the network's legal division, was clearly nervous. 'If the Securities and Exchange Commission gets wind of what we're doing, Leibe, figures we're sitting on inside information that bears on what's been happening today, they'll have this building sealed up tighter than a crab's ass at forty fathoms before we can say shit.'

'We're not gonna sit on it, we're gonna shout it from the rooftops,' Leibersen said. 'I'm pulling scheduled programming for a live news special tonight.' He scanned his audience. 'We start putting it together right now. We know what's coming. Aside from the boys that planned this, we're the only ones that do.'

Mack turned to Tyrell. 'Look, the authorities have had their shot at this. The Trade Secretary had my report before anyone. The DEA had Aid Watch's stuff. They blew it. Now it's our turn. Don't wait for these jerks to turn up here. Call 'em! The SEC, the FDIC, the FBI, the DEA, the US Attorney's office ... did I miss anyone out?'

Tyrell shrugged. 'Not many.'

'Tell 'em what you're doing and when.' Mack turned to Karen Kaufman. 'Show them how this should have been handled in the first place. And then lay it in their laps, keep the pressure on 'em till they make all the right moves.' The faces around remained frozen. 'I'm telling you, this second trading halt won't achieve a damn thing.' He looked at his watch and then at Karen Kaufman. 'It's up in three minutes and then NYSE is all out of options. The ninety minutes to the closing bell are going to be the longest of your life.'

Mack glanced at the bank of information screens ahead of him. The message still thundering down the lines from investors was: sell, sell, sell! On a program monitor, he could hear a report coming in from the NBS correspondent outside the Exchange building.

'. . . Already close on a billion shares have been traded today and the computer system here just can't cope with the volume. A deciding factor in the crash of '87 was the massive backlog of unprocessed orders that had built up in the system.

'They told us that couldn't happen again, but it has. Despite everything, new technology that was to safeguard against exactly this kind of situation, has failed. Even though the Federal Reserve Bank has stepped in to keep systems liquid, there can be no safety net for stock values . . .'

Mack studied the information screen ahead of him. Buy orders were down to a trickle. The two weeks of remorseless pounding the market had taken, capped by the worst five hours in Wall Street's history, had smashed the confidence of all but a handful.

'Sweet Jesus!' Paul Costello's shout caught everyone's attention. 'Look at this from Reuters! The Japanese have just announced they're pulling out of the Greenfield leverage buy-out.'

Karen Kaufman turned towards Costello. 'The frozen food giant?'

'Christ, this was the biggest deal of its kind in commercial history. Took years to set up . . . thirty billion to finance – seven billion of it Japanese money.'

'A syndicate put together by Nashiba.' Mack ran his eye quickly down the brief press statement. The final paragraph read: 'In the context of the present situation, our first responsibility must be to our own shareholders.' He looked at the studio clock. It was 2.55 p.m. and the Dow'd already lost almost 720 points on the day. There were rumours that a trillion dollars had been wiped off US stocks. Within minutes, he watched the Dow go into freefall, dropping so fast that no computer seemed able to track it. Watched as the dollar spiralled into the unknown.

Leibersen shook his head. 'My God,' he said, 'I never thought I'd live to see this.'

'You getting me, Steve?' The programme director leaned towards the microphone in front of her to speak to the presenter of the extended newscast in the studio. 'We need comment on the Greenfield pull-out and instant reaction to the new price low, okay?'

'Okay.'

'Right. Cue studio.'

Before NBS's financial analysts had finished their comments, the mood of the market shifted again. The trickle of buy orders suddenly became a torrent. The change hit like dye poured into a waterfall.

Saul Leibersen stared at the screen in front of him in disbelief. 'What the fuck's going on here! Why should the market suddenly rally now?'

Mack nodded slowly. Suddenly, it all made sense. Almost inaudibly, he said, 'The Rothschild Syndrome.'

'The what?'

'The Rothschild Syndrome. I just couldn't figure how the Japs would be able to monopolise the buying when the flag went down. But now I understand.'

'Speak English to me, will ya!' Leibersen shouted.

'Look,' Mack said. 'Battle of Waterloo, 1815. The British thought they were finished and before the battle even started, the London Stock Market went through the floor. Well, Lord Rothschild had observers out watching the battlefield. Once they saw Napoleon was screwed, they sent carrier pigeons across the Channel to Rothschild's London home. He read the news, rode quietly down to the Stock Exchange and bought everything he could lay his hands on. Later, that same news filtered through the normal channels. The market recovered and Rothschild's fortune was made.' Mack's voice-pitch hit a higher level. 'Don't you see, Leibe? That's what we've been going through the last two weeks here. The Battle of Waterloo. Only this time the winners don't need pigeons. They already know how the end plays out because they wrote the fucking script!'

The studio lights began to reflect in the beads of sweat on Mack's forehead. 'I discounted it at first but it has to be the answer. The logjam in the computer system, the massive delays it's causing. The Japs knew it would happen. They were relying on it. Transactions at the Exchange are dealt with strictly on a first come, first served basis. Right? They must've stacked buy orders into the system by the million, hours in advance ... That first spurt we saw was probably the signal Nashiba was waiting for. He must've known that within minutes the system would be deluged with their buy orders. So he delivered the *coup de grâce*.'

'The Greenfield pull-out.' Leibersen looked slowly up at Mack. 'You mean they zapped the market to floor and just waited for the buy orders to kick in?'

Mack nodded. 'And because of the delays on the system, no one else'll get a buy order processed this side of the closing bell.' He glanced at the studio clock. *'Fifty-two minutes. That's all the time they'll need. In fifty-two minutes the Japs'll have it all, Leibe. And there's not a damn thing we can do about it ...'*

Tension hung in the air of the control room like the rank odour of gelignite. The voice of the NBS correspondent stationed on the corner of Wall Street and Broad Street filtered through Mack's thoughts. '... In the last minutes the floor of the Great Hall here at the Exchange building on Wall Street has begun to fill with members in scenes not witnessed in eight years. Many have come equipped with mobile phones in an attempt to bypass the main switchboard, which has been jammed solid for hours ...'

Mack stared unseeing at the bank of screens in front of him. War, waged by computer; exactly as Morton had predicted.

The Japanese were using the Exchange computer system to snatch the whole economy; using the inadequacies of

357

the system, at that! The flaws. Mack shook his head. Reverse logic, incredible. But flaws in the system could be turned to a different advantage. Maybe there was some other weakness in the system that could stop this onslaught.

Time, I got to buy us some time. One night might be enough . . . If there's any way to force some of the Japanese buy orders through into a second day's trading . . .

An idea hit. In a flash, Mack was on his feet. He dived down the corridor to Leibersen's office, picked up the phone and dialled.

'Jay! C'mon Jay, pick up the goddamned phone!'

'Bodecker.'

'Thank God you're there. You following this?'

'You kidding?'

'Tell me, computer-delivered orders — transactions are only complete when they're put into the electronic order display books at trading posts, aren't they?'

'Yeah.'

'And the Exchange computers run on a network system, right?'

'Sure, I worked on it myself back in '85 when they were looking for programmers . . .'

'Great. So the network also links up the order books?'

'Yeah, yeah. What you looking for, Lasky?'

'There must be some central computer that controls them.'

'Sure. Somewhere in there there'll be a gateway computer that oversees the whole setup.'

'Without which the whole lot could go down.'

'Yeah, but . . . wait a minute, here. If this is going where I think it's going, the answer's No Way.'

'I'm not looking to shut the place down, if that's what you're thinking . . . just slow it up some.'

There was silence at Jay's end of the line. Mack took a breath. *Don't turn chicken on me now, Bodecker.* 'Out of your league, this, is it?'

'Is it shit!'

'So what's your problem? Look, I think I know how it can

be done. There must be some way of bringing down the bulk of the order books without affecting the dealers' information screens.'

'You're out of your fucking mind.'

'Is there or isn't there?'

'. . . Well yeah, it'd mean running a special program through the gateway computer, but sure, in principle you could do it.'

'So write me that special program.'

'Just like that, huh?' Mack could hear Jay lighting a cigarette. 'Listen, this is a lot tougher than you think. I mean, it'd be kind of obvious that someone'd been fooling around with the system if all the order books went down at once. You'd need to be clever about it. Take 'em out one at a time, every couple of minutes to really throw 'em. Make it look like happenstance, know what I mean?'

'Yeah, that's the effect I'm looking for. How long'll it take for you to cook up something to do the job?'

'Dunno . . . could be . . . Jesus, Mack, you're not a member, how in hell you gonna get in there, anyhow?'

'Let me worry about that. Listen, the roof's caving in here, Jay, I need that program as fast as you can give it to me.'

'Okay, okay. Put your laptop on line and give me half an hour. I'll see what I can do.'

'You're a jewel, pal. I'll be on my mobile phone number. You got that?'

'I got it.'

Mack's cab had just crossed the junction of Broadway and Fortieth when the program came through. He sat listening to the modem clicking off data bits as it downloaded, praying all the while that nothing was getting lost in the translation. By the time the taxi swung left towards Wall Street, he'd transferred the program from the laptop's hard drive to a floppy disk and wiped the memory.

A knot of people were standing on the sidewalk at the east side of the Exchange building on Broad Street. As his taxi passed, Mack turned in his seat to get a better view. Some members had taken to using a fire exit as a quick way out of the building. Others, who'd been heading for the main entrance, had seen the doors open and decided to use the exit as a short cut in. Mack put his face up to the cab's perspex partitioning and told the driver to pull over. He slipped the floppy disk into his coat pocket, clicked the laptop shut and passed it to the driver with a twenty-dollar bill. 'Leave this at reception at the NBS building.'

Mack hurried to join the crowd at the fire exit, slowly pushing his way through the steady stream of people trying to leave the Exchange. He watched them unclipping their identity badges as they reached the street.

As word travelled that the weight of buy orders pouring through the system had turned into a deluge, the human traffic in the narrow passageway between the street and the floor of the Exchange swelled until it was forced to a standstill. Tempers began to fray. Mack was trapped at the centre of an irritable mob; a few feet from him was Liam O'Connor.

O'Connor'd been all played out long ago. His last trip to the men's room had seen off the Bushmills and now he was almost too drunk to talk, much less bring his mind to bear on the changing events around him. He'd pushed his way across the floor, through the throngs of yelling dealers and towards the Broad Street fire exit. The Japanese were doing this, that's what Weinberg'd said – buying through nominee companies, most of them. He was never wrong about these things.

O'Connor was halfway down the passage that led to the street now. He jabbed out with his elbows to make a larger space for himself, seeing those around him only as a blur. This way out was hopeless, he thought. He tried to turn round and force his way back. Not a chance. He shouted to the man behind him, 'You shove me again, I'll break your face.' Then his eyes focused on a guy a few feet ahead, coming the other way. He took a good look at the face. It was oriental.

Jap, he thought. *Fuckin' Japs. Some slitty-eyed little bas-*

tard's probably sitting on most of my portfolio right now.

'You're doing this to us!' O'Connor started screaming at the Oriental as he struggled to keep upright. 'We should've fried the lot of you in '45! That's what we should've done!'

Trader Li Peng shook the sweat out of his eyes and shouted back that he was Korean-American, born in Brooklyn.

'Yeah. And all the Nazis were Austrians! I didn't fight in 'Nam to be fucked over by geeks like you now.' Something in O'Connor snapped. He threw himself forward and swung at Li, hitting a man in front. The man lashed back.

Mack was caught up in a flailing mass of bodies as all hell broke loose. People began to stumble. He watched powerless as the guy O'Connor'd hit suddenly disappeared, felt his thrashing body slide beneath his feet. The mob closed over him like a coffin lid. Mack was thrown violently forward, the breath crushed out of him. All around him, men were being dragged down and trampled underfoot. The animal screams of the dying sent those who might otherwise have survived into a frenzy. Mack's feet left the floor as he was impelled forward into the building with a rush. Then the jam tightened again. Ribs cracked as the press of bodies closed like the jaws of a vice. Mack's face was an inch from O'Connor's. Now the Irishman was fighting for breath.

'Pull back!' he screamed. 'For the love of God, pull back.'

Mack grabbed at O'Connor's coat as he saw him drawn downwards. A second later, he lost his grasp. O'Connor was swept up and slammed back against the wall, his skull cracking like a walnut on the hard stone.

Mack fought to hold his ground. He watched the life drain out of the Irishman's face, the eyes glaze over. Watched as his body was sucked down into the chaos that he had created.

The stampede ended as suddenly as it had begun. Injured men moved limping and blood-spattered out on to the sidewalk. Some dragged the bodies of friends behind them, unaware that they'd been dead for several minutes.

Mack broke free of the mob and plunged through the

corridor into the Exchange. A steel gate dropped in his mind. *Block out what just happened. Block it out! Right now all that matters is finding the gateway computer.*

Something was digging into his right hand. He looked down, opening his fingers slowly. In his palm was a piece of O'Connor's lapel, his identity badge still attached. Mack pinned it to his coat and pushed on through the crowd, heading across the floor like he had a right to be there. Where to start looking, that was the problem. The noise in the Great Hall was deafening; the tension amongst the members crowding the floor, struggling to get to traders, had the same raw urgency he'd felt in the crush to the fire exit. He turned around, slowly. The vastness of the room, the difficulty of the task ahead of him became clear at once.

The computer room could be anywhere. The possibilities were endless.

Mack propelled himself forward towards a door marked 'Private', to the right of the Exchange bell. He pushed in and walked down a short corridor. *What happens if I run into someone?* he thought. *Use the chaos.*

He reached the room at the end: janitorial supplies. He turned around and ran back into the Hall. *The whole thing's for shit*, he thought. *It could take a week to find the god-damn computer room!* He looked at the clock above him. Frustration welled up inside.

Every minute that passes, tens of millions of dollars' worth of stock falls into Japanese hands. And I'm just standing here!

His mobile phone rang. Then Jay's voice said, 'Where are you?'

'Inside.'

'All right!'

'This is hopeless, Jay. I don't have a prayer of finding this fucking room . . .'

'That's what I figured you'd say. I just hacked into the NYC Fire Department database. They have plans of all these buildings. As far as I can see, the room you want is second from the end of the main corridor in the basement.'

'Jay, you're a genius.'

'Where are you exactly?'

'Just in front of the bell.'

'Well, the nearest access point to you is . . . a staircase halfway down the west side of the building.'

Mack took his bearings and pushed off in the direction Jay had given him. 'Basement? This phone won't pick up down there. And I need you to tell me what to do with this disk.'

'Simple,' Jay said. 'You stick it in any floppy drive, type "FOO.BAT" and punch the carriage return.'

'That's all?'

'Well, unless I'm getting careless in my old age, FOO.BAT'll load BAR.BAT and BAR.BAT'll execute itself from a neat little command I wrote in.'

'Eh?'

'Y'know FUBAR, services slang for Fucked Up Beyond All Recognition.' Jay drew on his cigarette. ''Cos with any luck, that's what my baby'll do to the system – enjoy!'

Mack flattened himself against the wall to allow three women to pass him on the narrow staircase. From the little he could pick up of their conversation, it seemed news of the riot and the chaos on the Exchange floor had filtered through to the administration staff. He moved down a long corridor. The offices to the left and right of him seemed virtually deserted. The second door from the end was slightly ajar. A large sign across it read: 'Strictly Authorised Personnel Only'. Mack craned his neck to get a better view inside. All he could see was part of a work-station and the light of a computer screen. A cigarette burned in an ashtray beneath it; a woman's shoulder-bag lay at the foot of a chair. He put a slight pressure against the door. If it creaked . . .

The room was empty; the computer had been left signed on. Mack figured no operator would leave it unattended for long. Every instinct told him he had seconds rather than minutes. He tried to bring his mind to bear on Jay's instructions. His fingers hovered hesitantly over the keys. He flipped from the hard disk to the floppy. He muttered to himself, 'Put in the disk . . . type: "FOO.BAT."' He hit the carriage return and held his breath.

The program began to load; each second seemed to pass like a milestone in Mack's life. Sweat dripped through his eyebrows into his eyes.

Suddenly he heard the distant tap of high heels on the tiling floor. Through the hinges of the door he had a clear view of the corridor: a woman, dressed in a white cotton suit carrying a coffee; no purse. The shoulder-bag at his feet was white. Her bag; had to be. The office had one door. *It's either run or take what comes*, he thought. *First she'll take me for a thief. Then she'll see the disk* . . . His mind blanked as the footfalls drew nearer. The reader light on the floppy drive flickered and stopped. Mack punched the drive's eject button and snatched at the disk. With the disk out, no one would ever know the system'd been tampered with. He dropped it into his pocket. It hit something plastic: the radio frequency detector he'd bought to sweep Auburn's apartment for bugs – the suit'd hung unworn in the wardrobe ever since.

Any second now, the door would swing open. *Use the chaos.* Mack sprang up and stood defiantly, legs apart, moving the detector up to his mouth like it was a shortwave radio. He shouted angrily into it.

'. . . I don't give a shit about that, McClusky! I can't be everywhere, goddamn it! Right now, I got all the security problems I can handle, down here . . .' As the door opened, Mack stole a look at a memo on the woman's desk. 'On top of that, some damn fool has left the computer room unattended. I'm stuck here until . . .'

The girl stood staring at Mack. He glared at her. 'Ah! So there you are, Erikson! What the hell do you mean by leaving this room without signing off? What does it say on that door? Strictly Authorised Personnel Only! Any maniac could walk in here and screw up the entire system! I'm disappointed in you, Erikson. Very. How long have you been here?'

The girl blushed deeply. 'Almost a year.'

'Almost a year. Exactly! If you don't know the procedures

by now you never will. You never, repeat never, leave this room without signing off.' He started to push past the girl. Her face was crimson.

'You're right of course. I'm very sorry, I . . . I assure you it'll never happen again . . .'

'It damn well better not, Erikson.' Mack stalked off down the corridor, moving as fast as he could for the stairs.

A blast of heat hit him as he walked out through the Corinthian columns of the Exchange building into the sunlight of Wall Street. He turned towards Broadway and headed uptown, the sound of police and ambulance sirens following him down the street. A few yards ahead of him, a bag lady was picking through some trash in the gutter. Two small dogs on strings waited beside a stack of overstuffed tote bags. Mack took the disk from his pocket and spun it like a frisbee into a decaying pile of clothing as he walked by.

The sound of the private elevator invaded Nashiba's thoughts. Only he, Akitō and Fumiko had palm-prints the security system accepted. And his wife had been at her sister's apartment on Park Avenue all afternoon. Nashiba pulled his mind back to the latest reports that lay on the desk in front of him. Akitō's behaviour was an irritation to be addressed later.

'My mother is dead.' Akitō's voice shocked the old man out of his concentration. He spun round in his chair and stared at his son.

'No, not your wife.' Akitō's eyes menaced his father's. 'My mother. Yoshi Tosa. Remember her? She threw herself from the eighteenth floor of an apartment block in Queens early this morning.' He pulled a torn envelope, stiff with dried blood, from his jacket. 'The police found this note in her pocket.'

The expression that passed across the old man's face was unlike anything Akitō remembered seeing before. In an instant, it was pushed away, lest it betrayed any emotion. He turned back to his papers, writing hurriedly.

'I hope you're satisfied,' Akitō said quietly.

Nashiba fought hard to keep his composure. If the boy was hoping for an impulsive reaction he was going to be disappointed.

'You killed her as surely as if you had pushed her off that ledge yourself. You should have done it years ago, Father. Then I would never have known the truth.'

'And what do you know of the truth now?' Nashiba spoke softly, keeping his eyes on his papers. 'You have heard her truth. A truth distorted by time and by bitterness.'

'Don't you care about anyone, about anything that you've done? You ruined that woman's life!'

'You don't know . . . you cannot know how it . . . was.' Nashiba looked up, at last. 'She was a brilliant woman, with an extraordinary intellect.'

'Yeah, I bet you thought about that all the time you were humping her nice, tight ass.'

The old man moved so fast his blow sent Akitō halfway across the room. He landed on his back across a small lacquer table, smashing it to pieces.

'How dare you . . . how dare you talk like an . . . American.' Nashiba spat the word out like it described a disease. He slumped back in his chair, breathing hard.

Akitō sat up, ignoring the rising bruise on his jaw. *How pathetic*, he thought. *So he had loved her after all. So that was it. He'd never meant to, it wasn't part of the plan. He wanted to be rid of her as soon as she'd served her purpose. But he couldn't shake her off. Some part of her had clung to him. This same brooding violence must have been on his face then, the day he forced Yoshi to leave Japan.*

'I did what I did for you.' Nashiba rubbed his shoulder. He was too old for physical displays of anger. 'For the good of the only son I would ever have. To make him stronger, fitter for the tasks he would have to face. To give him a better chance of survival after I was dead. I've held the alliance together for fifty years, Akitō. I've done whatever it has taken to see this day come about. When today ends, the alliance will end with it, have no doubt about that. The Families will return to the way they always were. Blood ties will be the only thing that will bind them.'

Suddenly, his energy was drained. 'Fumiko was the wife my parents chose for me. She has many qualities but she could never have borne me the son I needed – Japan needed. I have given you both Nashiba wisdom and Tosa fire. When you marry Miyoko Ishihara, the Families will be bound together in blood as never before . . .'

'*If* I marry.' Akitō was on his feet, walking over to his father's desk. The old man's eyes dulled to black stones.

'Why should I honour a moral code that you break whenever you choose? I have followed your wishes all my life without a thought for what I wanted. Do you even know what I want, Father?'

'This American girl, so it would seem.'

'You always told me to think like an American – to know their strengths and their weaknesses. Is it so unnatural that I should fall in love with one?'

'Unnatural?' Nashiba toyed with the word. 'Let me tell you about our race and the American.' He walked to the window and looked down. 'When I was a student, I used to swim in a public baths down there. Every morning when I get up, it's the first thing I see from this window. They used to change the water on a Friday night. All weekend only Whites were allowed to swim there. Monday and Tuesday, they would let the Hispanics in. Wednesday through Thursday, the Blacks got to go. Friday morning, when the water was filthy, they let in the Japanese.

'I have swum in the piss and spittle of every breed of American there is. Now they're going to swim in mine.'

When Nashiba turned back to face the room, Akitō was gone. For a moment Nashiba was tempted to go after him. Then he turned back to watch *Tsumi*. *Give him a day or two*, he thought, *he'll soon see things in their proper perspective again.*

The TV screens set into the office panelling brought in more news of the day of days. Re-programming on every network reflected the impact of Nashiba's plan. But now, he felt no elation. He felt old, older than he'd ever remembered feeling. His whole ribcage ached. He'd pulled a muscle in his back when he'd hit the boy. Akitō had goaded him to it. He'd wanted him to hit him. Why?

How can I ask myself that! he thought. *Didn't I choose Yoshi for her fire, her freedom of spirit! She was her own woman to the last. And Akitō is her son.*

The essence was the mother's.

It was the one eventuality he'd never allowed for. Why had he never seen it before? Nashiba felt a gnawing emptiness in his gut. He'd loved Yoshi for that same fire. Pushing her away was the hardest decision he'd ever had to face. But what choice had he had? How different his life might have been if she had been by his side and not Fumiko. Yoshi was the rarest of women, her counsel would have been invaluable; her warmth, her lustre, a glory. Had it not been for the loathing the Tosas bore him, there might have been some way . . .

Now was not the time for regrets. At every turning point he'd stopped and weighed his options, the implications that every decision might have, with infinite care. The pain he'd endured was a part of the price he'd had to pay for all that he'd achieved. This American girl of Akitō's was a sexual diversion. That was all. If she were more, then she would simply be part of the price Akitō too would have to pay to become President of Nashiba. It was the way of these things. Akitō would understand that in the end. Such responsibilities, such commitment to one's obligations was no more a matter of choice to a Japanese now than it had been when he, himself, was young. Such disciplines were what set the Japanese apart as a race.

He walked back towards the window and looked down to where the public baths stood. What a thrill he'd felt, before the war, when he'd first come to America. How he'd longed to be part of this country, to be accepted by its people. In the street way below, he watched a yellow cab stop, pick up a couple and turn off on to Broadway. How many times, before the war, had a cab driver slowed for him, then seeing that he was Oriental, sped on? How many times had he paid for a ticket for an orchestra seat for a Broadway show only to be forced to sit with the other reject breeds, almost in the rafters of the theatre? Who were they to treat him like that? How many of them could trace their families back through two thousand years of matchless history? He had the blood of *Shoguns* and *Daimyos* in his veins! *They* were the rejects, a nation thrown together from the outcasts of every country of the world.

He had learnt to loathe the Americans. To despise their shallow values, their vulgarity, their noise. From the war, all through Korea he'd watched them in Tokyo and despised them. Were these fighting soldiers? he'd asked himself. Take away their ice-cream and their comic-books and they fall apart like frightened children.

Had Akitō become like them? Had his immersion into American life changed his attitudes, weakened his resolve? He had even talked of love — a word he had never heard Akitō use before. Never in all the times he could remember . . .

Nashiba opened the French doors on to the balcony. He needed air. *Tsumi* was almost over. The hegemony between the Families might be challenged within days. He needed Akitō here, he had to be seen to be ready to take the helm, firm and resolute. If the gap between them now was an unbridgeable chasm; if there was to be no union with the Ishiharas, no bond of three bloods, what then?

The old man bent forward, almost doubled up with pain. The boy had been right. He had killed the one woman he'd ever loved. Ruined her life and killed her. He had lost Yoshi and now he had lost his son.

Akitō must be installed as Chief Executive West, *Shacho* of *Shachos*. Alone, he was no victor. With *Tsumi* over, he was a toothless dog. The others would sit watching, waiting for him to die.

A wind blew in off the East River. It was not a cold wind but it cut through him, chilling him to the marrow. For fifty years, he'd cherished the old hatred. And what had he now? A sudden, unshakable fear: he would live to see the Nashiba supremacy ended and all that he worked for divided amongst the others. He would die without his son at his side, to the whimpering of a woman he did not love.

In the bowels of the Nashiba Building, Akitō stepped out of the private elevator and crossed the underground parking lot to the gun-metal limousine. The chauffeur checked his mirror as his boss climbed into the back.

'Where to, Nashiba-san?'

'South. Call up for the address. It'll be a new listing, an organisation called Aid Watch.'

'Now listen up, here's what we're doing.' The twenty-seven people crammed into the conference room at the NBS building fell silent as Saul Leibersen spoke. 'In case there's anyone here who doesn't already know, we're pulling scheduled programming from five till at least ten-thirty and running with a live newscast. The underlying message is going to be: "If you want to understand what really happened out there today, stay with us. And we'll take this turkey apart in front of your eyes."'

Leibersen held up his hands and waited for the noise in the room to subside. 'I take it all of you here have read the Lasky Report and the Aid Watch file. If you have, then right now you know more than anyone outside of the people who planned it. Now. Get this into your heads, all of you. This isn't finished yet. Not by a long way. The Japanese lost vital buying time today. If Mr Lasky here is right, and I believe he is, when that bell went twenty minutes ago, billions of dollars of Japanese buy orders were locked into the computer system. And there's not a goddamn thing they can do about it till tomorrow. One hell of a lot's gonna happen between now and then. And we're gonna make it happen!'

A man at the back lifted his hand to speak. 'I haven't finished yet, Mel,' Leibersen went on. 'The first thing we got to do here is start dealing in facts. Not perceptions.' He held up a long length of ticker-tape. 'This is paper, figures on paper, that's all it is. In reality, not a nickel has to change hands for five business days. We can get to the American people in two hours.'

Mack watched Leibersen pass round glasses of Scotch and brandy. The charisma, the leadership qualities that had put the man in charge of the second-largest network in the country at forty, seemed to transform the meeting into some kind of council of war. With his broad head and furrowed brow, it seemed to Mack that he cut an almost Churchillian figure. Exactly who the enemy was, still may not have been clear to all, but that they were witnesses to a momentous chapter in the network's history was evident enough.

'I want clear heads, so make this last.' Leibersen looked slowly round the room. 'First off, we got to get to as many of these Neutrals as we can. Ship them in here, into regional studios, take ENG units to their homes, drag 'em to the phone if we have to. We'll use the testimony of the guys we already have to make them realise they're not alone. After today, most of them must figure they've got nothing left to lose.

'Six hours ago the Lasky Report was just hypothesis. Now it's the underpinning to a reality. With that report, the Aid Watch file and the Neutrals, we can prove that what happened today on Wall Street was part of a carefully orchestrated plan which has already succeeded in part. And will wholly succeed, if the Exchange opens for business tomorrow morning.'

'You're aiming for a one-day freeze?' Mel Duggan got his question in at last. 'That's a long shot, isn't it, Leibe? The way the market was rallying before the bell—'

'Not if the authorities understand why it's rallying. It's the only appropriate move they can make. But that means we have to come through tonight. That means we have to pin enough on the Japanese involved in this to put a freeze on every nickel they have in this country. It means giving the authorities enough firepower to force every player out into the open – to take apart every deal they've put together here in the last ten years. And if, then, we get one sniff of anything other than roses, if there's one thin cent in the wrong pocket, or the right pocket for the wrong reason, a ton of shit's gonna

371

fall out of the sky on them that even Moses would have been proud of.' Leibersen gathered up the papers on the table. 'Let me tell you, whichever way it goes tonight, the youngest of you here is gonna be drawing a pension by the time the dust settles on this one.'

Leibersen put his hand on Mack's shoulder. 'Jesus, pal, you look terrible. I wish I could tell you that your part in this was over, but I need you here tonight, you know that.' Mack nodded. Leibersen turned back to his staff. 'Okay. Karen's going to talk about format . . .'

Mack left the conference and walked wearily to the elevator. Standing beside him was an elegant-looking woman he'd noticed amongst the group in Leibersen's office. She offered Mack her hand.

'Hi, I'm Bryony Cole, I'm with Aid Watch. I wrote the report on Western Pacific Pharmaceuticals. I think Leibe was planning on introducing us if things hadn't got so crazy.'

'Oh, right.' Mack shook her hand.

'I haven't read your report yet,' she said. 'I'm going back to the office to do that right now.'

'There seems to be a lot riding on it,' Mack said almost to himself. The elevator arrived and they got in. 'You know what worries me most? Leibe's standing up there trying to convince himself and everyone else we've got enough now to mount an effective counterstrike. But there's a whole part of me that says we're way too late. One night isn't long enough to dismantle something that's been building up steam for half a century. Nothing we've got even touches the men at the top, the men who planned and developed all this. And they're the only ones that matter.'

'Is getting to them so difficult?'

Mack smiled at her. 'They're beyond reach, believe me. If they weren't, they would never have started this. They exist on a different plateau to the rest of us. The guys I name in my report, most of them are old men with scores of their own to settle. Fundamentally, they despise Americans. Time has shown them we have none of their foresight or force of will. If we did, we'd have understood what was happening to us long ago and taken the appropriate steps. And they know that even if in the longer term, we do climb back, they won't be around to see it.' He looked at Bryony. 'I'm afraid there's no bunkers to bomb this time. I only wish there were.'

It was 5.30 when Bryony reached the Aid Watch office. Most of the staff had left for the evening. Rienderhoff's secretary sat in reception sorting through the mail. 'Oh good. I wasn't sure if you were coming back again tonight or not,' she said. 'You have a visitor. He's been here some time. I put him in your office.'

Akitō stood up as soon as he saw Bryony. Her eyes met his in an icy stare. 'Well, you're the last person I expected to see today.'

'Can we talk?'

'Short of calling the police and having you thrown out, it doesn't seem I have a choice.' She put down her attaché case and sat on the edge of her desk, her arms folded.

'I know what you think I am, what you think I'm a part of. That I was dishonest with you from the start. Three months ago you'd have been right on most counts. But a lot has happened in that time, Bryony. Things that made me question who I was, what I was becoming. I've spent my adult life in this country, and that makes me part of it. I watched what was happening on Wall Street, all across the United States today and all I could think was, this is *their* doing – a few men from a generation of Japanese that I am part of, in name and blood, but a generation that is separated from me by an aeon of time and all the changes in philosophy that that brings.'

'How very convenient for you.'

'Why else do you think I'm here?' Akitō continued quietly. 'You thought that the man you stood with, gazing out across the Cordilleras that night, was the real Akitō Nashiba. I knew that it wasn't. Perhaps the greatest dishonesty was that I didn't tell you at the beginning that I was already contracted to marry in September – a Japanese. It is not a marriage as you would understand it, so much as a business alliance, an expedient, like everything my father has a hand in. For me, perhaps it is a symbol. A key symbol. I have told my father today that I can no longer honour such an arrangement.'

'Akitō, I don't know what you—'

'Please. I can't tell you everything that has happened, all that I know, as much as I would like to . . .' Akitō followed Bryony's eyes. She was staring at the patch of dried blood on his shirt – Yoshi's blood. He buttoned his jacket to cover it. 'Some things no longer have a place in all this. Some things you must know if you're ever to have faith in me again. I can't change overnight, or change completely. I was forged too strongly in the flame of a proud and ancient culture. But I'm willing to learn; to use the best of the culture I was born into, with the best of the one that I have inherited. If you ever believed in me, ever believed that we might have some kind of a future together, believe that you will come, in time, to know that what I'm telling you now is the truth . . .'

Mack sat naked on the floor of Auburn's apartment, his head almost touching his knees. She sat behind him on the sofa slowly massaging his back. Hardly a part of his body had escaped bruising. Carefully, he craned his neck to watch television news footage of the aftermath of the riot at the Broad Street fire exit. Now, it seemed a miracle that he had escaped with his life. He switched to another channel. A newscast showed panicking depositors trying to break through a cordon of National Guard thrown around a bank building in Oklahoma City.

'What happens now?' Auburn asked.

Mack moved his neck slowly around. 'Depends on how swiftly the authorities act, if they act at all; what they uncover and how much of it they make stick. My guess is that the Japanese already have control of about three hundred of the Fortune Five Hundred corporations. Maybe more. Even if the switch is pulled before the first bell tomorrow, the best that can be hoped for in the short term is a measure of damage control.'

'And in the longer term?'

'The Japs spent fifty years planning this. Only they know how deep it goes.' A news report from another part of the country showed a mob turning its anger on the bank building itself, in an orgy of burning and looting. 'A professor at Harvard when I was there used to tell us the financial institutions of this country were once like separate windows. Now they're interlinked, one vast sheet of glass. Pitch one stone at it, you take out the whole front of the building. That's what Nashiba's done. Whichever way it goes in the next forty-eight hours, it's going to take a lot of putting back.'

'You did all you could.'

'No, I screwed up.' He sat motionless watching the television. 'I should never have trusted Brodie's judgement. I should have gone straight to the State Department a week ago.'

'How could you know Galbraith was going to sit on the report? Give yourself a break, you did good. No one could have done more. You saved the butts of friends; you activated Leibersen; you helped buy time.'

'I'm the kid who put his finger in the dyke. That's all.'

'Listen, by tomorrow, a lot of people are going to be saying, this guy Lasky, he predicted it all. We should have listened, we should have acted.'

Mack shrugged. 'So tell me why I feel so dissatisfied.'

'Maybe because this was the first time you committed yourself totally to something that wasn't just about you. Maybe your priorities have changed.' She slipped an arm around him and held him close. 'You're going to be okay, Mack Lasky, you know that. So give yourself a break, huh?'

The corner of Mack's mouth lifted into a smile. He leaned back and kissed her. Then he caught sight of his watch. 'Hey, it's 7.10. We need to be at NBS in forty minutes.'

It was still only 7.30 when they stepped out on to West End Avenue, so Mack decided they should walk to the NBS building. The air and the exercise would do more good than harm. He'd almost expected the city to look different. Then he thought, if the half-dozen bloody confrontations of the last century had left the buildings of the city unscathed, an economic war was hardly likely to mark them. But as they crossed

375

Seventh Avenue, Mack noticed a small gathering of people around the window of a thrift store. A window-dresser was standing amongst the clothes and gift items arranging price tags. As he and Auburn drew closer Mack saw that the prices were marked up in Yen.

'Is that meant to be some kind of joke?' Auburn asked another bystander. The man shrugged and moved off.

Mack felt the saliva in his mouth dry up. He and Auburn walked the rest of the way in silence. As he put his weight against the glass door of the NBS building a stab of pain shot through his right shoulder. He crossed the lobby and gave his name to the security guard at the desk. The man checked his list and lifted the phone.

'Studio Four. If you'd like to go to the twenty-sixth floor, Mr Lasky, someone up there'll meet you and take you through.'

They started towards the elevator. Bryony Cole was walking across the lobby towards them.

'Mr Lasky?'

'Hi,' he said. 'We're in Studio Four.'

'I'm not coming up. It was you I wanted to see.' She handed him a white folder. 'It's for the programme.'

Mack opened the folder. Inside was a black and white ten-by-eight photograph of a Japanese man in his seventies, and about ten sheets of closely-typed manuscript. The title page read simply: 'Tatsuya Nashiba.' He started to skim-read the first couple of pages. Then he began to turn them quickly, reading a paragraph here, a heading there. 'Where the hell did you get this?'

He looked up but Bryony was already gone. Through the high plate-glass doors, he could see her stepping nimbly across the cracked, uneven sidewalk and into a waiting cab.

He got into the elevator and flicked through the contents of the folder again. Between the photograph and the title page was a half-sheet of paper he'd missed the first time. Written in an immaculate hand, at the bottom, in black ink, were two words:

'For Morton.'